A
Sister's
Curse

❧

Jayne Bamber

A Sister's Curse

Copyright 2019 by Jayne Bamber

Cover design by Jayne Bamber

Cover artwork by Mary Ann Flaxman

***

***

ISBN: 9781688143920

Prologue

❧❦

June 1794, Derbyshire

A respectable family of the lower gentry were travelling on the Great North Road toward Lambton, a village of little consequence to any but those happy enough to reside there. The gentleman felt entirely indifferent to the notion of travelling thither with his wife, her younger sister, and his three young daughters; he occupied himself chiefly in reading his newspaper, idly stroking the hair of his second and favorite daughter, a lively girl of three who had finally dozed off in his lap.

His wife, seated opposite him, was equally engrossed in coddling her own favorite, a darling fair-haired angel of five, while the lady's younger sister sat beside her, cradling the youngest of the children. Though she quite longed to be as doting an aunt as ever there was, the young lady grew restless as the babe in her arms drifted to sleep, and the gentleman's hope of having silence at last was soon dashed; his wife and her sister resumed the tedious chatter that had been nearly constant during their three-day journey.

Their intention was not to attend the wedding to which they had been invited, but to prevent its taking place. Their brother, the jovial bridegroom, was a fine-looking and affable young man of thirty with a promising future in trade. Moreover, his sister had come up in the world, having married into the landed gentry these six years, and she felt her brother could now likewise do better than a penniless country miss from some remote northern backwater – he ought to marry a young lady of means, perhaps with younger brothers of an age and standing to some day look toward her own three daughters.

The lady found a ready audience in her younger sister, and with the hour of confrontation nearly upon them as they approached their destination, her wit flowed long. The gentleman could only conceal a smirk; he had resolved to wait until the very last to make his own sentiments known to his wife and her sister by pledging his full support of his brother-in-law's choice, for six years had taught him there could

1

be little pleasure in such a marriage beyond vexing his wife from time to time.

Unfortunately, it was his turn to be vexed by his lady, whose increasingly animated lamentations inevitably resulted in the disruption of her daughters' equanimity. The babe began to cry, and her aunt would insist on tending to the child herself, rather than handing her off to her mother. The babe's cries soon roused the middle daughter, who squealed a great deal, grappling wildly at her father in disorientation.

Still coddling her eldest, there was little else the mother would do; she scolded her sister and the babe, scolded her second child, and scolded her husband for the girl's distress until the gentleman was obliged to stop the coach entirely and claim a seat on top beside the driver, leaving the wailing of his daughters to his wife and sister, the responsible parties for the current uproar.

His lady wife let out a huff of indignation as he slammed the carriage door behind him, and a moment later deposited himself heavily on the seat beside the driver. He had taken the reins himself and gave the carriage a heavy, impatient jolt as he set them off toward the road leading into the village. Recovering from such a rustle about the carriage, the lady exchanged a look of shared annoyance with her sister, before chastising her second daughter again.

There was another disturbance a moment later – they were going far too fast – and then there was a great commotion of sound outside, on the road – all hooves and shouts. The lady met her sister's eye a moment before the carriage began to tumble. She cradled her eldest girl close, as her sister likewise held the baby, and both women had only just begun to reach out for the middle daughter when the carriage tumbled over.

***

Two great ladies, sisters, were travelling south on the Great North Road – had in fact just begun their journey – one sister had come north to accompany the other down to Bath, to see a doctor of a certain speciality, as a matter of some urgency. The elder sister was always happy to be of assistance to anybody, particularly her beloved younger sister, and a great deal more keen to be away from their husbands. Her own husband had remained behind at the manor, where he would no doubt debauch himself for the duration of her absence; her younger sister's husband, a much finer man, had ridden as far as the village to see them off.

It was not long after he guided his horse away from them, and their carriage began to pick up speed where the road widened at the edge of the village that their journey went amiss. What followed happened too quickly for either sister to recall with any clarity just what transpired, but when it was over, the younger woman sprang from the carriage. The elder sister was well enough recovered from the collision to instantly begin scolding the driver, while the younger sister hastened to assess the condition of the carriage they had struck.

It was in pieces. Both equipages had taken the curve at far too dangerous a speed, and only hers, the finer of the two, had survived the impact. She was immediately struck with no little dismay at just how many passengers had been within the battered carriage – all women and children, and two men riding atop, both now prostrate on the ground, their bodies twisted impossibly.

The lady cried out to her maid, who stumbled out of the carriage wide-eyed and shaking, but uninjured. The girl was dispatched to the village for help, and ignoring the dramatic fits of her elder sister, the sisters knelt amongst the wreckage to ascertain the injuries of the two women and three small girls, ignoring the pang in her heart at the certainty that the two men were beyond help.

The women and children were seen to – the fine lady felt some hope that they wanted only a little more assistance to be quite well. Assistance soon arrived in the form of her husband, the foremost gentleman of the area, who quickly took command of the situation. His wife, cradling one of the crying girls in her arms, watched with tears glistening in her eyes as her husband heard the final words of the man dying on the side of the road. He locked eyes with his wife, and gave her a solemn nod as the gentleman, assured that his wife and daughters would be safe, drew his last raspy breath.

1

George Darcy restlessly paced the halls of Pemberley; his home was in uproar. The worst of his fears had not come to pass, for when first his wife's maid had sought him in Lambton, scarcely sensible in describing the carriage accident, he had thought only of his wife. He had found Lady Anne Darcy not only unscathed from the collision, but commanding the situation and offering her aid to those in need; she was in every way a divine creature, and he was proud of her.

What had followed was horrible enough, and even his relief that his wife was unharmed was tainted by knowing that the family in the other carriage had been far less fortunate. His wife was alive and well, while the hysterical stranger upstairs with his wife had become a widow in the blink of an eye.

Anne joined him in the gallery some time later, still wearing the gown she had soiled with dirt and blood as she had assiduously tended to the travelers long after Doctor Johnson had answered their summons. He strode toward his wife, drawing her close to him, still not past the notion that she might have been lost to him. "What news, my love?"

"Our guests are beginning to speak sensibly now that the shock has worn off, and their injuries beginning to mend."

"And Catherine?"

"Sir Lewis has taken her to her room to calm her nerves – he thinks they had better return to Rosings tomorrow – surely our trip to Bath must be postponed." Anne sighed, and wrung her hands as she leaned into him. "Sisters, just like us… travelling to a wedding of all things. Can you imagine anything so horrible? My heart aches for them, George."

He nodded gravely and gave his wife a soft kiss on the forehead. "Where was the wedding to be? We must endeavor to find their family – the women and children must be looked after, and surely there must be someone who will worry when they do not reach their destination."

"That is the worst of it, I fear." Anne Darcy's voice quivered, and a tear rolled down her cheek. "They were nearly there – had my carriage departed the house but a moment later, they should have been safely on the parsonage road before I passed them by. Their brother is to marry Miss Fisher. I hope you do not object – that is, I have sent word to the parson and his daughter, as well as her betrothed – his sisters are asking for him, you see."

"Of course, my love. I daresay there are a great many arrangements to be made. By the bye, have you learned the names of our poor guests?"

"Bennet. The widow and children are called Bennet, the brother and younger sister are called Gardiner."

***

Edward Gardiner strode into the foyer of Pemberley with his fiancée on his arm, and her father at their side. They were met by the housekeeper, Mrs. Reynolds, and quickly led upstairs to meet with the Darcys in the gallery outside the guest wing.

Mr. Fisher stepped forward to perform the introductions, but Mr. Gardiner cut him off, caring nothing for formalities at such a time. "Where are my sisters?"

"They are upstairs, sir," Mr. Darcy replied. "Miss Gardiner is well enough, but for a broken arm and some other bruising. Your elder sister, however – I fear there may be some complications. And your brother, Mr. Bennet, I am afraid...."

"God, no," Mr. Gardiner sighed. Mr. Darcy exchanged a look of tender sadness with his wife, and nodded. "I long to go to my sisters, but I suppose I had better ask what happened."

Mr. Darcy hesitated, and glanced again at his wife, who took Mr. Gardiner's hand as she met his eye, before withdrawing it to wipe away a tear. Lady Anne appeared greatly affected by what she was saying, as she explained how the accident had come about. "The coachman broke his neck instantly, and I feared the same befell Mr. Bennet – they tell me now he survived the fall, but his ribs were badly broken, and had pierced his lung. I believed him already gone, and sent my maid to the village to fetch my husband, that we might assist your sisters and nieces. The oldest girl has a sprained ankle, but the younger two are quite well. I believe – I believe your sisters shielded the girls when they perceived the impact, at the cost to their own bodies. Miss Gardiner suffers only a broken arm and dreadful headache, but Mrs. Bennet is in a bad way, I fear, and Doctor Johnson fears for the child she carries."

Mr. Gardiner let out a heavy gasp – he had not even known Fanny was with child again. *That she should have come all this way!* "Good God, my poor sister. Does she suffer a great deal?"

Mrs. Darcy glanced up at her husband, who gave a barely discernible nod. "I should like to take you to them now," she said, and cast a glance at the Fishers.

Mr. Fisher, an affably disposed old parson, was stony as ever Edward Gardiner had seen him. "I shall accompany you, with Edward's consent, but Madeline will remain – I would not wish her exposed to anything... that is...."

"I perfectly understand, Papa," Madeline replied in a steady voice. "I am sure I shall wait for your report, and yours, my dear Edward."

Mr. Darcy offered Madeline Fisher a gentle smile. "Your family are all fond of reading, I understand. I shall escort you to the library, where you might wait for us all, my dear."

Mr. Gardiner and Mr. Fisher followed Mrs. Darcy through the guest wing, into the bedchamber that had been made available for Fanny Bennet. She appeared to be resting; the doctor left his post at her side and approached them, motioning for silence lest she awaken.

Mr. Gardiner moved to the corner of the room. "How is she? She will wake up, yes?"

"I have no doubt of that, sir, however...." Doctor Johnson paused and grimaced at the ground, apparently choosing his next words with care. "She has been in and out of consciousness, and though more vocal than some others I have seen after such an injury – well, Mr. Gardiner, to speak plainly, I believe you sister is under some confusion as to the circumstances of her accident."

"How so?"

Mr. Johnson grumbled under his breath, and led Edward to Fanny's bed side. He placed a cool cloth on her forehead, dabbing at her skin gently to rouse her. As Fanny's eyes opened, she broke into a broad smile at the sight of her brother. "Well, Edward! You are looking well!"

Mr. Gardiner smiled ruefully at his sister. "You are not, dearest. Whatever has happened?"

"Oh, la! I had a little fall, that is all! Cousin Pru has been ever so kind," she replied with a raspy laugh and a glance at Mrs. Darcy.

Mr. Gardiner cast a nervous glance up at Mrs. Darcy, who hovered nearby, her brow knit with concern. The lady *did* rather resemble their cousin Prudence, but he began to worry. "Fanny, Pru died six years ago...."

Fanny laughed nervously. "Whatever do you mean? She had her come-out last month, we were all there." She paused, her attention caught by Mr. Darcy, who had come to stand nervously in the doorway. "My goodness, Brother, who is your handsome friend?"

Mrs. Darcy looked up, her eyes twinkling with amusement that quickly gave way to alarm. "This is my husband, Mr. Darcy... ma'am?"

Fanny tittered nervously, and cast a wild look around the room. "It is a fine house, Pru – pray, where am I? Where is Phyllis, and Mamma?"

Mr. Gardiner looked over at Doctor Johnson, who nodded knowingly. "Young lady," said he, "your brother has come to ascertain your injuries, after your… fall. I shall speak privately now with him – he shall be returned to you in just a moment."

Mrs. Darcy took a seat beside Fanny's sickbed while her husband followed Mr. Gardiner, Mr. Fisher, and Doctor Johnson into the corridor. When they had closed the door, the doctor addressed Edward first. "You take my meaning now, sir?"

"She did have a tumble, when she was eighteen – the only other time I think she has ever been unwell, in fact. But what is to be done to make her remember?"

"Yes, she must be made to remember herself," Mr. Darcy agreed. "There are a great many cares for her at present – her children, and arrangements for her husband. Tell us, doctor, is she well enough to recover?"

The doctor drew in a deep breath, puffing his chest out and steepling his fingers in a gesture of consideration. "To be honest, it is difficult to say at present. I am rather astonished she has not spoken of being in any great pain, for her injuries are not inconsequential. In cases as these, it is possible that the part of the brain that processes pain is not responding, and given her current state I do suspect there is some damage to the brain – as to whether it will last, I must suggest that this may also depend on whether her other injuries heal sufficiently for her to survive long enough to recover her faculties."

Mr. Gardiner let out a small sound of surprise – guttural, jarring surprise. "You mean to say that she might not live? That she may perish without feeling the pain of her injuries, or recall ever sustaining them?"

Mr. Fisher interjected. "Perhaps it is a small mercy. *Of course* we must pray for her recovery, but if this is to be the end, would it not be better to spare her any pain, both physical and mental?"

"With all due respect, Mr. Fisher, I cannot agree," Mr. Darcy said, looking quite aghast. "Of course, that is all up to Mr. Gardiner, here, and the good doctor, but I cannot think it wise to allow her to remain in any state of delusion, however comfortable. Mrs. Bennet and all her family are welcome here as long as we may be of service – I promised her husband before he passed – but ought she not be made to remember? She must want a say in what befalls her husband next, not to mention the care of the children."

"Well said," Mr. Gardiner agreed. "I thank you for your kindness, sir, and I fear we may yet have to trespass on your hospitality for some time, until my poor sister is quite well again – I shall not give up hope that she may yet mend. I fear for the babe – she has most ardently desired a son, and if I know my sister, she must be determined that this child will at last be the heir she has hoped for – with Thomas being gone, it is their family's last hope…." A sob overtook him before he could say more. "Certainly she must know about Thomas. As to the girls, were it in my power – that is, I shall speak to Madeline about some possible arrangement...."

The doctor nodded his agreement. "I think it could only be to her benefit that we make her recollect herself." They were interrupted by a sudden shriek, and the four men rushed back into Mrs. Bennet's sick room.

Mrs. Darcy sat by, clasping Fanny's hand with a look of panic as Fanny grasped at her stomach with her other hand. "Eddie, what is this? What has happened to me?"

Good God, she has no notion of being a mother. The Darcys and Mr. Fisher shared a look of agreement before quietly retreating, and Mr. Gardiner sat down beside his sister. "Fanny, dear, I must speak to you about Thomas. You remember Thomas Bennet?"

Suddenly exhausted by her own distress, Fanny shifted awkwardly in the bed. "Brother, I hurt all over," she whined.

"You have been in a terrible accident," he said gently. "You did not have a fall. Listen to me, Fanny. Your fall down the stairs at our cousin's home happened seven years past. Can you remember nothing since then?"

Fanny gazed up at him in pained confusion. "What's this? I have been abed all that while?"

"No, dearest. You have married Mr. Thomas Bennet, do you not know it?"

She appeared to consider his words, but he knew the worst was true. She had no recollection of the husband she had lost. "I – I have? But when?"

"Six years past, my dear. Sweet girl, you must try to remember. Can you not think on his face?"

"I am trying.... I know him, but – we are wed?"

"Yes, my dear. You have three beautiful daughters, and even now you carry his son."

She pulled her hand from his to clasp at her belly, and began to weep. "But – he doesn't like me. He doesn't like me!"

Mr. Gardiner pursed his lips, and hesitated. "He loved you, my dear. He loved you very much, and gave you everything you ever desired when you wed. A fine house, lovely children, elegant gowns...."

Fanny only wept harder, and Doctor Johnson drew nearer. "Perhaps if we brought her one of the girls? Every mother knows her own child."

"If you think it best."

"She has a fever, Mr. Gardiner, but it is not the sort to be contagious. What I always prescribe is rest, rest above anything else is the great healer. But perhaps a moment with one of the children might jar her, if followed by a good rest. The mind *wants* to be well, you see. Let us show her some proof of her current life, and then let her rest a while, and she may wake up a little more sensible."

Mr. Gardiner glanced down at his sister, who had listened to the doctor's whispers with a mounting expression of sheer terror. He had no wish to alarm her, and even feared she might do the child some harm if the shock was too great. "I suppose… you are quite sure?"

"Certainly, sir."

They found Lady Anne Darcy in the nursery, where two of the girls, Elizabeth and Mary were sleeping – little Jane had sprained her ankle and was resting elsewhere. Lady Anne smiled warmly as they entered, clearly content to look over the cherubs in her care. "They have no idea what has happened to them," she sighed wistfully. "No idea at all."

"Their father gone and their mother unable to remember them," Mr. Gardiner sighed.

A queer look passed over Lady Anne's face, and she seized his hand for a moment. "We will make it right for them, sir. We shall look after them, and their mother, and we shall make it all right for them. They are such dear, sweet girls."

The doctor harrumphed, and Lady Anne looked away in sudden embarrassment. Mr. Gardiner approached the cradle where Mary lay sleeping peacefully. Though he knew but little of children, he was aware of the great lengths that would be gone to, to prevent their waking, and he regretted that he must disturb one of them. The babe was likely to make the greater ruckus, so he picked little Lizzy up in his arms instead, giving her a gentle bounce as she woke. "You know Uncle Edward, yes you do," he cooed at her as she peered up at him, her hand instantly seizing a clump of his hair.

Lady Anne smiled. "She certainly is familiar!"

Lizzy was tranquil enough as they carried her back to Fanny's room, where his sister looked to be waiting for them. Some recognition flashed in Fanny's eyes – Mr. Gardiner let out a silent prayer of thanks as he handed his niece to her mother. Fanny grappled to hold her properly, crying out from the pain of her injuries, and Mr. Gardiner pulled back, holding Lizzy on his lap as he sat beside his sister. "Here's your dear girl," he said gently.

Fanny continued to moan with discomfort from the movement, but her eyes were locked on her daughter, who after a moment grew disturbed by her mother's unrest, and the girl began to cry out. Fanny reacted instantly, giving a shrill shriek and squeezing her eyes closed. She failed wildly. "Hush Lizzy, hush! You've driven your father away, and, oh, my God! We are going to crash!"

Lady Anne instinctively moved to take the child from his arms, as

Mr. Gardiner stood and leaned over his sister. Careful not to injure her, he managed to subdue the woman, and coaxed her into opening her eyes. "Look at me, my dear. Right here, Fanny. There now. Tell me, what has happened?"

Fanny wailed loudly. "Mr. Bennet is dead, and we are all ruined forever!"

It took above an hour to subdue Fanny, but she soon regained what she could of her senses, and was subsequently dosed with laudanum; she was drifting in and out of sleep when he left her. His youngest sister was likewise resting, the doctor informed him, and Mr. Gardiner steeled himself for a very painful conversation with Mr. Darcy while his sisters and nieces rested.

***

Lady Anne hummed softly to herself, savoring the familiar tones of a song her mother had sung to her, and the warm perfection of the baby cradled in her arms – how she loved this feeling! She had politely refused Catherine's eager offer to send for a nanny from the village, and borne the looks of pity from her sister and Sir Lewis when she had insisted on looking after the girls herself. The eldest she had sat with for some time, promising her that her ankle would be well, until the flaxen-haired little angel had dozed off to sleep. Afterward she had come to the nursery, unable to keep herself away from the poor girls whom she knew she had robbed of something that could never be gotten back.

She was obliged to return the sleeping babe to the cradle when little Lizzy began to cry, and she exchanged one sister for the other in her arms, peering down with equal measures of pain and delight at the little girl's wide, expressive eyes. The child began to gurgle something, tugging at a stray wisp of Anne's hair as if to emphasize her slurred declaration. "Doll, doll."

Anne gave a gentle laugh. "Oh, do you want a doll? I suppose there must have been a doll amongst all your things. Good Mr. Reynolds went back for all your family's belongings, dear one, and we shall find your doll. In fact…."

She set the girl down on the floor, steadying the child as she found her footing, and then watched with joy as the precious girl rambled across the room and threw herself against a tufted ottoman, squealing with delight. Keeping one eye on the child, Anne approached a cabinet across the room and retrieved something she had purchased long ago, though her hopes had been so often disappointed that she had never made any use of it. She gave the doll's curly hair a little pat of affection and displayed it for young Miss Lizzy. "Here you go, my darling. Come and have a look at this doll here. What do you think of her?"

Little Lizzy gave a sheepish grin, and hugged the doll close to her chest. "Doll," she repeated shyly. "Pwetty."

"I believe the proper response is 'thank you,' little imp," came the reply; Anne gave a quick curtsey and brushed at her gown, embarrassed to have been caught in the nursery once more.

"I have always wished for a daughter – that is, I was happy to have something on hand to indulge her. The poor thing deserves something to lift her spirits, do you not think, Mr. Gardiner?"

Offering a forced smile, Mr. Gardiner crouched down beside his niece. "Lady Anne is all politeness, Lizzy. Shall we thank the nice lady?"

"Fank you, nice laly," Lizzy gurgled, giving her uncle a sly grin and hugging at his neck until he picked her up in his arms.

"I believe I must thank you as well, your ladyship, for your kindness and hospitality amidst this dreadful ordeal. I apologize if I have disturbed you – Mr. and Miss Fisher have gone back to the village, and I have been instructed to let my sisters have their rest for the time being. I find myself in want of any occupation other than fretting away many long hours, knowing there is nothing within my power to be done for my family."

"I quite understand, and your concern does you credit. If I may say, your sisters are in excellent hands with Doctor Johnson. He has saved my life more than once – that is, he has served our family well for many years. I shall leave you with your nieces, but I must mention that I believe my husband was wishing to speak with you regarding..." Anne hesitated, fidgeting with the lace that lined the cradle. "Regarding the arrangements for Mr. Bennet."

"Oh – yes. I've spoken with him, for quite some time, in fact. Fanny has regained her senses, thank the Lord, but the doctor and I are in agreement that it would do better to leave my sister out of the decision making for the time being. At any rate, I have accepted your husband's generous offer to remain a guest here until my sisters are well enough to return to London with me. Mr. Darcy and Mr. Fisher have both urged me to consent to burying Thomas in Lambton, as it is not advisable to remove him to Hertfordshire in all this heat. 'Tis a pity, but it cannot be helped."

"I think it a right thing, sir. You are all quite welcome here for as long as you require, and my family is entirely at your service. My husband gave Mr. Bennet his word."

Mr. Gardiner looked pained. "That is... thank you. I believe that must have given Thomas great comfort."

Anne wished to say something more, but what could possibly put any of this to rights? There was a nagging weight in her heart, telling her that this was all her own doing. Her carriage, her fault that this poor man's family had suffered a devastation from which they might never recover. Before she could formulate any manner of speech that might express the depth of her feelings, her niece Charlotte, a plucky little girl of six and a half, came bouncing into the nursery.

"Oh! Good evening, Aunt," Charlotte said with a nervous giggle and an attempt at a curtsey. "Uncle told me there's friends to play with?"

"Evening? Uncle? Good Heavens! Forgive me, Mr. Gardiner," Lady Anne sputtered. "I have lost track of the time, it seems, but I had no notion that my brother meant to come here. Then again, I was to have been dining tonight at an inn fifty miles hence. I suppose my husband must have invited him to dine – Sir Lewis can be such tedious company," Anne said, covering little Charlotte's ears as she whispered the last.

Mr. Gardiner gave a nervous glance at what Lady Anne supposed must have been a most incomprehensible speech on her part. "I should hate to trespass on your family gathering. I would be happy to take my meal here in the nursery – or perhaps I may take Lizzy in to see poor Jane. And you are very welcome to stay and play with us too, little miss," Mr. Gardiner added, offering Charlotte a friendly smile.

"Should you like that Charlotte? Mr. Gardiner will take you to meet Miss Jane, she is nearly your age, and has sprained her ankle. I think she would very much like to make a new friend this evening." As Charlotte gave an eager nod of assent, Lady Anne began to grow concerned about her brother's unexpected arrival. "Well, if it is nearly time to dine, I am sure they shall be ringing the gong soon, and I must go and greet my brother before I go up to dress. I do apologize – we would not dream of inviting anyone, not even family, at such a time – my husband must have forgotten to cancel his arrangements, and I was not aware…."

Mr. Gardiner held up a hand to stop her. "Your day was quite upended, Lady Anne, and I can only thank God that it was such an attentive and generous family that was on hand to see to my family's needs. I owe you more thanks than I could ever supply – you needn't apologize for the presence of your family in your own home."

"You are too kind, sir. Had I not been on the road at all – but no, I mustn't. I shall have a tray sent up for you in about an hour, if that suits, but if you decide you should like to come down and join us, please know that you are very welcome."

"I have no wish to cast a dark cloud over your meal, as I would be certain to do. At any rate, I shall be closer on hand up here, than in the dining room, should either of my sisters' conditions change."

"Of course. If there is anything else you require, the staff is at your disposal, as are we all." Lady Anne dropped into a parting curtsey, and hastened downstairs. As she approached the drawing room to greet her brother and hear some account for his unexpected presence, she heard several raised voices, and steeled herself for the ensuing Fitzwilliam chaos.

2

Lady Anne stood seething in the entrance of the drawing room as her husband and Sir Lewis de Bourgh yelled at one another, gesturing angrily. Her brother Henry, broad shouldered and powerfully built, stood towering over both of them; rather than having taken one side or the other in their argument, he appeared to be antagonizing both gentleman in equal measures. Beyond them, Anne spied her mother observing the argument with her usual wry superiority, no doubt waiting until the optimal moment to swoop in and make her own sentiments known. Catherine looked on with silent rage and the countess sat languidly on the sofa, as if they were only discussing the weather.

It was the indolent countess who first noticed Anne's presence and approached her, and just as Anne felt herself on the verge of delivering a withering set-down to everybody in the room, Lady Margaret took her by the hand. "My dear sister, it is good to see you are well. I understand there was some sort of terrible accident," she said flatly.

The gentleman ceased their bickering long enough to acknowledge her presence, and her mother broke through them to approach Anne, shooing the countess back to the sofa with a wave of her hand. "There you are. At last, now we might hear a few words of sense spoken about this whole matter."

Anne gave her mother a perfunctory kiss on the cheek before registering her own surprise. "I had not expected to see you... and everyone...."

"Yes, well!" The dowager countess punctuated herself with a firm stomp of her cane the carpet. "I shall spare these knuckleheads the trouble of repeating themselves – the last thing on earth I think any of us could bear – it appears your brother received two conflicting reports from Pemberley this afternoon. Your husband wrote Henry to rescind his invitation to dine tonight, while your sister sent a message of her own begging him to hasten hither directly, that a great calamity had befallen you, leading to your home being set upon by a pack of gypsies of questionable origins and indeterminate quantity."

Before Anne could make any reply, Catherine interjected. "I told you, I sent no such letter. What an ugly thing to say," she exclaimed, gesturing with what must have been the letter in question. "This is your doing, Lewis, I know your writing."

"So you would hide behind a woman, de Bourgh?" Henry rounded on Sir Lewis. "I should have expected no better of you, damned snake!"

"He had no business writing to you at all, no matter whose name he signed to his poison pen," George growled. "And shame on you for doing his bidding, Henry, when I had made it explicitly clear that we were not to be disturbed here. Do you think to question my judgment about how to assist these people? Or do you simply doubt my ability to look after your sister?"

"Calm down, old boy," Henry cried, clapping George on the back. "Nobody is questioning your judgment – at least, *I* am not – but I have some right to look in on my sister after such an ordeal, and so does her mother."

Sir Lewis began to sputter with rage. "I have told you how your sisters fared – and what sort of *people* your sisters have dragged in off the street to make a charity case out of. It is always something with you, Catherine; everyone within your reach must be in need of your high and mighty condescension. Your sister will grow just as bad. Damned soft of you to be bullied by your wife, Darcy – I certainly would not be, nor would I bend over backward at every turn for vulgar tradesfolk. And surely you, Henry, would never think of such a thing at Matlock."

At the mention of tradesmen, the countess looked up from playing with her bracelets and gasped, and Catherine glowered at her. "Oh, do shut up," she screeched.

Wishing she might simply scream at the top of her lungs, Anne burst into tears, as she often did when she grew angry. "Stop this," she said, raising her voice enough to silence her relations. "What is wrong with you? A man died before my very eyes today! Everyone in this room *knows* what it is to lose a father. Has it not occurred to any of you that it could have just as easily been me, or Catherine, lying in a crumpled heap on the road this morning? You bicker like children while upstairs that poor man's widow is fighting for her life! If any of you has a particular opinion about my husband and I acting in a Christian manner to suffering women and children, I shall happily escort you to the door myself." Anne paused, breathing heavily from the force of her ire; she cast a wild glance around the room, and six blanched faces regarded her with unmasked astonishment.

Finally, Sir Lewis broke the silence. "Catherine and I will be removing our daughter to Matlock immediately, and departing for Kent in the morning. I *will not* have our daughter exposed to whatever disease these people may have brought with them. She is not well."

"You are no more invited to Matlock than I was to Pemberley, you whinging old prat," Henry spat. "And as for your daughter, she's not a bloody invalid, she's a spoiled, lazy brat, and I can guess *where* she got that from."

"Now see here," Sir Lewis rejoined, stepping toward Henry as if to challenge him.

George met Anne's eye with a rueful smile, and he stepped between Henry and Sir Lewis. "Now see here, *all* of you. As my wife said, you would all do well to hold your tongues. A man lost his life today, in such a way as to involve Pemberley materially. Out of respect for the gravity of the situation, and the suffering of the *perfectly respectable* family I have welcomed into my guest wing, we will have peace in this house tonight. De Bourgh, you are very welcome to return to Kent as soon as you like; take a tray in your room if you cannot be civil for the duration of our meal. Henry, Margaret, you are welcome to stay and dine, as you have come all this way, and the boys have already run off together to God knows where, but it is to be a rather sober evening. This morning I promised that man in his final moments that his family would be looked after, and spending this evening quarreling with my own family seems to me to be in the worst possible taste."

Anne gazed at her husband in admiration and wiped the tears from her face. Her mother gave her an arch look as she handed her a handkerchief. "Well, if it were up to me," the dowager declared, "I am sure I would be sending all three of my children back to the nursery tonight, and boxing some ears besides, but I for one am perfectly willing to behave as one should when one is a guest in another person's home. Come, Anne, you must walk with me into the dining room, for I have a great curiosity to hear about your guests. We are the leaders in this community, and as Catherine would say, it is our duty to do what we can for the less fortunate within our reach, as befitting our station. Now dearest, I want to hear all about it."

***

Dinner was an awkward, grim affair, but it was gotten through. Sir Lewis's resolution to take a tray in his room while he packed for their departure at first light proved a blessing to the rest of the family. With the presence of her son and nephews and young George Wickham at the table, there were so many uncomfortable questions, stilted answers, and rather troubling speculations that Lady Anne scarcely felt herself up to sitting through it.

The countess, as was her custom, remained indifferent to most of the conversation, while Henry, no longer provoked by Sir Lewis, calmly continued questioning them about the Bennets and Gardiners. The dowager countess's interest was equally apparent, and she was, unsurprisingly, inclined to see things exactly as her youngest daughter did. That Catherine was so sympathetically disposed towards their unfortunate guests was more of a surprise to Anne, who wondered if her concern was borne more out of a desire to spite Sir Lewis than any genuine sentiment. However, Catherine revealed that she had apparently spent a few hours with Miss Gardiner while Anne had lingered in the nursery, and found her to be a pleasing sort of girl, just the right blend of deferential and genteel. Catherine *did* like to meddle, and had developed an interest in making Miss Gardiner her next pet project, once the young lady's injuries healed.

Anne answered her family's questions and made all of the appropriate remarks when necessary, but felt the entire time as if she was slipping away from the present moment, into a distant, murky haze. She found herself often losing the direction of the conversation entirely, replaying over and over in her mind the moment she had descended from her barouche to see the Bennet carriage strewn across the road.

To her tremendous relief, her brother had the good sense not to tarry over brandy with George after supper, and was prompt in commanding his family to retire for the evening, cordially asking them to keep him informed on how he might be of service. Anne, her husband, and her sister seized the opportunity to retire immediately.

Anne and George Darcy were a love match, and in twelve years of marriage they had ignored the custom of sleeping in separate bedchambers. As the two of them came out of their respective dressing rooms, attired for bed, George drew his wife into a gentle embrace before pulling back the bedclothes and gesturing for her to come and sit beside him. "I am sorry for that dreadful business this evening. You were right to be angry with all of us, carrying on like that. I am sure de Bourgh and I would have had words at some point during his stay, we always do, but tonight of all nights, it was horrible of me. Can you forgive me for being so beastly?"

Anne nestled in close to her husband, her head on his shoulder and one hand on his chest as they lay back against the pillows. "I forgive you, dearest. I am sure Henry must have come in already worked into such a state."

"And I ought to have known Sir Lewis would make this whole ordeal about *himself.* Not a thought for how close he came to nearly losing his wife today! When I think of it – when I think of how it might have been you...."

Anne raised her fingertips to George's lips. "Hush, my love. I am safe. Only I...."

"What is it? You are not concealing some injury from me, are you?"

"No, not at all. I was a little knocked about, of course, but nothing serious. Nothing at all like – oh, it was so horrible. I shall never forget the sight of it, that is all I meant to say. I feel as though I am forever changed by what I have seen today."

"I daresay we both are, my love. It is no small thing, to see a man die, to hear his final words. To see so much suffering – but I am proud of you. I always have been, but never more than today. You were like a lioness looking after her cubs."

Anne smiled sadly. "They are such dear children."

George placed his hand on hers. "I know it is your wish – that is, you have wanted to give me more children, but after today, Anne, I would beg you give it up. I cannot bear the thought of losing you, whether it be on the journey to some doctor in Bath who *might* be able to help, or if you were to conceive again, and...."

Anne sniffled, and brought her hand up to her face as if to stop the tears from coming. "Oh George, do not ask me this. Not tonight, I can scarcely think clearly. I almost agree with you, perhaps it is not worth it. My madness for more children led me to this folly, and it has cost a man his life, a man who will never see his own daughters grow up. Yet, all those hours I spent in the nursery today.... I ought to be ashamed of how happy it made me to be with those dear sweet girls. I want one so badly, George. I want to be a mother again."

George cradled his wife in his arms as she wept. "Let us not think of it now, dearest. It has been a difficult day, and nothing need be decided just now. If the Almighty wishes us to have any more children, we shall have them. For now, he has given us the Bennets to care for, and I daresay we had better get some rest so that we can do our best to face whatever tomorrow brings."

***

Tomorrow came far earlier than anyone could have expected. Just before dawn, a commotion in the corridor woke the Darcys, alerting them that all was not well. Quickly donning their dressing gowns, they rushed out of their chamber and were met by Mrs. Reynolds in the hall.

"Oh, thank the Lord, I was afraid to come and wake you," Mrs. Reynolds cried, coming towards them as a couple of other maids went rushing past with arms full of linens.

"Of course," Anne replied. "If anything is happening, we must be awake and present. Pray, what is going on, Mrs. Reynolds?"

"I believe it is Mrs. Bennet," she replied. "The doctor woke Mr. Gardiner, and sent for his helper in the village. Mrs. Bennet took a turn for the worse, and she is asking for her eldest daughter and sister, but they are both injured, and nobody wants to disturb them – that is, unless you think we ought to."

"I say let them rest a while longer, but we must consult Mr. Gardiner," George said. "Surely they cannot be moved? What does the doctor say?"

Mrs. Reynolds countenance darkened. "Oh, he is in such a state! Well, perhaps you had better come and see."

***

After spending a hellish half hour with his sister, Mr. Gardiner leaned against the wall just outside the door of her bedchamber, slumping back and breathing out heavily as he brought his hands to his face, trying to drown out the sound of Fanny's screams. Doctor Johnson had done everything he could to make her comfortable, despite Fanny being far from a cooperative patient, but the situation was rapidly deteriorating. The door opened once more and the Darcys came out into the corridor as well; he immediately straightened himself, embarrassed to have been seen so discomposed by his gracious hosts.

The Darcys both looked subdued, and no less distraught than himself; thankfully they said nothing of his tear-streaked face. Mr. Gardiner cleared his throat, not wishing to appear so entirely useless, and said, "We had better go and get the girls."

Lady Anne made a strangled sound and looked timidly between her husband and Mr. Gardiner. "Are you sure it is best?"

"Doctor Johnson seemed to believe it would help," Mr. Gardiner replied, so tired his voice was almost devoid of any emotion. "Lizzy and Mary won't remember it, perhaps not even Jane. Johnson is right; Fanny's need to see them outweighs the distress it may cause them. They will forget it."

"The decision is yours," Mr. Darcy said with a nod. "So be it."

They collected the Bennet girls and returned several minutes later, once the younger children had been reasonably comforted from their unexpected awakening, and were calm enough to be brought to their mother's room. Mr. Gardiner glanced over at Mr. Darcy as they stood on opposite sides of Fanny's bed. To his relief, Jane had been lifted from her bed without being woken – even now she lay with her head on Mr. Darcy's shoulder, sleeping peacefully. *More the better.* Doctor Johnson was correct that Lizzy and Mary would likely not remember this view of their mother, the look of pain on her face and the terrifying quantity of blood on her bedsheets, but if Jane were to open her eyes now, he feared the image would stay with her forever, as he knew it would for him.

Mr. Darcy took a step closer to his wife, who leaned into him as she buried her face in Lizzy's thick, dark curls and clutched the girl closer. Fanny had been coaxed by the doctor to open her eyes, even as she squeezed the bedding with both hands and suppressed another cry of agony long enough to focus on her children, and say what Mr. Gardiner knew in his heart might be her final goodbye.

He shifted the weight of the baby he held to one arm, and reached out with his free hand to clasp Fanny's. "You must be brave for them, Sister. Tell them you love them, and bid them good night, and then we shall see you through this, I swear it."

Fanny met his eye and tried to smile as she gave a slight nod, but in another moment her face was contorted and she let out a scream of pain. He squeezed her hand tighter. "Stay with us, Fanny."

She whimpered and looked frantically between her three daughters. "Goodbye, my darlings. Be good girls for your uncle, and remember your Mamma loves you." Fanny managed to choke the words out before ending her speech with a haunting moan and a sob.

"Enough," Mr. Gardiner said, noticing Jane's eyes begin to flicker open. "We've got to get them out of here."

As he and the Darcys turned to leave, Mrs. Bennet cried out, "I will see you in Heaven, my darling girls." Her weeping soon faded into another scream of agony, and Mr. Gardiner bit his lip and left his sister to the mercy of the doctor and his assistant.

In the corridor, the Darcys led the way back to the nursery, and Mr. Gardiner was approached by Mrs. Reynolds, who in one fluid motion divested him of the baby in his arms and handed him a freshly starched pocket square. "Your lip is bleeding, sir," she said. "I'll get the little one back to her sisters; the Fishers are here, in the gallery – Lady Anne said you'd want them here."

"Thank you, yes," he replied, dabbing at his lip as he moved away to seek Madeline's comfort.

The gallery was near enough that he could still hear his sister's shrieks as he entered and went directly to his fiancée, sparing a quick greeting for her father before he took Madeline in his arms. She embraced him back, letting him hold her for far longer than might have been appropriate as he gently wept on her shoulder.

Mr. Fisher was patient, but eventually cleared his throat, and when Mr. Gardiner broke away from Madeline to look around at him, he gestured for them all to be seated.

"What news, Edward," Madeline asked.

He took a deep breath, wishing to speak calmly in the presence of his fiancée and her father, though at such a time it was nearly impossible. "She has lost the baby."

Madeline gasped and brought her hands to her face. "Oh no!"

Mr. Fisher lowered his eyes sadly. "I am sorry, son."

"It is not the first child she has lost, but it is the first time it has ever been a boy. I cannot describe to you the depth of her despair. Knowing how close she was to saving the family estate, and with Thomas gone, even if she did survive this…." He stopped, ashamed to have given voice to such an awful thought.

"But she will survive it," Madeline said hopefully.

"She might. She has before. She lost one after Jane, and another after Lizzy. Johnson says he has seen this pattern before, but she was not so severely injured already the last two times. She has no broken bones, as Phyllis does, but shielding the child on her lap, she took the brunt of the impact, and her body is very badly bruised. She's been in and out of her senses, and briefly lost her sense of time once again. If this is the end, perhaps it might have been better that she did not remember the girls, but she did. She asked to see them and the doctor urged us to comply, if only to give her some little relief. I do wonder if it wasn't a mistake, but it is done."

Mr. Fisher nodded. "It is done, and I think it was done for the best. I believe your sister is in with her now; Mrs. Bennet was asking for her when we first arrived."

"Is she quite well enough to move? I think you said she had some broken bones," Madeline said softly.

Mr. Gardiner took her hand in his. "If the doctor allowed it, I must trust him in this. Everything is in his hands now."

"No, my son," Mr. Fisher replied. "It is in God's hands. Perhaps it might give you some comfort if we began to pray?"

"Yes, I believe I would like that," Mr. Gardiner replied, choking back a sob.

The three of them bowed their heads and Mr. Fisher led them in prayer for a quarter of an hour or more. Though Mr. Gardiner was not a particularly spiritual man, despite planning to marry the daughter of a clergyman, he tried to seek comfort in Mr. Fisher's words. Rubbing his thumb over Madeline's soft little fingers, he felt the parson's words begin to blur together, the sound of Mr. Fisher's deep baritone voice soothing and reassuring. He felt his shoulders begin to lean against Madeline, and it was her nearness more than anything that finally stopped Mr. Gardiner's tears. He would be strong, because of her, and for her.

A short while after they finished their prayers, they were joined by the Darcys, who entered the gallery hand in hand. "The girls are back in bed," Mr. Darcy informed them. "Little Lizzy required a glass of milk with a couple drops of brandy, but they are all three sleeping peacefully now."

Mr. Gardiner gave a hollow laugh. "I've always said she's all Thomas, that one."

"We saw Doctor Johnson – Miss Gardiner is still with Fanny, and she is asking to see you, Miss Fisher," Mr. Darcy added, helping the young lady to her feet.

Mr. Gardiner reluctantly released Madeline's hand, and she peered nervously back at him. "They are to be your sisters," he said encouragingly. Mr. Fisher nodded his agreement.

"Come along, my dear, I will show you the way," Lady Anne said, offering Madeline her arm.

Madeline shyly linked her arm through Lady Anne's. "Yes, of course. I am happy to give her whatever comfort I can."

As he watched Madeline go, Mr. Gardiner began to feel some doubt as to whether he ought to have allowed it – a young woman on the brink of marriage, and whose fiancé dearly wanted children of his own, should really not be exposed to what she would see in Fanny's sickroom. On the other hand, Fanny had asked for her, and if it would give his sister any comfort to meet his future bride, Mr. Gardiner could not deny her that.

Lady Anne returned after showing Madeline into Fanny's room, and sat beside her husband on the sofa, opposite Mr. Gardiner, while Mr. Fisher began to pace, peering out the windows as the first rays of sunlight crept over the horizon. Lady Anne leaned against her husband, her head on his shoulder and her hands clasped in his, clearly trying to hold herself together. After sitting in silence for a few minutes, she met Mr. Gardiner's eye and said, "I had the impression yesterday that your sister must have been quite lively and sociable in her younger days."

Mr. Gardiner smiled reminiscently. "That is certainly a delicate way of putting it. Very perceptive of you, your ladyship."

"I always wished for a sister," Mr. Darcy mused aloud. "I was an only child – I lost two brothers quite young. What was it like, growing up with your sisters?"

Mr. Gardiner felt his eyes begin to mist over as he chuckled. "Like having three mothers. My goodness, how they would fuss over me. Despite being several years my junior, they have both, since they were old enough to speak, known exactly what was best for me, and never hesitated to make their sentiments known to me. Marriage has certainly made Fanny even more of an authority on a wide variety of subjects. I have not always enjoyed being the recipient of such solicitude, but now I find I would not be content without it. It is good to feel so cared for, so looked after. They have always been my biggest supporters."

"They must have been so happy when you found yourself such a fine young lady to settle down with, to come such a distance," Lady Anne said, choking back tears.

Sensing what she meant, Mr. Gardiner met her eyes with an earnest look and replied, "I do not blame you for the accident, Lady Anne."

She nodded, weeping softly, and buried her face in her husband's shoulder.

They were interrupted then by Madeline's return to the gallery. Mr. Gardiner stood, hoping Madeline would come to him, but she only glanced his way before bursting into tears and running to her father. Mr. Fisher hugged his daughter, patting her head as he gently whispered words of reassurance that Mr. Gardiner could not quite make out. Madeline whispered something back to her father. His face grew somber, but he gently nodded.

"Mr. Darcy, Lady Anne," said he, "I think we must be returning to the village now." Madeline wouldn't meet Mr. Gardiner's eye as she hastened away with her father.

3

⮦⮤

Three days after the tragic conclusion of their journey north, Thomas and Fanny Bennet were laid to rest in the Lambton churchyard. The funeral was presided over by Mr. Fisher, and attended by Mr. Gardiner, Mr. Darcy, and, inexplicably, the Earl of Matlock and his two adolescent sons.

After everything was said that was right and appropriate for the occasion, Mr. Darcy and his brother-in-law had intended to ride back to Pemberley with Mr. Gardiner, but it had been two days since Mr. Gardiner had seen Madeline, and had heard nothing from the parsonage since she left Pemberley hours before Fanny passed.

The wedding was only two days away, but obviously must be postponed – there was much for him to discuss with his fiancée – not only the postponement of their wedding, but the arrangements that must be made for his nieces. He had hoped to start a family soon, naturally, but beginning their marriage with three young girls in their care was a matter of great delicacy, which he needed to discuss with the companion of his future life.

Mr. Gardiner expressed his intentions to Mr. Fisher, hoping that given the circumstances, he and Madeline might be permitted a prolonged period of private interview when they returned to the parsonage. Mr. Fisher was polite and obliging in this matter, acknowledging all the importance of what Mr. Gardiner must wish to discuss with his betrothed. To Mr. Gardiner's distress, Madeline was far less willing to speak with him. As her father led her into the front parlor to sit and speak with him, Mr. Gardiner expected some tender greeting from his beloved; he needed nothing so desperately as to fall into her arms and hold her for some time before he could begin to gather his thoughts into some semblance of rationality. Instead, his desolation was met with cold reserve, which even her father seemed to notice; his expression was one of sad concern as he closed the door behind himself and left the two lovers alone.

Mr. Gardiner move to embrace his beloved, but she took a step back and just gestured for him to sit across from her at a little table near the window that looked out on the garden. He leaned forward on one of the two embroidered arm chairs, hoping to take her hands in his across the table, but she withdrew again.

"You needn't be nervous, my love," he said. "I have assured your father that, given the circumstances, you and I must have a serious conversation in privacy. I am sure he would permit you to take my hand at such a time, for we have a great many matters to discuss."

"Indeed we have, sir," Madeline said softly, her expression inscrutable.

"To begin with, we must present your father with a new wedding date, as we cannot wed two days hence. Although it would be more expedient, regarding our moving to London with my nieces, I think it a right thing to wait a month before we wed. I can arrange for a short-term nanny or the like to look after the girls until then. I know we have only ever talked about starting a family *someday*, and it is a far different thing to take on the care of three small girls immediately upon marriage, but I have every faith in you, my love, and I know we shall rise to the challenge together."

Madeline's face crumpled, but she did not shed any tears. She only shook her head and said, "No, Edward, I cannot do it. I cannot marry you."

Mr. Gardiner recoiled. "Madeline, what are you saying? Do you wish to wait until I am in half-mourning?"

"No, not even then. Not at all, not ever."

"I know it is a lot to ask. It is not what I expected when I proposed, but we shall have my sister Phyllis there with us, too, to help with the children. And of course we can still have our own. My career is promising, and I *will* rise, I promise you that."

"No, I cannot. The children – I swear it isn't them. Had one of their parents survived, had they somewhere else to go, even then my answer should be no."

"But why?" He could feel his head spinning, overpowering his ability to speak. After everything that happened, now this? He could not make sense of it all.

"When I was with your sister – oh, it was too horrible."

Mr. Gardiner struggled to process what she was saying, and stammered, "No, no, this cannot be happening." And then it hit him. She had seen Fanny losing her child, and dying from it. He should never have let her in that room. "Dear God," he gasped, nearly weeping. "I am so sorry, Madeline. But you need never give me children, not if you do not wish it. I would not ask you to put yourself in that danger, if that is what you fear. We shall have the girls, and that will be enough. Of course you would not wish to bear my children after what you have seen."

She shook her head, not meeting his eye. "It is not what I have seen, but what I have heard – no, I will not speak of it. I cannot marry you, Edward. Not now, not ever. Your sister died, her children were orphaned, all for the sake of coming here, for this wedding – it cannot ever take place. That is all I will say. I must ask you to leave."

Madeline stood and began to withdraw, when Mr. Gardiner leapt to his feet and grabbed her hand. "Madeline, no. You cannot do this to me. I cannot live without you. I cannot get through this without you. I beg you, I beg you reconsider."

A look of disdain on her countenance, Madeline pulled her hand away, slowly retreating toward the door as she pressed her eyes shut. "No, Edward. Do not ask me to think about it any further; I am resolute. You must go now, and do not come back again."

Mr. Gardiner could bear it no longer; finally a sob escaped his lips. And that was it – as soon as he broke down, Madeline fled the room, and a moment later Mr. Fisher entered. He did not appear entirely surprised by what was passing. Mr. Gardiner looked at him with a mounting sense of dread. "She has broken off the engagement," he said flatly, in a voice not his own.

Mr. Fisher folded his arms behind his back and bowed his head slightly. "I see. I had suspected she might, but I did not wish to burden you until it was absolutely certain. I confess I had hoped your plans for the girls might sway her, however I will own it *is* a lot to ask."

"Yes I suppose it is, though she claimed that was not her reason for breaking the engagement. I do not know what to think, or what to do… I do not know how I shall get on at all…." Mr. Gardiner managed a grimace, still feeling dazed, and rather foolish now.

Mr. Fisher looked up, his eyes betraying more sympathy than his stern expression usually allowed. "I think you had better return to Pemberley. I am sure you would find a welcoming ear if you choose to confide in the Darcys. Your hosts are excellent people, and I give you leave to share the details of what has transpired here, if it would give you any comfort. Surely some arrangements must be made for your sister's recovery, and your nieces. You must prepare to resume your life, with your relations under your care. You are a good man, Gardiner; you will remain in my prayers. However, if my daughter has asked you – and I am sure she has, to keep some distance – I must ask you to respect that. I would not have her burdened if she feels that this is all too much for her."

Mr. Gardiner nodded absently and slowly moved to the door, scarcely feeling Mr. Fisher clap him on the back as they parted ways. He knew not how he made his way back to Pemberley.

***

Mr. Gardiner was accosted by an elegantly attired woman in her mid-sixties, who waved her cane at him as she exited the manor and approached a very grand carriage in front drive at Pemberley. He tipped his hat. "Good day, madam," he said, still feeling half mad with grief.

"That is not what I hear," she quipped with a sympathetic turn of her countenance. "I am Lady Eleanor Fitzwilliam, Dowager Countess of Matlock – Lady Anne's mother. You must be Mr. Gardiner, I presume. You have my condolences, sir. Indeed, I have just been paying them to your dear sister."

Mr. Gardiner was in too great a state of bewilderment already to form any rational response to this new, surprising development. The dowager waited a moment before realizing no response would be forthcoming. "Well," she said, stepping forward to clasp his hand in hers, "I have heard a great deal about you and your dear late sister from Phyllis, and I look forward to coming to know you better through Phyllis, as your sister and I grow better acquainted ourselves."

"Indeed?" Mr. Gardiner could only gape at the dowager, unable to express that he had not the pleasure of understanding her at all.

"Oh yes, my daughter Catherine sorted it all out before she left for Kent, a record success even for her. You see, young man, my last companion experienced the most perverse inclination to accept a proposal of marriage! I have not the least intention of moldering away all summer at the dower house by myself, and when your sister is recovered from her injuries, she will take up the position as my new companion. Perhaps we will go to Bath, or to Brighton. She is a lovely girl, and I do hope you are not unwilling to part with her."

Mr. Gardiner had winced at the word *marriage*, and scarcely absorbed any of the information that followed it. He nodded anyhow.

"Well," the dowager continued with a good-humored smile, "I can well understand your being reticent on a day like today, but another time I should like to speak with you further, as I have heard nothing but your praise every time I speak with dear Phyllis. You will call on me before you return to London, at the dower house at Matlock. Then you must visit, of course, once Phyllis is all settled in. How snug we shall be, when we are not traveling about. Oh! And here I am, you poor man, being *overpowering*, as my daughters would say. I shall leave you in peace now, but I shall be expecting that visit."

Mr. Gardiner felt as if he was watching through thick fog as the dowager countess was handed into her carriage, which quickly sped down the driveway, and he did not stir until it was long out of sight. Only then did it strike him that somehow, in the last three days, his sister had agreed to become the dowager's companion, without even mentioning it to him. "What is to become of those poor girls," he groaned.

And then he saw them. Perhaps fifty yards distant, Lady Anne and her brother the earl were walking on the lawn with his nieces. Lady Anne held Mary in her arms as little Lizzy ambled along at her side, and a boy of ten or eleven was pushing little Jane in the bath chair Lady Anne had procured the previous day. It had been brought to the house for Phyllis's use, and how tiny Jane looked in it! Mr. Gardiner could not help but give a little smile at the sight of it.

Lady Anne caught sight of Mr. Gardiner, and raised her free hand to wave at him, motioning for him to join them. He hesitated, still overwhelmed by all that had transpired that morning, but just alert enough to be sensible of the fact that he could not possibly hold a rational conversation with his hostess. She waved again, and this time was joined by the earl – Mr. Gardiner sighed, knowing he could not demur.

He took every step towards them with deliberation, struggling to recollect himself. He had buried one sister, lost the other, and had his heart broken all in the space of one morning, and after his encounter with the dowager countess, his capacity to speak with so many noble near-strangers was waning. Attempting to conceal his pain and confusion, he scooped little Lizzy into his arms as he joined their happy grouping.

"Your sister was worried when you did not return with Henry and George, but I am sure the walk must have done you good. I saw you speaking with Mamma," Lady Anne said. "If I had known you were to cross paths, I would have introduced you properly, and given you some warning."

"She can be... vocal," the earl drawled. "She sat with your sister for quite some time; I am sure she was glad of the meeting."

"Aye, she was very kind," Mr. Gardiner replied.

"Did she tell you anything in particular," Lady Anne asked.

"I was most astonished – she means to take my sister as a companion. I am very grateful, I am sure," Mr. Gardiner said, scarcely knowing what he was about. "I have only now to consider what is to be done with my nieces. They ought to have a mother figure." He frowned, the sight of little Mary in Lady Anne's arms tearing at his heart. She looked so maternal, so natural with them, and it was no longer a possibility he might envision of Madeline Fisher.

Lady Anne offered him a gentle smile. "Surely it will not be so long until your mourning is up, and you and Miss Fisher can wed, I am sure. We are at your disposal, should you require any assistance in making arrangements until you and your bride remove to London. Miss Gardiner mentioned you recently purchased a house in Gracechurch Street. I am sure it will be very cozy once you have your family settled in with you."

Mr. Gardiner looked away. "I believe I must – that is, I will not – we...." He broke off and looked away, drawing Lizzy close to him.

"William," the earl said, turning to look down at his nephew. "I believe our friends have been exploring with you long enough. They must get some rest. Why don't you help your Mamma get Miss Jane inside. Anne...." He reached for Lizzy, gently taking her from Mr. Gardiner's arms and giving her a pat on the head before setting her down on her feet at Lady Anne's side.

"Yes, of course," Lady Anne replied, concern in her eyes as she looked from Mr. Gardiner to her brother, and then down at little Lizzy, whose hand she clasped in her own. "Come girls, let us see if your aunt is still awake."

As Lady Anne and her son led the girls back toward the manor, the earl stood with his hands folded behind his back and watched them go before clearing his throat to address Mr. Gardiner. "You were not long in the village. I suppose you called on your betrothed – I understand she is the parson's daughter."

"She is the parson's daughter, yes, but she is no longer my betrothed," Mr. Gardiner said evenly.

"I see. If you will permit me the liberty of speaking candidly with you, sir, though we are not well acquainted...."

"Yes, of course." Mr. Gardiner was past the point of being astonished by anything that transpired anymore. Though he had never been the object of interest to an earl before, the unfortunate circumstances that had thrust him into the Darcys' lives must be a concern for their relations, to some degree.

"Good, good. You strike me as an honest, respectable man, and I have heard nothing of you that would contradict my impression. My sister feels very deeply toward your family, even a measure of guilt for what has befallen you. It is perhaps more my brother's place to have this conversation with you, but as he is resolving some tenant matters at present, I believe I am within my rights to speak candidly with you now. Beyond my condolences for your loss, and for the dissolution of your engagement, I should like to offer you a word of advice. You must be weighing your option as regards the future of your nieces, given that they have lost their parents, and now they shall have neither their Aunt

Gardiner – for which you might rightly fault my mother and sister – nor your intended bride as a mother."

"I see you understand me, sir," Mr. Gardiner replied, still uncertain why the earl should wish to discuss such things with him. "However, I can assure you that I have no intention of trespassing on your sister and her husband's kindness. My troubles are my own, and I was raised to be my own man."

The earl nodded. "I do not doubt it. However, if you have any doubts – any uncertainty as to how you are to raise three young girls on your own…."

"I confess I have a great many doubts at present; I have only just learned it is what I must plan for."

"Indeed. As to that, if you would allow me to hint that the Darcys, as you know, are excellent people – they would be willing to do a great deal for the girls, I believe, by way of assistance, should you be interested."

"That is very kind, and I am certain you must be right, but I cannot ask that of them. Perhaps Phyllis will reconsider her plans. I dare not hope that Madeline would change her mind."

"And if neither of them is willing to budge? What then? I am sure your sister is a good sort of girl, who would happily forego the opportunity of becoming my mother's companion, if you asked it of her; indeed, my mother would not have offered her the position if she were not such a person. However, I hope I am not too bold in saying that you must think carefully before you would ask this of her. My mother's last companion married far and away beyond what she might ever have imagined. In five years she was able to put by a small fortune of her own, and married a man of some property. Though I have no doubt your sister would gladly return to London with you for the sake of her nieces, taking this position might be the making of her."

Mr. Gardiner frowned as he considered this. "I could never ask her to give up anything she truly desired, certainly not after all that she has been through. If this is what she wants, what is best… but it does not answer the question of how I am ever to raise those poor girls on my own. They need a mother, and I cannot imagine that I shall ever marry, if Madeline will not have me. And yet, how could I ask her to shoulder such a responsibility, when it terrifies me?"

"I saw it in your eyes, when you looked at my sister. Those girls need a mother."

"They need a mother," Mr. Gardiner repeated sadly. "Well, unless you happen to know how any heiresses that would have a heart-broken tradesman with three young wards, I cannot say I know what I am to do next."

The earl gave a rueful laugh. "No, I cannot say I have any of those on hand at the moment. But I can tell you, if my sister has not, why she was in her carriage that day. Has she mentioned it to you?"

"I know nothing of her reasons for traveling, other than that she bitterly regrets it."

"I am sure she does, and I am sure she is afraid to mention it."

"I understand she must feel awful for her part in the accident, but I do not blame her and her sister. "How could I? How could I want to hear that there is one more heart broken in this tragedy?"

The earl was quiet for a moment, then replied, "She was going to Bath. My sister is a busy woman, you see – Catherine takes great pleasure in making herself useful whenever she can, and in this instance she had convinced Anne that she had found a physician in Bath who could give her what she has wanted these ten years – another child."

"I see. With all due respect, I am not certain you should be telling me this."

"I think you need to hear it. Indeed, I think that on some level you must have sensed it yourself, the maternal instinct Anne has already come to feel for your nieces. I have."

"She is a very kind woman. I assure you, I am fully cognizant of the good fortune my family has had in finding ourselves in such capable hands. They could have just as easily collided with the carriage of a much less generous family."

"They *are* a generous family – I do not know if you realize just how much they may be willing to do. I know my sister and her husband well, Mr. Gardiner, and if you were to speak to them candidly about your plans for the future of those three girls – including any doubts you might have about raising them yourself, Mr. Darcy would agree to raise them here at Pemberley."

"And Lady Anne desires this?"

"She desires it so deeply that she will likely be unable to give voice to it. That is why it must be Darcy. He knows his wife's heart, and he would give her anything she desired in this world. It must be for him to work through her guilt, and persuade her to accept it. The guilt she feels over causing your sister's death will lead her to deny herself that which would give her the greatest joy, should you wish for them to take in your nieces. Darcy will agree to it, to spare her the burden of taking what she wants, for she believes that she is to blame for their being orphaned in the first place. And yet, she would be a good mother to them. Do you think you might be amenable to such an arrangement?"

"To be perfectly honest with your lordship, I cannot even imagine ever presuming to ask such a thing of them."

"And if I were to speak on your behalf? Let us suppose their agreement is a certainty — could *you* like such an arrangement? Does the challenge of raising them outweigh the pain of being separated from them?"

Mr. Gardiner let out a heavy sigh. They had been walking about the lawn for some time, and he approached a bench nearby. "I believe I must sit down for a moment, if you will permit me. This is a lot to think on, and today has been… taxing."

"Yes, of course," the earl replied, though he remained standing.

"To answer your question, I suppose what *I* feel in this matter is of the least importance. Let us say, for the sake of argument, that your sister and her husband would agree to such a thing. It would certainly be in the best interest of the girls, that is an indisputable fact. Your family could give them things I certainly never could – the advantages are almost incomprehensible to me. To have a mother, a kind and gentle one, a father, brother, and even cousins nearby – not to mention your sister's situation in life…. Even if I thought myself up to the hardest task of bringing them up in London, which is daunting but not impossible, I daresay – how could such an upbringing possibly compare? How could I face them, knowing what I had denied them? No, I cannot deny my sister the opportunity that has been offered to her, and I could no more do the same to my nieces. I could not live with myself. But I should hate to think them lost to me forever – that is, I would not wish to seem as though I were putting myself forward, but I should still like to see them, to be permitted visits, especially if Phyllis is nearby. And what of my sister? Would my nieces know their aunt only as the companion to their lady grandmother?" Mr. Gardiner realized he was babbling – he must seemed a damned fool to the earl.

"It sounds as if there is a long conversation with Mr. Darcy ahead of us, sir. Think it over for the day; I could ride over tomorrow, if you wish it."

"I will think it over, and speak with Mr. Darcy in the morning, if he is available. I thank you for your interest in the matter, and I shall send word to you if anything is resolved."

"Very good, Mr. Gardiner. I do hope I have done all of you a favor – I believe it will all work out to everyone's satisfaction." The earl extended his hand, and Mr. Gardiner stood to shake it before returning to the manor, where he sat in the library in quiet speculation for quite some time.

4

❧

December 1794, Derbyshire

"I have brought you a cold compress – I thought it might be time to change out your bandages," Lady Anne said meekly, giving a perfunctory knock on the open door to the library.

Mr. Gardiner nodded and gestured for Lady Anne to take a seat beside him as he set aside the damp rag he had been holding to his bruised face for the last few hours. Lady Anne busied herself with changing out the bandage at his temple before offering him the cold compress and taking a seat near the window that overlooked the lawn. "How is your headache?"

"No worse than I deserve, I suppose," he replied, flinching as he pressed the cold compress against his bruised face.

"I cannot agree with that," she chided. "How could you have known? I blame myself. I reside but five miles away – I ought to have known of Miss Fisher's new attachment. I could have warned you."

"And I ought to have exercised better judgment, and heeded her father's warning to keep away," Mr. Gardiner side. He had struggled to remain strong in the face of his heartbreak, but finally succumbed to his desperate yearning to see Madeline, to win her back. He had been soundly throttled for his efforts by her new beau, a man of considerable means as well as muscle.

"Are you quite sure you do not wish to report that awful man to the magistrate?"

Mr. Gardiner considered. "I cannot see what it would accomplish. If he is jailed or fined, Madeline will despise me even more than she does now."

"You do not suppose – he would not harm Miss Fisher, would he?"

Mr. Gardiner knew not what to say. The truth, which he could hardly bear to admit to the woman who had through six months of correspondence become quite a dear friend to him, was that he rather deserved the thrashing he had received. He had disregarded Madeline's wishes and proper decorum itself by returning to the parsonage to see her, only to make some rather spiteful comments once he had discovered how quickly his former fiancé had recovered from their broken engagement and bestowed her affections elsewhere. In short, he had provoked the man, and gotten what he deserved.

Unable to own up to his own behavior – he recalled with a near certainty that he had thrown the first punch – Mr. Gardiner thought it best to change the subject. After all, this was the Christmas visit he and his sister had long looked forward to, and he could not bear the idea of ruining it for her, or for their nieces and the Darcys. "Lady Eleanor is going to have a conniption when she sees me."

Lady Anne laughed. "Indeed, Mamma has taken quite a fancy to you. She dotes on your dear sister, and takes an eager interest in the letters you send Miss Gardiner, as well as myself. She calls you her young beau."

"Oh my," Mr. Gardiner said, both mortified and amused. "Perhaps she might change her mind on that score, when she sees me like this. I hope I do not frighten the children!"

"We must come up with a story for their sake, I think. Perhaps we could tell them that you fell out of a tree, rescuing a kitten? George told me the tabby in the barn had another litter, and thought one of the kittens might make a fine gift for the girls, though I would have preferred a puppy."

"Fanny loved animals – I think the girls would do well with a kitten, and it is certainly a better tale to tell them about why I am looking rather worse for wear."

"They shall think you quite the hero," Lady Anne said with a smile, and gestured for him to join her by the window.

Mr. Gardiner stood near her and they peered outside together. The snow had started just the day before, when he had arrived at Pemberley, and there was just enough of it on the ground as to render the landscape unspeakably beautiful. Indeed, nothing could be more picturesque than the sight before him, his nieces playing on the lawn with the earl's three children and young William Darcy.

"My brother's children have come to stay with us for a while – he has a house full of visitors at Matlock, and thought it best the children remain someplace... quieter."

"I see," Mr. Gardiner replied, uncertain why Lady Anne should appear so concerned by her brother's house party. "More Fitzwilliams come to enjoy the festivities?"

"Something like that," she said with a thin smile. "It is the countess's family. Her father is the Earl of Abingdon. He has brought his youngest daughter, the countess's sister – perhaps you have heard of her? Lady Olivia Bertie – I believe her name has been in the papers lately...."

"It sounds familiar, but I cannot recall why. At any rate, it is good to see the girls getting on with their cousins."

They were interrupted by Mr. Darcy, who ambled into the library with his steward's son, a boy of about nine or ten, trailing behind him excitedly. "There you are, Edward! I was worried I would not know your face, old chap – Anne said it was all black and blue, but I daresay you shall be right as rain by Twelfth Night!"

Mr. Gardiner glanced at Lady Anne, who gave a sheepish shrug as her exaggeration was exposed. "I am well enough, though my battle scars are gruesome to behold," he said wryly.

Mr. Darcy laughed. "Very good, very good. Well, if you are of a mind to ice those bruises and scrapes, you must join young Wickham and me – we are to surprise the other children with a snowball fight. Dare I hope you shall go easy on me?" He winked.

Lady Anne swatted at her husband. "Shocking, George!"

"I should be happy to join you," Mr. Gardiner replied, "though as I am the one who is nearly injured past recognition, perhaps it is you who ought to show some mercy."

***

The twelve days of Christmas were merry enough to keep Mr. Gardiner's mind off of his troubles, with frequent visits between Matlock and Pemberley, and finer food and company than he was accustomed to. All this, and more importantly, the delight his nieces felt at his inclusion in the festivities, served to heal not only his physical wounds but those of his heart. Seeing Phyllis content, both valued and indulged by the dowager countess, pleased Mr. Gardiner immensely. Knowing his nieces were likewise treasured, not only by the Darcys but all of their extended family, brought him an even greater joy. He had made the right decision in leaving them at Pemberley to be wards of the Darcys, rather than trying to raise them alone in London.

His time at Pemberley passed faster than he would have wished. Each day was so full of activity, and warm affection from his new friends that he felt some glimmer of hope that all would be well. Thus, when he arrived with the Darcys at Matlock Hall for the Twelfth Night ball, he was determined to be of good cheer.

He had yet to dance with anyone aside from the dowager countess, who enjoyed his company in spite of the fading bruises on his face, but he was several drinks in when Mr. Darcy approached and drew him aside. "Come, Edward, I must have you dance. I hate to see you standing about by yourself in this stupid manner – you had much better dance."

"I am sure I should like it very much, but I am not particularly acquainted with anyone in the room." Knowing the dowager countess was well within earshot, Mr. Gardiner winked at his friend and continued, "I have already danced with your mother-in-law, the handsomest woman in the room – it would be a punishment to stand up with anyone else after such a pleasure."

Mr. Darcy laughed. "Not still pining for Miss Fisher, I hope."

Mr. Gardiner shook his head, and tried to sound convincing. "I have put her from my mind entirely, I assure you. I have far too much to be grateful for, to dwell on the disappointment."

"Good man. Well then, what say you to partnering Lady Olivia Bertie? I daresay she must be handsome enough to tempt you." Mr. Darcy inclined his head in the lady's direction, but Mr. Gardiner was aware of who she was. They had been introduced when the Fitzwilliams had come to Pemberley on Christmas Day, though they had spoken but little. At the time he had been too occupied with his nieces to spare much time for anyone else, and he could just as easily suppose that the bruises on his face had not been particularly alluring to such a beautiful woman.

"She is quite a sight," Mr. Gardiner acknowledged. Lady Olivia was spectacular in the truest sense of the word. Her person was very elegant, her curves exquisite, and her gown obviously expensive and tailored to flatter what nature had given her, even to the point of pushing the bounds of propriety. The spectacle was completed by the wide variety of reactions he had seen her inspire in those around her. The dowager countess would not speak to her, her sister the countess and Lady Anne seemed to look at her with inexplicable pity, and the other ladies present merely gave her a wide berth, which he supposed must be due to the amount of interest she seemed to inspire in the gentlemen.

Mr. Gardiner had never been the type of man to find himself drawn to the loveliest girl in the room; he liked a pretty face well enough, but preferred it to be coupled with a more reserved demeanor, and Lady Olivia struck him as far from shy. As if sensing his eyes on her, she glanced over and gave him a coy smile, then flicked open her fan to hide everything but her dark, piercing eyes.

"It is a shame she is not dancing more," Mr. Darcy observed. "Come, let us go and speak with her. I am always moved to pity the poor young ladies who are slighted by other men."

It was true; though Lady Olivia was attracting a great deal of attention from the gentlemen present, none had stood up with her. Mr. Gardiner decided that should not deter him, and he followed Mr. Darcy across the room. Lady Olivia watched with obvious pleasure as they made their approach. She rose from her seat and flagged down a footman carrying a tray of champagne, and took a long sip from her glass as she observed them.

"I hope you have brought me some amusing company, Mr. Darcy. I find the entertainment tonight rather disappointing compared to London."

Mr. Darcy looked rather taken aback, but Mr. Gardiner schooled his countenance into a determined smile. "If it would amuse you to dance the next with me, Lady Olivia, I hope I shall not disappoint." He gave a little bow and watched with pleasure as Lady Olivia broke into a wide smile.

"And if you do, how shall you make amends?"

"Well, let me see. The last time I disappointed a lady, I acquired quite a fine arrangement of color on my face – here, you can still see what's left of *that* reproof, so I shall simply have to do my best to entertain you."

Mr. Darcy looked on with nervous approbation, and Lady Olivia gave a coquettish nod of her head. "Very well then, sir, but you must be forewarned, my standards are very high."

Mr. Gardiner took Lady Olivia by the hand and led her to the set that was just forming. She was an intimidating woman, despite appearing quite young – she couldn't have been more than eighteen. And yet, there was a look of great sophistication and intelligence about her, a wit that wanted some occupation, and it was rather fearful to behold.

"Did a lady really give you those bruises, sir? I have wondered about them since first we met. I concocted a story in my own mind, one dull night at Pemberley, but I am sure my own version of events is far more thrilling than reality – that is often the case."

"It was not a lady," Mr. Gardiner replied. "It was her new fiancé. And since you were hoping for something quite shocking, I shall tell you candidly that I quite deserved it."

Lady Olivia's eyes were wide and bright as she laughed. "My goodness, what luck for me – an interesting man at last – and finally one to whom even *I* seem a wiser choice!"

Mr. Gardiner could tell from the trace of challenge in her voice that this must be some allusion to what Lady Anne had hinted at, what seemed to be some thinly veiled secret about the stunning creature before him. And yet, he found he did not care. Intoxicated by her pertly expressed interest in him, he simply wanted to enjoy a lively dance with a beautiful woman, and keep the memory of Madeline Fisher tucked away where it belonged.

"If you have no broad-shouldered beau with a penchant for boxing lurking about, I think we shall both be quite safe," he teased her.

"No," she said in a breathy voice, "I haven't got one of those."

Their dance together was a pleasant one; her willingness to flirt was gratifying, and he was emboldened by the ease with which he was able to recommend himself to his partner. He had little to say of himself that would not instantly expose him as far beneath her notice, but she seemed bent on turning the conversation to her own amusement, and he was content to listen to her speak of her time at court, while he soaked in the sight of her.

As he led her from the dance floor toward the refreshment table afterward, they were approached by the Earl of Matlock. Mr. Gardiner began to fear he had crossed a line in so openly enjoying the company of the earl's sister-in-law, but Lord Matlock clapped him on the back and smiled. "Well done, Gardiner. What a splendid couple the two of you made out there. Well done, indeed."

Lady Olivia gave the earl a sardonic look before curtseying to Mr. Gardiner. "If the two of you are going to discuss me as if I am not even present, I suppose I shall leave you to it." She winked at Mr. Gardiner and gave her brother-in-law one last impertinent roll of her eyes before she moved away.

Indifferent to Lady Olivia's behavior, the earl remained focused on Mr. Gardiner, and led him toward the edge of the ballroom. "The two of you certainly seemed to get on well."

"Yes, I suppose so. I hope I have not offended your lordship in any way."

The earl guffawed and clapped Mr. Gardiner on the back again. "Far from it, my good man, far from it." He glanced around them, noticing as Mr. Gardiner had that Lady Anne was standing at some remove, her arms crossed, her countenance full of disapproval. The earl looked away, pretending not to notice, and continued addressing Mr. Gardiner. "It occurs to me that we ought to continue this conversation somewhere more private. I hope you enjoy cigars and brandy as much as I do."

Mr. Gardiner agreed that he did, and followed the earl to the library, away from the condition of the ball. Lord Matlock gestured for Mr. Gardiner to be seated and poured them each a generous amount of brandy before he retrieved the cigar box from his desk and sat down across from his guest. Still unsure as to the nature of their conversation, Mr. Gardiner accepted the proffered cigar with some hesitation, and thanked the earl.

"Pah. I ought to be thanking you. Lady Olivia is... difficult, to say the least. I was most impressed to see how civil she was with you."

"She was very civil indeed – do you mean to say that this is out of the ordinary?"

The earl studied Mr. Gardiner, twirling the cigar in his hands as he considered his answer. "If I was to say yes, would you think any less of her?"

"I do not know, sir. I suppose I should prefer to judge her based on what I have seen of her, rather than what I hear from others, though I mean no disrespect. I respect the value of your advice, of course, however…."

"Come, come, you need not stand upon ceremony with me. Let us drink until you stop thinking so much of rank." The earl reached for the brandy and refilled both their glasses.

"Very well then – might I ask what all this is leading to?"

"Ha! I should bloody well hope you'd come to the point of it! I am asking you to marry her."

Mr. Gardiner downed his glass of brandy and stared at Lord Matlock in disbelief. "What?"

The earl laughed, puffing thoughtfully at his cigar. "I must surmise that you do not know about Lady Olivia."

"Your sister hinted that there was something in the papers, but I have been too occupied with my family to think of such things."

"Yes, your halo is quite radiant," Lord Matlock drawled. "Well, I suppose I ought to tell you the truth. My father-in-law, Lord Abingdon, is one of the oldest peers in England. I fear he has outlived his ability to control his children, his youngest daughter in particular. To put it plainly, she is with child, and she must marry quickly."

Mr. Gardiner set down his drink and reeled for a moment at the shock of the earl's casual revelation. "And the father of this child?"

The earl smiled wryly and sipped at his brandy. "An Englishman, whose name I serve the crown best by concealing. He is engaged to a certain lady of Brunswick, and soon to be wed. Olivia was not best pleased by his dismissal, but if we can keep her quiet about it, out of his sight and away from court and Carlton House… there may be a knighthood in it for you."

"If she would have me," Mr. Gardiner said with no little incredulity. "I cannot imagine a tradesman of little standing and a fortune still yet to be made would be high on the list of suitable fathers for a child of this nature."

The earl guffawed again. "I like you, Gardiner. In all honesty, you are far from the first man I've asked. I have already spoken to six of the most eligible, Tory bachelors here tonight, and they have all turned me down flat. However, just because you were not my first choice, it does not follow that you are not a good choice. She is still my sister by marriage, after all, and I am confident that you would be good to her. Your fortune is of less importance to me; as you say, it has not been made *yet*. If Olivia behaves, there may yet be some provision made for the child in that regard, and I was quite serious about the knighthood, you know. It would not be the first time such a thing as happened. But it would be the first time such a thing has happened in *this* family, and that is something I will absolutely not allow. Olivia will marry, from this house, as soon as a special license can be procured. I understand if your answer is no, after all that you have been through this year, but I will hope you will give it some thought – and quickly."

Lord Matlock sipped at his brandy before refilling the glass. "She is not an ideal choice of bride, of course, but she could be the making of you, and you may yet be happy together. She has an active mind that turns wicked when it is not occupied, but she can be loyal and even pleasant when she wishes it. As you are one of only a few in attendance tonight that she has not been astonishingly rude to, I would say you stand a fair chance of happiness with her."

Mr. Gardiner let out a heavy sigh and gestured with his empty glass toward the bottle of brandy – the earl poured him another drink, and he took a long draught of it. "Lady Anne, no doubt, has made you aware of what transpired with Miss Fisher?"

The earl nodded. "I was damned sorry to hear it, Gardiner. For what it's worth, your face is looking a lot better."

Mr. Gardiner touched his fingers to his face, where one of the bruises had actually burst open and bled – Doctor Johnson had said it would require stitches, but he had refused. The black eye had begun to fade, but the scar would remain. "And what does Lady Anne know of our conversation here? I saw you exchange a look before. I have no doubt Mr. Darcy must have understood your intentions when he introduced me to Lady Olivia, but I should like to know what his wife thinks on the matter. Or the dowager, for that matter."

Lord Matlock smiled with bemusement. "You wish for a second opinion? I will tell you candidly, you'll not receive a sterling character reference from either of them. Shall I send for my mother? I am sure she would love to have a drink with us and tell you exactly what she thinks of Lady Olivia."

"No, I am sure that will not be necessary, though I have no doubt it would be edifying to say the least."

"I understand you may need to think it over. The knighthood is a near certainty, in my opinion, and I am sure in time there would be some financial provision for the child, though likely no public acknowledgment. Spend some time with her tonight, if you can. She is not ignorant of my actions on her behalf tonight, and you are one of the only options I can imagine her being amenable to, after seeing you together."

Mr. Gardiner finished his drink and the glass when the earl offered another. With a heavy sigh, his thoughts drifted back to London – to some improvements he made in the front parlor of his house on Gracechurch Street, the vision he once had of Madeline writing her letters there, sitting with their children there, or jumping up from the window seat to give him a kiss whenever he stepped in to surprise her with flowers for her writing desk. The image faded as he watched the thick smoke curling around his cigar, and the earl looked expectantly at him. "I need no time to consider – how could I say no? If you will assist me in the arrangements, I would be happy to marry your sister."

Lord Matlock grinned. "Excellent! I shall speak to Abingdon, and we can proceed. I suppose you must wish to speak to Olivia yourself now."

"Truth be told, I cannot imagine telling a lady she has been effectively bartered off to me. I never imagined such a thing would happen, my marriage a business transaction. Perhaps she ought to hear it from her father. I shall speak to her after... after she has had some time to process the news."

"Ha! Smart man!" The earl guffawed. "You are going to make a most amusing brother-in-law, Edward."

"There is one thing more," Mr. Gardiner said, panicked that it had not occurred to him to ask sooner. "Will this change anything about the arrangement with my nieces?"

"I do hope not. My sister would be deeply disappointed, for she has grown attached to your nieces these six months. However, they are *your* nieces."

Mr. Gardiner understood completely, and gave a firm nod of his head. "I cannot imagine that Lady Olivia should desire to take on three young girls, especially in light of her current condition. I suppose it is better that we begin a family of our own, and make no alteration to the current arrangement."

"Very good." The earl extended his hand for Mr. Gardiner to shake. "Well then, Edward, let us go and speak with Abingdon. If all goes well, we can make a formal announcement tonight, and have something put in the papers directly."

5

❧❧

Derbyshire, December 1804

Lady Anne looked about her drawing room and let out a sigh of contentment as she cast her eyes about everything before her – everything she had ever wanted. The Yule log her husband had collected with their son and young George Wickham was blazing brightly in the fireplace, and Mary and Elizabeth were hanging up garlands of holly with little Rose Gardiner and their Fitzwilliam cousins, who were bearing up cheerfully on their first Christmas without their mother. George was turning the sheet music for Jane as she practiced at the pianoforte she had been given for St. Nicholas's day, and the sound of the traditional carol, mixed with the crackling of the fire and the laughter of her children, was sheer bliss.

Upstairs, the rest of her recently arrived relations were settling in from their journey; Catherine, Sir Lewis and Anne, the earl, dowager countess, and Phyllis Gardiner – soon to be Phyllis Fitzwilliam – would join them soon. Sir Edward Gardiner ambled into the room with a broad smile, and Anne patted the sofa beside her.

"How are you this evening, Lady Anne?"

"The same as I am every Christmas – incandescently happy."

"I am glad to hear it," Sir Edward replied, seating himself beside her. "That is just what I love about visiting Pemberley. This place is always full of happiness and laughter."

"It is, is it not?" Anne gazed at her daughters and smiled. "I suppose I owe a great deal of that to you, my old friend. You have given my husband and I three very good reasons to be happy. I only hope that you are half as contented as I am."

Sir Edward smiled sadly; he must have known what she was really saying, and the question she could not bear to ask. "I am well enough. Rose is a delight, in her own way. She is every bit a little princess, you know, and stubborn like her mother."

"Is Lady Olivia well?"

"She will be, after her confinement. She sends her regards, of course. I think she really would have liked to be here this year. It is my hope," he confided in a low voice, "that after the babe comes, she may yet return to her former self. There are still traces of it about her, at times...." He sighed and broke off.

Anne looked away, recalling her attempts, all of which had been in vain, to dissuade him from the match that had brought him wealth and a title, as well as a decade of misery that he had not been able to conceal. Fond as she was of Sir Edward, she had often been forced over the years to remind herself that he was a grown man, capable of making his own decisions. She had long felt little but doubt at his attempts to assure her, whenever Lady Olivia acted up, that he had made his peace with his marriage, if not his wife.

"I have given some thought to your last letter," he said. "If you wish to formally give the girls the Darcy name, I have no objection to it. I think it would be better if I were with them when you and George tell them about it, if only to assure them that they need not feel any uncertainty about the matter."

"Oh, Edward, thank you. Truly, it means the world to George and me. And of course it will be a fine thing for Jane, too, with her going off to school in the new year. She is so very shy, and I think the Darcy name might help her make friends in spite of her reserve."

Sir Edward regarded his eldest niece and smiled warmly. "She is nearly a woman grown, is she not? The years certainly have flown by. She is a fine young lady, and I appreciate your influence on her."

Anne swatted at him. "And what of the other girls?"

"Lizzy is still all Thomas, and I daresay she ever shall be."

"I could not wish her any different. She gives me the most trouble of the three, but between you and I, I confess I rather adore it."

"And little Mary, how she diverts me! I should never have imagined Fanny having a daughter who would be so very serious, and so bookish. She rather reminds me of your William. I see his influence in her, as much as your own."

"And dear William is entirely his father, as I am sure you are aware."

"He has got a good head on his shoulders, and is every bit the gentleman."

Anne smiled to herself as her eyes drifted over to her son. Her husband had shaped William into a fine young man indeed, and she was tremendously proud of him. She only wished that he might, in time, grow closer with the girls. She supposed it was a great disparity in their ages, and the fact that he was already of an age to begin schooling so soon after the girls first came to them, that must have produced this reserve she sensed from him. He was certainly not as outspoken as young George Wickham, their steward's son, but he was easy and open enough with Richard and John Fitzwilliam.

"I think he is rather mortified by Catherine's new notion of his marrying Anne someday," she felt herself blurting out. "He shows the same reserve to poor Charlotte as well."

Sir Edward chuckled. "They are all of them far too young to be thinking of such things yet, but given how time does tend to fly, I am sure we must all be thinking of such things ere long. Soon it will be our girls."

"Perish the thought!" Anne shook her head teasingly, and was on the point of changing the subject entirely when her mother swept into the room. She greeted her family warmly, saving Anne and Sir Edward for last.

"You are looking well tonight, Daughter," she said cheerfully as she took a seat nearby. "And how are you, dear Edward? I hear you have left Lady Olivia in London on this visit. Tell me, how does your charming wife?"

Anne could perceive the barb by the turn of her mother's smile, and suspected Sir Edward could as well, but he only replied, "She sends her love."

"Oh yes, I am sure. Well now, Anne, I suppose the rest of our party will be down soon. Have you asked him?"

Sir Edward quirked his eyebrows knowingly, and Anne laughed. "Well Good Heavens, Mamma! I suppose if I had not, you would have quite muddied the waters, putting him on edge by making such a speech!"

"Yes, well, I like to keep my *beaux* on their toes, you know."

"We have spoken of it, Lady Eleanor," Sir Edward said with humor in his tone. "I have given my hearty approval to the girls taking the Darcy name."

"I am glad to hear it. I was quite your supporter, I shall tell you that. I told them how it would be, that you would think it the most natural thing in the world, and most advantageous. You are a fine uncle indeed! Now then, when shall we tell the girls?"

"Oh, I do not know," Anne sighed. "To own the truth, I am rather nervous. George assures me I am making a fuss over nothing, but I worry about Lizzy."

As Sir Edward gave her a nervous look, her mother harrumphed. "Yes, well, I worry about all thirteen-year-old girls. It is a difficult age!"

"I hardly know – Jane was not like this, two years ago. Jane and Mary are both so sweet and gentle. Sometimes I think Lizzy is so very clever that it causes her to worry overly much about everything. I do not know how much of the accident she remembers, but I wonder if this proposing of a name change might cause some distress for her."

"She has never asked questions about... the past, not as far as I am aware," Mr. Gardiner replied, and Anne nodded her agreement. "Well then, if she has any questions now, we shall simply answer them."

"Edward knows what he is about, my dear," the dowager said. "Your husband is quite right that all shall be well. Lizzy is only a little jumpy because Jane is going off to school in the new year, but she shall settle down. Let us get through the holiday first. You are hosting Twelfth Night this year, and Henry and Phyllis's wedding breakfast – let us wait until after the ball to broach the subject."

Anne shook her head at her own foolishness. "Oh, you are both quite right. I am sure it will turn out well."

***

A few days after the arrival of her relations, Elizabeth found herself wandering the halls of Pemberley in want of some occupation. She and Mary would have been content to spend the day in the library, but for William occupying it with their older cousins. The drawing room was strictly off-limits, as her mother and aunts were making final preparations for the wedding, and her mother's favorite parlor was full of flowers, fabric, and a flurry of activity.

Mary had decided to make herself a nuisance by following Jane and George Wickham into the orangerie, and so Elizabeth went off in search of her cousin Charlotte. Though they were three years apart in age, the two had always been thick as thieves whenever they were together. Eventually, she found her cousin lurking outside the music room, her ear pressed against the door.

Instantly curious, Elizabeth hastened toward her as Charlotte motioned for Elizabeth to keep quiet. "What are you doing," Elizabeth whispered.

"Shh. Spying, of course!"

Elizabeth grinned. "Who is in there? Is Sir Lewis fighting with someone again?"

Charlotte snickered. "For once, no. It is Miss Gardiner and Uncle Edward, only I am not sure if they are quarreling or not."

"We cannot spy on Uncle Edward!"

"I can if I wish it! She is to be my Mamma, and help me with my come-out next year. And I want to hear what she is saying about my Papa, so hush!"

Charlotte gave Elizabeth a gentle nudge, and Elizabeth considered a moment before her curiosity got the better of her. If Charlotte wished to know what was happening, it must be something worth hearing. Standing beside her cousin, she leaned her ear against the wall, which was thin enough that she could hear every word spoken within.

***

Sir Edward offered his sister a handkerchief, and she dabbed at her eyes with it. "Oh, Edward, this ought to be the happiest time of my life – why must I feel so wretched?"

"It is only natural for you to feel some agitation on the brink of marriage, I am sure."

"Did you?"

"I was marrying a woman I had known less than a fortnight – you have known Henry these ten years. Surely you can imagine what I felt, but it does not signify, Phyllis. This is not a patched-up business transaction – he loves you very much, and I suspect he has for quite some time."

"I know he does. He is such a dear man. I love him so very much, but that is what distresses me so! I feel so terribly guilty for being this happy."

Sir Edward took his sister's hand in his. "Henry has nearly finished his year of mourning, and I am sure Lady Margaret is in Heaven, and not begrudging either of you this happiness."

"It is not that," Phyllis whimpered. "It is Fanny."

"Fanny? What is this about, Phyllis? Let us not reopen old wounds, my dear. There is no need."

Phyllis began to weep harder. "Yes, brother, there is. It has haunted me these ten years or more. Every good thing that has happened to us has been at her expense. You made such an advantageous marriage, you were granted a knighthood, and your business is one of the most prosperous in London. I went to reside at Matlock and now I am marrying an earl. Even the girls have grown up amongst luxury and privilege beyond anything they might have known, had their parents lived. They shall have dowries and likely marry lords themselves, and for all this, it cost our dear Fanny her life."

Sir Edward let out a shaky breath. He could not deny that he had been prone to similar notions more than once in the last decade, and he could well understand what his sister was feeling now. "I can only ask," said he, "what good does it do you to dwell on such thoughts now? We cannot change the past, Phyllis, but our sister would never wish you to deny yourself any happiness on her account."

Phyllis laughed bitterly. "Your memory is kinder to her than she deserves."

"I suppose that is always the case, is it not? She was not a perfect woman, but she loved those girls, and she loved us. She would not wish us ill."

Phyllis sniffled, seeming almost determined to wallow in her own misery. Do you not ever think of what life would have been like, if she and Tom had lived? I might have stayed at Longbourn a while longer with them, perhaps married our father's handsome clerk in Meryton. You might have wed Miss Fisher...."

Sir Edward held up his hand to stop her. "I am sure we might have all been quite happy a hundred different ways, if this or that had been different, but this is what fate had in store for us, and we must accept it. You need not berate yourself for having had a happy life since the accident. It was not your fault."

"I fear it was, sometimes. We were chattering away about –"

He cut her off. "I remember that day like it was yesterday, Phyllis. You have told me before. You and Fanny for speaking with great animation about my wedding, and woke the girls from their slumber. Elizabeth grew cranky and started crawling all over Tom, as she was wont to do. Fanny attempted to placate her, to no avail. Tom got cross, and got out of the carriage to sit up top and drive. He took the curve too fast, as did Lady Anne's coachman, and that was that. I do not see how any of that was your fault; nobody at all was to blame, that is what an accident is."

Phyllis wept into her hands for a moment before leaning forward and resting her head on his shoulder. "Oh brother, there was more to it than that, I fear."

"What is it, Phyllis? Is there something you need to tell me?"

"Tom was not cross with Lizzy, he was cross with Fanny and I – at least I suspected he was. Just before he got out of the carriage, we were speaking of our plans to... forgive me, Brother... to prevent the wedding from ever happening."

Sir Edward went rigid instantly, and drew away from his sobbing sister. "What?"

Phyllis clung to him. "I have wanted to tell you, all these years I have wanted to tell you, but I could see no good that could come of confessing the truth, and how it has weighed on me!"

Sir Edward felt as though the room had begun to spin, and he rested his arm on the sofa to steady himself. The events of that fateful day, and the horrible weeks that followed, were crystal clear in his mind, which turned to the moment Madeline Fisher had walked out of Pemberley without sparing him a backward glance. He groaned. "Madeline spoke to Fanny on her deathbed. You were there, Phyllis. What did she say to her?" He pressed his eyes closed, bracing himself for the worst. In some small way, he had known, he had always known.

"She told Madeline that your marriage could never take place, that Tom's death and her own, and the loss of her child, her boy, had cursed your union, and that if Madeline married you, she would share the same fate. She said that any mercenary match in this family would be cursed."

"Good God! She *cursed* us? And you sat by and allowed her to bully my fiancée?"

"She had me all twisted up, Edward. She said you ought to marry a fine lady, one that could someday put the girls into the paths of rich gentlemen. She said that she had married up, and that you and I ought to as well."

Sir Edward let out a bitter sound that was almost a laugh. "She has certainly gotten her way, hasn't she?"

"I tried to stop it, Edward. You must believe me. She had Miss Fisher in tears, and she was laying there, bleeding out. It was the most ghastly thing. I tried to stop it, but she turned on me at the end. She cursed me too, and now I am so afraid to marry Henry."

Phyllis was shaking from the force of her sobs, and Sir Edward was moved at last to embrace the poor woman. "Hush, Sister. There is no such thing as a curse. Our Fanny was not in her right mind after the accident, I am sure you saw it. Whatever her intentions were before... well, it does not matter now, does it? We must move on with our lives. Besides, you love Henry, and he loves you - yours shall not be a mercenary match."

Phyllis nodded and wiped her tears. "I do love him so dearly, but... oh, Edward, I am so sorry for my part in all that happened with Fanny. I might have discouraged her sooner, warned you or Miss Fisher.... You might have been ever so much happier. I know it is not well with you and Olivia, and I am so sorry."

Sir Edward closed his eyes and leaned into his sister. The last ten years had been kind to him in many ways, yet even now he struggled to reassure his sister that all was well. *Of course there is no curse. It was the ramblings of a dying woman who was out of her mind with grief. There is no curse.*

"I am not so very unhappy. Olivia is a... troubled woman, a complicated creature, but we have our sweet Rose, and another babe on the way. We have had some good years, and may yet expect more. You and Henry, I am certain, will have a wonderful life together."

Phyllis nodded sadly, and was on the verge of speaking when they heard a noise outside, and Sir Edward crossed the room to open the door.

***

"Tom got cross, and got out of the carriage to sit up top to drive...." Elizabeth abruptly drew her ear for the wall and raised her hands to her mouth to conceal a gasp. Beside her, Charlotte has frozen in place, her eyes wide.

Elizabeth whimpered softly, her countenance crumpling into tears as she hid her face in her hands. Charlotte put a hand on her shoulder. "Hush Lizzy, do not cry," she whispered.

Elizabeth drew away from the wall, pacing wildly. "Do you not see? It is all my fault. That is why they never talk about my real parents, because it is all my fault they are dead!"

Charlotte looked on helplessly, wringing her hands as Elizabeth continued pacing and weeping pitifully. Then, she pressed her ear back against the wall. Elizabeth wiped her tears, her mind spinning with a thousand questions. "What are they saying?"

"Hush, I cannot hear!" Charlotte leaned in, her face somber as she listened. After a moment she replied, "Your aunt is weeping so much I can scarcely make it out – something about a curse."

"A curse? What curse?"

"Hush!" Charlotte listened a moment longer. "She says your real mother cursed them from her deathbed."

Elizabeth felt as though someone had struck her. She knew so little of her birth parents; she could not even remember their faces. Her uncle and mother had given her only the barest information over the years, and she struggled to connect the specter of her birth mother that existed in her imagination with this new discovery. "My mother put a curse on Uncle Edward and Aunt Phyllis? It must be all my fault – my fault that she died!"

Charlotte was still eavesdropping. "Uncle says there is no such thing as curses... ah, but he also says he is very unhappy because of Aunt Olivia. She is rather scary at times, is she not?"

Elizabeth had sunk down onto the floor to softly cry into her hands, and Charlotte finally came away from the wall to help Elizabeth to her feet before embracing her. "Do not cry, Lizzy."

"But what am I to do?"

"I do not know – what *can* you do? I am sure there is no such thing as a curse, not really! It is the stuff of fairy tales, and your mother was on her deathbed. I think she must have given them a fright."

Still Elizabeth wept. "My mother and father died because I could not behave myself in the carriage – and we were nearly to Lambton. If I could have kept quiet a little longer, my parents would be alive."

"But then you would not live at Pemberley! Don't you like it here?"

"Of course I do, but that just makes it worse! If I am happy here, then I must be happy that I killed my parents," Elizabeth whimpered.

"What a horrid thing to say," Charlotte gasped.

Elizabeth could only gape at her with a sense of horror and no little fear, which she had not the words to describe. And then the music room door opened, and her uncle was gaping at her in dismay. His face was stained with tears, and his astonishment at discovering her there seemed on the verge of turning to anger. She could not bear to face him; she took off running around the corner, and bolted down the hallway.

***

Richard Fitzwilliam had lingered longer than his brother John and cousin William in the library, but decided he ought to go out riding with them after all, even if that prat George Wickham was to be one of the party. As he stepped out into the hall, he was struck by a force that nearly bowled him over – his young cousin running at full speed down the corridor like an absolute lunatic. After staggering backward for a moment, Richard steadied himself and grabbed his cousin by the shoulders; she looked at him with silent, tearful panic as he pulled her into the room and sat her down on a chair by the door. "Dizzy Miss Lizzy, whatever is the matter?"

He crouched down in front of her chair and waited patiently as the tale came spilling out of her, and at the end of it he patted her head and replied, "Well, Cousin, I daresay you have been duly punished for dropping eaves!"

What he had meant as a gentle reproof only resulted in more tears, and Richard winced at his own folly. Would that he had gone down to the stables with John and William directly! "Now Lizzy," he said, hoping some wisdom would follow.

Instead, Charlotte slipped into the room; after seeing them there, she sighed with relief and closed the door. "Uncle Edward is looking for you, Lizzy, but I shall not give you up."

Richard scowled at his younger sister. "Charlotte, was this your doing? Lizzy is quite upset – it was not for either of you to be spying on an adult conversation. Now we are harboring a little fugitive; look what your mischief has done!"

He instantly regretted scolding his sister, for it only heightened Elizabeth's distress as she pleaded with them not to tell her uncle where she had gone to hide. It tore at his heart to see her thus, for he knew how much Lady Anne, Uncle George, and even Sir Edward doted on the girls, and how assiduously they had worked to shield their young wards from knowing too much of their own tragic history.

"It must have been quite a shock," he conceded. "I am sure my aunts and uncles must have wished you to be older yet before they told you the truth of it. It was a dreadful time, better left in the past, I fear. Can you not see why they should wish to keep this from you?"

"Indeed, Lizzy," Charlotte said, still looking white as a sheet from the incident. "Let us pretend we heard nothing at all."

"But Uncle saw, he knows that I know the truth, and that it is all my fault. I will be in trouble for spying, and now that I know the truth, they are all at liberty to hate me for it!"

"Hate you?" Richard patted her hand. "My dear Cousin Lizzy, your aunt and uncle could never hate you. All this business about the curse, it is simply stuff and nonsense. I understand you mother was not quite sensible at the end... you must not think anything of it, and you certainly cannot blame yourself. "

"But there *must* be a curse, for my aunt and uncle are so very unhappy, and all because I made my parents crash their carriage. I am the reason they are dead!"

Elizabeth was weeping so loudly that Richard could only wonder at how half of the family had not descended on them already, in such a state. "Do be calm, dear one. Charlotte is right. You must put it all from your mind. I am sure Uncle Edward will wish to speak to you about it, and then it will all be well again. You need not have run away from him." He ran his fingers through his hair and began to pace, wishing desperately he didn't feel so damned responsible for putting it all to rights.

The look on Elizabeth's face was frantic, her eyes flickering about so much that he could almost see the rapid barrage of thoughts and doubts piling up on her. "Mother and Father have been so good to us, but I do not even deserve it, not now that I know what I have done. I ought to be banished for it! That is what Aunt Phyllis said."

"I am sure it was not!"

"She said we have all prospered from my parents dying, and it is true."

"What an idea! Lizzy, you must not torment yourself like this. You did not, at the tender age of three, concoct a vicious scheme to crash your father's carriage so that you might be adopted into a wealthier family. Nobody is going to punish you or banish you. It was an *accident.*"

"But I am still to blame," Elizabeth wept, and she rose from her chair to pace beside Richard. "I cannot bear to know the truth of it."

"You must bear it, or better still, put it from your mind."

"I cannot."

"You must! We must *all* do difficult things in life, even silly little girls," Richard cried with no little vexation at Elizabeth's abundant supply of tears. "It is in the past, and there is nothing to be done. You cannot punish yourself for some imagined crime against your family."

Elizabeth looked at him with wide, frenzied eyes, and she wept once more. "I do deserve to be punished! I am sure I do!"

He wanted to rip his hair out, but instead he drew his cousin into an embrace. As he looked helplessly to Charlotte for some assistance,

Elizabeth screamed into his chest and pounded at his shoulders with her fists. He sighed with resignation, and allowed her to spend her ire. "Alright then. Let it out, get it all out." After a minute or two, Elizabeth had vented her emotion – and given him something of a beating – before she sat back down, deflated. Charlotte sat beside her and took her hand, murmuring little soothing sounds.

Richard observed the act with curiosity, confirming his own suspicion that he had not the talent for conversing with teenage girls at all, which was quite fine by him. He had tried to reason with the girl, but Charlotte's nonsensical muttering seemed to have more of an effect. Shaking his head in frustration, he warned the girls that he would leave them be for now, but they must begin to collect themselves, and prepare to face Sir Edward. Closing the door to the library to afford them some privacy, he headed toward the front parlor in search of his Aunt Anne, hoping it wouldn't break her heart to face Elizabeth's emotional discovery.

***

There was an old staircase in a little-used corridor at the back of the ballroom, which could easily be accessed by another passageway at the back of the west gallery upstairs, that led to a little ornamental balcony overlooking the ballroom. Elizabeth had always imagined it must have been used for visitors who were very grand – the King himself might have visited and stood up on this balcony, looking down on the guests in the ballroom and waving before he made his grand descent. She had discovered the spot by accident, and it had become one of her favorite haunts when she played with her cousins.

She and Charlotte were hidden away there, sitting cross-legged on the floor, concealed from sight by the shadows and the thick stone railings, taking in the spectacle of the Twelfth Night ball. "It is so very grand," Charlotte whispered.

Elizabeth looked out across the ballroom in wonder. "Everyone looks so fancy," she breathed. "Is this what London will be like?"

"It will be for me, when I come out next year. I cannot wait!"

Elizabeth knit her brows. It was all very dazzling, but frightening, too. "I wonder how I shall get on in London."

"You are determined to go, then?"

"I must," Elizabeth said, tearing her eyes from the ballroom below to look over at her cousin. "Mamma and Uncle Edward said I do not need to go away, that I am punishing myself for no reason."

"That is what Richard said, too."

"I know." Elizabeth sighed, feeling as though she were full of swirling, angry emotions that she could not gather into words. "I want to go."

"Jane will be cross with you."

"I know. Oh, what does it signify? She is going away to school in a few weeks, when William goes. She will not even miss me."

"Lizzy, there you are!" Jane peeked her head into the alcove behind them, and Charlotte swatted at her. Jane grimaced, and crouched down to hide herself from sight of the ballroom. Sitting down on Elizabeth's other side, she said, "You are always getting up to something without me, Lizzy."

"That is because you never want to sneak around with us."

Jane gave her a gentle but reproving look. "You will get into trouble. Mother and Father are already worried about you, and Uncle was very cross with you last week."

"They need not be. Look, they are having a very fine time." Charlotte smiled as she pointed out Lady Anne and Sir Edward dancing together halfway down the ballroom.

Jane flicked her eyes over to Charlotte, and then back to Elizabeth. "You are wrong, you know, Lizzy. I *will* miss you when you go to London. I think it is very unfair that Uncle Edward should take you away from Pemberley."

"William goes away to school, and soon you shall, too. Why should I not go to London?"

"But why *should* you?"

Seeing Charlotte on the verge of speaking, Elizabeth nudged her. "Because." *Because I do not deserve to live here.* "I want to."

"*I* am happy you are coming to London," Charlotte said. "You will not be able to go to balls and parties with me – not yet, anyway – but I shall be happy to have you close. Your aunt is to be my new Mamma, so I am sure we shall be together very often. It will be such fun!"

"I am not going to London for *fun*," Elizabeth snapped.

"Well, I wish you would tell me why, then," Jane said with frustration. "I saw Mamma crying about it. If you will have no pleasure in going, then you had better stay here!"

"It would make Uncle happy," Elizabeth said, averting her eyes and watching the dancers below.

"He does not seem happy about it to me," Jane retorted.

"He does not seem happy about *anything*," Charlotte observed. "I suppose it must be the curse."

"What curse?"

"Hush, Charlotte," Elizabeth whispered, sticking out her leg to kick at her cousin.

"I was only joking," Charlotte said. "Of course there isn't a curse. Richard said so, and he is the smartest person I know."

"William said Richard is a blockhead," Jane quipped. "*He* is the smartest person *I* know."

"William does not say *anything* to *me*," Elizabeth snapped, "and I think Uncle is the smartest. I know he is very sad, but I will go to London to make him happy. And I can see Aunt Olivia's new baby. I am going to be her helper, and make Uncle happy."

"Hush," Charlotte scoffed. "Someone will hear us. I want to stay awhile and look at all the handsome gentlemen. I shall get to dance with them next year, and I am trying to decide which one to set my cap at."

This elicited a giggle from Elizabeth and Jane; their quarrel momentarily forgotten, they all sat silently for a few minutes as they peered down at the ballroom in youthful admiration.

"Cousin Richard is very handsome," Jane whispered with a bashful smile, "even if my brother says he is a blockhead. I like his new uniform very much."

"I do not," Charlotte huffed. "If he goes to war, it shall break my heart."

"Maybe that is why William called him a blockhead," Elizabeth said absently.

"Cousin William is looking well tonight," Charlotte sighed, leaning closer to the railing. "He is the finest dancer I ever saw!"

"Shall you dance with him when you have your come out?"

"Cousin Anne would probably tear my hair out if I tried! Anyhow, I daresay I am not handsome enough to tempt him. My mother told me I am quite plain, and I suppose she was right."

"No, Charlotte," Elizabeth hissed. "You are perfectly lovely. You always have the prettiest gowns, and your hair is like chocolate."

"Or mud!"

"I like mud."

Charlotte nudged Elizabeth playfully, and Elizabeth smiled back at her cousin before glancing over at Jane, who was eyeing their exchange with wounded suspicion. She had tears welling in her eyes, and her lip began to tremble as if she might cry. "I think I understand," she whispered. "You two shall be the best of friends together in London, and I shall go off to school, all alone among strangers!"

"Jane, it is not like that! I have to go!"

"Why? You will not tell me *why* you must go."

"I cannot tell you. You would hate me if I told you the truth."

Jane scoffed with disgust. "I do not believe you. If you do not wish to tell me your secrets, as you do with Charlotte, so be it. Go to London. I shall go to school, I shall take the Darcy name, and I shall make loads of new friends who do not break my heart – or our mother's!"

Elizabeth chewed her lip and averted her eyes as Jane wiped away a tear and leapt to her feet. "She is not our mother."

Jane clenched her fists and let out a snort of exasperation. "You are a wicked, ungrateful girl, and I am going to tell Grandmamma you are up here!"

Elizabeth met Jane's eye and gave her sister a ferocious look. "Go on then. You have nothing to cry about, as I do. Tell Grandmamma whatever you like. I do not care what happens to me." Jane looked back at her with confusion and fury on her face before she spun on her heel and ran away.

6

❧❦

May 1805, Gracechurch Street, London

Lady Matlock paused silently in the open doorway to her brother's study, observing with fond bemusement as he stared abstractedly at the book he was holding upside down, his face crunched into a steady cringe as, right above them, upstairs, two infants shrieked and cried. A moment later, Edward's eyes came back into focus; he quickly grimaced at the book as he discarded it, and then started as he looked up and noticed his sister. "That is *it* – we are moving the nursery as far away from my study as possible, or I shall lose my mind. Oh, good afternoon, Phyllis. Did you know, twins run in the Bertie family? Her grandmother had two sets of twins! *This*, but twice!" He leaned back in his chair and sighed, deflated from his outburst.

Phyllis smiled reminiscently. "You sound like Tom Bennet after Fanny had Mary. Once one of the three started a ruckus, the other two soon followed suit, night and day!"

Edward chuckled softly. "Every letter I got from Tom for five years seemed to have the word 'caterwauling' heavily underscored."

Phyllis took a hesitant step into the room, and inclined her head as if asking permission to enter.

"Come in, sit down. Where are my manners?"

"I take it I am forgiven, then?"

"You are. I ought to have come round more since you got back to Town, but...." He waved his hand idly.

"No, I do understand. And we have been...." She mimicked his hand gesture. "It has been strange, to say the least. It was something of a shock to return from such a pleasant wedding trip, and see Henry so instantly occupied with business affairs and Parliament. We worry about Richard being sent to the continent. And then... well, I do not know what to make of my new position. From companion to countess, it sounds like something out of a novel. I have three step-children – they are quite grown, used to their old ways and missing their mother. With the girls... the Darcys got to start so young with them."

"I wish I had some words of wisdom for you, my dear, but I am certainly no expert. I suppose we both have faced the same obstacle – marrying up, as Fanny once said. I got a younger start of it, and was on more equal footing in *some* respects, you know. But you are very worthy of Henry. You will make him a fine wife and Countess; I suspect you have loved one another for some years now. The children might have known you only as their grandmother's companion these ten years, but you are the aunt of their cousins, and you have been family to them already."

"Are you quite sure you are not an expert? That was wonderfully said of you, Brother."

"Pah. It is always easier to dispense wisdom to others than to heed it oneself."

"That is very clever – who said that?"

"Sir Edward Gardiner."

"Well!" Phyllis grinned at him for a moment, then turned serious. "How is Olivia?"

"A little better since she had the twins."

"It was good of her to call them after Fanny and Tom."

"After naming her daughter Georgiana Augusta Rose, it was about time for something...."

"Less ostentatious?"

"Precisely."

Phyllis laughed. "So, Olivia is... better?"

"A little. I've crumpled up a dozen letters to George and Anne these last three months."

"You have something to get off your chest?"

"I suppose I do. The truth is, Phyllis, I feel damned awful for taking Lizzy. She begged me and I... I realized I needed it very much myself. It was utterly selfish of me not to insist she stay at Pemberley, and I fear the Darcys will hate me forever – not to mention how much it may ultimately harm Lizzy's prospects."

"I think I see what you mean. Things were not well with Olivia, and you needed a friendly face about the house."

"I have Rose, but she is so young, and too like her mother at times. Lizzy is different. Even at thirteen she is so... so old for her age. I think that after recent events she has grown up so much, and it is such a comfort to have her here. There are days when she provides the only rational conversation I have all day."

"Is she still as gloomy as she was?"

"A little less, perhaps. She is fond of the twins, and Rose; I am sure she would like to see more of Charlotte. She seems to have an inexplicable calming effect on Olivia, like nothing I've ever seen."

"That is odd. I never saw Olivia pay Lizzy any particular attention before."

"I think it was different, before. In so many ways, Lizzy's childhood abruptly ended that day at Pemberley, when she heard us speaking about the accident. As to Olivia... I suspect there is a great deal about her childhood that she has never spoken of – things perhaps just as unpleasant. When she is with Lizzy, it is as if they understand each other perfectly; they can communicate so much with just a look. The way they speak together is so quick and clever – they could talk circles around one another for hours and laugh it off. It has brought back the Olivia I married, and it is a delight for me to behold."

"You ought to pick up your pen once more; tell George and Anne exactly what you have just told me. I think they should be very glad to hear it."

He smiled and nodded. "I suppose I shall. You are for Derbyshire soon, I hear."

"Yes, in about a fortnight. We must get Lizzy and Charlotte together before then. Better still, why not come up with us? Surely you have enough clever men in your employ to be able to take some time away from Gardiner Imports?"

"Perhaps. I shall mention it to Olivia. Will you be often at Pemberley?"

"I hope so. John is taking William with him to see the estate in Scotland – we are thinking of fixing it up for Richard someday, perhaps coax him into giving up his commission. I think Jane and Charlotte had a row at Christmas."

"Did they? That is not like Jane."

"I am sure she was upset about Lizzy coming to London, and perhaps because it means Lizzy will see more of Charlotte... I shall speak to Anne about it. The girls were very cold to one another when we collected Charlotte after our honeymoon. And it was just after... well, perhaps it is unrelated."

"Perhaps bringing Lizzy back to visit Pemberley so soon would only add to the friction. Speak to Anne about it first."

"I shall, but you really ought to write as well."

"You have my word."

"Well then, I had better be off. I do believe Miss Lizzy has been rattling away at Henry since we arrived!"

Edward nodded and waved her off. "Off with you, then. Send word if you have a free afternoon, and I shall bring Lizzy round. Otherwise... if anyone asks, do speak well of us."

"I shall, Edward."

***

Elizabeth set aside her book and smiled. "Good day, Uncle Henry."

"Happy birthday, Miss Lizzy!" The earl reached into his coat pocket and withdrew a present for her – he hadn't wrapped it properly, but had tied a generous length of very lovely pink ribbon around a leather-bound book, which he presented to her with a cheerful grin.

Elizabeth accepted the book with thanks, and then looked down at the title. Smirking, she held up the book she had been reading before – it was the very same, *Letters for Literary Ladies* by Maria Edgeworth.

Uncle Henry guffawed. "Well, my goodness!"

Laughing, Elizabeth said, "It is quite a coincidence – Richard sent me a copy last week."

"And how do you like it? Rather daring reading for a lady of fourteen!"

"It is certainly edifying! I am glad to have another copy, for I have been discussing it with Aunt Olivia, and now it will be easier for us to go through it together."

"And how are you and your aunt getting on?"

Elizabeth raised her hand to her forehead and laughed. "Well, I certainly think she would be scolding me for having gone on for so long without offering you some tea, and making her apologies to you – she is resting presently. I have been learning my way around playing hostess since she was in confinement. Let me call for some refreshments. Here, come and sit in Uncle Edward's chair – he will never know."

Uncle Henry sat down where he was bid and watched her with a look of pride. "Well, go on then, my dear. Show me how it's done."

Elizabeth called for the tea, and when it arrived she poured him a glass, embarrassed that she was not quite sure how he liked it, and so she compensated by slicing him a rather large piece of cake.

"You spoil me, my dear. Tell me," he asked, sipping his tea, "how do you like living in London?"

Elizabeth considered, swirling the spoon in her own tea. "I like talking with Uncle Edward; we have such interesting conversations. And with Aunt Olivia. She is very smart – frighteningly so, at times, but I admire her. I know there is some great secret about her that no one will tell me, but I think I can get her to confide in me." She gave her uncle a look of triumph.

He smiled back at her. "Is that so? She speaks candidly with you, does she?"

"More and more, yes. I think she is quite frank with everybody."

"How long do you think before you wheedle it out of her?"

She smiled wolfishly at him. "So there *is* a secret?"

He laughed. "You have got until your eighteenth birthday – ten pounds on it."

She shook the earl's hand on the wager. "With such an inducement, I am sure to succeed."

Her uncle leaned back in his chair, studying her with an expression of affectionate curiosity. "Something about you has changed. You are far more... grown up, different since we were all at Pemberley."

Elizabeth blushed. She knew precisely what it was – her courses had begun for the first time a week after she had arrived in London, but she couldn't imagine telling her uncle such a thing. At least she had Aunt Olivia's unfailing candor to turn to for questions of that nature.

"Well," her uncle said, seeming not to notice that she had not answered him, "I am very glad of it. I had hoped you would do well here in London. I know my sister was hoping to hear good tidings of you."

"I am content, sir," she replied. She felt her will to converse suddenly recede, knowing now that everything she said would likely be relayed to her parents and sisters – to the Darcys. There had been not so much as a single letter exchanged between Pemberley and Gracechurch Street in five months, though she knew her uncle's waste bin was just as full of crumpled, unsent letters as her own was. She wondered if this might also be the case at Pemberley, a painful thought. "Are you going to Matlock this summer?"

"We are, in a week or two more. We thought to bring you all with us."

"Oh."

"We might perhaps visit Pemberley a few times."

"Naturally. Well, perhaps I might send a letter or two up with you, maybe a few little presents. Would you... would you tell them all to write to us?"

"I could, unless you wish to tell them yourself?"

Elizabeth hesitated and replied, "Aunt Olivia has gotten me a book about Lyme Regis, and we thought to go to the seaside...." The disappointment in his eyes tore at Elizabeth's heart, and she looked away. "But I should like to have some letters...."

❧

Pemberley, Derbyshire
7 June, 1805

Dear Sir Edward,

George and I are remiss in sending you not one but two sets of congratulations. Phyllis has been singing the praises of little Tom and Fanny Gardiner all week, and I am looking forward to making their acquaintance when we are in London this winter. All Charlotte can talk about is her come-out, and so I am sure it shall be for the next six months.

We had hoped you would all come and visit us this summer, but I can well understand the temptation of the seaside, in all this heat. No, I must be honest – I can well understand why you truly have stayed away. I suppose it is too soon for Lizzy to return as a visitor, without it feeling a rather forced homecoming – that is what George thinks, at least. I miss her desperately, but I am determined to accept the change in her situation for as long as she wishes it, and I shall love her nonetheless. I should always wish her, and all your family, to feel welcome at Pemberley, no matter what comes.

I shall bid the girls to write Lizzy, and if she wishes it, I shall write her myself. I hear she is grown quite the adventurous reader, and an assiduous hostess while Lady Olivia was in her confinement. I look forward to hearing tales from Lyme Regis very soon.

Your loyal friend,

Lady Anne Darcy

***

Matlock Park, Derbyshire
4 September, 1805

Dear Jane,

Thank you for your letter. I was sorry to hear about Miss Bingley's unfortunate remarks, but if she is not to return to school after Christmas, at least you will not have to bear her distemper much longer – and I for one think your French is quite good! As to your troubles with Miss Jensen, have you considered a frog under her pillow? Rose left one under mine last week, and I can confirm that it is a shocking experience.

Lyme-Regis was quite pleasant, thank you for asking. Sea-bathing is great fun. Uncle Edward thought Rose and I might be afraid, but I liked it very much, and Rose was bold as ever. The inn was quite grand, and the scenery was indescribably lovely. I attempted a few rubbish watercolors, and Uncle and I laughed at my folly. I had high hopes of capturing all the majesty of the Cobb – the light glimmering on the water, the blasted fragments of shipwrecks along the shore, and every picturesque aspect, and to my disappointment I am left to remember it only by a lithograph Aunt Olivia purchased at the circulating library.

Aunt Olivia wanted to go to Brighton and see the Royal Pavilion, and I confess I grew so curious about the place that she bought me a book about it (featuring many sketches far better than my own!) and told me some stories about her last visit there, the summer before she met Uncle Edward – she met the Prince! She says he is fearfully handsome, and I hope I might catch a glimpse.

So, too, shall Charlotte in a few months, and he presentation is all she has spoken of since I have been visiting Matlock. Mamma says it was quite the same all summer, and I suppose it must make you consider your own debut, the year after Charlotte's. I am glad I shall have the two of you to come out ahead of me, and lend me the benefit of your experience.

Do write again soon, for I am longing to hear that you are more content with your schoolmates. Charlotte and Aunt Phyllis send their love.

Your loving sister,

Lizzy Bennet

***

Pemberley, Derbyshire
4 May, 1806

Dear Lizzy,

Happy Birthday, Sister. I am glad to hear you are to come to Matlock again this summer. Mamma says you will come up with Uncle Henry and Aunt

Phyllis when they leave London next month. William and Richard were thinking of going into Kent, since they did not visit at Easter, as William was on his Grand Tour, though of course it was a rather curtailed trip. He has asked if I should like to go along and spend some time with Cousin Anne. Uncle Lewis writes that Anne has been ill lately, which as you know simply means that she is out of humor with somebody. However, I believe I ought to go, if William thinks it will cheer her. We shall only stay through half of July, and so if you are still at Matlock then, we shall see one another in Derbyshire after all.

I received a most astonishing letter last week – would you believe it? From Miss Bingley! She writes that her older sister is lately married, and she is very dull at home with her brother and step-mother, and asks if I would like to visit her in Scarborough this summer. Between the trip to Kent, and your coming to Matlock, I think I had better tell her no, but I am surprised she wrote to me at all, as she never seemed to think much of me when she was at school.

Ah, here is Mamma at my side, reminding me that William is friends with a Charles Bingley – perhaps a relation? I shall ask William about it. Perhaps Miss Bingley wishes to make some amends, if William is friends with a brother or cousin of hers. In the meanwhile, I think I ought to attempt some civil reply.

I look forward to hearing the latest news from London – do give my love to Uncle and Rose.

Your loving sister,

Jane Darcy

***

Gracechurch Street, London
17 February, 1807

Dear Jane,

Uncle was sorry to receive word from Mamma that you will not be coming to London this season. At least we had Christmas, though it was a shame to see Papa looking so ill – I do hope he is recovered by now, and that is not what has caused you to cancel your journey. Uncle would not say, and just smiled as he does when he is trying not to look unhappy. Aunt Olivia was very disappointed to hear of it – I think she is finally growing fonder of Mamma. She only wishes you would spend more time in London, and I do agree. You ought to have your season!

At least your upcoming visit from Miss Bingley will give you some consolation, I suppose. I wonder that you could forgive her for being so unkind to you at school, but if she has been the devoted correspondent you paint her as, then I am happy you shall have a friend to come and stay with you at

Pemberley. Aunt Olivia is here, asking me to send you her love, and she bids me ask if Miss Bingley will bring her brother to Pemberley? She says she hopes for your sake he is very handsome!

And now you see, dear Jane, how it would be if you came to stay with us in London! Aunt Olivia would be finding you some 'very smart beaux', as Grandmamma would say. She and Aunt Phyllis are doing their best with poor Charlotte, who is enduring her second Season, and quite making me dread the time when my turn comes! I had better leave off here before I am tempted to share with you the shocking tales of Charlotte's suitors, and utterly dissuade you from ever setting foot in London again!

Your Loving Sister,

Lizzy Bennet

***

Pemberley, Derbyshire
28 June, 1807

Dear Lizzy,

So, Charlotte survived her second Season! She has been visiting Pemberley since returning home for the summer, and appears greatly relieved to be out of London. Her disappointment nearly equals my own that you will not be joining us here, too, but I am pleased for your sake that you will finally get to visit Brighton. Aunt Olivia must be delighted – she always looks so very happy when she speaks of the seaside.

Caroline Bingley has been here with us this past month – even now she is commending my penmanship, and bidding me send you her warm greetings. She is so very elegant herself, so it is quite the compliment. Her brother did accompany her here, but only stayed one night, as he was keen to go with William and some of their friends to the Scottish estate – another project for Uncle Henry. At first, I thought Caroline was rather disappointed to see them go, but now I begin to suspect she is more disappointed to hear that Cousin John is soon to be married. She seemed quite smitten when first they met, but of course he has been promised to Miss Lucy Gainsborough for years.

We shall certainly be in town for the wedding – until then I must leave off, for I believe I see William's carriage coming down the lane. Yes, it is him, back from Scotland already!

Your loving sister,

Jane Darcy

PS –
29 June
My dear Lizzy, what a fool I was to be writing to you with others in the room! I have left some space so that I might come back now, in privacy, and write you something of the greatest import – I am to be married! About a week ago, my dearest darling sought me out and proposed, and I have accepted him. It has been a great secret between us this past year, but George Wickham and I are in love, and we have been given permission to marry.

I am sorry for telling you nothing of it sooner – how I feared you would guess it! This is why I did not wish to have a season last year, even though Papa recovered well enough. I could not bear to dance with anyone in London, if I could not have my dear George. But now we are saved! George had been waiting until he might make something of himself, and saw the opportunity when old Mr. Rivers retired, and he resolved to ask Papa for the living at Kympton, so that he might be able to afford to take a wife – me!

Mamma and Papa agreed, of course. Grandmamma was not best pleased, but Mamma is happy I shall have a love match. Papa was nearly convinced to give George the living, but William came home yesterday, and after sitting half the day with Papa, has convinced him that George had better not go into the church. It was a disappointment, but William believes that I deserve better, and so it has been resolved that George will instead take a commission in the Navy to earn his fortune. Papa is hoping that he will be sent to the Mediterranean or the Adriatic, where he might do well if they capture many merchant vessels. Even though I shall have to wait two long years to marry George, and shall miss him dearly and be frightfully worried – oh, Lizzy, I am still so very happy!

***

Matlock Park, Derbyshire
20 September, 1808

Dearest Brother,

Another summer passes with no visit from the Gardiners, and Pemberley is a very somber place at present. Mr. Darcy is not well, though he attempted to appear so at Christmas. I know he and Anne deeply regretted having seen little of you since then, but they do not wish to beg, Edward. Lizzy is still their daughter, after all these years, and they wish to make it right while there is still time.

Henry is here at my side, using such language as I cannot dream of putting to paper, but he does wish you would come, if your business will spare you the time. If it is Olivia, I am sure that between Henry's connections and Lady Eleanor's, we can keep the entire incident out of the scandal sheets. I hope you are not serious about wanting a divorce. Think of Rose and the twins! I can well imagine you burning the midnight oil in your warehouses or in your study, but if you can do no more than hide from it, you would do better to hide here, and bring Lizzy home at last, if only to say goodbye to her father.

Your impatient sister,

Phyllis

***

Pemberley, Derbyshire
28 September, 1808

Dear Edward,

I hardly know what to write, but George is fading fast. He was doing so well last year, but these past few months have been worse than he wished to let on. The girls are inconsolable and wishing for their sister now, and I beg you would bring her in all haste. Whatever it was Jane and Lizzy were fighting about at Christmas must be put aside, for we are all in such a state, and I need my dearest old friend at my side as much as the girls need their sister. Please, Edward.

Your desperate and devoted friend,

Anne

***

Gracechurch Street, London
30 September, 1808

My dear Lady Anne,

I received your express only moments ago, and am responding in kind. Of course we will come, Lizzy and I. She is packing a trunk now, and my valet is seeing to mine. I cannot begin to make amends for how the years have got away from us – I've been a stupid man indeed, and fully intend to throw myself at your feet and beg your forgiveness, and George's as well. I have let Olivia break my heart a dozen different ways, when it ought to be Lizzy I put first, and the good of this family, as Henry and George do.

I can scarcely write, for I am overcome with shame at what I have become, and a tremendous sense of guilt for letting Lizzy slip away from you all. I cannot promise she will want to stay, for she too is still in the awful grip of that useless emotion, as I am sure is all my own doing. I had not wanted to ever speak of it again, but it is time Phyllis told her the truth, the full truth, and have done with it. This time, nothing will be said or done without your approval, lest I make another horrid mess of it.

I digress – George is in my prayers, as are you and the girls, and poor William, for I know he must be feeling the weight of so much responsibility at a time like this – he is already a better man than I. You shall be ever-present in my thoughts as we travel north in all haste. Until then, God bless you, my friend.

EG

***

Gracechurch Street, London
18 April, 1809

Dear Jane,

I thought it only right I should write to you, on this, the day we go down to half-mourning for Papa, despite the contents of your last letter. I know it was wrong of me to jest about not having a Season – I only meant to dispel some of the awkwardness at supper when we were at Matlock, but when only Aunt Olivia laughed, I saw how wrong I had been. Oh, why does Christmas always have to be so awful? I know it gives you pain, but William was so very cold to me, and Mamma so very insistent that I come back to Pemberley.

I cannot do it, Jane. I will not. It would ruin Uncle Edward if I left – Uncle Henry was only just able to persuade him out of seeking a divorce and Aunt Olivia is quite sick over it. I fear she is in some sort of trouble, and I worry for Rose and the twins. Whatever Mamma and Aunt Phyllis may say, I know my place is here, where I can be useful rather than comfortable.

I am still your sister, Jane, and though I may not see you and Mary often, nor Mamma, I do love you all, and I wish we wrote more often. I beg you do not let Miss Bingley fill your ear with such awful notions of melodrama, and instead simply try. We need not live our lives like a Greek tragedy, no matter what befalls us.

Well, then. If you are still reading this letter, I can only hope that it means you are of the same mind, and we might be friends again. As such, I shall inform you that I have scored quite a little triumph over our Uncle Henry, and have consequently won a boon of ten pounds. It is an old wager existing between us these many years, and though I am sworn to secrecy as to the particulars, I can tell you that I am now a wealthy woman indeed! I shall save it for now, and buy myself something pretty when it comes time for your wedding.

Speaking of wealth and weddings, I hear the Amphion captured two merchant vessels in February – what a fine thing for your dear Wickham. I still stand by my resentment of William's interference in sending the poor man out to sea, when you might have been a happy parson's wife already, but I was pleased to read in the paper that he and his shipmates have also won quite a boon, and thought instantly of you, my dear sister, and the comfort it must bring you to know that in a few months yet you may be settled, and signing your next letter Jane Wickham – how well that sounds.

I remember all the fuss Mamma made over Aunt Phyllis's wedding, and I am fully prepared to do my share of swooning and selecting flowers and fabrics for you, when it is time for you to come to London to purchase your trousseau. Poor Charlotte – if only there was such a man for her!

I am running out of space on the page, but I send you, Mary, and Mamma all my love, and have enclosed a particularly commendable drawing from little Tom, imagining you and I as pirates on the high seas – you must show it to your Mr. Wickham, for I think it shall give him a hearty laugh.

Yo-ho, yo-ho, a pirate's life for me,

Lizzy

PS –
I have just overheard Uncle Henry in the study with Uncle Edward. Richard is soon for Portugal, and Charlotte and Aunt Phyllis are quite beside themselves. Do write to them of happier tidings.

***

Pemberley, Derbyshire
14 June, 1809

Elizabeth,
I am writing you this letter, after which I must ask you direct your correspondence to Mary or Mamma. To answer your question, Christmases are generally awful when you make them so with your behavior, just as it has been

since the year you ran away. You sulk in corners with Charlotte, whispering of curses, or strut about like Aunt Olivia, flaunting your irreverent wit. William says you have grown far too like her, and he tried to warn you. How can you begrudge his interference in Wickham's career, when he was only trying to help us? He has been the kindest, most attentive brother since you left, and if you had stayed, if you were here to see it, you would know how very wrong you are to judge him.

Meanwhile, you make light of everything going on about you, boasting of money and secrets with Uncle, professing your loyalty to those who, quite frankly, do not deserve it, defaming a very dear friend of mine – and you clearly have not learned your lesson about eavesdropping, either! Richard going to war merits only a postscript, and you go on about Charlotte remaining unmarried, when Aunt Olivia wounded her so at Christmas – she is so very plain, you needn't always remind her of it, and put yourself forward to outshine her. It breaks our mother's heart to think you are growing up so like Aunt Olivia, and I am ashamed of you.

I threw your letter directly into the fire, and if you write again I will not open it first before doing the same again. I beg you do not come to Pemberley and spoil another Christmas this year.

Jane Darcy

***

Pemberley, Derbyshire
11 November, 1809

Dearest Lizzy,

I have wanted to write you this letter for so long, have prayed about it, and wept over unfinished drafts. At last, today, I believe I have found the strength to sit down here at my desk again, and finish what I start. Pemberley has been a wretched place for so long – it would pain Mamma for me to say it, but you and Charlotte did well to go with Aunt Phyllis to Bath this summer, instead of coming north, even if you did have to bear Aunt Catherine and Cousin Anne – wicked of me to say, but I know you agree.

In truth, I think Mamma is rather avoiding Aunt Catherine - but I am sure you have heard all about it, in Bath. I imagine she is still quite put out with all the de Bourgh relations that have been vexing her since Sir Lewis passed, but now she begins to write Mamma that William must marry Cousin Anne; Mamma does not like it, but she only demurs, saying it would not be right to talk of weddings at all, with Jane in such a state.

You must have heard by now, George Wickham was lost at sea in May, and you may have surmised that Jane had recently learned of it around the time she received, and burned, your letter. I was with her when she read it, and I retrieved it from the fire in time to have seen a glimpse of it. No doubt, you see that all your talk of wedding plans was particularly painful for her.

She has been entirely disconsolate for months – indeed, she still feels Papa's loss as keenly as we all do, and to lose George so soon – she is in a sorry state indeed, and I can only guess that she lashed out at you. I would beg you forgive her. Leave her be for a time, but I know that one day she will come to regret her anger toward you, misplaced as it was. All I ask is that when the time comes, you forgive her with open arms, because her heart is completely shattered right now, and the rest of us are nearly just as wretched.

I miss you so very much Lizzy, even though I believe you have done right in staying away. I know Mamma longs to see you again, and it is my secret wish that she might be persuaded to go to London soon, for we are out of mourning for Papa, and Aunt Phyllis says you are to have a little Season this spring. I have been deflecting all of Aunt's hints about my coming out next season – in truth, Charlotte is the only one in the family who has had a Season, and it sounds rather dreadful by her account of it. I should much rather come to London and be very snug together, as we once were, long ago. Do you not miss those days?

I shall let you know if I have any success in my scheme for London, as I really believe it would be such a fine thing for all of us who desperately need such cheering. In the meantime, do send me another reading list, for I have completed the list you gave me at Christmas, and you have excellent taste!

All of my love,

Mary Bennet Darcy

***

Gracechurch Street, London
6 May, 1810

Dear Mary,

Your birthday present arrived early this year – thank you for the handkerchiefs you sent; they are positively lovely. I will cherish them all, perhaps especially the one Jane made. It was very good of her, and it warmed my heart to receive it on what had been a rather awful day.

Aunt Olivia is expecting another babe in the autumn, and she has been ill quite frequently. Uncle Edward is so very delighted, he seems ten years younger, and my aunt as well. Oh my goodness, I hope you are not reading this letter aloud to anyone, it is meant to be a secret for a little while longer!

I suffer from a rather different malady – a plague of gentlemen callers, for I am nearly nineteen now, and both of our uncles are quite fed up with me for not being keen on anyone yet. I have only been to a few balls and parties, and I have made some new acquaintances, but the only bit of it I really enjoy is sketching so many different characters – the human race is certainly an amusing one, is it not? It is also, unfortunately, not one that is abundant with rich, handsome, gentlemen who desire to sweep an outspoken Cheapside girl of unusual origins and ready opinions off her feet!

Fortunately Aunt Olivia's condition has caused her enthusiasm for my cause to wane, and I have recently taken Aunt Phyllis into my confidence, and it has done me such good to unburden myself as I have never been able to before. Charlotte and Richard understand me well enough, but now Richard has gone off to war and Charlotte has a great many cares of her own. We are for Weymouth this summer, Charlotte and I, with John and his wife, and I am eagerly awaiting my escape. Perhaps you and Mamma might join us?

Aunt Phyllis has lent me her support in taking my first Season rather slowly – she understands I have certain apprehensions about the marriage state, and we had a good long chat about it one snowy night at Matlock House last month. I told her things I had never dared put into words, and she in turn told me a great many things I did not know – about the past – things that shed a new light on parts of my life that have been very troubling. I wish very much I might share some of this with you, and with Jane and Mamma too, if they could bear it. Do give them my love.

Your loving sister,

Lizzy

***

Pemberley, Derbyshire
28 November, 1810

Dear Edward,

My old friend, I was heartbroken to hear of Olivia's passing. I was sitting with Phyllis at Matlock when Henry received your express, and our sister went white as a sheet at the news. I know it was not always right between you, but it must be a devastating loss, her and the child. I can only imagine what poor Lizzy, and the children must be feeling at such a time, and of all people I can well relate to the pain of losing a partner.

Mary and William want us to come to London for Christmas, but Jane is still in such depressed spirits, and I confess I am much the same. If you are as afflicted as I was after George died, I am sure you would not want your relations descending in such a state, and adding to your woes, yet it pains me that this Christmas will make two years since I have seen you, and my dear Lizzy.

She writes Mary and I often, and it has been a great comfort to us both. Even Jane is coming round, and seems genuinely interested in sitting with us when we read a letter from Lizzy, which gives me great hope. Pemberley feels so very gloomy and oppressive of late, and Lizzy's letters are so bright, it is like opening a window and letting sunshine into my heart – you see how sentimental I am grown. I do wish you would write more, particularly now. I shall worry for you a great deal, but at least I can trust that it will be a comfort for you to have sweet Lizzy at your side.

I find I am grown tired - old, weary, and tired, but I shall write again soon, and hope that you do the same.

All my love,

Anne

***

Gracechurch Street, London
7 January, 1811

Dear Anne,

I find myself more lucid today than I have been for some weeks, and I have been hoping to find the time and presence of mind to write you. I cannot promise my letter will bring you the same cheer as Lizzy's, and yet you have been my faithful correspondent these seventeen years or more.

You might imagine how I feel, and what my struggle has been since losing Olivia. For better or worse, I loved her, and the child she carried was to be the first of mine – we both wanted it so very much. It has made me think back on Fanny, a troubling thought, given what she said to Madeline and Phyllis before she died. After all these years, there is still a part of my heart yet broken over it all.

I even thought I saw Madeline the other day in Mayfair, with a couple of young ladies at her side. I suppose it is old eyes and a wounded heart playing tricks on me, but perhaps it really was her. The man she married could certainly keep her in such fine clothes, I am sure, and perhaps the girls were her daughters. I never told anyone, but the man she married had three children of his own – his situation was no different than mine. I shall never understand it.

I hear William has resumed his project in Scotland, to help John fix up Nettylmoor. Henry would do better to sell it, I think, but I suspect he has some sentimental attachment to the place. Still, we hope it might tempt Richard to resign his commission and settle down – this family needs a happy marriage to rejoice in.

Your mother sent me a very kind note last month, and I hear she is to come down in a few weeks. She is quite worked up about her fear that Charlotte will end up "on the shelf" and I fear it is only a matter of time before she comes to the same conclusion about our dear girls. Still, she has always been my supporter, and it will be good to see her. Lizzy finds her brand of expression quite inspiring, and I am looking forward to watching her reaction to Lizzy's new haircut – she has cropped it quite short, and I am told it is quite the fashion in ladies' magazines. She looks quite fetching, and as Rose is growing quite accomplished in her sketching I shall have her make a little portrait of Lizzy for you, so you can decide for yourself if you like it. I am certain, however, that it will earn her at least three rather severe stomps of Lady Eleanor's cane when she beholds it.

Well my old friend, I cannot recall when I have last written such a long letter, and I had better leave off while I remain quite sensible.

Yours ever,

EG

***

Pemberley, Derbyshire
25 November, 1811

Dear Lizzy,

We have done it! William has spoken with Uncle Henry, and we are for London this Christmas! After three long years of separation, I am so delighted I shall see you again! Mamma has agreed to it, and I think even Jane is looking forward to the journey. I know they were both hesitant to come down in the summer, while Richard was recovering, but it shall be wonderful to see him too, now that he has recovered. I daresay you all shall scarcely recognize Jane and I, for we are both grown taller, and I hear you have as well – we are all quite grown up now.

Oh Lizzy, I am so very filled with hope that all shall be well in the family at last. We are all out of mourning, and old enough to attend balls and parties.

I do hope that finally everything will be as it should again. Mamma and Jane both send their love. I shall keep this letter short, for I shall see you very soon, and tell you a great many more things when I am looking upon your sweet face!

Your loving sister,

Mary

8

❧

December 1811, London

"Damn it, Richard, sell the place in Scotland for all I care, but you'll not be running off to war again just because your arm is healed. Not now, when Anne is finally bringing the girls down to London. After all the work Darcy has put into the place it would be a shame to let it go, but if the funds will keep you here in England, so be it. But only if you take a wife – you are nearly thirty!"

"Father, I am still on the mend – a little – John is not even out of half-mourning for Lucy."

"That is no excuse," the earl replied. "He ought to start looking for a wife again himself, though he would not deign to attend our family meeting. His daughter needs a new mother."

"Lest history repeat itself," Sir Edward drawled. Though he schooled his countenance into a studied sort of neutrality, Elizabeth knew by the look in his eyes that he was not best pleased by the direction her Uncle Henry's visit had taken.

"I am quite firm in the matter," Uncle Henry carried on, as Elizabeth shifted uncomfortably beside Richard on the sofa, fearing what would inevitably follow. "William and I have put our foot down, and Anne will bring the girls to London for Christmas. Three years of nonsense, and we have nothing to show for it but melancholy – I shall not allow it to continue any longer. I do not blame you, Edward, but even Mary ought to have had a season by now. Think of how it would help Charlotte, to have a pretty cousin by her side."

Charlotte blanched. "Papa!"

"Well," Uncle Henry grumbled, giving his daughter an apologetic look. "Have you not said you wished for company at all those balls and parties?"

"Lizzy has come along sometimes…."

Richard drew closer to Elizabeth and laid his hand protectively over hers. "I think you all quite forget what poor Lizzy has suffered, what we all have been through. We have been in mourning for most of the last three years."

Uncle Henry looked from Richard to Elizabeth with a curious glint in his eye. "To be perfectly honest, I'd not be opposed to a match between the two of you. What do you say, Edward? Phyllis? There is merit to it."

As Elizabeth glanced at her Uncle Edward with wide eyes and a mounting sense of dread, he answered the earl with a grimace, "If you mean it will keep her money in the family."

"What I mean is that the two of them have been thick as thieves since you brought her to London! Why should they not marry? With her dowry and the sale of the Scottish pile, they could settle wherever they choose, and they get on better than most couples who meet on the marriage mart...."

"I beg your pardon, Father," Richard interjected, his hand remaining on Elizabeth's, "I have been away for years! This has never been discussed before, and I cannot like the subject being broached in such a matter now."

"Come, come, Richard, you have been back nearly six months, recovering your arm, and who has been faithfully at your side?"

Richard began all the protestations Elizabeth was too stunned to give voice to, and then abruptly fell silent. He pulled her hand toward him, stroking it thoughtfully as he met her eye. "What do you think, Lizzy? We are not so much brother and sister – have you been tending my war wounds, hoping for such an alliance?"

Elizabeth stammered, feeling her heart sink into the pit of her stomach. She knew – or at least, strongly hoped – that he was only jesting, but for once she had no clever retort. Surely Richard, who had indeed been as a brother to her these seven years, was not suddenly proposing to her in a room full of their nearest relations.

"Richard is quite right, this is hardly appropriate talk – not at all how we had intended to broach the subject. There are a great many eligible prospects for all three of the girls, and John and Richard besides. William too. We have begun compiling lists, but nothing need be decided today."

"Yes, yes," Uncle Henry conceded. "I do get carried away, but of course there is the whole Season ahead of us yet, and a great deal to accomplish. The separation in this family has gone on long enough, and we are going to be a true family this Christmas, but I'll be damned if we do not have a few weddings to look forward to at the end of it."

Elizabeth flinched at her uncle's language, and glanced back at Richard, trying to gauge his reaction.

"I shall admit the idea has merit, but I do have some questions about these lists," he said warily.

"Of course you have," Uncle Henry drawled and rolled his eyes.

Elizabeth looked frantically back at her aunt. "But I have no wish to marry at all! You know I never shall. I thought you understood."

"Well, of course we have all tried to understand," Aunt Phyllis replied gently. "We have all been very patient, but of course we hoped you would eventually change your mind."

"What about me," came a giggling voice at the corner of the room; Rose had snuck in.

"For Heaven's sake, child," Uncle Edward burst. "You were not invited in, young lady!"

Seizing the opportunity to extricate herself from the situation that had quickly become very deeply uncomfortable, Elizabeth sprang up off of the couch and seized her cousin Rose by the hand, dragging the young girl down the corridor and upstairs.

"It's not fair, Lizzy," Rose whined as Elizabeth led her up the stairs. "Why can I not come out a year early, and go to balls and parties? You and Jane and Mary and Charlotte shall do everything without me."

"Your come out is not until next year, and you must understand it may be a little... different. At any rate, perhaps you would do better to think of ways you can show your father that you are ready. If you can stop pulling tricks like you did downstairs just now, they might at least let you dine with the family more this year."

"Dine with you? I want to dance!"

"Well, ask Cousin Charlotte how well she has liked most of *her* dance partners, and I daresay you may yet change your mind!" Elizabeth, her hands on Rose's shoulders, steered her cousin toward her bedroom, and half-teasingly nudged her inside. "I shall ask Aunt Phyllis to bring you dress shopping with us on Friday, if only you stay in your room and give the rest of us some peace!"

Rose scrunched up her face with displeasure, and shut the door in Elizabeth's face. Elizabeth breathed a sigh of relief and went into her own room, desperate to be alone with her thoughts.

It was too much all at once! It was enough to think that she must face Mamma and her sisters again after three years of separation, and though Mary was optimistic, Elizabeth was rather frightened. Would Mamma despise her? Had she sided with Jane? Was Jane really as eager to reconcile as Mary let on?

And now, to all this, she must add the looming threat of marriage. *They thought I would change my mind?* The idea was insupportable. She had encountered a few hopeful suitors over the years, but none that hadn't been easily discouraged by her total lack of interest. But Richard?

He had been as a brother to her these last seven years, since the moment he had calmed her tears at Pemberley when she had learned the truth. At least, that is how she had always felt. It was alarming to think that Richard might actually consider her in *that* way, that his feelings might go beyond familial affection, when the thought had never occurred to her.

"Oh Lizzy, look at you hiding away, vexing yourself; you are always quite determined to do it." Charlotte peeked in the doorway at Elizabeth before coming into the room and sitting in the window seat next to her. The two had been nearly as close as sisters could ever be since Elizabeth had come to London, and had grown up a great deal since their days of spying on their family at Pemberley. No longer was Charlotte a carefree, mischievous girl, but a thoughtful, pragmatic young woman who had been passed over for several seasons, despite Elizabeth's loyal belief that her cousin was one of the finest women in London.

Elizabeth knew she had changed, too – she had felt so grown up from such a young age, and her knowledge of her uncle's unhappy marriage and the alienating tragedies in her family had darkened her once sparkling wit. Aunt Olivia would have wanted her to be bold at such a time, but in truth she could face neither the arrival of her family, nor the prospect of marriage.

"Do not think of marriage," Charlotte chided her. "You will see how it shall be. My father can scarcely arrange seven marriages all in the space of a single season! Do not dwell on it, I am sure it will come out right. Think of your sisters and your mother. Occupy your time mending your relationship with them, and I daresay you shall have no time for a courtship."

"Perhaps you are right. Mary is so sure it shall be well, and I do wish for it. I shall do my best with Jane and Mamma."

"And William too?"

Elizabeth shrugged. "I do not see the point in that – I know he despises me. So much the better. I could never allow him to meddle in my affairs as he has done with poor Jane."

"And yet I hear he has played a rather large role himself in bringing this Christmas visit about."

"I cannot think why, except that he hopes to cheer Mamma."

"He is still your brother, Lizzy."

"Indeed he is not! Whatever regard Jane and Mary have for him, I do not share it. He did not deign to trouble himself over his sisters until long after I went away. It hardly matters – I do not care a whit."

"Oh yes, I can see that."

There was a knock on Elizabeth's door. "Not now, Rose," Elizabeth cried, and muttered under her breath.

Aunt Phyllis opened the door and slipped into the room. "Richard has asked me to convey his apologies, if he gave you any alarm, Lizzy."

"But of course he – no, no. It is well, aunt. I am sure he was just as surprised as I was."

"Were you really so shocked? You have never thought of it, not even recently? You *have* been very diligent in visiting since he has been home."

"I was only trying to help his recovery! He is like a brother to me."

"Well, I am sorry your uncle sprang it on you like that. You know how worked up he gets when he has some scheme in his head, but nothing is certain just yet, my dear. Only think on it is all we ask. Perhaps if you start to consider Richard in a different light... well, he had not seen you in years, until he came home injured, and suddenly you were a woman grown, and always at his side...."

"Aunt! Are you suggesting he has *feelings* for me? That I have somehow done something to, to...."

"I am not suggesting anything, just thinking aloud, I suppose. You are not children playing together anymore, Lizzy."

"I have not been a child in a long time, Aunt."

"I know. And for that I am sorry – we all are. But it is time to let go of the past and think of the future. It need not be a future with Richard, if you decide against it, but it ought to be a future that brings you fully back into this family. You have been walking about with a dark dreary cloud over your head for years, child, and you must ask yourself if that is how you really want to go on. Or, do you want to open up your heart and let your family back in, and maybe someone to share your life with, too?"

Elizabeth sighed and turned to Charlotte, who quietly nodded her agreement. "Very well," she sighed. "You are both quite right – as regards the family. I am ready to make more of an effort, and to be happy again."

***

Fitzwilliam Darcy looked up from his desk as his cousin Richard sauntered into the study. "Imagine my astonishment, Darcy, at finding your mother and sisters were gone off to see Sir Edward and Lizzy, yet you had remained at home, after all of this working my father into a frenzy about being a proper family at Christmas! What are you about, Darcy? You ought to be at Sir Edward's new house on Upper Brook Street – he bought it just to spite Olivia after she passed, or so the story goes...."

Darcy fixed his cousin with a dark look before turning back to his work and scribbling a few notes down in a journal. Richard only laughed at him. "You make a fine show of it, but I know you are not really doing anything but brooding." He took a seat across from Darcy, lounging in an idle and indecorous posture. "So, let's out with it, then."

"I have no interest in visiting Elizabeth, or hearing of Lady Olivia, either. Indeed, I daresay they are one and the same."

"You cannot still hold a grudge against your poor sister – she is but a child!"

"She is neither a child, nor my sister, and if Uncle is to be believed, she is soon to be your betrothed." Richard shrugged and Darcy studied him, hoping his cousin's nonchalance indicated the match was merely some fancy of the earl's. "Well?"

"Well *what*, Darcy? I already know what you are thinking, as always, but this time I think I shall make you say it."

"Very well then, I shall," Darcy said, his temper rising. "I think it would be a disaster. She is too much like Olivia, and I should hate to see you end up like Sir Edward in a few years. That woman ruined him, and she ruined Elizabeth Bennet, who shall in turn ruin you. Her foolishness has already hurt Jane and Mother, and I should hate to see you be next. Uncle and I have worked too hard on your behalf, fixing up the estate in Scotland – you might keep it or sell it as you like, but now that we have finally gotten you to leave the army, you might settle down and be happy. I do not think you would be, with Elizabeth."

Richard folded his arms and glowered at Darcy for a moment, before stalking over to the sideboard and pouring them each a glass of brandy. "Well cousin, have you gotten the stick out of your arse? Are you quite finished?"

Darcy took a drink and stared silently back at him. If Richard wanted to hear more, he would be happy to vent his spleen at length, though he knew it was not wise.

"Good," Richard snapped. "I left the army because I wanted to, and if I had not wished it myself, none of your carping or my father's would have accomplished it. As to Lizzy, you have been beastly and you know it. You are far too hard on her, and she does not deserve it. She is a good girl – a fine woman, I should say. You barely even know her, but for her letters to your mother and sisters. You have not seen her these three years, and I can assure you she is quite grown up."

"You just said she was a child."

"Damn it, Darcy. Listen, when I came back this summer, she was so different. With Olivia gone... and just to set matters straight, you know, I have always thought Lizzy made Olivia more pleasant, rather than Olivia influencing Lizzy. She has always been mature for her age, even when she really *was* a child. I have the highest opinion of her, whether she agrees to marry me or not."

"She would dare to refuse you?" Darcy was relieved to hear it, yet offended on his cousin's behalf, and disgusted that Elizabeth would be so foolish.

"Father sprang it on her so suddenly – I do not blame her for being dismayed. Perhaps she was only embarrassed. At any rate, her uncle has put by some money for her dowry – rather more than he will bestow on Jane or Mary, and it *would* be a prudent match. Beyond that, I happen to care for her a great deal, and I enjoy her company. This makes her a far better choice than any of the other names on the list my father has made, and I think she shall be saying the same of me, ere long. And," Richard said with a laugh, "I have seen your list, too – poor man!"

Darcy rolled his eyes. "Uncle Henry is not my father. I am not of a mind to marry at present – that is by no means what has brought me to London."

"What, then? You were most keen to be here."

"As I told your father, I have made the arrangements to come to London for my mother's sake, and for my two sisters. Pemberley has been a dreary place since father died, and it pains me to see it. I have not the talent for cheering them, though God knows I have tried. I would keep them with me always, and far from Elizabeth and even from Sir Edward, but I fear nothing short of a complete reunion will make them happy again. At any rate, it is time Jane and Mary had a proper Season."

"You and Father are in agreement about that."

"Perhaps, but in their case, I think Mother and I ought to have the final say in whatever list our uncle has taken it upon himself to compile for them. I will not see them wed without anything but the deepest love and mutual respect."

"That is awfully sentimental talk from you, Darcy. And if I were to tell you I was most ardently in love with Elizabeth Bennet?"

Darcy tried not to let his lip curl with disdain. "Are you?"

"I might be – I think I *could* be, in time."

Darcy gave his cousin a sardonic look. "And here I had hoped you might save me from Cousin Anne."

"Ha! Never. I was rather surprised hers was not the only name on your list."

"Even Aunt Catherine has given up on the idea, after all these years. As I said, I have no mind for matrimony at present – I shall have my hands quite full looking after Jane and Mary."

"You are a diligent brother, I shall give you that. After this sad business with Wickham, vile fellow that he was, I do hope Cousin Jane might find some happiness."

"As to that, I am thinking of speaking to Uncle about a name to add to her list."

Richard raised his eyebrows in exaggerated surprise. "Playing at matchmaker? That is not like you."

"No, I suppose not. I am not *playing at matchmaker* precisely. It is only a little notion that occurred to me – you remember Charles Bingley."

"He and his sister do leave a lasting impression, different though they are. I daresay we shall be seeing a lot of her when she finds out John is available again."

"We shall be seeing a lot of Bingley too, I hope. He wrote recently – he has been inquiring about estates to let, perhaps even purchase, and hopes I might assist him in finding one, and in getting the feel for estate management. I think he might be of a mind to settle down soon."

"And you think a lively fellow is just the thing to help Jane forget about Wickham?"

Darcy shook his head, trying not to let old resentment get the better of him. "He never deserved her in the first place."

"You are damned right about that. I suppose it is well enough he died at sea, before she had the chance to find out what he was really like."

Darcy regarded his cousin evenly; he had dreaded his cousin ever guessing his secret, and hoped this would not be the day he must be fully honest with Richard. "I am sorry it pained Jane, sorry it took so long for me to look after her interest as a brother should, but yes, it was for the best."

Richard eyed him curiously. "I wonder if such a thought crossed your mind when you suggested a naval career instead of the church?"

Darcy went rigid. "I take no pleasure in Jane's pain. Her grief has been considerable."

Richard continued his probing look a moment longer, then clucked his tongue at Darcy and stood up, making a great show of checking his watch. "Well, Darcy, I think I shall be off. I might catch your mother and sisters at Upper Brook Street if I head there now. Shall I give Lizzy and Uncle Edward your regards?"

Darcy glowered at him and said nothing as his cousin sauntered away, as cheerfully defiant as he had been when he came in.

***

Elizabeth paced in front of the drawing room windows for a quarter-hour, the anticipation almost too much for her, but at length the Darcy carriage could be seen coming to a stop in front of her uncle's grand new house in Upper Brook Street. He had intended to be with her for this first meeting, and she knew he was as eager to meet with them as she was, but a message had arrived not ten minutes earlier from one of his warehouses, and his presence was urgently needed there.

Instead, Rose sat with Elizabeth in the parlor, doing her best to allay some of Elizabeth's anxiety. Well, perhaps it was not her *best*. "I hear William is grown tall and handsome – I cannot wait to set eyes on him."

Elizabeth rolled her eyes. "He has always been tall, and – Rose, that is not helpful."

"Well! What shall I say? It is sure to be awkward, but they are here now and it will be over soon."

Elizabeth groaned and seated herself on a chaise, positioning herself so that it would not be so obvious if nobody chose to sit beside her. Rose reclined merrily on the sofa, fidgeting with her bracelets. Elizabeth knew not which had been worse for her spirits, her uncle's sober silence until he had been called away, or Rose's unyielding exuberance. She was right, at least – it would be over soon.

She heard the sound of their visitors removing their coats in the foyer, and in another moment the three women stepped quietly into the room. Elizabeth felt her heart pounding as she looked upon her Mamma – the only mother she had ever really known, and though she rose to greet them, her feet were rooted in place as she held Lady Anne's gaze. It broke her heart to see so much sadness in her mother's eyes.

Rose was the first to fill the heavy silence with her own effusive greetings, and Elizabeth shook herself out of her reverie to call for tea before she finally came forward to greet her guests. Mary quickly embraced Elizabeth, burying her face in Elizabeth's shoulder as she whispered, "Just be yourself, Lizzy."

Elizabeth held Mary close for a moment longer before releasing her, and by the time Mary drew away, Elizabeth's tears had begun to fall. Mary caught her by the hand and led Elizabeth forward, toward their mother, and with each step she took, Elizabeth lost more of her composure, until at last she was weeping.

Her mother stepped forward, closing the last space between them, and cupped Elizabeth's face in her hands. "Oh, my dearest girl, I have pictured your dear face in my mind every day, I am sure." She gently ran her soft fingers across Elizabeth's cheeks and said, "I hope these are happy tears, my love."

Unable to speak, Elizabeth raised her fingers and hesitantly placed them atop her mother's, holding her mother's hands against her face as she wept. "Oh, Mamma, I am so sorry."

Her mother embraced her, slowly rocking as she stroked Elizabeth's back. "We are together, at last, my dear girl. All shall be well. Your Uncle Henry has commanded it," she teased.

"And so it must come to pass," Elizabeth laughed, savoring the feel of her mother's soothing touch. "You smell... so wonderful. I forgot... I forgot how much...."

"Hush, dearest. I love you too."

Elizabeth shed the last of her tears and pulled away, wiping her face with a sardonic smile. "Am I not in very fine looks, Mamma?"

"You always are, in my book." Her mother gave her a reassuring pat on the arm, and then reached up to stoke Elizabeth's hair, which hung just past her shoulders when loose. "You let your hair grow out," she said with a smile. "I am so pleased."

"Now it is Rose's turn to vex my uncles," Elizabeth said, mustering a playful smirk. She gestured to Rose, who had recently gotten the same short haircut that Elizabeth herself had sported the previous year.

Lady Anne shook her head with bemusement. "It is very fetching, I am sure, as was yours, Lizzy, in that sketch Miss Rose made of you last winter. Still, I am old-fashioned, and prefer more elegant arrangements. I suppose I must be like my own mother, and begin to keep smelling salts in constant supply."

The tea service arrived, and Rose quickly offered to serve, nearly pushing Elizabeth toward Jane, who had yet to speak. Elizabeth glanced nervously at Jane. "Sister…."

Jane stared at the carpet, wringing her hands for a minute before finally meeting Elizabeth's eyes with – was that hope? Elizabeth stared back at her, too anxious to speak. "I must have tried to write a hundred times."

Elizabeth continued to stare back at her, still too overcome with emotion to speak sensibly. "Me too."

"I hope… I hope we shall be friends again, Lizzy."

Elizabeth took Jane's hand as they sat together on the sofa. "I want to, very much. It would make me so happy."

"Oh, Lizzy," Jane sighed. "It feels so long since anyone has really been happy, does it not?"

Elizabeth held her sister's gaze and whispered, "Do you blame me for that?"

"I wanted to. For years, it was easier. And you did not come back, after Papa died."

"I did come back. We stayed a month."

"I mean – we wanted you to *come back*. When you did not stay, it was easier to be angry with you than to feel anything else, and losing poor George only compounded it for me," Jane said softly. "Several times over these three years it occurred to me that I could finally understand what you must have felt all those years ago when you went away; at times I felt as though it were my fault George went away to sea, and was drowned."

"Why did you not tell me that?" Elizabeth pressed Jane's hand in her own, grateful for Rose's determination to keep Mary and Lady Anne occupied in conversation, affording Elizabeth and Jane some privacy.

"It was too hard, too humiliating to admit my own error in

judgement, and there was too much to keep old resentments alive. And there was always so much talk about Aunt Olivia; I feared it was true that you had grown rather too like her."

"Aunt Olivia was – we all *know* what she was, myself more than you, perhaps, but I saw past it, you know. Even Uncle Edward did, at times. Rose does not know the truth, not any of it," she said, dropping her voice even lower. "Better that we remember the years that were good, for her sake. In truth, I have learned a great deal about emulating that which I admired about her, and understanding the difference between those traits – her wit, her vivacity – and her... other characteristics. I hope I am not like her in *some* respects, though I suppose I can guess who might have led you to draw such conclusions."

"Oh, Lizzy," Jane sighed again, fighting back tears of her own. "Our brother is... you do not know him as Mary and I do. After you went away, he became so very attentive to us. He is protective, and loving, and though he has not quite the talent for it, he *has* tried to cheer us, to bring some happiness to Pemberley. William is...."

Jane was interrupted; she had caught Rose's attention. "Oh, yes! Where is Cousin William, Aunt?"

Elizabeth looked over at her mother, who smiled weakly. "William is at home – that is, he had some urgent business to attend to. He has been such a diligent master of Pemberley since... these last three years. I believe he had a letter from his steward."

Elizabeth turned to glance at Mary, who nodded sadly. She knew very well why William had not come. "I suppose it does not matter," she whispered to Jane. "It is you three that I wished to see. I suppose he has done me a favor in staying away."

Jane looked stricken. "Oh Lizzy, I wish you knew him as I do."

Elizabeth scowled and turned her face away. She was relieved at William's absence, almost happy at having all the triumph of being the slighted party, rather than all the discomfort of having to face him.

Lady Anne likewise observed Sir Edward's absence, and Elizabeth was horrified to think that it might be attributed to the same reasons as William's, that her mother and sisters might draw such awful conclusions. "He wished very much to be here," she stammered. "He was waiting with us, in fact, when he was called away to his warehouse on some urgent business of his own. It is a pity we do not still live so near, on Gracechurch Street, else I am sure he would be returning to us any minute."

Her mother was all politeness, expressing a hope that Sir Edward would soon return. They heard footsteps in the hall twenty minutes later, and Lady Anne looked toward the doorway with a face full of hope, though it was not Sir Edward but Richard who had to come to save them from a conversation that was, despite Mary's best efforts, inevitably awkward.

His face lit up as he paused in the doorway, and he beamed at Elizabeth, who sat happily ensconced on the sofa between her two sisters. "Cousin Richard! I had not expected to see you today. How is Charlotte?"

"Beset with suitors – Viscount Milton and Mr. Harper have come to call and Phyllis has quite cast me out of the house, lest I make a nuisance of myself, as I am wont to do."

"Well, I am glad you have come here to be a nuisance," Elizabeth replied, teasing him as was her custom, until she suddenly recollected herself. There had been no further conversation, as far as Elizabeth was aware, regarding Uncle Henry's hopes for a match between her and Richard, but she had no doubt the matter would be revisited. She reminded herself that she ought to take a less familiar tone with him until she had made up her mind about the idea, lest she encourage him too soon. She invited him to sit, and after a moment of glancing about for a seat, and then drinking in the sight of Jane, who was looking every bit the prettiest of the three sisters, as ever, Richard sat between Elizabeth and Jane.

Elizabeth watched Jane blush and greet Richard with a strange sort of giddy shyness, but Richard addressed Lady Anne. "What a fine thing, all of us together at Christmas! We have William and Mary to thank for that, I think, though my father would take all the credit."

"It was Lizzy's idea, I am sure," Mary said, giving Elizabeth a smile of encouragement.

"Uncle Henry can take all the credit he likes," Elizabeth replied with a pert smile, and out of habit she nudged Richard with her shoulder before recollecting herself. "I am content to enjoy the result."

"So are we all, my dear," her mother replied with a sigh of contentment. "Myself most of all."

***

Richard remained at Upper Brook Street after Lady Anne had taken Mary and Jane home, though she waited for Uncle Edward for quite some time. To Elizabeth's dismay, Rose perversely decided to venture upstairs and look in on the twins, leaving Richard and Elizabeth alone in the drawing room.

To Richard, it seemed the most natural thing in the world, and he did not leave his seat beside her on the sofa as he turned to address her, asking how she felt after the visit.

"Relieved, I think," she answered.

"I can well imagine. After so long a separation, the first visit could not be easy, but I think it went rather well, though I suspect there must have been a great deal of waterworks before I arrived."

"Indeed there was – and yet, I felt so happy, so... whole again. As if perhaps being together like this at Christmas might somehow be a chance to make up for all the other Christmases that have gone so wrong. It was painful, but a pleasant sort of pain. I must sound quite mad."

He nudged her shoulder with his. "It has been many years, I am sure, since I thought you were mad."

"Shocking reply! And here I thought you wished to hear my feelings."

Again Elizabeth felt a strange sort of anxiety in her stomach, and as she met Richard's eye, she saw that he felt it too. "On one subject," said he, "I very much wish to know your feelings. You need not feel obliged to consider anyone's opinion but your own, but I should like to know how you feel about...."

He had taken her hand in his, when they were interrupted by the sound of Uncle Edward returning. "About Christmas," Richard finished, looking away from her with some embarrassment as he withdrew his hand.

"Christmas?" Elizabeth stared at him with bewilderment, relieved to see her uncle striding into the room.

Uncle Edward glanced nervously between Elizabeth and Richard, who repeated, "Yes, Christmas. Sir Edward, what a shame you just missed Aunt Anne and Jane and Mary. Lizzy and I have been speaking of our plans for Christmas this year."

Uncle Edward eyed them incredulously. "We are still to dine at Darcy House for Christmas, are we not?"

"Indeed," Elizabeth answered, "and we have been invited to dine there day after next, as well."

"Exactly so," Richard agreed. "With two happy gatherings in the space of one week to look forward to, Lizzy and I were hoping it should really feel like Christmas again at last, as it did in years past. I know it would mean the world to Aunt Anne."

Elizabeth smiled, relieved at the life line he had thrown her. Not only had he deftly skirted the matter of what she suspected he truly wished to speak to her about, but he had subtly suggested a way she might really make amends to her family. "I remember what a happy time it once was for us all, how festive it once felt, all of us gathered together, singing Christmas carols, hanging holly, exchanging gifts and making merry. Can we not attempt to recreate the atmosphere? I am sure Mamma would be so pleased, and I should like to make her happy."

"They have only just arrived at Darcy House, and there is not a trace of holiday cheer to be found there," Richard said with a playful glint in his eye.

Uncle Edward took his usual chair and stoked his chin pensively. "What an idea. We shall have to bring it to them."

9

❧

Elizabeth, her uncle, and her cousin Rose were able to time their arrival perfectly with the party from Matlock House, and they disembarked their carriages together as they arrived at Hanover Square to visit the Darcys. They had been invited to dine, but had come early, and nine merry revelers – two of whom were very nervous indeed – made their way into Lady Anne's drawing room bearing baskets, boxes, and bags overflowing with holly and garlands and St. Nicholas Day gifts.

Lady Anne leapt to her feet as her family made their entrance in a noisy, affectionate cluster; she greeted them each warmly, saving Sir Edward and Elizabeth for last. "Oh Edward, Lizzy dearest, what a lovely gesture. It has been so many years since Christmas has felt like – well, like Christmas at all."

Elizabeth could see Lady Anne's eyes beginning to mist over with tears, and she impulsively came forward and wrapped her arms around her mother's neck. "Happy Christmas, Mamma," she whispered, pressing her eyes shut to avoid shedding tears of her own.

Jane and Mary approached, their smiles shy but sincere; each of them latched on to one of Elizabeth's arms as the whole family made their way into the drawing room. Elizabeth was pleased that they had sought her out, but once she was seated near them, she found herself suddenly uneasy. What was she to say? After so long a separation, and such a history as they shared, how could she possibly begin to converse comfortably with them?

Fortunately, Rose could always be relied upon for lively conversation, and after a few mundane remarks about the weather, Elizabeth was relieved when her cousin came to join them. "La! How dull you all are, sitting about when there is holly to be hung! Come, Lizzy - Cousin Jane, Cousin Mary, I must have you all help me. I remember hanging holly at Pemberley when I was a little girl, it was such fun!"

"Why not?" Elizabeth seized eagerly on the idea. After all, she, her cousin and her uncle had worked diligently putting together all the trappings of Christmas; but of course this was the logical conclusion.

Perhaps if she tried to simply act naturally, the rest would come.

She and her sisters followed Rose, laughing shyly together as they began the business of hanging boughs of holly. It was still a few days before Christmas Eve, and it felt a little silly, especially as it had been so long since Elizabeth had felt such a festive impulse, but the encouragement they received from the rest of the family served both to put her at ease, and to provide a means through which she could converse with her sisters without fearing any awkwardness as they went about their activity.

Elizabeth was surprised to notice the dynamic that existed between her two sisters. Before – when she had lived at Pemberley – Mary had always been the more serious sister, even at a young age, and though she certainly still was, Jane's shy temper had grown into such a sorrowful, sedate sort of reticence that Mary seemed far livelier. It was an adaptation likely borne out of necessity, but the result was quite pleasing. To Elizabeth's complete astonishment, it was Mary who asked if they had included a kissing bough in all of their greenery.

"Unlike you and I," Jane said with a mournful look, "Mary is quite eager to be fallen in love with this Season."

"I am sure I should not object to it either," Rose giggled.

"I know Jane has her reasons, but surely *you* are not so opposed to our Uncle's scheme for us, Lizzy," Mary chided, betraying an impish smile.

"I am trying to remain open-minded," Elizabeth admitted, unwittingly casting a nervous glance in Richard's direction. "At least – I have decided that I ought to be open-minded, but in truth I have been given little opportunity to put my resolution into practice yet."

"I am sure there shall be time for all that," Jane said, her voice and countenance betraying her discomfort with the subject. It was no secret she still pined for her lost love, and Elizabeth hoped that they might soon have the chance to speak privately about it.

"Well, the time for mistletoe is *now*," Rose declared, tickling Elizabeth's nose with a sprig of rosemary before she resumed her rummaging through the basket of evergreens. "By the by... where is cousin William tonight?"

"Oh," Jane said sadly, "he made other plans, before he knew you were all to come to us tonight. He is dining with an old friend – Miss Bingley's brother, in fact. He had not expected to meet with you all before Christmas."

Elizabeth had made a conscious effort not to comment on William's absence, but was relieved that Rose had done so, as she had felt some little curiosity as to his whereabouts. And yet, it was a relief; Elizabeth had feared that her attempts to converse with her mother and sisters might be strained if he was constantly observing her, holding her in contempt as he had long been disposed to do.

"Well, I am glad you are both here," she told her sisters. "I have brought some little gifts for you both." Reaching into one of the baskets she had brought, Elizabeth produced two small, simply wrapped gifts. Mary opened hers first – it was a book about Hertford Castle. "You always did like my reading recommendations, particularly those that were suggestions from Aunt Olivia, and they were not *all* so very racy, you know. This was the first book she ever gave me. Hertford Castle predates the Norman conquest, and has a fantastically rich history – I thought you might enjoy it, as it is in our native county."

Mary opened the book reverently, running her hands over one of the illustrations. "It is lovely, Lizzy. Oh, thank you, Sister. I shall treasure it."

To Jane Elizabeth presented a gift she was rather nervous about; she feared it may be perceived as ironic, rather than earnest. It was a stationery set with lovely paper tinted lilac and scented the same. Jane looked into Elizabeth's eyes as she opened it, her countenance offering Elizabeth some assurance that the gift had been taken as it was meant. "This is beautiful, Lizzy," Jane whispered. "We shall be together many months yet, but whenever we are not you may depend on having a letter from me."

Elizabeth rested her hand on Jane's. "That is precisely what I would wish."

Mary smirked at them. "My goodness, you make me feel quite silly, Lizzy. I have only gotten you both some new sheet music."

"Well, I hope it is something that can be played as a duet," Elizabeth chided her sister. "I have not exaggerated in my letters – I play very ill indeed! I shall have to rely on Jane to save me, if I am called upon to perform, else I shall surely disgrace myself."

"Oh, no, Lizzy. I am sure you play very well – Aunt Olivia was always boasting of your abilities," Mary said.

"Which was hardly a favor!" Elizabeth managed a laugh, despite the grief she still bore for her late aunt. "Much better to understate my talents, lest people expect true excellence from me – they should be sorely disappointed."

"I – I have not played in years," Jane admitted softly, her eyes flirting between Elizabeth and Mary.

"I know," Mary said.

Elizabeth regarded her sister with compassion. "But you have always played so well! Mamma has always said there was nothing that gave her more pleasure than hearing you play."

"Yes, I know. George always said the same. I suppose that is why I stopped, after…."

"Oh dear," Mary sighed. "I – I hoped you would like it. I did not mean to make you sad."

"I think I should like to play again – a duet with Lizzy would be lovely." She offered Elizabeth a warm smile.

Elizabeth reciprocated with a grin. "I shall never forget Aunt Catherine always pestering you about it." Mimicking the great lady's voice, she said, "You will never play really well if you do not practice more. If I had ever learnt, I would be a great proficient!"

Jane and Mary laughed, and for a moment Elizabeth felt perfectly at ease, as if they were all children again, laughing at their elders in secret. "Where is Aunt Catherine, anyhow? Is she coming for Christmas?"

"Of course she is," Mary replied. "She has still not given up her efforts to make a match between Cousin Anne and William."

Elizabeth laughed. "Really? My goodness, she has been on about it for so long – in truth, it has been many years since I have heard anything of Cousin Anne, and I suppose I had imagined she must have settled somewhere."

"No," Jane said. "She is still at Rosings. I kept up our yearly visits for a time, but she has grown rather like Sir Lewis, very disagreeable."

"Poor William," Elizabeth said, enjoying the gossip with her sisters that felt so natural.

"I shall be very sorry for him, if he does marry her," Jane said defensively. "Whatever you may think of our brother, I hope you would not wish such a fate on him!"

"No, of course not. I am sorry Jane. It is only an amusing notion, that is all."

"Perhaps he shall be spared such an awful fate – I suspect Rose has an interest in him," Mary said, gracefully steering the subject in a more amicable direction. "She certainly asks about him a lot."

"Rose is interested in *all* gentleman," Elizabeth replied, casting a glance of bemusement in the direction of her young cousin, who even now sat speaking to Charlotte and the viscount with a look of fervent interest. "Poor Uncle is certainly going to have his hands full when she comes out next year."

"It is a shame she cannot come out in my place," Jane said. "I am quite dreading it. I have never wanted a London Season, but William says it is for the best."

Elizabeth bit back a caustic remark and gave Jane's hand a gentle squeeze. "It is some relief that we shall all be together, and not have to come out alone, as we might have done. Of course, I confess there is a certain allure to the notion of using Rose as a stand-in, and I am sure she would be most eager."

"I shall keep that in mind," Mary said with a gentle laugh, "if I encounter any unpleasant suitors. Apparently Uncle Henry has a list for each of us!"

Elizabeth caught herself once more glancing over at Richard, who was likewise staring in her direction – but no, he was looking at Jane. He caught her eye and smiled. She briefly wondered if his name was on her sisters' lists as well, or only hers, before reminding herself of her promise to Charlotte and Aunt Phyllis. Their Season had not started just yet, and tonight was about her sisters and mother. Excusing herself from Jane and Mary, she went and sat at her mother's side, earning her a look of loving approbation from her mother.

**

For once, Elizabeth felt her excitement equal to her younger cousin's as the two prepared together to attend the Christmas supper at Darcy House. They had each ordered new gowns a few days earlier with their Aunt Phyllis, whose status as the Countess of Matlock ensured that the dresses were ready in time to wear this evening.

Rose had completed her toilette ahead of Elizabeth, as her thick brown hair was cut so short there was little to be done with it, while Elizabeth's full chestnut curls were finally long enough to be arranged in an elegant chignon. When Elizabeth's maid had finished tucking back the loose tendrils of hair with the delicate gold and ruby pins Lady Anne had gifted her on the last Christmas they were all together, Elizabeth wrapped a shawl around her shoulders and declared herself quite ready. She wrapped her arm around Rose, and the two beheld their reflection in the mirror together.

Elizabeth was more simply dressed in a flattering shade of green, and her deep emerald shawl with gold vines delicately embroidered on it completed the ensemble. Rose was more elaborately attired in red and silver, her gown more detailed with trim and lace than Elizabeth favored. Despite the disparity in their tastes, they both knew themselves, and one another, to be in very fine looks.

"We could be sisters, could we not?" Rose laughed as she stared at their reflections.

"Perhaps if my hair were still short, like yours. And we shall not be the same height for long, you know, for I am done growing, but you are not."

Rose turned and smiled at Elizabeth. "At any rate, you are a thousand times prettier than me, I am sure."

"If only I could believe it! I suppose it is a pity I shall not have you at my side for the Season, for you do bolster my confidence."

Rose rolled her eyes. "You need only speak to Papa."

Elizabeth shook her head, causing a few stray curls to break free near her face. "You know what the answer would be! At any rate," she said, turning serious, "I hope you shall stay close to me tonight. I find I am still rather nervous. There was a moment, last time we were at Darcy House, I thought I had rather offended Jane, and with William there tonight, undoubtedly eager to provoke me as ever, I am sure I shall be in constant danger of giving offense!"

"I shall not leave you alone with him for a moment," Rose said, squeezing Elizabeth's hand. "I only wish you were not so very afraid – I adore you, Lizzy, and you ought not fear what anyone else thinks, because if they do not agree with me, they are simply wrong."

Elizabeth smiled, taking heart from her cousin's encouragement, and gave her an affectionate kiss on the cheek before hastening downstairs as she heard her uncle calling out that they were in some danger of arriving late.

They were the last to arrive at Darcy House, and Elizabeth was startled at what a large party they made. Her mother and sisters made a great deal of fuss over her, as well as Uncle Edward, Rose, and the twins, and they were subsequently greeted by her Uncle Henry and Aunt Phyllis, Charlotte, and the Dowager Countess; it felt a quarter-hour had passed just in exchanging pleasantries with those she had seen less than a week prior.

William did not escape Elizabeth's notice, and she felt vindicated in her continued dislike of him when he did not even rise from his seat to greet her. He was sitting across the room, apparently too engrossed in a game of chess with John to acknowledge her party at all. Anne de Bourgh was looking on, and Elizabeth exchanged a glance of amusement with Mary as Cousin Anne laid her hand on William's shoulder, only for him to instantly shrug it off. Richard was with them, and he looked up with a smirk as he met Elizabeth's eye across the room.

Elizabeth made a droll face at him, her eyes landing on William once more, and she watched as Richard leaned forward and whispered something to him. William turned then and let his eyes linger on her and Rose for a moment; he inclined his head in their direction before turning back to the game. Elizabeth glanced back at her mother, who was speaking with Uncle Edward and had not noticed her son's incivility, and then looked back at William himself, her stomach in knots.

Richard said something else – something that appeared to amuse none but himself, before approaching two gentlemen Elizabeth did not know. They had been speaking with Lady Catherine, who had also neglected to acknowledge her, but Richard now led the two gentleman forward to perform the introductions. "Cousin Lizzy, Cousin Rose, may I present a dear friend of William's and mine, Mr. Charles Bingley. Bingley, my cousin Elizabeth Bennet, and my cousin Georgiana

Gardiner – Rose for short. And this is Mr. Bingley's friend, Mr. Will Collins."

Elizabeth knit her brows at the name. "Collins?"

It was the handsomer of the two gentlemen, Mr. Bingley, who answered her. "Yes, my good friend Collins has come down to London to stay with me, and when Darcy came round to invite me to Christmas, he was so kind as to include Will as well, else we should have had a sorry time of things by ourselves – no offense, Will."

Mr. Collins smiled graciously at his friend, and then at Elizabeth. He was plain and ruddy faced, rather short but athletic, and he had a kind look about him. Seeming eager for Elizabeth's attention, he replied, "I quite begged Bingley to allow me to come and stay with him. I am sure I should have done so at any rate, as it is my first Christmas without my poor mother, may she rest in peace. However, when I heard that Bingley had been invited by Mr. Darcy to London to meet the Bennet sisters, I knew I had to be one of the party. I can see you have anticipated me, Miss Elizabeth – I am William Collins of Longbourn, and I am delighted to make your acquaintance at last."

"Longbourn," Rose cried, squeezing Elizabeth's hand as her enthusiasm drew looks from several of their relations, including the perpetually scowling Fitzwilliam Darcy.

"I am all astonishment," Elizabeth replied. "I confess I was aware my father's estate had passed to a distant relation, but I had never thought to encounter – that is, I am pleased to meet you, sir. It is kind of you to take an interest in becoming acquainted with my sisters and I."

"Dearest Cousin Elizabeth," he said, taking her hand, "I apologize if I have made you uncomfortable. I should hate to be indelicate, and I would never have dreamed of trespassing on such a happy family gathering here, were it not for my resolution, as soon as I became aware of my old friend Bingley's connection to your adoptive family, that I might join Bingley in meeting with you all, and make myself known to you – you are my only living relations, after all. I hope I am not too forward in declaring that I have eagerly been looking forward to coming to know you and your sisters, and all of your dear family. Such excellent, hospitable people!"

"That is very kind of you," Elizabeth replied, not quite sure what to make of the man. Perhaps his friendliness seemed overpowering simply because it presented such a stark contrast to how some others in the room had received her arrival. She was equally struck by Mr. Bingley's allusion to having come to London for the express purpose of meeting her and her sisters, and without any discernible reason, as his friend had. It seemed odd indeed that William should wish to invite two gentlemen so wholly unconnected to their family to Christmas, and then remain so unsociable himself. Odder still, he had begun to stare at her.

***

William Darcy made a dedicated effort to remain focused on his game of chess as Sir Edward Gardiner arrived, his children and Elizabeth Bennet in tow. It was to be a large enough party that he might reasonably manage to speak very little to *her*, and not at all to Lady Olivia's by-blow. And yet, he could not help that his eyes were drawn to them as they came into the room. He recognized Elizabeth, for though it had been three years since they had met, and many years longer since they had spoken at any great length, he had seen the drawing she had sent his mother a year ago depicting her short-cropped hair. She was still sporting the brazen style, and wore an over-trimmed red gown. Her cousin Rose appeared surprisingly demure by comparison. She wore a simple green gown that flattered her complexion and slight build, and her thick chestnut hair was elegantly arranged with little gold pins that had let a few loose curls to escape. He realized he was staring, but could not resist – she was breathtakingly beautiful.

Anne had possessively laid a hand on his shoulder and he shrugged her off, chastising himself for having such thoughts. Rose was not truly his relation, but she was so young – he did not think she was even out yet. After a few minutes of attempting to focus on the chessboard, his eyes found her again. Elizabeth had drawn the attention of Bingley and his friend Collins. Though he was seated too far to hear any of their conversation, nearly everyone in the room heard Elizabeth cry out, "Longbourn." It seemed she had identified Collins as a man of some property, and Darcy began to fear it may become necessary to reprimand his erstwhile sister for her lapse in decorum, when Rose appeared to make a comment that put the gentlemen more at ease. The four of them sat down with Jane and Richard, and Darcy watched with some relief as the scene unfolded before him.

Rose had engaged Mr. Collins and was speaking to him with great animation, and listening intently in turn as he spoke exclusively to herself. Beside them, Elizabeth was rather determinedly vying for Richard's attention, occasionally running her little white fingers through her short-cropped hair and laughing at everything – in short, presenting herself as every bit the hoyden he had expected. He might have felt moved to intervene, were it not for the fact that her insistence on dominating Richard's attentions had allowed Bingley to speak more privately with Jane.

Darcy turned his attention back to the game, making a foolish move, and was thoroughly chastised for it by his cousin John. "Your mind is not on the game, eh, Darcy?" John chuckled.

Darcy grimaced as his bishop was captured, and cousin Anne laughed derisively. "I am sure he is too busy admiring his sister and cousin, John, but he has been soundly punished for that."

Ignoring his cousins, Darcy debated between focusing on the game to salvage his dignity, or sabotaging himself to end it quickly so that he might better observe his friends and relations; he opted for the latter, moving his remaining bishop into a dangerous position.

John gave him a sardonic look. "You wound me, cousin. If you do not wish to play anymore, simply say so."

Darcy shrugged. "I should be happy to observe you play, if you can find any better partner."

John glanced over at Anne. "Shall we show him how it's done?"

Anne grinned. "Indeed, Cousin John. Do move aside, Darcy, but stay close. You might learn a few moves."

Despite her attempt at a provocative tone, Darcy felt nothing but contempt for his cousin Anne after such a speech. But no, he also felt some relief that he might still have the means to observe Jane, Elizabeth and Rose from a distance. He happily offered Anne his chair and moved to lean against the wall nearby, pretending to observe the game as he watched his sister from afar.

By now Bingley had managed to elicit a smile from Jane, and then a gentle laugh. *Good, very good.* It pained him that he had not taken an interest in his sisters sooner – he could not have told them what Wickham really was without being wildly indelicate, exposing Jane to such things as no lady ought to hear, but he might have at least prevented the attachment from growing too serious. He had waited too long to take his role of brother as seriously as he ought, but he had done everything in his power to salvage the awful situation after the engagement, and two years later he was still cleaning up the mess.

His eyes drifted back to Elizabeth, who was leaning forward provocatively and whispering something to Richard, causing him to color and glance helplessly at Rose. Bingley must have perceived it as well, for he spared her a slight cringe before turning back to his conversation with Jane. Darcy considered Elizabeth Bennet as she fidgeted with her bracelets and then adjusted the neckline of her bright red dress, which plunged far too low for a family gathering, even with the fichu. How could such a girl be the sister of sweet, innocent Jane?

Then he watched Rose, who had continued speaking with Mr. Collins, turn to subtly admonish her cousin, somehow managing to make a joke that aroused laughter from all her companions. There was something absolutely magnificent about her poise and the curve of her mouth as she spoke, as if she knew some secret that no one else did. Her rosy lips turned up into the most enchanting, if asymmetrical smile, and her fine eyes sparkled with wit. But of course, Lady Olivia had been quite the same.

"Oh, Cousin William, I am quite undone!" Anne glanced up at him with a sickening smile. "I am sure my poor knight is in some danger; what am I to do?"

Darcy flicked his eyes down to the chessboard. Pushing the vision of a pair of hauntingly fine eyes from his mind, he deftly scooped up the queen and removed the hidden threat from the board on his cousin's behalf.

"Devil take it, Darcy! You were not playing like that before," John said in feigned indignation, scowling down at the game.

Darcy shrugged and, ignoring Anne's effusive thanks, took a few hesitant steps closer to the conversation he had been watching, in the hope of overhearing just a little of it.

***

After several minutes of chatting about Longbourn, a topic Elizabeth felt a tremendous interest in, she began to fear she had monopolized Mr. Collins's conversation for too long, and turned the subject to a more general topic so that her companions might be included. She spoke of music, which she enjoyed despite her own limited proficiency. She had spent a few days practicing the piece Mary had gifted her, and expressed a wish that Jane might perform it with her.

Jane had not the chance to respond to Elizabeth before Rose interrupted, leaning across the space between the two sofas to whisper to Richard something about her desire to dance. Rose might have said it aloud – it was certainly audible enough – and yet leaning in to speak afforded both Richard and Mr. Bingley a rather ample view of her bosom.

"I shall not press Jane if she does not wish it," Elizabeth replied, "though I am sure you make a convincing argument," Elizabeth chided her younger cousin.

"Do you play, Miss Gardiner," Mr. Collins inquired.

"Of course! I must, if I am to be considered an accomplished young woman before I come out next year."

"If a worthy performance at the pianoforte is the requirement to attend balls and parties, I may yet remain at home," Elizabeth teased.

"You misrepresent yourself, Cousin," Richard teased. "You play very well indeed. I must confess I should like to hear Jane play alongside you. From what I recall of your playing, Cousin Jane, your taste and style are rather different than Lizzy's, and I imagine the contrast might make for an interesting fusion."

Jane shook her head shyly. "Another time, perhaps, when I am better prepared. I should hate to disgrace myself, and fall short of the mark of accomplishment."

"I am sure you could never be found wanting, but I shall not press you," Elizabeth replied. "On the other hand, if I were to perform first, you might attack the instrument with your toes and still give a better performance!"

Mr. Bingley laughed. "That I should very much wish to see!"

It was at this moment that William finally left his post in the corner and drew nearer to their conversation. Heartened by her good-humored companions, Elizabeth ignored William's piercing gaze and asked Mr. Collins his opinion on the matter.

"It is amazing to me how young ladies can have patience to be so very accomplished, as they all are," he said congenially.

Rose laughed. "All young ladies accomplished! I scarcely know if I should feel slighted or flattered at such talk!"

Elizabeth made a droll face at her. "When there is a choice, you must always choose to be flattered if you possibly can."

Richard laughed. "Quite right, Cousin."

"I agree," Mr. Bingley said with a merry smile. "I *do* think all ladies are quite accomplished. You all paint tables, cover screens, and net purses. I scarcely know any woman who cannot do all this, and I am sure I never heard a young lady spoken of for the first time without being informed that she was very accomplished. Indeed, it is just what my sister Caroline told me of Miss Darcy, and I see that she was right." Mr. Bingley and Jane exchanged a look of mutual appreciation, and then Mr. Bingley caught sight of William. "Ah, there you are Darcy! Come to defend your sisters?"

"I am sure that is hardly necessary, when you have done it so admirably already," William replied.

"Shocking reply," Elizabeth said to him, raising her chin defiantly. "Have you nothing to contribute? You are a man of experience who has lived in the world; I daresay you have firmer opinions than anyone else amongst us."

There was an unexpected look of approbation on William's countenance as he gazed at Elizabeth. "You provoke me to be contrary, and observe that there is too much truth in this common list of accomplishments. I find the word is applied to many young women who deserve it by no more than netting a purse or covering a screen. But I am far from agreeing with my friend's estimation of ladies in general. I cannot boast knowing more than half a dozen in the whole range of my acquaintance that are really accomplished."

"Nor I, I am sure," Richard said with a droll expression, and he turned his face away from William to roll his eyes for Elizabeth's amusement.

Suppressing her laughter, Elizabeth replied, "You must comprehend a great deal in your idea of an accomplished woman."

"Yes, I do," William said.

"I believe my brother is right," Jane said, speaking softly but firmly in her brother's defense. "No woman can really be deemed accomplished who does not greatly surpass what is usually met with. A woman must have a thorough knowledge of music, singing, drawing, dancing and the modern languages to deserve the word. Is that not so, William?"

William gave Jane a slight smile and a nod of approval, and Elizabeth couldn't resist a momentary grimace. *Is that what Jane has learned at school? More likely, she has learned such rubbish from William.* Elizabeth was on the verge of a scathing reply, when her cousin interjected.

"Oh, yes," Rose agreed, taking on a haughty posture as their companions turned to look at her. "And besides all that, she must possess a certain something in her air and manner of walking, the tone of her voice, her dress and expressions, or the word will be half-deserved."

William looked askance at Rose for a moment before turning his eyes back to Elizabeth. "All this she must possess, and something more substantial besides, in the improvement of her mind by extensive reading."

Ha! Her Aunt Olivia had been the most voracious reader Elizabeth had ever met, and William had never done other than scorn her. "I am no longer surprised at your knowing only six accomplished women. I rather wonder at your knowing any," Elizabeth deadpanned.

Mr. Collins gave a little gasp at Elizabeth's retort. "Are you so severe upon your own sex as to doubt the possibility of all this?"

Elizabeth grinned. "I never saw such a woman."

Rose laughed. "And yet you have no further to look than your own home!"

Mr. Bingley observed Elizabeth and Rose exchange playful looks with evident bemusement before insisting that he knew a great many young women who answered this description. William ignored his friend and cast Rose a look of inexplicable displeasure as he declared that he had only ever beheld such perfection at Pemberley, and then he moved away.

***

Richard knew well enough, or at least strongly suspected, that Darcy's animosity toward Rose and Elizabeth was chiefly born out of the contempt which all of the elder members of their family had long held for Lady Olivia. He likewise knew both Rose and Elizabeth to be fully capable of holding their own should the banter deteriorate into an outright argument, but Darcy withdrew, lurking once more in a corner.

Elizabeth and Rose had their revenge by moving away to speak with Charlotte, and he could tell not only that they were repeating the particulars of their exchange with Darcy to Charlotte with humor, but that Darcy himself was aware of what they were about.

After staring at Elizabeth and Rose for quite some time, Darcy turned and stalked silently out of the room, and on a lark Richard decided to follow his cousin, who went into the dining room. Richard hung back as he watched his cousin go down the length of the table and survey the place cards, throwing his hands up in frustration as he got to the end.

"Let me guess – Aunt Catherine was in here?"

Darcy looked up and grimaced. "Why she thinks such behavior is acceptable in another person's home is simply beyond me. I have endured quite enough tonight, and sitting beside Cousin Anne through an entire meal is unsupportable." Darcy walked down the side of the table and snatched up Charlotte's place card, switching it with Anne's.

Standing on the other side of the table, Richard quirked up his eyebrows. "I am sure Charlotte will be flattered by your placement, but are you sure it is wise, given my father's matrimonial state of mind? And blast it, Darcy, now you've placed Anne right across from me!"

"You shall suffer far less than I," Darcy drawled.

As his cousin plucked up a couple other place cards and began indecisively considering a few more switches, Richard took advantage of Darcy's distraction to make a couple changes of his own. "Indeed I shall, I am sure," he muttered. On his left side, he switched Mary's name with Jane's, and on his right side he switched Rose's name with Elizabeth.

***

Lady Anne had the satisfaction of watching her daughter speaking so warmly and naturally with Mary and Jane; it was clear that everyone who had the pleasure of speaking with her was quite delighted. Even William seemed rather warm to her in his own way... eventually.

It had not escaped her notice that her son had avoided Elizabeth for quite some time after her arrival, nor the fact that he had stared at her nearly the entire time. Anne had grown quite inattentive to her conversation with her mother and Phyllis as she caught herself reveling in what she could hear of Elizabeth and William engaging in rather civil repartee with Jane, Rose, and Mr. Bingley.

She suspected she knew what her son was about in inviting his two friends, for with Henry determined to make matches for anyone he could, William must be wishing them to have eligible options who had already at least merited his approval as a friend; it was very sweet of him. And, given the unexpected degree of civility he had shown to Elizabeth, after first giving her some rather harsh looks, Anne hoped that in time he might begin to show Elizabeth the same attentive affection he bestowed on Jane and Mary. After her blissful reunion with Elizabeth, and the wonderful surprise of Christmas holly, Anne had finally begun to let herself hope that this awful rift in their family would at last be healed.

Just before supper was called, Elizabeth approached and offered Anne a gentle smile.

"Hello, sweet girl," Anne said, reaching out and giving Elizabeth's hand a quick squeeze as she took a seat nearby. "Are you having a happy Christmas?"

Elizabeth nodded, her smile widening. "It is really wonderful, us all together like this. In truth, I had quite forgotten the feeling, and after all these years I find it almost intoxicating."

Anne drew nearer to her daughter. "I was so worried about you, dearest. You looked nervous when you came in, but then I saw you speaking with your sisters, and it looked so right, so natural and easy. Are things well between you at last?"

Elizabeth chewed her lip for a moment and then said, "As to Mary, it has never not been well between us. Jane is more reserved than I remember, but I suppose I am more used to Rose's open temperament now. I think it could be well with us, though I confess I think it must require more effort on my part, to draw her out. I am perfectly willing, and I believe she is as well. I have come to understand why she has changed so much."

"Oh, Lizzy, that is so good of you to say. I always knew how it would be. You two just had to get there on your own, I suppose."

"I am sure we shall. Mary is determined, and I know I can count on her to help us along. Mamma, I am so very proud of Mary."

Anne laughed wistfully. "How she used to vex you when she was a little girl! She followed you around, when you only wanted to play with the older girls; she admired you so much."

"Yes, I remember. Well, she is welcome to do so now – I shall encourage it."

"Rose certainly does! She has hardly left your side all night."

"I must confess, I asked her to. I *was* nervous. I know William is not fond of me, and I suspect Aunt Catherine is not either. Rose is always so full of praise and reassurance; she is my staunchest defender."

Anne sighed, and offered her daughter a sad smile. "I am sorry to hear you say such things about William, though I do understand. I think he is beginning to come round, in his way. Would it make anything easier for you if I were to speak to him about it?"

"Oh no, I beg you would not, I should be mortified. I do not wish him to know I am afraid of him. Indeed, I intend to teach myself not to be – my courage shall rise at every attempt to intimidate me!"

Despite Elizabeth's smirk, Anne knew her daughter to be only partially in jest. "I shall say nothing if you do not wish it," Lady Anne said.

Elizabeth nodded. "I know you wish us to be a family again – I wish it as well, and I am sure it is all my own fault that we are not – believe me, no one could possibly blame me as much as I blame myself, not even William."

Anne let out a heavy sigh, sorry to hear her daughter speak in such away. She knew not how to begin to explain to Elizabeth that it was herself who had been the most to blame, perhaps even George and Edward. They had been the adults and Elizabeth a mere child when things had gone so terribly wrong.

She was interrupted from her reverie by the dinner gong, and Rose approached to slip her arm through Elizabeth's as they prepared to go into the dining room. She was on the point of following them when Sir Edward moved that way and detained her.

Anne met his eye with a hopeful look; they had spoken little that evening. "Anne," he said, and gestured for her to sit as the rest of their relations began filing into the dining room. He sat down beside her and reached into his coat pocket, withdrawing a rolled piece of paper tied in a red ribbon. "I have a gift for you – I've not had time to frame it, as I finished it only yesterday."

Anne took the gift with curiosity and untied the ribbon, letting the paper slowly unfurl in her hands. The charcoal drawing was the most beautiful thing she had ever seen. It was a view of Pemberley, and a very accurate one at that. In the foreground were four figures, a woman and three small girls walking across the front lawn, a field of flowers before them. "Oh, Edward," she breathed, running her fingers over the illustration of her daughters.

Edward lightly brushed her hand, wiping the charcoal that had gotten onto her fingers. "I shall never forget the first time I saw you walking with them at Pemberley. I knew in that moment that you were destined to be their mother. I think of it often, especially of late. I... I have wanted to tell you for so long...."

"What, Edward?"

"I ought never have changed a thing. It was wrong of me to take Lizzy away, and I am so sorry for the pain it caused you."

Blinking back tears, Anne looked up from the drawing to meet Edward's eye. They were quite alone in the drawing room now, and she began to think he might also shed a tear. "Oh, my old friend," she sighed. "I have long forgiven you for it. I needed those girls so very much when they came into my life – Doctor Johnson told me that having another child of my own might very well kill me. But I knew the same was true for you as well, when you took Lizzy away. It broke my heart, not only to part with my darling girl, but to see how desperately you needed her as a companion in your loneliness."

"I fear I did her no favors."

Anne clasped his hand. "Edward, no. Let us look upon the past only as it gives us pleasure."

He laughed ruefully. "A pretty philosophy. I am glad of your forgiveness; I hope we might be friends again."

"Of course, Edward... I have always... cared for you." Anne heard her voice crack as she fought back tears, and he reached into his pocket again to offer her a handkerchief. She dabbed at her eyes, running her thumb over the soft corner embroidered with EG, and then rose to her feet, fearing they had tarried too long.

"I shall have this framed and hung right here in this room," she said, gesturing with the rolled up drawing as she placed it on a shelf for safekeeping, and tucked his handkerchief furtively into her pocket. Edward offered her his arm and led her into the dining room.

The table was already humming with lively conversation as they made their way in, and Rose, seated nearest them, called out to Edward as they entered the room, gesturing with her eyes to the bough of mistletoe the girls had hung in that very doorway earlier in the week.

Edward turned and looked at Anne with a smile tugging at the corner of his mouth as he raised her hand to his lips. She smiled back, and before he could release her hand she stood on her toes and placed a soft, quick kiss on his cheek, and then, for just an instant, hoping no one in the room could perceive it, she tilted her head and let her forehead brush against his.

***

Elizabeth and Rose watched with matching smirks as Lady Anne gave Sir Edward a little kiss on the cheek beneath the mistletoe before taking their seats in the dining room. Near the door, Lady Anne was seated at the head of the table, with Edward on her right side and Rose at her left. Elizabeth was just next to Rose, and though she wished to be directly beside her mother, Lady Anne declared she was delighted to be seated near Rose and have the chance to come to know her better, as she was so important to Elizabeth.

"She is in many ways my opposite, and in some even my superior, I believe," Elizabeth said with a warm smile at Rose before turning to her mother. "Aside from Charlotte, she is my dearest friend, and I am delighted that you wish to know her better."

"She is certainly unlike any young lady in England," Uncle Edward quipped with mirth in his eyes as he raised his brows and took a drink of wine.

As the first course was served, Lady Anne began speaking with Rose and Elizabeth turned to her left, listening to Richard speak across the table to his sister Charlotte.

"I am sure I was not offended, not really," Charlotte said to Richard, and then she met Elizabeth's eye. "Oh, Lizzy – before you came into the dining room, what do you think? I was seated beside William, and Aunt Catherine commanded me get up and change places with Anne!"

"I suppose his punishment for allowing such a thing to take place shall be his company over the meal," Elizabeth whispered, sparing William a roguish glance.

Richard laughed and leaned in toward Elizabeth. "You wish it out of spite, or perhaps because you think one marriage in the family will placate my father for a time."

Elizabeth arched an eyebrow at him. "Until I have seen this infamous list, I must refrain from comment."

"Well! And here is my comment for you – as to the matter of cousins, I have the best seat in the house tonight."

Elizabeth flicked her gaze to Jane and then back to Richard. "I see what you are about."

He grinned at her. "I would not have it otherwise." Richard held her eye for a moment and Elizabeth gave him a nod; it seemed they understood one another, and perhaps they needn't ever say more about it.

As he struck up a conversation with Jane, Elizabeth turned back to Charlotte across the table. Mr. Collins had begun speaking to her about Longbourn, relaying the same general information he had told Elizabeth.

While her mother was speaking with obvious pleasure to Rose and Uncle Edward, Elizabeth indulged in listening to Mr. Collins's conversation, and upon perceiving he had an audience in her, he began to address her directly.

"The neighborhood is an excellent one – I dine with four and twenty families quite regularly. The foremost family in the area are the Lucases – Sir William Lucas was knighted when I was still a boy, a most jovial man indeed. His son is a great friend of mine and has gone into the church, and the two oldest girls were friends of my sister's before she married and settled in Ireland. The great estate of the area, Netherfield, is a fine manor indeed, but alas it has been vacant these two years."

"Why?"

"The previous occupant was my brother-in-law, Mr. O'Rourke, who shortly after marrying my sister, inherited a small but enchanting castle in Ireland, and my sister had a great desire to reside in it. They moved away two years ago, and a fine thing it was for Miss Lucas – poor girl was quite on the shelf, but Amelia took her along to Ireland and just last summer she married a baronet. Her mother, Lady Lucas has talked of little else since then, and I daresay it shall be the same when I return home this spring."

Jane, who had been speaking softly with Richard, suddenly leaned closer, speaking nearly across him as she looked from Elizabeth to Mr. Collins. "Lady Lucas? Oh my – I remember her!"

"Do you?" Mr. Collins smiled at Jane. "I am sure she shall be glad to hear it. She has always spoken very highly of your late mother, Cousin Jane. They must have been very great friends."

"I envy my sister's ability to remember such things," Elizabeth observed. "I was but three years old – I would not even recognize Longbourn, I am sure."

"I remember the garden," Jane shyly observed. "Our mother was very proud of her roses."

Mr. Collins nodded with enthusiasm, his smile rendering him almost handsome. "Yes! My mother was most diligent in preserving them, which always vexed Lady Lucas – I daresay they enjoyed the friendly competition."

"You liked the garden too, Lizzy," Jane said. "There was a prettyish little wildness at the back of it that you liked to run around in, and a swing our father built. You always liked being out of doors, just like at Pemberley."

Elizabeth felt her eyes misting with tears, though she knew not if it was for the memory of her childhood home, or that which she could not remember of her birth place. Blinking rapidly to disguise her heightened emotion, she addressed Mr. Collins. "And what is your favorite part of Longbourn, Cousin?"

"My goodness, it is difficult to decide. I was always fond of the stables as a young lad. My father and Sir William Lucas shared a venture in breeding horses, and we always had first-rate animals. I was quite a chubby little fellow when first we came, but after a few years of riding – well, it is quite a passion of mine. I am fond of the library, as well. The window is happily situated, affording a fine view of Oakham Mount in the distance, and the collection of books is excellent. I believe your father added substantially to the collection, as most of the books bear his nameplate. Some of them even have the most interesting footnotes and musings scribbled in the margins."

Seated beside Mr. Collins, Charlotte laughed and looked pointedly at Elizabeth. "That sounds like somebody I know. Who would have thought it was an inherited trait?"

Jane and Richard both laughed. "You *do* do that, Lizzy," Jane said.

Richard smirked as he looked between Jane and Elizabeth. "We shall have to make a count of it – which house is more full of books Lizzy has made her mark on – Pemberley or Matlock House? I am sure she has left quite an *impression* on my sister's collection of novels – I recall a particularly lurid passage she underlined in *Camilla*." He waggled his eyebrows.

"And you were accusing me earlier of misrepresenting myself!" Elizabeth nudged Richard with her shoulder as she joined him and Jane in laughter.

"Ah, but on both occasions it was a virtue you wished to deny," Jane gently chided her.

"So defacing the property of my relations is a virtue, is it?" Elizabeth grinned, delighted by Jane's teasing.

Richard laughed as he looked between Jane and Elizabeth. "It is a compliment to you both, I think, that she should find your imperfections so endearing."

Elizabeth smiled. Certainly it had not always been so, but she was pleased enough that Jane was making the effort, and amongst such lively company she passed the rest of the supper very cheerfully indeed.

***

Dinner was a penance for Darcy, whose gambit to attain some better company for the meal had backfired abysmally. Seated at the end of the table, he did his best to remain civil and attentive to his cousin Anne without giving her any encouragement, and fortunately John, seated on his other side, managed to sustain enough conversation with her that Darcy was often enough at liberty to observe the other conversations taking place at the table without having to participate in any himself.

At the opposite end of the table, which was at some remove due to their large party, his mother was speaking with Sir Edward and Elizabeth, and he begrudgingly admitted to himself that at least she was behaving herself at present, and paying his mother all the attention she deserved.

Beside her, Rose was absolutely radiant. She was speaking chiefly with Mr. Collins, her demeanor playful and yet magnificent as she drew in Jane, Richard, and Charlotte, seated between Mr. Collins and herself. Though he was too distant to catch the tone of their conversation, whatever they were discussing had her wholly engrossed. Her eyes sparkled and her mouth was fixed in an artless, serene sort of smile that made him envy the companions that had inspired it.

He was obliged to check himself upon experiencing a little jealousy that he was not seated near enough to her to inspire such rapt attention. She was Olivia's daughter, after all, and a few months yet from turning seventeen. Even if he had been of a mind for marriage at present, she was surely not a candidate. And yet, what an unexpectedly fine woman she seemed to be. It was clear that Mr. Collins thought so, as well as Richard and even Mr. Bingley, who was eventually drawn into conversation with her, after speaking almost entirely with Mary for the first half of the meal.

Bingley, as usual, seemed delighted with everybody and everything – he had smiles for Mary, Jane, and even Rose. *Especially* Rose, toward the end of the meal, it seemed. He had been drawn into Mr. Collins's conversation, and whatever Rose's contribution to the discussion, Mr. Bingley appeared quite keen to speak with her despite the considerable distance down the table between them. *This will not do.* Not only was Darcy mortified to find Bingley interested in the same woman who had captivated him – a woman he still considered a child, and would never actively pursue, or even admit to admiring – but he had hoped Bingley would direct his considerable charm toward drawing Jane out. It was time she return to the world of the living.

To his chagrin, Rose was doing a rather impressive job herself of drawing Jane out, often leaning into Richard to speak across him to Jane, who began to do likewise. He watched with satisfaction; whatever his prejudices about Lady Olivia and the two young women she had raised, it did his heart good to see Jane laughing again. He had not seen her converse so openly, so naturally with anybody but Mary and their mother in two long years.

After their meal, there was no separation of the sexes, and when they returned to the drawing room the doors to the music room were opened; Richard applied to Rose to give a performance on the pianoforte, as she had promised. Unsurprisingly, Elizabeth joined her – the two had been inseparable all evening. Rose decried her own abilities, claiming she preferred Elizabeth to accompany her to mask her deficiencies in playing and singing alike. Though her execution was not as technically perfect as Jane's and Mary's, she played and sang with tremendous feeling, which he had always felt was of greater importance.

Toward the end of the performance, Mary approached Darcy where he had been watching from the back of the room. "I am glad Lizzy is playing the music I gifted her," she said. "It is rather impressive she has learned it so quickly. Do you not think she plays very well, Brother?"

Darcy agreed, to please Mary, though in truth he found Rose to be the superior performer, despite being some years younger. "You ought to play next," he said. "If both you and Elizabeth give a performance, perhaps it might convince Jane to do the same."

"I do not think she wishes it."

"She would be so much happier if only she would try. It once gave her so much pleasure to play and sing. Even Elizabeth acknowledged that it is the sort of thing expected of a young lady during the Season."

"Last time she played, it was very mournful indeed," Mary sighed. "I cannot think anyone would wish to hear such a thing now. Perhaps – perhaps I might play something we could all dance to."

"I am sure that would pleasure *one* of your sisters," he drawled.

"I am sure it would please a great many people present," Mary retorted, "even if you are not among them." She moved away to approach the instrument.

Dancing was soon called for and Rose was coming that way, as if to go and speak with Sir Edward, when the Countess intercepted her, just as she was moving past Darcy. "What a charming amusement this is for young people," she observed to Darcy. "There is nothing like dancing after all. I recall you being quite adept at dancing yourself. Well now, here is my niece. Why are you not dancing yourself, child? William, allow me to present you a very desirable partner for such a happy family gathering."

Lady Phyllis had taken her niece's hand, and was on the point of offering it to Darcy, who, though surprised, would have happily taken it, when Rose drew back and with some discomposure said, "Indeed, Aunt, I have not the least intention of dancing. I entreat you not to suppose I moved this way in order to beg a partner."

"I should be happy to dance with you," he replied evenly, smiling with admiration at the sight of her as she nervously toyed with a loose curl that had escaped her chignon.

"William is all politeness," she said, focusing on their aunt.

Lady Phyllis persisted. "How could he not be, considering the inducement?"

Rose stammered some reply and abruptly excused herself. Lady Phyllis moved away from Darcy and began whispering with his mother, and he watched Rose as she stalked across the room. The first strains of music had begun, and Rose was applied to by Richard to join in the dancing. Rose continued to demur, though far more amiably than she had done with Darcy.

"Surely you'll not deny your favorite cousin," Richard chided her.

"My favorite cousin?" Rose made a great show of looking about the room. "Hmm, I do not see her." She tapped thoughtfully at her chin with one of her elegant little fingers.

"You wound me," Richard laughed.

"I suppose it must be some recompense for your teasing at supper," she replied.

By now Bingley had approached Rose as well. "*I* have not teased you at supper. Shall you grant me your favor, and join the dance?"

Offering Richard a wicked smile, Rose agreed that she would be delighted to, and offered him her hand. Richard shook his head and laughed it off before looking up and catching Darcy's eye. He grimaced and waved Darcy off before he could speak. "Do not say it, cousin." He stalked off and sat down beside Jane on the sofa.

Darcy was drawn once again to the sight of Rose, watching her graceful form with pleasure though she had accepted his friend after refusing himself, when he was accosted by his cousin Anne.

"I can imagine the subject or your reverie," said she.

"I should imagine not."

"You are considering how insupportable it shall be to have to pass so many evenings in company with certain members of this family, and I quite agree. How insipid, and yet how self-important I find certain persons present to be. You shall not convince me you disagree."

"Then I suppose this conversation is fruitless indeed," he said before abruptly moving away. He approached his cousin Charlotte, who was sitting by herself, and offered her his hand before joining the other two couples in the dance.

There was but one set danced, which was a happy thing for Darcy, as he feared he might have been tempted to make quite the fool of himself in importuning Rose a second time. After the dance, it seemed their party was on the verge of breaking up, and he approached Bingley, hoping to encourage him to speak with Jane a little more before the evening was over.

"Your sister Elizabeth is absolutely enchanting – they are all three lovely girls, Darcy."

"I trust your dinner conversation with Jane and Mary was enjoyable?"

"Very much so. Miss Mary is certainly well-informed – rather more so than myself, I fear. She and Jane are both perfectly amiable – it is a shame they have been hidden away at Pemberley for so long."

"I quite agree. I am glad they have come to London."

"Quite right! I shall be happy to know more of them, if that is your wish. And Miss Elizabeth as well – I enjoyed dancing with her very much."

Darcy gave his friend a dubious look. "You mean Rose Gardiner, my... cousin."

"Miss Rose is very friendly as well, certainly, but it was Miss Elizabeth I danced with," Bingley replied. "Surely you saw us together."

"I think you must be mistaken. The woman you danced with is Miss Rose Gardiner. The young lady in red, with the short-cropped hair is my sister Elizabeth."

Bingley colored and laughed at his own error. "Well, that is embarrassing! I am sure I have been calling them by the wrong names all night and no one has corrected me until now. I was correct about Jane and Mary, I hope? Jane there in the blue, and Mary in white?"

"Yes. I am sure that Rose and Elizabeth were too polite to undeceive you, and it is an honest mistake after all; the two have been inseparable all evening."

"Well, Darcy, your entire family is universally charming, and I am sure Collins quite agrees with me. It was very kind of you to invite us, as we would be boring one another to death tonight if we had stayed at home. My stepmother and Caroline will be returning from Bath next week – might I dare hope they shall be included in the invitation to the Twelfth Night Ball?"

"Of course. Jane is very fond of your sister, and I would by no means suspend any pleasure of hers."

"Good, good. Well, it is getting late – I think Will and I shall be off before I make an ass of myself any further." Bingley clapped Darcy on the back and went to collect Collins before making their goodbyes.

Darcy smiled with satisfaction as Bingley tarried longer with Jane than any of the others before departing, and soon afterward the rest of their guests took their leave, allowing Darcy some much needed respite after so large a gathering.

10

❧

London, January 1813

Over the next week, visits between Darcy House and the Gardiner home were a daily occurrence, and Elizabeth awoke each morning looking forward to seeing her mother and sisters with a degree of excitement she hadn't dared to hope she would feel so soon. A few days before the earl's much awaited masquerade ball in honor of the Twelfth Night, Elizabeth was preparing to visit her mother and sisters when she was met in the foyer by her cousin Richard.

Elizabeth had not seen much of him over the last week – every time she had been to Darcy House, William had gone off with Richard to his club. She had mixed emotions about seeing so little of each man, but perhaps it was for the best.

Though she still felt years of bitterness and distrust toward William, she was bothered most of all by the fact that she had caught herself, as they had briefly bantered at Christmas, actually wanting his good opinion for the first time in many years. He had already bestowed it on the three women she loved the most, making it well worth the earning. Still, it felt like a weakness – one she could not bear to let show – and it bothered her exceedingly.

She had been so frightened when he had approached to speak to her, though she had summoned the courage to conceal her unease. And then, his conversation had been at once so severe, and yet challenging, as if daring them all to suppose he was professing an opinion not really his own. It had been amusing and surprising... until his jab about Pemberley. And then he had asked her to dance! Whatever he meant by it, Elizabeth was determined to put him from her mind entirely. She had never sought his approval; there was no reason to start now.

Though she was tremendously fond of her cousin Richard, they had still not spoken of her Uncle Henry's suggestion, in large part due to Elizabeth's deliberate effort. She had tried to take her aunt's advice to heart, to focus her energy on her mother and sisters; to reconnect with them. To right the wrongs of her past felt like such a tremendous undertaking of the heart, that she could not allow herself the chance to think of romance.

She had done her best to avoid speaking alone with Richard when she and her uncle had dined at Matlock House the previous evening, talking chiefly with her aunt and Charlotte, or conversing with Richard only in the presence of his siblings. It was cowardly of her, she knew, but she needed time. Certainly she could not keep avoiding Richard forever, even if she wished to, but she had not imagined he would seek her out so soon. Then again, since he had already attempted to speak once, perhaps she ought to speak to him now.

"I was not expecting you, Richard," she said evenly. "I was on the point of going to Darcy House – my mother sent over a note that our costumes for the masquerade are ready to look over."

Richard cocked his head to one side. "You are going by yourself?"

"Uncle is at his offices and Rose is indisposed. I was just on the point of calling for the carriage."

"There is no need – let me walk with you."

Elizabeth quirked an eyebrow at him. "Our costumes are to be a great secret amongst us ladies. You may walk with me, but you shan't get a peek of our costumes until Friday."

Richard laughed and offered her his arm, and they stepped out onto the street together. "You forget, Cousin, I am to be in the receiving line with my parents – I shall see everybody come in, and I daresay guess everyone's costumes the moment they are announced."

"Then at least I shall know yours, as well. I can only imagine what shocking thing you will come up with. The year you dressed as Shakespeare was very amusing."

"I am quite sure you and Charlotte were taking secret notes on some of my... ah, language."

"Mmhm," Elizabeth chortled. "Perhaps a little less wine this year?"

Richard laughed. "Dearest Lizzy, you know me well. We get along so well, is what I mean. With you I can be myself, and you make me laugh."

"I laugh at everybody, sir."

They had gotten to the end of Grosvenor Square, and ought to have stayed on Brook Street to approach Hanover square, but Richard guided them around the stately green instead. "I hope you do not mind if we go once around the square before heading over to Hanover. I think you must know what I wish to speak to you about, but I am sure it shall not be improper, us being alone like this, as long as we remain in motion, do you not agree?"

Elizabeth had felt a great swelling of anxiety the moment she suspected his intentions, but she suppressed it. "Of course you must wish to speak about it. Yes, let us go around the square. I am sure we shall be quite safe, in as much as you have ever cared for the rules," she quipped, but felt that her joke had fallen flat.

Richard smiled weakly. "I understand it was a shock, but it has been weeks now since Father brought it up. I think you know that is what he and Uncle Edward were speaking of last night after supper, for when John and I came into the drawing room alone you instantly flew to the pianoforte and started playing. I understood why you ran away that day, at your uncle's house. It was a great shock, I am sure, but have you not given it any thought in these three weeks? Surely you can understand that you cannot dodge me forever without wounding me. Have we not always been friends?"

"We have – and you are right. I am sorry for avoiding you as I have."

"And... have you thought about...?"

"Of course I have."

As Elizabeth looked away, Richard drew her closer and stopped walking, tilting his head in toward her until she looked at him. "Should I be wishing my father's words unsaid, so that we might be friends again?"

Finally Elizabeth met his eye. "If you expect me to know how I feel about the idea, I am sorry to say I cannot oblige you just yet." She looked away briefly and took a small step back before addressing him again.

"Do you mean to say that you have thought about it? You... agree with this notion?"

"I have thought about it – indeed, I had before my father said anything at all."

"Oh." Elizabeth knew not what to say, but as she gave his arm a little tug and began to start walking again, she knew she must say something. She owed it to him to at least speak about it. She had loved him in some sort of way, for many years now.

"I have always confided in you," she said, slowing her pace around the square. "Surely you must know that the years I have lived with my uncle have... affected me."

"You fear a marriage like Sir Edward and Lady Olivia's?"

"Everyone says he was so happy when first they were married."

"Come now, Lizzy, you know the truth about it. She was not the best of women."

"And yet my uncle loved her always, and it tore him apart at times."

"He had his heart broken by another woman, just before he met Lady Olivia, and he knew their marriage was to begin as a... peculiar one."

"And could you desire such a union? I do not know about you, but I have never been in love before. What if I were to fall in love someday, and be already wed? What if you were to meet someone, someone you could give your heart to, rather than settling for an amicable business transaction?"

"I have been in love before, Lizzy," Richard sighed.

"Oh."

"There would be no pressure for you to ever fall in love with me, and you yourself have long proclaimed you shall never do so at all. And yet you would escape my father's machinations and avoid being made to spend your life with someone with whom you have not even the comfortable camaraderie we share – surely a life of friendship and good humor must be enough to tempt you. I am not the viscount – I needn't even ask for children unless you wished it."

"And if I did?" Elizabeth clamped a hand over her mouth, scandalized by her own thoughtless question.

Richard stopped walking and grabbed her gently by the shoulders, turning her to face him. "Yes, Lizzy. If you wanted children, we could have twenty. Whatever you wanted, we would have it. I am a man, after all, and you are a beautiful woman."

Elizabeth held his probing gaze for as long as she could bear it before turning away. She regretted knowing that he had had such thoughts of her, and was even a little fearful of letting herself dwell on such ideas. "And if I did not wish it? You would take a mistress."

"I am a man – not a monk. But Lizzy, I would never disgrace you. I would be discreet. And if you ever changed your mind about – well, I would be faithful to you."

"I see. So are you... are you proposing to me?"

"Not yet, if you do not wish it. Certainly not if I have no assurance that I would be accepted." He offered her a smile, but she could see the disappointment in his eyes.

"As I told you, I have not yet arrived at any sort of... decided opinion on the matter."

They had started walking again, and were nearly around the square now. Elizabeth was eager to be on her way to Hanover Square and replied, "I shall think on it, Richard. Much of what you say is true – I am sure I shall not like everyone on my uncle's list as much as I care for you. I would not have you think that this is what gives me pause. I only wish better for you. Perhaps I may never give my heart away, but as you have before, you may yet again. How can I be married to a man who came to love another? I should feel guilty, and you would come to resent me. I have seen what that looks like." Though she did not have the courage to say it, Elizabeth had imagined at Christmas that Richard might have taken an interest in Jane.

Richard nodded. "I admit, you have every reason to feel as you do. I only ask you not to dwell on the past. The time will soon come when you must look to the future. I am willing to face it with you, if that is ever your wish."

They turned the subject to happier things as they continued their walk to Darcy House, and the upcoming Twelfth Night occupied much of their conversation. Though Elizabeth still felt a great deal of apprehension about the list of possible partners her uncle had taken it upon himself to compose for the young people in the family, she could not resist feeling some excitement about the prospect of a masquerade ball. She was a young lady after all.

***

The sound of the pianoforte filled the corridor as Richard and Elizabeth divested themselves of their coats in the foyer and then moved into the music room. Richard waved away the footman that had come to announce them, and lingered in the doorway, his eyes fixed on the pianoforte. Beside him, Elizabeth experienced the same reaction at the sight of Jane seated at the instrument. She was completely absorbed in the music, a mournful, hauntingly beautiful melody performed with feeling and precision; tears streamed down her face, though her eyes appeared closed. Richard let out a slow exhale as Elizabeth continued watching with sorrowful admiration a moment longer before stepping into the room.

Jane looked up, and nearly recoiled in surprise. "Oh! Lizzy, I am sorry – I did not expect to see you before Mamma and Mary returned."

"I did not expect to arrive before them – I had understood she wished me to come look over our apparel for the ball. I was surprised to hear you were home alone."

Jane blushed. "I confess I asked to stay home while they went to the shops to retrieve our things. Perhaps they were detained. I... I have been practicing my instrument again recently – ever since our conversation at Christmas. It is only that I do not wish to make it known quite yet. I feared I would perform amiss, after so long."

"I can assure you that is not the case," Richard replied.

"No indeed," Elizabeth agreed. "Your playing has only gotten better. But that was not the music Mary gifted us – I did not recognize the tune at all."

"My own composition, in fact," Jane said shyly. "My goodness, where are my manners? Shall I call for tea?"

Elizabeth and Richard took seats on the sofa at Jane's behest, answering that the refreshments would be most welcome. Though Elizabeth suspected her timid sister had tried to turn the subject away from herself, Richard pressed on once the tea was brought out to them.

"I had no notion you were a composer, Cousin Jane."

"Oh, no – not really. It is what I do to acclimate myself at the instrument before I truly begin to apply myself, especially when I have not practiced in some time."

Richard leaned into her, smiling quixotically. "You mean to tell me that beautiful playing was the idle work of a moment?"

"Yes, I suppose." Jane blushed again and looked away. "Tell me, how does Cousin Charlotte?"

"She is well. You ought to come and visit more, I think she would like that."

"Then I shall," Jane replied, smiling brightly.

Elizabeth watched their exchange with some curiosity. "I went to see her yesterday and she was asking after you," Elizabeth said. "I daresay she was quite wishing me away, however, for she had a rather handsome caller when I arrived."

"Did she?" Richard looked askance at Elizabeth.

Elizabeth frowned. Richard had been away when she had called the day before, and she suspected she knew why. Every time she had come to Darcy House in the last two weeks, with the exception of Christmas, and every time her mother and sisters called on her, Darcy and Richard were away at their club or visiting friends. William was clearly avoiding her, and seemed bent on pressing Richard to do the same. After all, if his feelings for her were what he professed, surely he was not staying away on his own.

She considered all they had discussed, and his determination to blame her for their having spoken so little; Richard had let William claim all of his afternoons, keeping him away from her. Provoked, she replied, "Indeed – Mr. Steventon was there with his sister, Miss Amelia. I know her a little, and we chatted together while her brother was occupied with Charlotte, but eventually Mr. Steventon would address me too, and he asked for my first two dances at the ball."

"What a shocking thing," Jane gasped. "Was Charlotte very much offended?"

"No indeed – she laughed about it later, when we were alone. I was relieved that she was not cross with me, but it occurs to me now that if she would not repine over a man so handsome, he must be very unpleasant – now I am quite dreading my opening set."

Richard smirked at her. "You are so determined to keep your costume for the evening a great secret – perhaps he will not recognize you."

"Ah! A fine idea," Elizabeth laughed. "I am sure I might evade everyone on Uncle's list in a similar fashion, and not have to dance a single set!"

Richard and Jane laughed, and Jane even gave Elizabeth a playful swat. They were interrupted by more callers – a footman entered to announce Mr. Bingley, Miss Caroline Bingley, and Mr. Collins. Jane gave a genuine smile as she rose to greet her visitors, and Elizabeth was no less eager to meet with the two gentlemen again. Toward Caroline Bingley, of whom she had heard varying reports over the years, she was less effusive.

Miss Bingley was civil to Elizabeth, but no more, though she was warm and familiar with Jane and appeared eager to ingratiate herself with Richard. "I hope your brother and sister are well," said she. "I have had the pleasure of making their acquaintance on my visits to Derbyshire."

"They are, thank you. Charlotte will be very well pleased to hear she is so popular today, for my cousin Elizabeth was just asking after her as well."

Miss Bingley glanced at Elizabeth with a thin smile before turning her attention back to Richard. "Indeed? I confess I heard some talk of dancing as we entered the house – I wondered if you were all as eager for the upcoming ball as I am."

Jane smiled diffidently. "My sisters and I have been working together on our costumes – they are...."

"A great secret," Elizabeth interjected, arching her eyebrow at her companions. Richard made a droll face at Elizabeth, and the others merely laughed.

"I say," Mr. Bingley cried, "I can well imagine it is appealing to maintain the mystery, but how are we to ask you to dance with us?"

"Why yes, Jane," Miss Bingley said sweetly, "I am sure Charles meant to ask you for your first set."

Jane looked over at Mr. Bingley, equal measures hopeful and fearful, and he smiled back at her. "I came with no other purpose, I assure you, Miss Darcy."

Elizabeth studied the look exchanged between them. Though Elizabeth thought Mr. Bingley a very amiable fellow, she was still trying to decide if some particular regard existed between him and Jane. He had called on Elizabeth once, just after Christmas, only to discover with no little mortification that he had confused Elizabeth with her cousin. She had seen him thereafter at Darcy House on two other morning visits, but after his gaffe it was clear that his attentions had shifted to Jane.

She could not begrudge her sister for it, as she had no interest in being courted by anybody, particularly a man so wholly unsuited to her in temperament, and only hoped such a man could better please Jane. He was such a stark contrast to both of them with his lighthearted affability.

Elizabeth had seen little of Mr. Collins since Christmas, and as she had no wish to watch Mr. Bingley's attempts at flirting with Jane, Elizabeth turned her attention to her newfound cousin. "I hope you are well, Mr. Collins. I have been looking forward to meeting with you again."

Mr. Collins placed his hand on his heart and smiled, nodding deeply to her before replying, "That is very kind of you, Cousin Elizabeth. In fact, I went to Hertfordshire a few days after Christmas and returned last evening."

"My goodness, but I understood you had only just arrived in London. I hope you were not obliged to return by anything amiss."

"No indeed, it was an errand of my own devising – that is, I was very struck by our conversation at Christmas dinner. I resolved to return to Longbourn for the express purpose of retrieving certain possessions of your parents from my attic, that I had hoped I might offer to you and your sisters in the spirit of the season."

"Mr. Collins!" Elizabeth broke into a wide smile, struck speechless by his gesture.

"Please, I beg you would call me Will – we are cousins, after all. I hope I might call again tomorrow and bring a few trunks I have packed up. There were a great many books belonging to your late father, as I mentioned. There were also several personal articles belonging to your parents, which my mother had carried into the attic when we took possession of Longbourn. I hope you and your sisters might enjoy looking over them – that is, they are yours to keep."

Elizabeth thanked him for his generosity, leaving it to Jane to make the final decision as to when they would be at home to receive him. After that, they all chatted for another quarter of an hour; Bingley and his sister remained focused on Jane, as Mr. Collins did on Elizabeth, and Richard wavered between the two separate conversations a few times, his face inscrutable.

When Lady Anne and Mary returned, trailed by footmen bearing the fruits of their shopping trip, Richard stated his intention to depart, signaling to the Bingley party that it was time for them to do likewise. Elizabeth passed a cheerful hour looking over their garments with her mother and sisters, and after all their finery had been admired and proclaimed quite perfect for the occasion, Lady Anne declared herself to be rather tired, but encouraged her daughters to walk out in the back garden together for as long as they liked.

Mary begged off, telling them she was too tired from her morning of shopping to walk in the garden, but when Jane and Elizabeth stepped outside into the crisp winter sunshine, Jane smiled happily at her sister. "I think she means for us to talk more together," Jane observed. "You and she are already so close; I envy that."

Elizabeth smiled wistfully back at Jane. "It need not be like that."

Jane nodded. "It is all my own doing – that is what you are too generous to say. Oh Lizzy, I can hardly justify what my actions have been. I ought to have apologized to you sooner for writing you that horrid letter. Is that why you stayed away for so long?"

"Of course it is," Elizabeth said, knitting her brow. She had already faced one surprisingly serious conversation that day, and felt herself ill-prepared for another.

"I just thought – I always wondered if there was more. You never got on well with William, and... and you never told me why you left in the first place."

"Mamma never told you?"

Jane shook her head. "No, she did not. She told us it was because Aunt Olivia needed help in her confinement, and after she had the twins, I thought you would come back, but... sometimes I wondered if it was because you were always close with Charlotte, and that made you happy to stay in London."

"Jane, no! I *am* fond of Cousin Charlotte but *you* are my sister. That was not my reason at all."

"Will you tell me?"

Elizabeth sighed, hugging herself as a cold breeze blew through the garden. "I do not know if it is best... I do not want to hurt you, Jane. I was very distressed when I left Pemberley. There was something – it has become a burden I have borne for many years, and I have done my best, but I would not put that burden on you now, when you are still grieving for George Wickham."

"Oh." Jane nodded. "I still miss him so very much, Lizzy, but I know everybody must think it has gone on for long enough. It has been more than two years. I know Mamma is afraid I shall end an old maid, and I do not wish to. It pains me that you all see the need to treat me so... differently. William is an excellent brother, but I do not always need to be shielded from everything. I think he was right to listen to Mary about coming to London. I *do* wish to be more in society, to return to my former self."

"That is good to hear, Jane. I have never seen this side of William you speak of, but I am proud of Mary for carrying her point with him. As to being shielded from things, as you say, perhaps that is something I envy you. I have seen and heard much that I wish I had not. Ever since that Christmas... my eyes were opened far earlier than I was prepared for, Jane, and I have never been the same since then. I do love Uncle Edward with all my heart, but he is rather the opposite of how you describe William. He has shared a great many burdens with me, and it has made me rather less optimistic about being more in society, as you say."

"Oh. I understand that you do not wish to marry because of what Aunt Olivia was like?"

"Not exactly. I knew her better than anybody, Jane – sometimes I think I knew her better than Uncle Edward, or at least I understood her better. I think she was just as damaged as I was from such a young age, and growing up I understood how such a thing could completely shatter one's ability to fully love and trust another person. I do not know what I fear more, Uncle Edward's fate, or Aunt Olivia's."

"This is why you dislike William so much, because he was always unkind to her?"

"He was, when he was around at all, and I believe he still sees me as tainted by my affection for her."

They had made a circuit around the garden, and Jane gestured for Elizabeth to take a seat beside her on a bench next to a little fountain. "I suppose that is the problem – he was not at Pemberley so much before you went away. He was always at school, then. After he finished and came back from his Grand Tour, he was so different. He became such an attentive brother, even attempting to help poor George in his career. He took an eager interest in Mary and I, and all our pursuits, and when he saw how much it pleased our parents, he doubled his efforts. I am sorry you were not there to come to know that side of him."

"I do not know that I wish for his brotherly affection, such as you and Mary enjoy. I have long since come to care not at all for it; I should merely wish to be judged on my own merit."

Jane was quiet, and nodded her head slowly as she stared abstractedly at the fountain. Elizabeth reached over and took Jane's hand in hers. "You say you do not wish to be shielded... shall I tell you, then?" Jane gave a slight nod, rubbing her thumb across Elizabeth's fingers, and the two sisters did not look up at one another until after Elizabeth had told Jane everything.

"Oh dear," Jane sighed at the end of it. "That must have been very difficult and confusing for you. And so you felt yourself unworthy of taking the Darcy name when Mary and I did?"

"I felt I did not deserve anything the Darcys had ever given me, not even their love."

"It was because of their love they have given us so much."

"Yes, I know that now. It has taken me many years, Jane, to accept the truth of what I heard."

"I wonder that Aunt Phyllis did not speak to you of it sooner."

"Even when she did, I was not fully ready to hear it. My spirit at thirteen, even at seventeen... I felt everything so intensely, and the notion of a curse brought on by my own actions... well, it warped my heart and soul for so long. I am a little older now, and the dramatic heaviness of it all has settled in my heart somewhat. I do not feel everything so very intensely anymore, but I am not the same as I might have been had I never known of it."

"I can see how that would be. I am two years older than you and it still hurts to hear of it. I cannot imagine what I would have done if I had learned of it so young, or how I would have acted."

Elizabeth squeezed Jane's hand. "I cannot tell you," she whispered, her lip quivering as though she might weep. "I cannot tell you what it means to me to hear you say that. To have told you the truth at last. Oh, Jane!"

Jane embraced Elizabeth and the two girls held one another for several minutes before Elizabeth pulled away. "To think of all the wasted years...."

"No, Lizzy. You said yourself that it is only recently that you could bear it better. I am only sorry you had to bear it alone for so long."

"Well, Mamma and Uncle Edward have known. And Aunt Phyllis, Richard and Charlotte. Probably Uncle Henry, too. Nearly everyone, really, but no one ever wanted to speak of it."

"True. Mary and I have asked a few questions over the years, but Mamma and Papa would always get so quiet, and seem so wounded."

"I suppose it was hard for them, too. They both saw our father... you know."

"Oh. I suppose they did. And our mother."

Wishing desperately to turn the subject to happier things, Elizabeth said, "When I spoke with our cousin Collins today, he said that he went to Longbourn after Christmas and has brought us all some of their things. He wishes to call again soon and bring us these mementos of them."

"How very kind! Oh, I should like that so much. I had wondered what you two were speaking of. I thought perhaps you had made another conquest."

Elizabeth made a teasing face at her sister. "No indeed! I have no intention of doing any such thing, not with anyone. Although, I was supposing the same of you and Mr. Bingley."

Jane blushed. "Mr. Bingley is amiable. He is so cheerful and open, I daresay he did all the talking, and between him and Caroline there was little need for me to say much of anything. We were simply speaking of the ball."

"Yes, Miss Bingley seemed most keen."

"She was very smitten with Cousin John before he married, and now he is a widower. I know it has only been six months, but I have heard their marriage was not a love match, and I promised in my last letter I would help her cause if I could."

"She seems eager to do the same for you, with her brother."

"I suppose so. William wishes it, too."

"And do you?"

"I am far better acquainted with Caroline than her brother, but both she and William speak so highly of him. I only fear he thinks me too insipid – he is so lively and always at ease. I cannot see what would possibly attract him to me."

"I am sure the encouragement of his friend and sister must be something."

"I suppose it may. I thought he might ask me for my first set, but Richard beat him to it."

"Did he?"

"He said that as you were already engaged for the first set, he would have to dance with us in descending order – me in the first, you in the second if you manage to survive the first, or something like that."

Elizabeth laughed. "That sounds like Richard."

"You and he are very close. I heard William say that our Uncle Henry wishes for you two to wed. Should you like such a thing? I shall not dance with him, if you do not wish it."

"By all means, you have given him your word! I am far from objecting, though I suspect Mr. Bingley might. He smiled at you far too much to think you insipid."

"Mr. Collins smiles at you a great deal," Jane teased.

"He is very kind, but I think we are each simply pleased at the discovery of an amiable new relation. At any rate, I remain resolved I shall never marry."

"But what if Uncle Henry insists?"

"Would such a thing move *you* to bind yourself to someone you did not love?"

"Certainly not! I have known true love, Lizzy...."

"I am so sorry, Jane. My heart aches for you for losing your love, and for myself a little, because I do not even know if I believe in it."

11

❧

Despite being in very fine looks and having received an abundance of enthusiastic praise from Rose before leaving home to attend the Twelfth Night ball, Elizabeth's evening was off to a rather disappointing start. In fact, she was quite racked with horror from the moment she made her entrance with her uncle. Aunt Phyllis and Uncle Henry greeted them, with John, Richard, and Charlotte at their side.

Richard approached Elizabeth after she had greeted her aunt and uncle, and he took her hand, eyeing her appreciatively. "I understand my sister's costume tonight," he said. "I did not know she meant to coordinate with you and your sisters, but the effect is quite exquisite. A robin, a raven, a peacock and a swan."

"You have seen my sisters?"

"They are here already," Charlotte replied. Dressed as a swan, Charlotte was absolutely stunning. Her uncharacteristically flattering gown, made of ethereal white silk and lace, was complemented by the splash of black feathers in the center of her mask, with longer white plumes splaying out in an elegant arrangement.

"Waiting for you, as we all were," Richard added with a wink. He kissed her hand, and then asked for her dance card. She handed it over to him, and he penciled in his name for the second set.

Uncle Henry glanced over, and before Richard could hand her the dance card back, Uncle Henry had taken it and the little pencil, and began scrawling down a few extra names. He met Elizabeth's wide-eyed gape of astonishment with a teasing smile. "Do not worry, my dear, I have spoken to a few gentlemen on your behalf. I shall introduce you when the time comes."

Elizabeth stammered some protest and glanced up at Uncle Edward, who merely nodded at the earl. Ignoring Elizabeth, he turned to Richard and said, "You may have a second set with her, after supper, if you wish it."

Richard took the dance card from his father and handed it directly back to Elizabeth. Chewing his lip a moment, he said, "I shall seek you out later – I leave it to you to decide if you wish it."

Elizabeth's only response was to glare at him, and at her uncles as well, before taking Charlotte's arm and storming off, into the ballroom. She was, for once, too mortified and angry to say anything at all.

"I thank you for the rescue, Lizzy – there was no one else left to greet who I should wish to meet with. Are you well, Cousin?"

Elizabeth shook her head, tightening her grip on Charlotte's arm as they slowly entered the ballroom together. "I shall be."

"Come now, Lizzy, it is not so very bad to be a desirable partner. You have thirty thousand pounds, and are the niece of an earl!"

"I have twenty thousand pounds, but is that all I am to these people?" Elizabeth waved her cousin off. "No, do not answer me, I have no wish to hear the truth at such a moment. I shall simply have to muddle through until supper, and then I suppose I might have some choice. Or perhaps I might sprain my ankle in the first set!"

"What an idea! Might you take me down with you, if you have a fall?"

"And save you from dancing the second with Mr. Steventon? Never!"

"He is not so very bad – when he is silent, he is quite a sight to look at. But then, he inevitably starts speaking…."

Elizabeth laughed softly, for they were approaching her mother and sisters. "What dreadful luck," she whispered, "for it is a *masquerade*, Charlotte – I shall not be able to look upon his handsome face at all – I shall *only* be able to converse with him, and you know his conversation is his greatest defect!"

They were very near the Darcy ladies now, and Mary rushed forth to take Elizabeth and Charlotte by the hand. "There you are! Oh Lizzy, how splendid you look! And is not Jane looking simply divine? I even feel rather pretty myself, though I am sure I am the last one amongst us who should have been the peacock. I am sure every man in the room shall end the night in love with one of us!"

Elizabeth knew not what to say to such a speech, but was spared having to formulate a reply by Jane, who squeezed Elizabeth's hand as she greeted her. "Oh, Jane, Elizabeth sighed happily, "How well you look!"

Jane's costume was by far the most delicate. Her silk gown was pale gray, with intricate red and orange embroidery across the bodice, and red feathers trimming her neckline. Her mask was on the smaller side, with just a few small white feathers and a red jewel in the center.

Jane replied with a smile that did not reach her eyes. "I confess it is rather good to be back in grey this evening. I – I am sorry, I do not know why I said that."

Elizabeth smiled back, and gave her sister a reassuring pat on the arm. "Trust me, I feel the same," she whispered. "I contrived to wear black, after all. And yet, it has not put anyone off at all." She winked at Jane and Mary, showing them her dance card, which was already half full.

Mary and Jane produced their own, which looked much the same, and Lady Anne sighed. She had hung back as her daughters greeted one another, and now she frowned at the sight of the dance cards. "I am sorry, girls – my brother is quite firm, once he sets his mind to something."

"I suppose it must a family trait," Elizabeth replied with a grin.

"I do wish we might dance with Mr. Bingley," Mary observed. "And dear Mr. Collins, too."

Elizabeth could not help but smile at Mary's optimism, and Jane's gentle blush. "Our uncles liked both of them at Christmas – of course you will be permitted to dance with them if they ask you," Elizabeth replied.

"Oh yes, I am sure our brother would approve," Jane added.

"Where is your brother?" Elizabeth glanced around.

"He went to the card room as soon as Aunt Catherine informed him he must open the ball with Cousin Anne," Mary laughed.

As Lady Anne smiled weakly at Elizabeth, Jane whispered, "I cannot make out Cousin Anne's costume at all. There she is just over there."

Elizabeth instantly knew what her sister meant. Though Anne's costume was ostentatious in the extreme, she could not make out what her cousin was meant to be. A queen, perhaps? Daring indeed! Not wishing to say anything unkind, Elizabeth turned her eyes back to her mother, filling the silence with a laugh. "I am so very pleased by your costume, Mamma."

Lady Anne wore a gown of shimmering mahogany silk, with downy brown feathers lining the trim and sleeves, and a few of the same feathers arranged in her hair. A simple red satin mask completed the ensemble, and she looked every bit the mother hen.

The ballroom had begun to fill up; like so many of the earl's fetes, it was going to be quite a crush. It was not long before the three sisters were each claimed by their partners as the music began, and though Elizabeth could only steel herself for the coming tedium, she was determined to be pleased that at least her sisters did not look so very unhappy.

After the opening set, Richard led Jane toward Elizabeth, who had extracted herself from the voluble Mr. Steventon and was lurking near the refreshment table with her second glass of wine. The two were all smiles as they approached Elizabeth, who did her best to appear equally cheerful.

"Richard has been regaling me with tales of your youthful folly," Jane said with a bashful smirk.

"A rather bold move, Cousin, as I might pay you back a hundredfold, I am sure."

"I daresay we are in the midst of one of my tales of folly even now," He said with a wink, gesturing to his ridiculous costume. He was dressed as a dandy, his narrow-waisted tail coat rendering his silhouette very lean, as the narrow sleeves accentuated his muscle. And yet, the ornate blue and gold embroidery of the tail coat and satin striping at his waist coat, coupled with form-fitting breeches was rather lurid, evocative of a fashion not seen in twenty years are more.

"Not as shocking as Shakespeare," Elizabeth chided him, "but very near."

"Whatever would Beau Brummel say?" A lady and a gentleman had appeared behind them, and from Jane's warm greeting Elizabeth deduced it was the Bingley siblings. Miss Bingley, her posture haughty as ever, was dressed in a shimmering orange gown covered with a rich blue velvet pelisse, and a mask covered in blue feathers and jewels. "Why, Jane," she said with tittering laughter, "we are certainly birds of a feather, are we not?"

"What a fine coincidence. You are a… parrot?"

"A kingfisher, my dear," Miss Bingley replied boldly.

"And you are a king, I think?" Elizabeth spared a brief grimace for Miss Bingley before addressing Mr. Bingley.

"Richard the Lionheart, at your service," Mr. Bingley said with a sweeping bow.

Beside them, Richard looked cheerfully affronted, and puffed up his chest. "Now see here…."

Mr. Bingley held up his hands and laughed. "I surrender! That is, I shall not draw swords, but I had hoped Miss Darcy would help me make a hasty retreat to join the dance."

"I am engaged for every set until supper, but I shall save you that one if you wish," Jane replied meekly.

Elizabeth had not the pleasure of hearing her sister's reply, for Richard loudly cleared his throat as the music started up again, and reminded Elizabeth that she was promised to him for the next set, leading her away with a nod to their companions.

Though she spent the dance with Richard too agitated to fully enjoy herself, determined not to think upon their last conversation together, it was still one of her better sets of the evening, for her subsequent three partners were all gentlemen on her uncle's list, and each more unpleasant than the last. Mr. Leigh had warts and a leer, Mr. Clifton, who danced abysmally, waxed poetic in ranking her just below both of her sisters in matters of appearance and comportment, and her partner for the supper set, Lord Chawton, lavished her with praise that bordered on proposition.

Passing the supper with such a dreadful companion was almost as much of a punishment as standing up with him, and though Elizabeth did her best to make her sentiments known to the man, he persevered in believing she was just as enchanted by him as he claimed to be with her. It was not without considerable effort that she was able to detach herself from the cad as she returned to the ballroom, and he detained her a little longer yet to kiss her hand flamboyantly. "Fare thee well, for now, my fair lady raven," he said, attempting a seductive look before she hurried away in disgust.

***

Darcy managed to evade the first half of the ball, lurking in the card room with the old married men. He congratulated himself on the achievement as he joined his cousin John for supper, taking a seat in the corner where he might observe without being much observed himself. John and Darcy spoke but little, as was often the case between them without Richard present, and yet it was a companionable silence. Happily, he was able to observe his mother and his two sisters from across the room. Lady Anne was chatting with Sir Edward and Lady Phyllis, and he was pleased to see her looking very cheerful.

Near their mother, Jane was listening intently to something Bingley was speaking of, and Darcy was gratified at the sight of them together. Though Darcy was not one prone to oversentimentality, he was exceedingly fond of Charles Bingley. Theirs had been an unlikely friendship, struck up in their days at Eton. Darcy had long surrounded himself with friends too like himself, serious and diligent in their studies, young men from fine families who knew what was expected of them, the price of their privilege. Bingley was nothing like Darcy's regular set, but he was so much more. He was ambitious and energetic. He had not been raised with the gravity of his future responsibilities weighing on him, but rather witnessing his self-made father rise in station. But behind this new-money optimism, there was a true wealth of good character, sincerity and affability, and above anything, loyalty.

Bingley was the kind of friend his parents had always wished Wickham could be to him, a man who could smile at Darcy's scowls and laugh him into better cheer. After Darcy lost his father and Richard went off to war, it was Bingley who held Darcy together, both with enough conversation to keep him quite sane, and a persistently hopeful outlook on life.

Seeing Bingley with Jane felt right. If anyone needed his reassuring, amiable presence, it was Jane, and Darcy hoped she would at last be moved to put aside her grief for Wickham, a man who did not deserve her devotion.

Darcy finished his meal and was on the point of leaving the room when his uncle approached him. "There you are, my boy! You have been hiding from us all night; waste of a damn good costume, I say! William the Conqueror indeed; you will not even face the ladies! Your Aunt Catherine is determined you shall dance with Anne."

Darcy grimaced. The costume had been all Bingley's idea, and though it had seemed amusing at the time, in truth he had felt rather ridiculous since arriving. He wore a deep crimson tunic that hung to his calves, velvet with darted gold embroidery, and a lion emblazoned across the chest. His boots and gloves had been painted to look like a suit of armor and a gold and red cape trailed down his back. The helmet was real – a relic on loan from John, who had found it in the attics at Matlock years ago and used it in a number of antics over the years. The golden crown attached was merely paper, Mary's contribution to his costume.

John pulled himself out of his usual sardonic languor and leapt to his feet, taking the helmet off of table and popping it over Darcy's head. Darcy lifted up the visor and fixed his cousin and uncle with a droll look. "I am quite ridiculous."

"That is the spirit," John cried. "Off to battle with you!"

The earl clapped Darcy on the back. "Come on then, the ladies only want to dance, not run you through!"

As the earl steered Darcy back toward the ballroom, Darcy happened to glance around and caught sight of a breathtakingly beautiful woman. She had been seated on the other side of a large marble pillar that had obstructed her from his view, else he might have stared at her through the entirety of the meal. He watched as she left the ballroom, visibly eager to detach herself from her dinner partner. Without realizing what he was about, he broke away from his uncle and drifted toward the beauty in black.

No, it was not black, not entirely. Her form fitting silk gown was covered with an iridescent gossamer netting, embroidered with gold and violet, making the black gown shine brilliant blue and purple in the candlelight as she moved into the ballroom. She wore an elaborate black wig, her curls held up by little gold and silver pins shaped like stars, and there were delicate white stars adorning the bodice of her gown and her black feathered mask as well.

As Darcy drew nearer, she had just managed to extricate herself from Lord Chawton, a rake of the first order who had only been invited because he was a political ally of the earl. He was also more than ten years older than Darcy, and the way he clutched the young lady's hand as he kissed it was revolting in the extreme.

"Fare thee well, for now, my fair lady raven," Chawton said to the woman before moving away. She abruptly turned and moved the opposite way, putting her into Darcy's path, and as she moved past him she muttered, "I am *not* a raven."

"You are a starling," Darcy blurted out as she walked his way, and she looked up at him with surprise before breaking into a smile.

"Yes," she breathed. "Nobody has noticed it, and I thought it was so clever of me."

Darcy smiled and stepped closer as the delightful creature began to laugh at herself. "It is a fine costume, and plain to me what you had intended."

"That is kind of you to say, sir."

"Perhaps, as I am the first to guess it correctly, you might favor me with a dance, Miss...?"

Her eyes sparkled, and though the beautiful starling did not volunteer her name, she offered him her little white hand. As he led the radiant starling to the set, he could not keep his eyes off of her. The elaborate mask shielded much of her face, but for her remarkably expressive eyes and a delicate pair of rosy lips. It did not matter to him – he was already convinced that under the mask she was very likely the most beautiful woman in the room – she was certainly very shapely, and her dressmaker must have known what they were about.

"You said you felt rather clever about your costume," he prompted her as they began to move through the steps of the dance.

"Oh," she said, twisting her lips into a mischievous smile. "I suppose it is something of a rebellious impulse on my part."

"Rebellion?" Darcy grinned, though it was hidden by his medieval helmet. "You seem rather satisfied with yourself."

"In my family, one must claim what victories they can. They are... difficult, at times."

He laughed. "I know just what you mean. So, your costume is a triumph. I suppose you mean you have outshined all your sisters?"

"No indeed, that is quite unlikely to ever happen, nor would I wish it," she replied. "I meant to say that there is a hidden meaning to my costume, intended for my own private amusement."

As Darcy turned in time with the other dancers, he smiled to himself at the impertinent candor of his partner – he had never undertaken such banter with a beautiful woman, and could only marvel at her artless charm. He considered her words – secret rebellion against her difficult family, perhaps not something a gentleman should condone... and yet her poise rendered her quite flawless. And then it struck him.

"I believe I must venture a guess," he said. "Are you a great reader?"

"I should think I am," she said with a wide smile.

"Laurence Sterne?"

She gave a single breathless laugh and then nodded, as if embarrassed. "*The Hotel at Paris.* It is one of my favorites."

Keeping time with the music, Darcy and the starling placed their hands together as they spun. "*'I can't get out, said the starling.'*"

She locked eyes with him as she recited, "*'I can't get out, I can't get out.'*"

"*'God help thee said I, but I'll let thee out, cost what it will,'*" he said, completing the quote. Darcy held her gaze for a moment, feeling as though he was seeing her for the first time. She was witty and magnificent, but there was something almost sorrowful about her.

She was the first to turn away, seeming suddenly embarrassed. "Oh, my goodness, I am being rather too maudlin for a ballroom, am I not?"

"Certainly more honest than one usually finds in such places."

Darcy considered. He did not know her identity, nor she his, and yet she had spoken forthrightly. Perhaps *because* she did not know him, she had spoken so openly. It occurred to him that he might do likewise, and for once simply enjoy the company of a pretty woman without being known as nothing more than Darcy of Pemberley with ten thousand a year. He might be anyone, to her; yet she seemed to like him on his own merit alone. It was not something he frequently experienced in London society.

He was suddenly overcome with a desire to really make himself agreeable to her, to discover if he might be able to exert his full powers of pleasing a woman who knew nothing of his wealth, and he was fascinated enough by his partner to want to know more about her as well.

Still feeling all the intensity of what she had said before, Darcy asked, "Do you really feel trapped by your family?"

"I ought not to have said it."

"I do not know you, nor you me – why should we not speak freely?"

"Do you speak as a general rule while dancing?"

"In fact, I do not. I have never been thus intrigued. I should like to hear whatever you wish to say."

She laughed nervously. "Do you seek to gratify my feelings, or your own?"

He braved a little wink. "Both, I should imagine."

The starling looked down as they spun to the music again, and he suspected she might be blushing under her mask. "To answer your question, I suppose I have felt trapped. I know every family has its own particular complications. Mine are... as Mr. Sterne would say, *'twisted and double twisted.'* Being thrust out onto the marriage mart is...."

"A ghastly business. Oh yes, I do understand you."

She looked probingly at him. "Do you? Hmm. I had always imagined it different for gentlemen. You have all the freedom."

"And a great deal of responsibility."

She playfully rolled her eyes at him. *Little minx!* "Such as directing the lives of others?"

"I hope I would never do such a thing. You mentioned having sisters. I have two, and I hope they never feel trapped, or that they have been put in any kind of cage."

"Then you are far kinder than anyone in my family. That is — they are not unkind. They do their best, but now that there is so much expectation upon me, I find myself rather recalcitrant. You must be wishing you had chosen a more pliable partner," she said with a smirk.

Darcy could not imagine taking pleasure in partnering with any other woman in the room, and said so, eliciting another gentle laugh from her as she turned her face away.

"I confess," said she, "you are the pleasantest partner I have had all evening. The first of my own choosing, in fact."

"And the first to see you are clearly a starling, and not a common raven." *A very spirited starling.*

"The first to see me at all, really. All night I have listened to dull men talk about themselves."

"*Foolish* dull men," he replied, finding the teasing coming easily to him. "They ought to have asked more about you."

She bit her lip for a moment as she considered. "As you said yourself, sir, I do not know your name, nor you mine — for now we might say what we like...."

"And if you speak of your family, or anything too personal, I may guess your identity? Oh yes, that would take all the mystery out of it."

"Yes, it would," she said, looking up at him with intensity as the steps of the dance brought them together. "We cannot have that. I have been so bold already."

"I pray you would continue," he replied. "If you would not speak of yourself, tell me of your pursuits. Do you enjoy reading?"

***

Elizabeth laughed to herself for a moment, remembering what William had said about accomplished women and reading. Surely her handsome knight would never profess such a stuffy opinion! Of course, she could not be *sure* he was handsome, for she could see only his eyes through the visor on his helmet, but she was quite certain he must be incredibly dashing. He was tall, muscular and well-built, and the medieval costume that might have seemed clownish on some men, such as Mr. Bingley, simply accented her partner's masculine frame.

Answering his question, she replied, "I love to read anything I can get my hands on. I am of the opinion that books ought to be enjoyed, rather than read to make oneself a great reader. I recently acquired a veritable treasure chest of books from my father and I look forward to savoring their delights."

"That is just what I think is right. Do you enjoy music?"

"I am enjoying it right now, sir," she said, daring to wink at him as he had done to her before.

He laughed. "I meant to ask if you play or sing?"

"Both, when forced. I am far from of the finest performer in my family, but I do my best and I am usually praised more than I deserve for it."

"You have very indulgent oppressors, then?"

Elizabeth was startled by his jest and missed a step in the dance. "Oh! I...."

"I should not have said such a thing."

"No, do not apologize. We have both been a little impudent. Indeed, sir, you are rather near the truth. I love my family and I know they love me too, but it seems that the older I get, the more I grow to question how that affection has been expressed throughout the years. Protectiveness at odds with selfishness... sometimes I really have thought we may all simply be cursed."

"You sound like a gothic heroine out of a novel," he quipped.

"Pah! What do you know of novels?"

"What my sisters tell me, which is not inconsiderable, I assure you."

"And can you tolerate it with any equanimity? My aunt was always so very fond of them that I am sure my uncle wished to toss half of her collection out the window and into the thoroughfare."

He shook his head and said with mock gravity, "Literary defenestration is quite indefensible, even when I have spent many hours hearing of the plights of *Camilla* and *Evelina*."

Elizabeth threw back her head and laughed at her handsome knight.

"Your sisters are lucky to have such a brother. If only mine were...."

"Were what?"

Elizabeth turned her head away, falling nervously silent. She knew she ought to hold her tongue. He might very well be acquainted with William – after all, he must have at least known her uncle to have garnered an invitation. And then another notion struck her. She had not seen this gentleman at all before the supper. Could he have snuck in later? Was he perhaps a roguish gatecrasher, come to steal her heart?

She shook her head and laughed. She was smitten, and it had made her nonsensical. "Well, suffice it to say, if he knew how well I was enjoying this dance with you, I expect he would think very ill of me."

He dropped a hand to his hip, patting about as if looking for something. "And I have forgotten my sword."

Elizabeth laughed again. "Next time, sir, see that you do not. At any rate, I have managed to evade his unceasing judgement so far this evening, I had better not jinx myself, or he shall creep up out of nowhere with a heavy dose of ready censure."

He looked intently at her, and for a moment Elizabeth feared she had taken her impertinence too far. She simply could not help herself. She felt such a strong magnetism to this gentleman whose name she did not even know, and it occurred to her that she had spoken with a greater ease to him than she had with a great many people much closer to her, in recent days.

The dance came to an end, but both Elizabeth and her partner stood fixed in place in the middle of the dance floor, each unwilling to shatter the magic of the moment. Slowly he reached for her hand and took it in his. "If you would tell me your name, I am sure I should call him out," he gently teased.

"Hmm," Elizabeth mused, imagining William squaring up against her knight in shining armor. "An offer I intend to consider."

"Perhaps you should consider another offer," he said, and slowly lifted her hand to his lips, placing a soft kiss on the black satin. "Dance the last set of the night with me. If you enjoy yourself as much as I have enjoyed this dance, tell me your name, and I shall tell you mine... and call upon you tomorrow. I cannot bear to think that we might never speak again."

Elizabeth met his eyes and saw nothing there that was not in her own heart at that moment. Before she knew what she was about, she replied, "Nor I. You shall have the last dance, sir."

"I shall look forward to it, my beautiful starling," he breathed, and released her hand at last.

As he turned to walk away, Elizabeth hurried in the opposite direction, suddenly aware she might have made something of a spectacle of herself after such an exhibition in the middle of an empty dance floor. It was beginning to fill again now as partners were exchanged, and, feeling some turmoil at the unexpected stirrings of her heart, she was relieved her next set was not promised to anybody, for she required a few minutes of private reflection.

She wished to seek out her sisters, but saw Uncle Henry standing nearby, staring at her with a most curious expression on his face. She would need to move his way in order to approach her sisters, and meant to do so quickly, hoping he would not detain her and thrust her at any of the dreadful men on his wretched list.

"Ah, Lizzy," he said as he intercepted her. "That was quite... unexpected of you, just now. I take it you enjoyed your dance?"

"I did," she said. At the sight of some discomposure in his countenance, Elizabeth grew contentious and squared her shoulders back. Thrusting out her chin, she said, "I daresay it was the most wonderful dance I have ever had. I suspect his name is not on your list, but perhaps it should be."

"Lizzy," he cried her with apparent astonishment, and she folded her arms and held his gaze. "I should not think — that is, I suppose it is not impossible... but are you quite sure?"

"If I am at liberty to decide at all for myself, then I suppose I am."

He furrowed his brow. "I shall have to speak to your mother about it."

Heaven forfend I make any decisions myself. Giving him her most ferocious glare, Elizabeth silently held her uncle's eye a moment longer before she swept away to speak with her sisters.

***

Elizabeth was still fuming at her uncle's interference when she reached her sisters. "Where is Mamma?"

"I think she is still speaking with Uncle Edward," Jane replied. "They have been whispering together all evening."

"And dancing together," Mary added.

"Oh, that is very kind of her to lift his spirits," Elizabeth said. "He was so quiet on the way here, as if he were going to a funeral and not a ball." Looking round, Elizabeth was pleased to see him in better humor now as he spoke to her mother.

"Who is in better humor? I hope it is you, Lizzy," Richard chided as he approached them, his sister on his arm.

"Look who I have retrieved from the card room," Charlotte drawled.

"Playing cards at you own ball! Shocking, Richard," Jane laughed.

"I might be willing to reform myself most thoroughly if you dance with me again, Cousin," he said to her.

"I shall not keep a straight face the whole time, I am sure," Jane giggled, gesturing at Richard's ostentatious costume.

"I mean to bring back the fashions of old," he said, striking a preposterous pose, "and cast Beau Brummel back into obscurity! Oho, you laugh now, Lizzy, but you are next. And you, Mary. You shall all suffer the indignity of standing up with me once more." He winked at Elizabeth.

Charlotte, Mary and Elizabeth laughed, waving him away and urging them to be off, when they were joined by Mr. Bingley and his sister.

"There you are, Miss Darcy! Charles says he shall not dance at all if you will not have him," Miss Bingley purred.

"Oh! I have just promised the next set to my cousin, but you may have the one after that, Mr. Bingley."

Elizabeth observed Mary smile brightly at Mr. Bingley, but he had turned to address Charlotte, whose acceptance was readily given. As the two couples joined the set, Elizabeth and Mary were left alone with Miss Bingley, who smiled vacantly at them. "Well, what charming birds we all make, I am sure. I believe I must go and give my regards to your mother." She hastened away.

After Miss Bingley left then, Elizabeth laughed and linked her arm through Mary's, leading her sister along the perimeter of the ballroom. "Shall we go find you a partner? You seem eager to dance."

"Oh, Lizzy," Mary sighed.

"What is it, dearest?"

"What do you make of Jane and Mr. Bingley?"

Elizabeth considered for a moment. "I suspect his sister and her brother desire the match more than she does at present."

Mary smiled sadly at her sister. "I hoped someone else would see it as I do." She chewed her lip for a moment, looking as though she might say more, but she did not.

"Mary, whatever is the matter? Surely you do not fear she will be pressed into a relationship she does not desire?"

"I do fear it, Lizzy, but... not for the reason you suspect."

"Mary...."

"I... I like Mr. Bingley," Mary whispered.

"Oh dear. That is a problem."

"I know that, Lizzy. I feel awful. The truth is, I suspect Jane does not like him so much herself."

"You think she is being pressured into it by William and Miss Bingley, and goes along with it for their sakes, without any idea she is wounding you in the process."

Mary nodded. "Exactly."

"You ought to ask Jane about it. If she does not like him, there will be no harm done, and if she does, well...."

"Then I shall be simply wretched! I already despise myself for it. I am sure William would be furious with me, too. Jane deserves such a man as Mr. Bingley. She has been unhappy for so long, and William thinks his friend is jolly enough to life her spirits – I daresay he is, he is quite perfect! Besides, I know William and Mamma fear Jane shall never marry. I like Mr. Bingley, but perhaps I shall find someone else. I should not wish to take him from Jane, if he could make her happy. It is entirely hopeless."

"Oh, Mary," Elizabeth sighed. "I do not know what to tell you. You really must speak to Jane. Why should you care what William thinks? He is just like our uncle, thinking he can arrange peoples' lives as he chooses, and if I were you I would not put up with it!"

"No, Lizzy, it is not William's fault. Besides, I do not even know if Mr. Bingley remembers that I exist. That is no fault of William's."

"Oh, yes it is! He has made no effort to put you forward as he does Jane. It was not enough for him to meddle with George Wickham, now he must interfere again with poor Jane, and it may cost you both dearly! I have half a mind to hit him on the nose!"

Mary looked distressed. "No, Lizzy, please. I ought not to have spoken – I beg you would put it from your mind. Please, do not tell William."

Elizabeth made a face at her sister. "You would put your own feelings aside to spare his? Fitzwilliam Darcy is a selfish, boorish beast whose opinion does not signify, and I beg you would not credit it at all." Elizabeth realized she had begun to raise her voice, and recollected herself. Nearby, Miss Steventon and Miss Leigh were walking past them, and they exchanged hushed whispers as they glanced at Elizabeth.

Mary turned on her and crossed her arms. "Stop it, Lizzy. I wish I had not confided in you at all!" She turned and ran away. Elizabeth stood stunned and alone, angry with herself for earning her sister's rebuke. *Stupid William Darcy, this is all his fault!*

***

Darcy could not escape his cousin Anne's notice, for she accosted him almost immediately after his dance with the beautiful starling.

"How well we look together," she drawled, "a king and a queen. I have been waiting for you to make an appearance on the dance floor, though I hoped I might claim you myself first." She latched her arm around his with determination. "How well Richard looks with Jane," she observed. "What fine couples cousins can make."

Darcy thought it better to get the inevitable done with at once, and he silently led her to the floor. Anne was content to lavish him in syrupy compliments and make suggestive remarks about the advantages of spring weddings, but Darcy could scarcely attend her.

Instead he thought of his previous partner, with whom he could not wait to dance again. He was bewitched by the mystery and intimacy of their conversation, and eager to discover who she was. She had spoken of her misgivings about the marriage mart – perhaps her portion was small? Then again, her costume was clearly expensive, and it was evident that she had been well educated. And she had just received a "treasure chest of books" from her father, a rather lavish and erudite gift. It caused him to wonder about her.

As to her portion, he decided it did not matter. He had never desired a mercenary match, not after seeing the genuine love his own parents had shared. Her fortune was of no consequence to him, and if she had not a penny to her name, he would gladly give her *his* name.

Darcy laughed to himself. *Well now, that was certainly a rapid leap!* From admiration to love, and love to matrimony in a moment. Though he had no plans to marry currently, she might be the sort of lady to change his mind. He relished the idea of what she might say when next they danced, what secrets she might share with him, and what questions he might ask to come to know her better. He desired to – no, he *needed* to know everything about her, and more than anything he wished to look upon her face, and speak her name.

As if he had conjured her up through sheer willpower, he looked up and caught her eye, and she smiled widely at him. He observed that she was speaking with Mary, and wondered with a smile if even now she was trying to discover his identity.

By now Darcy had been exceedingly inattentive to Anne, and as he led her down the dance, they collided with a passing gentleman at the end of the set, who splashed them both in wine. Anne, her white undergown drenched in red wine, let out a shrill screech and glowered at Darcy before abruptly stomping away.

Some wine had gotten on Darcy as well, and though the color of his tunic was perfectly suited to hide it, he had no wish to reek of alcohol when he had his next dance with the starling. He flagged down a footman and asked for a cloth to clean himself and after it had been brought, he ducked behind a marble pillar at the edge of the room to discreetly pat at the wine stain on his chest.

Once he had done what he could to preserve his costume, he discarded the wine-soaked cloth and leaned back against the pillar, letting out a heavy sigh. A moment later he was laughing at himself, no common occurrence, and yet he could not resist. It was worth it, he supposed, to be away from his cousin somewhat sooner than planned, and might make an amusing anecdote to tell his beautiful starling. He was amazed at how easy it had been to speak with her. He had always been abysmal at speaking to beautiful women, and yet *she* had put him at ease with her candor and her teasing. She was artless, intelligent and witty, which was all the more a virtue because he suspected there was a great sadness in her life.

Darcy's reverie was interrupted as he heard his name spoken on the other side of the pillar. "I have not seen Mr. Darcy," one young woman was saying. "I am looking for his cousin, myself."

"Why Caroline, the viscount is barely in half-mourning, you sly thing!"

"Yes, but even in half-mourning he is more amusing than Mr. Darcy. Oh, he is a great friend of my brother's, and I am glad of it, but he scarcely speaks at all, and he always looks completely miserable!"

The other young woman laughed. "My goodness, you are almost as wicked as Miss Bennet!"

Miss Bingley huffed. "I should hope not!"

"I was walking with Miss Steventon, and as we happened to pass Miss Bennet, she was abusing Mr. Darcy in the strongest language – it was quite shocking! She called him a selfish, boorish beast, and said that she cared nothing at all for him! Can you imagine anyone speaking so cruelly of their own brother?"

"How dreadful! I am sure I should never dare speak so to dear Charles, even when he gets on my nerves. I wonder that my poor friend Miss Darcy could be related to such a person! Miss Eliza ought to be punished."

Darcy drew away, not wishing to hear more, though for once he rather agreed with Miss Bingley. The music of the dance had ended, and Darcy hoped Miss Bingley and her friend would soon move away, so that he might come out from behind the pillar without alerting them to his presence. He listened once more, finally hearing his cousin John approach and claim Miss Bingley's hand, and waited a moment longer before he came out from behind the pillar.

Richard was nearby, and caught Darcy's eye. "If looks could kill, Cousin!"

Darcy grumbled under his breath and drew his cousin aside. He needed to remove his damned helmet, yet he still wished to maintain the air of mystery until he unmasked himself for the starling. He led Richard out into the corridor, and then took off the uncomfortable helmet and tucked it under his arm.

"Well, Darcy, what is it?"

"I have only just learned that I am a selfish, boorish beast."

Richard laughed. "And you mean to amend your wicked ways?"

Darcy grimaced. "Am I truly these things? Do I deserve such accusations?"

Richard's smirk turned into a frown. "You are serious."

"Tell me truly, Richard, am I any of these things?"

"Of course you are not. What had given you such a notion?"

"Apparently Elizabeth Bennet has been parading about the ballroom disparaging me to all and sundry."

"Damn and blast, what has gotten into her? She seemed out of sorts earlier, but that is going too far. Shall I speak to her about it?"

Darcy raised his eyebrows at Richard. "You are always her staunchest defender."

"Come now, surely you know me well enough to suppose that I cannot defend such language as that! Something is bothering her tonight, and I shall discover what it is. She confides in me, you know. At any rate, I daresay I have a stake in reconciling the two of you, if she and I do marry."

Darcy sighed. "You are still considering it? You might have anybody."

"No indeed, Darcy. I am a second son, and I do not wish to be anyone's second choice. Lizzy and I get on well enough, and she is determined not to have anyone else on my father's list."

Darcy shook his head, trying to subdue his ire. "Do you really think she could make you happy?"

Richard clapped a hand on Darcy's shoulder, knitting his brow as he looked earnestly at him. "She is not Olivia, Darcy. I shall speak to her, but it could only help if you made an effort to get to know her. In seventeen years, you never have. Besides, your mother has been speaking to Sir Edward tonight, and I think she means to ask Lizzy to come and stay at Darcy House."

This was new information to Darcy, who merely blinked stupidly at his cousin.

"Ah – I have said too much. I am sure she means to speak to you about it. Give it some thought, Darcy. You have *three* sisters, and it is time you started acting like it." At that, Richard turned on his heel and went back into the ballroom, leaving Darcy alone, angry, and confused in the empty corridor.

***

Elizabeth had gone out onto the balcony to take some air after her confrontation with Mary, and had been sitting alone, savoring the tingle of the January chill in the air for she knew not how long before Richard slipped outside to join her.

"I thought I would find you here," he said.

"Oh – yes – you wished to dance again."

"Only if you wish it. Before you decide, however, there is something I would speak to you about."

Elizabeth was filled with dread – he must have heard about what she said to Mary. *If he has come to make me apologize, he is quite mistaken!* As Elizabeth's shoulders tensed up, Richard sat down beside her and laid his hand atop hers. "I am not going to scold you, Lizzy, if that is what you fear."

"You... you do not think I deserve it?"

"I do think you deserve it, but it would give you pain that I do not wish to inflict. I only wish to say that I am very sorry there is no affection between you and Darcy. I have a great regard for both of you, and I wish that you could each see one another as I do."

"I fear it is impossible. I... I do not even wish it."

Richard sighed and intertwined his fingers with hers. "I wish it was easier for you, Lizzy. I know what you have suffered all these years, and I think your time away from Pemberley has been a very ill thing indeed."

"I know, I know," she sighed. "Jane says that I have missed out on seeing the side of William that she and Mary do. It is all my own fault for running away, and not a speck of blame on William, who took more than ten years to come around to the notion of being a proper brother to the sisters who remained!"

"And you are made bitter by it. You are right, Lizzy, but have you ever simply told him that this has hurt you?"

"Of course not! How could I? After all of his disparagement, his rudeness to poor Aunt Olivia, how could I say such a thing to him, allowing him the opportunity to...."

"To hurt you further?"

"To judge me! I shall not allow it. At any rate, his opinion means nothing to me. You and John have been more brotherly to me than William ever has."

Richard leaned in a little closer to her, sighing with dejection. Of course it was not what he wished to hear, when he hoped for more from her. "I shall not say William is blameless. I only think that if you actually spoke to him, and if both of you simply listened, really *listened* to what the other had to say, life would be so much easier. How much misery might have been avoided all these years, simply by us all being more open with one another?"

"Myself most of all, I suppose."

Richard wrapped his arm around her shoulders, and Elizabeth allowed herself the indulgence of leaning her head on his. He was warm, and it felt rather nice.

"You are too hard on yourself. Lizzy. You were just a child when everything went so wrong. I shall never forget the state you were in, when...."

"Oh, Richard. You have always been there for me. I daresay you understand me better than anyone. You know why I could not stay there. At any rate, Uncle Edward needed me."

"Sir Edward was a forty year old man who allowed a thirteen year old girl to make her own decisions, at the expense of your mother and father, and your sisters... and even you."

"I know. Of course. I have always known that, Richard, but it was still my choice. At any rate, there is nothing to be done about it now."

"There is, though, Lizzy. That is what I am trying to tell you. Make peace with Darcy, I beg you. If not for him, or for yourself, do it for your mother. She misses you, and this rift between you and Darcy – you know she must feel it."

Elizabeth sighed. "Very well, Richard, I shall try."

"That's my girl," he said and smiled at her. They held each other's gaze for a moment and Elizabeth suddenly grew nervous. There was one gentleman she might perhaps wish to be alone in the moonlight with, but it was not her cousin. She knew he was going to mention it, what he wanted from her, and she could not bear to think of it at present. Not now, when her head was so full of the handsome knight.

Richard sensed her hesitation and offered her a hopeful smile. "You look beautiful tonight, Lizzy."

She laughed. "You look ridiculous."

"It is worth it, to see you smile. I would always have you so happy."

"I know."

"Do you?" He held her gaze still, moving his arm from around her shoulder to the back of her neck, and he drew her closer. "I had not intended to pressure you about, but I wish you would think of it, Lizzy. If you could be willing to improve your opinion of William, could you not begin to think of me as more than a cousin?"

Elizabeth froze in place, unable to speak, to protest, as Richard reached up and stroked her cheek before leaning in and kissing her gently on the lips.

***

Darcy was in no mood to speak to anyone, and wished nothing more than some privacy to clear his mind. He was angry with Elizabeth, and even annoyed with Richard. He wished he had never heard Miss Bingley's vile gossip, for he had no desire to be so out of sorts when he was granted his next dance with the starling.

He wished only to think of her – *she* liked him, and did not think him a selfish, boorish beast. He longed for the moment when they would dance again, and when at the end of it he might learn her identity and reveal himself. Whoever she was, she was certainly bound to feel all her good fortune in discovering who he was.

Darcy stepped out onto the balcony, which wrapped around the side of his uncle's house. Feeling a great tumult of hurt and anger at odds with the hope his starling offered him, and the almost surreal experience their dance had been, Darcy paced on the balcony and finally drew his cigar case from his pocket to indulge his anxiety.

Still he paced, his mind a whirl. He was not pleased that his mother would wish Elizabeth to reside with them, though he knew what it meant to her. And in the end, he knew he could not possibly deny her anything that would bring her joy. Richard was in favor of it, and urging a reconciliation, but even if Darcy could come to terms with allowing Elizabeth to come home, he could not approve of Richard's pursuit of her. Richard could do far better, second son or not.

He paced and paced, and at length he put out his cigar and walked around the corner of the balcony, when he heard voices and stopped. It was more dimly lit on this side of the house, but not twenty paces away he could make out the figure of his garishly dressed cousin sitting on a bench, his back to Darcy, beside a woman, though the lady was cloaked in shadow.

He watched Richard lean forward to kiss the woman, and Darcy was on the point of withdrawing when the young lady's movement caused her dress to rustle, and as the fabric shifted around her feet there was a shimmer of blue and purple on black – it was the starling.

Darcy stood, rooted in place by his own horror as he watched her draw away from Richard, her eyes glistening with tears, and then she stood and ran away. Richard sat still for a moment, letting out a heavy sigh, and then he rose to his feet and pursued her.

It was several minutes before Darcy could move, though he had no wish to return to the ballroom yet. His heart ached and his stomach was in knots. He had not wished for Richard to pursue Elizabeth, but this was so much worse! Richard has turned his attention to the one woman to whom Darcy had been able to recommend himself. Had it been his disapproval of the match with Elizabeth that had driven Richard to look elsewhere? But of all the women here, why her? She was *his*; in some small way that he could not describe, he felt it completely. They had connected in such a way that she had, in that moment, seemed to belong to him, and it was little comfort to see that she had not welcomed Richard's advances. How could he pursue a woman he knew his cousin would covet?

The emergence of Caroline Bingley and his cousin John onto the balcony made Darcy draw back into the shadows, and though his mind was still reeling, he could not escape the sound of her preening laughter. And then, the sound of more kissing.

Darcy rounded the corner and forced himself to re-enter the ballroom. By now Richard had managed to make amends to the starling, for he was dancing a lively reel with her. Darcy quickly walked past the dance, avoiding the sight of her and his cousin together, and paused only to speak to Mary, who was being led to the set by Bingley.

"I am for the card room, my dear," he said. "Tell our mother she may send for me when she wishes to return home."

***

Elizabeth muddled through her dance with Richard as best she could; she had not been given much of a choice. She had been accosted by Lord Chawton almost as soon as she entered the ballroom, and solicited for another dance before she had even time to compose herself. Richard had appeared at her side then, telling Lord Chawton she was promised to him for the next dance, and she scarcely had time to inform the odious man that her final set was also taken, before she was whisked away.

Richard was silent for several minutes before saying, "I am sorry I upset you." Elizabeth scarcely knew how to reply, and so she remained silent. Richard sighed. "I only wanted the chance to find out ... to see if there might ever be anything between us," he whispered as the steps of the dance brought them closer.

"I told you, I am not ready," she replied, and at that moment she saw the handsome knight walking past. She stared at him, hoping he would glance back at her, but he did not. He stopped to speak to Mary and Mr. Bingley, and then disappeared into the great crush of revelers.

The handsome knight did not appear when the last dance of the night was called, and deflated by her uncomfortable set with Richard, Elizabeth hung back, hoping *he* would come for her.

He did not, and as the dance began, Elizabeth wondered why. Had she given some offense? Had the intensity of the connection existed only in her mind? She felt foolish for letting herself hope, as she had never imagined she could. But of course, it was doomed to end is disappointment, everything always did.

At last she was joined by her mother, who took a seat beside her. "Are you well, my dear?"

Elizabeth shook her head, fighting back tears. "I hardly know."

"Oh, my dear girl. Poor Lizzy, whatever is the matter?"

Elizabeth had no desire to embarrass herself by sharing the particulars, and merely leaned into her mother, resting her head on Lady Anne's shoulder. "Have you seen my uncle? I wish to go home."

"You do look tired, Lizzy. Let us go and find Sir Edward, and get you home." Her mother stood and took Lizzy by the hand. "I know it is not the right moment, my love, but there is something I have been wishing to ask of you. When you said you wished to go home, oh Lizzy, how I wished that you meant *my* home. I have spoken with Edward about it... Lizzy, what if you were to come and stay at Darcy House for a time?"

"I...." Elizabeth froze with panic.

Lady Anne squeezed her hand. "You do not have to answer now, my dear. I only supposed you to be upset because of Henry's insistence on pushing you at all his dreadful 'eligible men.' I know Edward does not wish to stand up to Henry – it has always been this way – but I am not afraid of my brother. If you were to come and stay with us at Darcy House, you might escape the pressure, and you shall always have your Mamma on hand to comfort you at times like this. Only think on it, my dear. I find I have grown tired of letting others make you cry, Lizzy. I wish you would come home."

Elizabeth felt the tears begin to flow behind her mask, and she nodded feebly as she looked up at her mother. She was in such a state that she wished she could do as she had done when she was a girl, and simply hide in her mother's skirts. To go home, to be with her mother, to flee her uncles' designs... it was exceedingly tempting, and yet, it would be such a betrayal. Even if Uncle Edward approved, Rose would be wounded, and the twins would not understand. And it would mean living in the same house as William.

She considered what Richard had said to her about William, and then, inevitably, everything else that had transpired with Richard flooded her mind. "I shall think on it," she said at last.

"Oh, Lizzy, thank you. I cannot bear to see you looking so miserable, and feel so powerless to do aught about it."

"Would you really go up against Uncle Henry and his matches for me? *All* of them?"

Her mother looked at her, understanding. "Yes, my dear. I am your mother, and there is nothing in this world I would not do for you."

***

After Caroline Bingley had been divested of her finery, prepared for bed, and sent her maid away, she crept down the hall and knocked softly on her stepmother's bedroom door. "Come in," came the feeble answer.

Her stepmother, a woman in her late thirties, still quite beautiful if a little pale, sat propped up against a great mountain of pillows. "Good evening, Mother. I wanted to look in on you before I retire. I hope you are feeling better."

Mrs. Bingley nodded. "I am well enough now you are come home, my dear." She patted the space beside her on the bed. "Come and sit with me, dear. I hope you had a fine time at the ball."

"It was so beautiful, Mamma – the earl's home is simply spectacular, and the ball was such a crush. Everyone was in very fine looks."

"You most of all, I daresay, my dear."

"Oh – I do not know about that. Miss Darcy and her sisters all looked very beautiful. I hear their uncle means to marry them all off this Season, and I am sure they must have had suitors falling at their feet after tonight."

Mrs. Bingley smiled. "Which of them does your brother fancy? I know he cannot resist a pretty face. Miss Bennet perhaps, or even Miss Gardiner?"

"Miss Gardiner is their cousin, I believe. She was not in attendance tonight; she will not be out until next year."

"I see."

"I believe Charles danced twice with Jane Darcy, and I am very happy."

"I had heard him speak of Miss Bennet when first we arrived in Town, but I suppose she has already been thrown over in favor of Miss Darcy. Ah, well, that is good, too; and he may yet change his mind again."

"I should not think so. Miss Bennet, I understand, is rather less refined in her graces. But Jane, you know, is a dear, sweet girl. It is very sad that she should have such an unfortunate sister."

"Ah, well, I should like to meet her anyhow – she sounds a most interesting creature. And though you have been friends these many years with Miss Darcy, I have yet to set eyes upon her. It is a pity she could not come to us in Scarborough, after that beau of hers died."

"Oh, Mamma, I wish you could have been there to meet her." Her mother coughed. "Can I get you anything? Some water perhaps?"

"I am feeling much better, child. I am sure I shall meet with them all very soon. Now, tell me of your partners – was the viscount among them?"

Omitting their romantic interlude on the balcony, she said only, "He was – we danced twice, as well. Oh, Mamma, he is still so very handsome, just as he was the summer I met him."

"I hope you behaved yourself, child – you must contain your enthusiasm, for a languid ennui is much more the fashion now."

"I did my best, as you have taught me, but I like him so much, Mamma."

Mrs. Bingley smiled widely. "If Charles is already besotted with the viscount's cousin, that bodes well for you, my dear. One alliance between our families may lead to another."

"I do hope so. I should like nothing better."

"Nor I, my dear," Mrs. Bingley said, patting her daughter's hand with a wistful smile. "Nor I."

12

❧

As was his custom, Darcy woke early the next morning and took his horse out for a ride in Hyde Park. And, as was not uncommon for the master of Pemberley, he had quite a lot on his mind. He had struggled to find sleep, fighting every hour to push the starling from his mind. There was something about her that had captivated him in a way he could not fully understand, as if her vulnerability and manner of confiding in him had somehow bound them together. Seeing Richard kiss her had been like a knife through his chest, which even the starling's adverse reaction could little assuage. He had never felt – never known it was possible to feel – so much, so quickly, and he could not get her words to him out of his mind. *'I can't get out, I can't get out.'*

He felt protective, even possessive over her, and whatever distress had led her to speak to him as she had, his starling was in some sort of trouble, and it filled Darcy with dread to think that Richard might be involved in it. Moreover, Richard's involvement with the starling, whatever it may be, was likely Darcy's own doing – he had pressed Richard to abandon his pursuit of Elizabeth, practically pushing him into the arms of the woman who had awakened these sensations within him.

And he had run like a coward. He had regretted his weakness the minute he departed Matlock House, trying to account for why he had not acted differently, why he had not pursued her, or confronted Richard. And yet, would it be worth it to pursue her at the risk of causing a rift between himself and his favorite cousin? The idea had seemed insupportable at the time, but now he wondered.

And then there was Elizabeth. Darcy sighed. His problems were many, but somehow she seemed to be at the root of them all. He knew he must prepare himself to speak to his mother about her wish to ask Elizabeth to reside with them. He would have preferred to learn of the plan from Lady Anne directly; hearing of it from Richard, at such a moment, had been mortifying in the extreme.

And how could he allow such a hoyden to come and live under his roof? He knew his mother loved Elizabeth, and Jane and Mary were fond of her, but he believed they were blind in their affection, and had been ever since Elizabeth fell under Lady Olivia's influence. *That* lady had been a royal mistress, an adulteress, and a silver-tongued harpy; it was impossible for Elizabeth not to have learned her wicked ways in seven years.

Given what the little chit had dared to say about him in a room full of people, he feared her influence on their sisters. He would not allow her insolence to wound the girls, nor risk their learning some of it themselves. And yet, he loved his mother dearly. She was the finest woman he knew, and had suffered a vast deal. Losing his father had changed her. Even losing Elizabeth all those years ago had wounded her, and causing the deaths of the Bennets haunted her still.

Their first night in London, the nightmares had returned. His mother had never spoken to him of it, but the servants talked, and Mrs. Reynolds had confided in him years ago that his mother still occasionally had horrific dreams of the carriage accident, even after all these years. He had brought his loyal housekeeper to London with them, for she, too, had been there that fateful day, and had made him a solemn, secret promise to attend his mother personally whenever the nightmares seized her.

Since Christmas, there had been no recurrence, and he was begrudgingly obliged to admit that seeing Elizabeth had done his mother tremendous good. How could he refuse what would give her such comfort?

Perhaps Richard was right. For his mother's sake, he must make the effort to reconcile with Elizabeth. He might never like her, nor truly esteem her as he did Jane and Mary, but he would be civil and courteous and welcome her into his home. Perhaps it would do *her* some good, as well, as she would have three daily examples of female perfection around her.

He found such feminine grace waiting for him when he returned an hour later, his head barely clearer than when he had gone out. Jane was in the breakfast room, though their mother and sister Mary were still abed.

"Good morning, Brother."

"Good morning, Jane. I trust you slept well?"

"Oh, eventually. I stayed up rather later than I had meant – that is, there was so much to think about. So much that happened."

He fixed himself a plate at the sideboard and then sat down at the table across from his sister. "Good things, I hope? You appeared to enjoy yourself."

Jane gave him one of her characteristic gentle smiles. "I did, more than I expected to. Some of the partners recommended to me by Uncle

Henry were, as Elizabeth said, rather odious, but then Cousin Richard and our new cousin Mr. Collins were so very pleasant – and Mr. Bingley too, of course."

"He is quite taken with you, I think."

Jane blushed prettily and pushed the food around her plate with a fork. "I shall have to accustom myself to such things."

"Jane," he said, reaching his hand across the table. "There is something I would ask you. You do not feel that you are in a cage, do you? That you are trapped, and cannot get out?"

Jane made a queer expression at him. "No indeed, William. I am doing my best to overcome my grief, I promise you. It is just such a change, all at once."

"I understand. It was a shock for me, rejoining society after we lost our father, perhaps made worse because I was alone."

Jane's eyes widened with distress. "Oh William, I am so sorry!"

"No, no – I am not blaming you, Jane. You did well to stay at Pemberley, where you were needed. I only meant to say that I did rejoin society alone, and perhaps it may prove an advantage for you to be amongst so much family as you have around you for your come-out. You are gentle and kind, but so very shy. Your sister Elizabeth may be a little too... brash, but she is confident and has little trouble conversing with others. Perhaps you might temper one another, learning more of one another's strengths while polishing the weaknesses. You might grow more voluble under her influence, and likewise lend her your sweetness."

Jane smiled widely at him and laid a hand on his. "Oh, William, what a lovely thing to say! It is just what I have wished to hear from you! Lizzy is... oh, Brother, she has suffered a great deal, and yet she is so bright and easy to be around. I know you have never known one another as I know you both, but if only you could!"

"That is just what Richard said last night."

Jane blushed again. "I am gratified to hear that I am not alone in hoping you and Lizzy might get along. I have wronged her before, and I am striving to make amends – to know that you would do the same... oh, Brother, it means so much to me."

Darcy was stung by her words – she had suggested that he had wronged Elizabeth. Richard thought the same, but he was always so brusque – yet if Jane could say such a thing, he must wonder if it was true.

"Well, my dear, if our mother has not already told you, she wishes Elizabeth to come and live with us."

Jane's eyes lit with delight. "Oh, William! Might I tell Mary? She will be so very happy, too. You are so good to us, Brother. When is she to come?"

"That I cannot say. I had thought I might pay her a visit, to make my amends to her and discuss the particulars with Sir Edward."

Jane giggled and gave him a mischievous look. "You must go this morning. What a fine joke if Lizzy was in the house, unpacking her things when Mary and Mamma finally awaken!"

Darcy laughed indulgently. "I doubt it may be that swift, but for you, my dear, I shall do my best." At this Darcy stood and gave his sister a quick kiss on the top of her head – not a gesture he frequently made, but in his resolution to act it simply felt right – and then he strode purposefully out of the house, toward Upper Brook Street.

***

Sir Edward met Darcy in the foyer and welcomed him into the house. He led Darcy into the sitting room, saying, "Yes, I was on the point of speaking to Lizzy about your mother's proposed living arrangements – your arrival is most fortuitously timed."

Only Rose was in the sitting room; she had evidently not been expecting company. Her long brown hair hung loose about her shoulders and she was looking rather pale. She had been curled up in the window seat of the front parlor, a book in her lap, and her knees tucked into her chest, though she had assumed a more formal attitude upon his entrance. She gave Sir Edward a rather sour look behind his back at the mention of Elizabeth moving to Darcy House. Despite the cheek of it, Darcy felt a little sorry for the emotion in her eyes – she must be disappointed to lose the constant companionship of a dear cousin. Perhaps something might be done for her benefit as well – she was far more poised than he would have expected Lady Olivia's daughter to be, despite her current displeasure. She might do well to stay at Matlock House with Charlotte and their aunt Phyllis for a time.

"Yes, I have come to discuss the matter with Elizabeth. Indeed, I believe I have some amends to make."

Sir Edward nodded. "Well then, I shall leave you to it."

Rose set the book aside entirely now, drew her shawl tighter around herself, and looked up expectantly at him, wearing just a trace of a smile. "Amends?"

"Indeed. I have spoken with both Jane and Richard, and consulted my own conscience – I suppose it is time I begin to behave as a brother, where I have not always done. Pray, forgive me – are you quite well?" Without knowing what he was about, he had sat down beside her on the window seat and taken her hand in his. "Truly, you look rather distraught. Might I get something for your present relief – some water, or tea perhaps?"

"No, forgive me. I... I ought to have thought of calling for the tea myself... I am always forgetting. You must think me quite hopeless."

"No indeed, but it is clear that you are not yourself."

"I – my mind is quite distracted at present."

"I am sure. You must be dreading the separation from your cousin."

"Yes, among other feelings," she said, giving him a wary look.

"Well, perhaps you ought to go and take some rest. I mean to speak with Elizabeth, and I am sure she will go to you after."

Rose's eyes went wide, and she smirked at him with no little incredulity. "Speak with Elizabeth? Do you not even know me, William?"

Darcy flinched, dumbfounded. "Rose...."

She merely shook her head and laughed at him. He gaped at her, unable to speak as he was struck by the full weight of his mistake. *This* was Elizabeth? *Good God, it was she I admired at Christmas?* He knew he ought to feel revolted for feeling anything like attraction to her – was she not his sister? And yet, she was not – he had never truly felt that she was. She was certainly not the timid child who had come to Pemberley. She was a woman grown, and a woman he barely knew.

At present, she was a woman who was laughing derisively at him; she asked, "Well, am I to expect no reply?"

Elizabeth's laughter faded, she pushed herself up off the window seat and began to pace the room, her countenance unreadable. "You said you had come here to make amends."

"I did – I have. I spoke with Richard and with Jane, and thought perhaps I ought to extend the olive branch. It was an honest mistake, thinking you were Rose...."

"*An honest mistake?* You are so keen to forgive yourself, you needn't even ask it of me!"

Darcy recoiled. She was right – he had not even apologized. "I am an ass," he sighed.

"Well now, we agree on something! Richard and Jane shall be delighted."

Darcy paced toward her, his eyes boring into hers. "I would have you know, Sister, I promised them that I would make an effort, if only for their sakes, and my mother's."

Elizabeth sneered at him with intense contempt and she pounded her little fists against his chest, pushing him away. "Do not call me your sister. I have never wished to be, and you have made it clear for nearly twenty years that you feel the same. I am sorry to pain Jane and Mamma, but I daresay they have long been pained by your treatment of me, and I rather wonder why it only now begins to matter, long after I have given up any hope or desire to be on amicable terms with you."

Darcy gritted his teeth. "So this is your opinion of me? Thank you for explaining so fully. I have done you no greater wrong that assume you still wore your hair short, as your portrait last year indicated. A small error after three years of separation, and for this you would seek not only to berate me, but in doing so punish the woman who welcomed you into her home, who has only ever cared for you, loved you as a daughter?"

"I have no doubt of my mother's affection for me, sir; I can only wonder at how such a woman could have such an unfeeling, judgmental, manipulative son."

"Unfeeling and manipulative?" Darcy scoffed. "I may have judged you – I would have been happy to admit I was wrong for it, had you given me half the chance, before you confirmed my every censure by railing at me in such vulgar terms. But I am not without feeling, Elizabeth. I care deeply for our mother and sisters, and would put aside my prejudices about you to welcome you into my home, so you cannot say I am unfeeling."

"Your prejudices about me? So, you shall not deny that you have held me in contempt all these years?" Tears were streaming down Elizabeth's cheeks, but she looked far from defeated. "What have I ever done to you, to deserve to be treated so differently from Jane and Mary?"

"*You left,*" Darcy bellowed.

Elizabeth crossed her arms in front of her chest and continued to pace the room like a wild animal. "You have no right to speak of such things! You know nothing about it! I had to leave. Mamma knew my reasons, and my uncles, and Jane knows, too. I owe you no explanation. I was a child!"

"You are Lady Olivia's creature through and through – a spoilt child, mouthing off in the ballroom like a petulant little brat!"

"How dare you? I am a petulant little brat?"

"And I am a selfish, boorish beast!"

"Yes you are! You pretend to care about Jane, when you have been the cause of all her troubles!"

"I have only ever tried to protect her."

"Have you? You have protected her fiancé right into an early grave, and now you think pushing her at your friend will fix everything."

"You would tell me not to speak of what I know nothing about? You have no right – you know nothing of Wickham!"

"I know he was an amiable young man who loved Jane. But that was not good enough for you, was it? You interfered in his taking orders and sent him off to his death, causing me to lose my sister and giving Jane a heartbreak of the most acute kind! Yet now you think to interfere again, to push Mr. Bingley at her as if that will make up for your costing her the life of her fiancé. You have no regard for how any of them actually feel about it!"

"My crimes, in this assessment, are great indeed! Yes, I am a rotten, heartless brother who wishes his sister to stop mourning a wastrel and give a decent man a chance to bring her back to happiness!"

"You are immovable then – you shall admit to no wrongdoing whatsoever. Very well, I think I must bid you leave now."

Elizabeth turned her back to him and stalked back to the window seat; she threw herself down heavily and picked up her book. After a moment she looked back up at him, and growled, "*Get out.*"

Darcy was too incensed to move. "So that is it, then? You refuse to oblige me, you refuse to acknowledge that I have this family's best interests at heart – so much so that, might I remind you, I came here to make amends despite your disparaging remarks last evening?"

Elizabeth slammed the book shut and fixed him with a withering glare. "I merely wish to hear no more of your self-congratulatory vitriol. You are just as blind and obtuse and, frankly, disappointing, as every other man in this family. You would bully others until they bend to your will, hiding yourself away in your own pointless selfish brooding, and locking us ladies away in a cage as if we belong to you! Have you even bothered asking Jane how she feels? Or Mary, for that matter? You seem ill-qualified to be any kind of brother to me when you cannot even claim to know their hearts at all!"

Darcy flinched at her allusion to the cages, his heart tearing just a little as he thought of the starling. He strode over to Elizabeth, determined to gain the upper hand. "As a matter of fact, I spoke with Jane just this morning about her feelings, and she is favorable to Mr. Bingley. I told her I should not wish her to feel, as you say, *caged*, like a starling... indeed, it was brought to my attention last night that I ought to ask her such a question."

Elizabeth's eyes went wide and her face turned white as a sheet. "Oh really, sir? And might I inquire how that came about?" She rose to her feet, her body inches from him, clutching her book to her chest so hard her knuckles were white. Darcy glanced down, just able to make out the title – it was Laurence Sterne's *A Sentimental Journey.*

Darcy felt all the air rush out of his lungs as he looked down at Elizabeth. She was the starling. *No, no, no....*

She was choking back tears now. "I can't get out," she breathed, before raising her voice to say, "*Get out.*"

His feet would not move, but he reached out to grab her by the shoulders, even as he closed his eyes and began to purse his lips, hardly knowing what he was about to do.

He didn't see it coming when she slapped him with all her might across the face, and by the time he opened his eyes, she had wrested herself from his grasp and was running away from him.

***

Darcy strode down Upper Brook Street at a brisk pace toward his house in Hanover Square, the frigid January wind stinging his left cheek, which was still throbbing from the force of Elizabeth's slap. He was furious with her, and even a little with himself – he had deserved it, and yet he hated her a little bit for making him so aware of his own failings. Even so, his heart ached over the discovery that she had been the starling. Everything he had felt about *her*, every impulse of compassion and desire... and it had been Elizabeth. Her words of disdain for her brother were meant for him, and the cage she had alluded to was one she imagined him complicit in creating. If he had misjudged her, she had certainly done the same to him.

As he approached Bond Street, he saw Richard coming from the direction of Hanover Square with Jane on one arm and Lady Anne on the other.

"Brother!" Jane waved to him, and Richard steered the ladies toward Darcy.

As they approached, his mother's eyes went wide as she looked at Darcy's face. "William, what happened?"

He winced as his mother ran her fingers across his cheek. "Elizabeth struck me. I would rather not discuss it on a public thoroughfare."

Lady Anne was dumbfounded. "What?"

Jane looked panicked. "We were just going to see her. What happened?"

Richard narrowed his eyes at Darcy. "What did you do?"

"Richard!" Lady Anne swatted at him. "Oh dear, there must have been some terrible mistake. That is not like Lizzy!"

"I assure you there was," Darcy said.

"Well?" Richard gave him an expectant scowl.

"William, I want to know what this is about," his mother said, her voice calm but her face quite firm.

Darcy had no desire to discuss it in a public street, and as they were so near Grosvenor Square, he gestured with his walking stick and led them back the way he had come. He was quiet for a block or so, waiting until the crowd of Bond Street thinned out closer to the Square.

Finally he met their silent, seething dismay with an answer. "I went to speak with her about your offer, Mother – that Elizabeth come live with us. I thought to persuade her, to please you and Jane. There was a misunderstanding – about another matter – and we quarreled. She struck me, and what pains me most is that I believe I deserve it."

"Will you not say why you quarreled?"

"She may tell you, if she chooses. I have no wish to speak of it. I beg you would convey her my apologies."

Lady Anne's jaw set in a thin line. "I was going to see her myself to speak about her coming to stay with us, but I see it would be impossible now. Well, William, I had better go to my daughter now."

This was the angriest he had seen his mother since he had been a boy. Though she was too mild to display it in a more obvious way, he knew his cousin and sister were familiar enough with his mother's manners to perceive it as well – the posture of her shoulders, the hardness of her voice, the flare of her nostrils – though she appeared composed enough, inside she was clearly raging.

"We shall discuss it more another time," Darcy added lamely. "Richard? Might we take a walk?"

Richard had been looking at Jane with some concern, but his expression turned mutinous as he fixed his eyes on Darcy. "I had much rather go to Lizzy, and clean up your mess."

"Richard!" Lady Anne grimaced at Richard, and Jane looked at him pleadingly. "I wish you *would* come with us," said she. "Poor Lizzy, I am sure we can clear up the misunderstanding for her, Richard. She is so fond of you, and I know she trusts you."

Darcy closed his eyes as his sister twisted the knife in his heart. He knew she did not do it on purpose, but it stung nonetheless.

It was Darcy's turn to look beseechingly at Richard. "Let the ladies speak with her first; I am sure she is in quite a state – I... I know I did some damage, and I am sorry for it. But Richard, I would have a word with you. Please."

Richard regarded him evenly. "You wish to make your side of it known to me before I hear it from Elizabeth?"

"You make it sound so... unchivalrous...."

"No," Jane said, speaking up for him. "It is only fair. I am sure I shall hear why Lizzy was distressed enough to strike William, but William did not go to her with the intention of quarreling. I beg you would hear him, Cousin Richard."

Richard looked inquiringly at Jane for a moment. "If you wish it, I shall." He turned to Darcy. "Walk round Grosvenor Square with me, Darcy, and we can meander back to the library at Matlock House."

They parted ways with Jane and Lady Anne as the ladies continued up Brook Street, and Richard and Darcy headed around Grosvenor Square.

"Well?"

Darcy looked over at Richard. "She despises me."

"Forgive me, Cousin, but that is not precisely new information. I had thought you in a more pensive state – last night you questioned whether you deserve her recriminations, and Jane said you were of a mind to make amends."

"I admit I have been hard on her – I believe I have been rather prejudiced about her for many years; I assumed she would be more like the woman who has raised her. Yet even as I raised this point with her, she proved me justified in believing that it would be so."

"Darcy, your mother raised her, too."

"You know what I mean," Darcy snapped. "At any rate – I am *trying* to say I was wrong. I was wrong about her and I did not realize it until last night. She was the starling."

"Yes… your mother and sisters were birds together – bloody hell, Darcy, did you not know it at the time?"

Darcy sighed. "I did not. I… Richard, I flirted with her. I liked her. She did not recognize me either, and we said things to one another that we might never have spoken of, had either of us known…."

Richard clenched his jaw, his tone brusque. "I see. You *flirted* with her. And you believed she was flirting back? You developed… sentiments, of some sort, in the space of the dance, without learning enough about her to discover her true identity? Forgive me, but do you not hear how that sounds?"

Darcy bristled at Richard's hostility, beginning to recall his own distemper with his cousin. "Well, I did not kiss her on the balcony."

Richard glared at him. "What, are you demanding an explanation from me?"

"I daresay I hardly need one."

"I certainly do not owe you one. I should rather wonder if you are asking as her brother, or her lover?"

"That is out of line, Richard. She fled straight away from you, and I will tell you what else – when we were dancing together, she told me she came as a starling because she felt trapped. '*I can't get out,*' she said. '*I can't get out.*'"

Richard looked as though he had been struck, and stood silent for a moment, his expression grim. He sat down on a nearby bench along the square and let out a loud groan. "That is… difficult to hear, Darcy."

Darcy sat down beside his cousin. "Yes, well, I suppose now we both know what she thinks of us."

"Damn and blast," Richard breathed. "So, she was angry when she discovered that you had been her mysterious dance partner?"

"She was angry that I did not recognize her."

"That does not make sense – she was so determined to be mysterious about her costume. But truly, Cousin, I am sure we all thought you knew it was her. You did not figure out the three birds were your three sisters?"

"She is not my sister," Darcy replied automatically. "And no, I did not. What's more... well, I did not recognize her at Christmas, either. I walked into her house this morning and asked her if I could speak with her cousin Elizabeth."

"You thought she was *Rose*? But how?"

"They were inseparable all night, and I do not know... I thought she had short hair!"

"So, all this time that you have been judging her so severely, the remarks you have been making to me these two weeks about what a hoyden she seemed – you were judging her for the behavior of a sixteen year old girl?"

"Yes, and I feel like a damned fool."

"You are!" Richard shook his head, still clearly angry. "You thought so little of her, you did not even know her face, and then in one conversation and a dance at a ball, you flirt with her?"

"That is the sum of it, and then I walked in on *you* stealing a kiss," Darcy snapped.

"My name is on her list, Darcy. You are her brother."

"She despises that list. And do not think for a moment that I am not completely flummoxed by the sensations I experienced when her identity was unknown to me. It was by no means deliberate; I am deeply unsettled by it."

"As you well should be!"

"Because we are so very much brother and sister? I was away at school more often than not when she was at Pemberley. These seventeen years I must have spent no more than six weeks a year in her presence – she is a stranger to me. She is not like Jane and Mary, and you know it. I think your righteous contempt signifies other motives entirely."

"Well if it does, at least I have some right. She did promise to think on it, about us. Even after she danced with you Darcy, and after I kissed her, she still said she would think of us."

That was it, that was the absolute knife through his heart. It was too much – to have experienced the chagrin of feeling attraction to his sister, who was perhaps not his sister, but who clearly despised him, and to watch her kiss his cousin, to choose his cousin, his best friend.... Darcy had preferred simply despising her from afar. He abruptly rose from the bench. "I will leave you now – I have urgent matters to attend to."

***

Lady Anne found her daughter in the back garden, skirt tumbled about her legs as she sat on the soft, cold grass, weeping. Her head was buried in her arms, which were folded in front of her on a little stone bench, and she did not look up as Lady Anne and Jane approached.

"Oh, Lizzy, my poor girl." Anne rushed to her daughter's side and sat down on the bench. She pulled Elizabeth's head into her lap and ran her fingers through her daughter's disheveled hair. Jane crouched down beside Elizabeth, removing her shawl to wrap it around her sister. Jane said nothing, but peered up at Lady Anne with a look of agony; her lip trembled as if she would cry too.

As Lady Anne stroked her second daughter's hair, she could only wait until Elizabeth's shoulders ceased to shake with the force of her weeping; these were not the feeble tears of hurt feelings, but sobs of utter loss and despair. After all the misery that had befallen their family, she should know.

"Hush now, Lizzy," Anne whispered. "Hush now, dearest, Mamma is here and all shall be well. Come now, tell us all about it."

Elizabeth calmed herself, her sobs coming slower and softer until they had subsided enough for her to speak. She looked up at Anne, her face red and puffy, and she leaned into Jane's embrace, her body going limp against her sister as she buried her fingers in Anne's dress, seeking out her mother's hands.

"Oh Mamma," Elizabeth moaned.

"Tell me what has hurt you, my love. I saw William a few minutes ago."

Elizabeth's tears began again. "Did he tell you...."

"No, but he looked as though he had been struck across the face, and now I find you in such a state."

"I do not understand," Jane said softly. "I saw William at breakfast, and he wished to make amends. Lizzy, what happened?"

"It is too awful – too humiliating!" Elizabeth buried her face is Anne's skirts once more, her cries guttural and piteous.

"I shall not force you, my love," Anne said gently, "but I think it would do well for you to tell us. Let us help you, let us sort it all out."

It was some time before Elizabeth had collected herself once more. This time she drew back from her mother and sister, sitting up and wiping at her face as if resolved to weep no more. "Have you ever cried so much, so deeply and at such length, that you forget what upset you in the first place, and begin to feel as though you were weeping for absolutely everything that has ever caused you pain?"

Gentle tears had begun to pour down Jane's face as she took Elizabeth's hands in hers. "All the time, Sister."

"It is too horrible," Elizabeth groaned. "I am truly cursed."

Anne flinched. Though Lizzy had never spoken of it, she must have known. When she heard Edward and Phyllis speaking of the accident all those years ago, she must have heard of the curse too. Anne had convinced herself there was nothing in it – it was the lament of a dying woman, nothing more. But with every death in the family, every tragedy, Anne had thought of it, particularly when Lady Olivia had passed.

She sighed. "There is no curse, Lizzy," she willed herself to say. "There is only too much that has not been said in this family, and perhaps it is time to remedy that. Where is your uncle, my love?"

"He left me," Elizabeth whimpered. "William came to speak to me, and he left me and did not come back, not even when...."

"When you quarreled with William?"

Elizabeth nodded feebly. "He must have heard the shouting, but he did not come. I suppose I have displeased him."

"Oh, Lizzy, I do not understand," Jane sighed. "I am sure William had the best of intentions – I do not blame you, but there must have been some great misunderstanding."

"Indeed there was! He did not even know me, Jane. He spoke pleasantly with me for the first time in I cannot remember how long, and then asked to see Elizabeth. He thought I was Rose!"

"He thought you were Rose!"

"And when he learned it was me, he said such awful things – oh, I said such awful things! I was so angry at him for not knowing me, and so miserable already, because of – oh, but I cannot tell you."

"I do not understand," Jane said. "How could he not have known you? The two of you seemed to get on well enough last evening – you look very well pleased with one another after your dance, and I thought for sure that you were very nearly reconciled already."

Anne shifted uncomfortably on the bench, still holding onto one of Elizabeth's hands. Their dance together last evening – it had certainly given her pause. Henry approached her just before she left and said that Elizabeth had asked for Darcy to be added to her list of possible suitors, and it had given Anne such confusion that she could scarcely sleep that night.

Anne let out a shaky breath. As fractured as things had been in their family at various times over the last several years, she suddenly felt this was the breaking point for her, and she could bear it no longer. "Lizzy, where is your uncle now?"

"In his study, I suppose. He is always there this time of day, if he is at home."

"I should like to speak with him at once. Go inside and warm yourself by the fire, my dear. Whatever has happened, you need not be embarrassed; you must speak to your sister, for I know Jane is eager to help. Can you do this for us, Lizzy?"

Jane stood first and helped Elizabeth to her feet. "Shall we go in, Lizzy?" Elizabeth stared blankly at them for a moment before nodding and standing up, and Anne watched with a sad smile as her two girls walked hand in hand into the house.

Sir Edward was in his study, just as Elizabeth said he would be, seated not at his desk but in a chair by the window, staring out onto the street. "Edward," Anne said, knocking on the door even as she entered. "William was just here – did you know it? He and Elizabeth quarreled."

"Yes, I know of it," he said sadly.

"They had quite a row – how could you abandon her at such a time?"

"I did not expect them to become so overwrought," he sighed, his voice numb. "I thought he meant to make amends – that was his claim. Eventually, I heard raised voices and came to see what it was all about. I was in the corridor, nearly on the point of entering the room, when I heard Elizabeth say – oh, Anne, I could not face her. I am a bloody coward, a useless old fool."

"You are not, Edward. You are a man just out of mourning, and your difficulties have been many." Anne wished to console her old friend, yet Elizabeth must be her priority, and Edward had let their girl down. "I have always been so fond of you, Edward, and it once pleased me to know that Lizzy gave you comfort, but at what cost? She is beside herself weeping and you would just hide in here? Is this what her life has been these seven years?"

Edward closed his eyes and let out a heavy breath. "She told William I was a disappointment to her – that the men in this family have let her down, that we have all been blind and useless. I daresay she is right. Through my own actions I have taught her to wallow in melancholy, and to expect the worst in others. Henry has shown her that the feelings of the adults matter more than the children, and though he may now have the only happy marriage in the family, he cannot expect *that* to solve Lizzy's problems. He cannot orchestrate a parade of the most tedious bachelors of the ton, in order to present Richard in a favorable light, and I can only wonder that Richard would stand for such a thing. I know nothing of her quarrel with William, and yet I am sure she was quite right about us all. We have used her so very ill these many years, and now I suppose the time has come for our reckoning."

Anne felt a tear slide down her cheek. "I daresay we have all failed her, and each other. I know little of what has transpired, but... I am very worried."

"You are right to believe it is all my doing," he said, looking ten years older as he stared ruefully at her.

"I do not believe that, Edward. You did not set out to do harm."

"But harm was done."

"Yes," she warily agreed. "Great harm, I believe. As you say, we are all complicit, you and Henry and even me. Lizzy does not even know William, nor he her. He came here today and mistook Elizabeth for Rose – these two weeks he has not even known his own sister, and Elizabeth is devastated. It is all because such distance has grown between us."

"They have been separated so long," he said with a shake of his head.

"Yes, and we allowed it. We have both of us allowed our own feelings to keep us apart, hidden away in our grief, and Elizabeth has paid the price. She did not even know William last night, Edward, and after dancing with him she told Henry that she wished him added to her list of suitors. She is humiliated."

Edward raised his eyebrows with apparent alarm. "I did not know – Henry said nothing to me."

Anne shook her head, unsure of where to direct her mounting frustration. "I suppose that is the problem. There is no conversation, no understanding at all in this family. Lizzy still feels everything so deeply and we stand by, doing nothing about it. If you could have seen her, heard her...."

"I ought to see it, I ought to be made to see what damage I have caused."

"Edward, please. I do not try to wound you. Can you not see, it is not about us – it has never been about us. Lizzy is hurting." As Anne began to weep, Edward came over to her and perched beside her on the edge of his desk, offering her another of his handkerchiefs. "I shall grow quite a collection of these," she said, dabbing at her eyes.

"There was a time when our friendship made you smile."

"It may yet still. Oh, help me, Edward, I beg you would help me. I cannot do it alone – I do not even know what I am to do, but I would cut out my heart if it meant healing Elizabeth's."

Edward reached out and took Anne's hand. "We shall make it right, my old friend." He gave her hand a lingering squeeze and then moved around to the side of his desk and took out a sheet of paper. He reached decisively for his pen and began to write. "I am sending word to Matlock House – as of this moment you and I are taking control of Elizabeth's well-being, and her future – we are taking the active interest that I ought to have done years ago, and together we shall make it all well." He looked up, smiling sadly. "I promise you, Anne, I shall make this right. For you, and for Lizzy, I shall begin to exert myself."

***

Elizabeth followed her sister indoors and they settled themselves in the music room, as Elizabeth could not bear the sight of the front parlor

161

at present. She drew her shawl around herself and curled up on an armchair, her mind almost numb from the purgative cry she had indulged in.

"You look a thousand miles away, Lizzy," Jane said as she settled on a sofa nearby.

"No, I am still here," Elizabeth sighed.

"Will you tell me what happened?"

Elizabeth looked skeptically at her sister. She was still rebuilding her trust in Jane, who was Williams's champion. "I think perhaps you will be angry with me."

"No, I... I shall not defend William if you do not wish to hear it. He was in such a state when we met with him – I have never seen him so angry, and I cannot imagine how dreadful it was for you to speak with him in such a state. I think he upset you a great deal."

Elizabeth considered. Jane had said she had no wish to be shielded from the truth; this would certainly test her resolve. "Oh Jane, it was so horrible. The worst part was, when he thought I was Rose, he was actually pleasant to me."

"I cannot believe he mistook you."

"It was mortifying. And then, as soon as he learned who I am, he became so churlish, casting the worst sort of aspersions at me and... and then I did the same to him, because I wanted him to feel just as hurt as myself."

Jane furrowed her brow, her eyes moist with tears, and her countenance all tender dismay and sympathy. "What did he say?"

"That my anger at him would wound Mamma, and that he cares so much about you all and your happiness that he would put aside his justifiable prejudices against me and *allow* me into his home. It was beyond the pale, Jane. He refused to apologize for anything, despite his claim that he wished to make amends. – he only gave offense! Jane, he called me a petulant little brat."

Jane's eyes went wide with surprise. "Oh no! Oh, Lizzy, I am so sorry. What did you say to him?"

"A great many cruel things. I said that I had no I wish to call him Brother, as he has been a terrible one to you, and that he and all the men in our family have disappointed me. I called him a selfish, boorish brute – again – and manipulative and unfeeling, and... I said that he caused George Wickham's death."

"Oh." Jane's expression crumpled, and a few tears slid down her cheek. "Oh my, Lizzy. Even at my lowest, my most forlorn, I could never had said such things to William." She was quiet a moment before meeting Elizabeth's eye, and her voice was barely audible as she said, "I *did* think it, though."

"Do you blame me, Jane? I ought to have kept such thoughts to myself, as you have done...."

Jane shook her head. "I have no answers for you, Lizzy. It is done, and your words cannot be unsaid. I am only so very shocked. You and he seemed to be getting on well when you danced together last night."

Elizabeth groaned. "I did not know it was him."

"Oh. Who did your think he was?"

Elizabeth could not bear to tell her sister the whole truth, even after Jane's small but shattering confession. Her own actions this morning had been shameful enough, losing her temper as she had – she need not add to her humiliation by making it known to all her family what she had felt the night before. She had actually been *attracted* to him, and had been open and honest with him. She had dared to hope she might have met a man who could change her mind about his entire sex, and all along it had been a man she despised. When she had heard him speak of the starling, her heart had broken just a little bit, as if until that moment she had never known herself.

"I thought he was a stranger," Elizabeth said – it was not untrue. "In fact, we had a pleasant conversation."

"And he did not know you either?"

"No. Nor this morning when he saw my *whole face*. He does not know me at all Jane, and I do not think I hold him in enough esteem to wish it otherwise."

"I am so sorry to hear you say so."

"I know, Jane, but it is the truth. We got along so well as strangers, but as soon as he knew me for myself, his sense of superiority and judgement instantly returned. He proved my point, that he is prejudiced against me – he even admitted it!"

Jane nodded sadly. "Oh, Lizzy, it must be true."

"It is, Jane."

"I do not understand him. This morning at breakfast he spoke of wanting my happiness, of wanting to make sure I did not feel caged...."

"That was true? He really asked you that?"

"Yes. I thought it so odd. But he does care about my happiness, and he seemed really resolved to ask you to stay at Darcy House. He said that you are confident and converse easily with others, and that I might learn this from you, as you learn sweetness from me."

Elizabeth grimaced. "He thinks I am confident... and rude?"

"Oh, I am sure that is not what he meant."

"How can it be otherwise? I told you what he said about me!"

Jane chewed her lip. "He was wrong to say such things. I can see why you struck him! Oh, Lizzy, I think that I am beginning to feel rather angry at him, and I have never been cross with William before."

Elizabeth suppressed a triumphant smile. "Thank you for understanding, Jane."

"I do wish to try, Lizzy. You have been through so much, and you and I and Mary and Mamma are trying so hard to be a real family again. But William – he came with the intention of making amends with you and has insulted you in every possible way. Richard has gone to speak with him, but I cannot imagine how he could defend the great disparity in his actions and his intentions! I am so disappointed in him!"

Elizabeth now found herself obliged to comfort Jane, but it was rather sweet that Jane was such a gentle creature as to be so affected.

"Lizzy, when you said you were disappointed with all the men of our family...."

"I did not mean Papa!"

"Oh, I know. You meant our uncles?"

"Yes, and even... even Richard, too."

"Really? But you are so close!"

"We are close. Richard has always been so kind to me. But I believe you can love someone very much, and still let them down."

"Like you and I," Jane said, lacing her fingers through Elizabeth's.

"Not anymore," Elizabeth replied, meeting her sister's eye. "Last night was awful. Uncle Henry pressing those awful suitors at us – he filled half of my dance card as soon as I arrived, and when I turned to Uncle Edward for help, he did nothing about it. Just his usual shrug of resignation, as it has ever been. I know he is only just out of mourning, but he is so like a ghost. It broke my heart that he did not stand up for me, not last night when we arrived, not later in the night when I grew so distraught, and not this morning when William and I quarreled. Ought he not to have told William off for speaking to me in such a way?"

"I am sure Uncle Henry would call him out, if William ever spoke to Charlotte in such a way!"

Elizabeth felt a rush of vindication and smiled at her sister.

"You said you grew distraught later in the evening – what happened?"

Elizabeth looked away and shook her head. She could not tell Jane of the foolish disappointment she had felt at the handsome knight failing to appear for their second set, nor the wild confusion she felt at realizing the knight had been William. "I cannot imagine why Uncle Henry should wish to push me at such dreadful gentlemen," Elizabeth huffed, trying to turn the subject. "Perhaps he means to make his son look like the best option for me."

"*Richard?*"

"Uncle Henry suggested it just before you came to London. I was shocked – I had never imagined such a thing."

"Does Richard desire it?"

"He says he has considered it and has asked me to do the same, but I cannot. The idea of making such a match is insupportable to me."

Jane gave Elizabeth a gentle smile. "You cannot love him?"

"I do not think I can love anybody in that way," Elizabeth groaned. And then she thought of the handsome knight again – the hope she had briefly felt, only to have it dashed as she looked up into William's eyes that morning. "Perhaps I might have thought… but I cannot force it. I will not."

Jane leaned her head on Elizabeth's shoulder, wrapping both of her hands around Elizabeth's. "Oh, Lizzy," she sighed. "It is a pity about Richard – that is, I am very sorry for you both…. I do know what you mean about not wishing to force what does not come naturally."

"Oh, Jane," Elizabeth sighed. "Wretched as I am, at least we understand one another at last."

***

That evening, the Earl of Matlock answered the curious summons of his old friend and brother-in-law, bringing Lady Phyllis, Richard, and Charlotte to Upper Brook Street with him for dinner. It was no ordinary family meal – indeed, Lady Anne and Sir Edward were united in insisting that not one morsel of food would be served until they had all come to some sort of understanding within the family.

Rose was relegated to a tray in her room, and Charlotte volunteered to keep her company upstairs, lest the child be tempted to intervene in what must be a serious family discussion.

Elizabeth sat numbly through it all, her vehement emotions all spent. She felt only a mild pang in her heart when William did not arrive with her mother and sisters, and a distant, vague apprehension at Richard's proximity when he came and sat near them.

Though the earl and countess, Lady Anne, and Sir Edward spoke a great deal, there was little that any of them could say to Elizabeth that could bring her comfort at such a time, little for them to chastise themselves for that she has not already thought to herself, and little that they could promise which would undo the years of emotional anguish that had exploded out of her that morning.

Lady Anne and Uncle Edward were firmer than they had ever been with the earl, and in the end the stalwart pair carried their point; Elizabeth would remove to Darcy House, and would be released from the earl's matrimonial schemes, however well intended.

Throughout the lengthy discussion, Elizabeth's attention was all for her letter; William had been gone when their mother and Jane returned to Darcy House that morning, and he had left behind one note for Lady

Anne, and one for Elizabeth. She ran her fingers idly over the paper, reading it over and over to herself as the rest of her family argued about how to behave as one.

Dear Elizabeth, for dear to me I believe you must be,

I write you this letter after some hours of reflection, some conversation with Mary – who was cross with you last evening, and is now doubly so with me – and several crumpled drafts lying at my feet.

I must begin by apologizing for my behavior these past weeks – but no, I must go further back than that. You said I knew nothing of your reasons for leaving Pemberley, and the truth in that is that I knew nothing of you at all, or even Jane and Mary at the time. I was a young man more concerned with my studies and my friends at Cambridge, and that must be my paltry excuse. By the time I had my eyes opened to the fact that I needed to be a better brother, it was too late for me to bestow upon you the same consideration, or so I believed.

As to your assertion that I hold you in contempt because of your defense of Lady Olivia – this I cannot deny, but I am resolved to rid myself of the notion that you were unable to love her without being tainted by her sins. It is strange, but when I thought you to be Rose, I rather admired your poise, wit, and grace, thinking you a far better woman than Lady Olivia.

It has been jarring to realize that I had held you in such high esteem without realizing it. Even last night at the ball, I gave credit to all your assertions when we spoke during our dance. Not only did I instantly find myself at ease with your candor and manner of expressing yourself, I was moved by all that you told me – I felt a protective instinct over you, as a mere stranger, that I had not allowed myself to extend to you, Elizabeth.

You may imagine my shock and dismay at discovering that you were the starling that had captivated me, had moved me with the bleak description of a such a hostile brother. That the man you believed would scorn you for merely enjoying yourself has caused me more pain than anything you said to me this morning.

I am mortified at how I have deserved it. What did you say of me that is not true? What are you feeling that is not wholly justified by my actions, and my ignorance of your character and worth? My thoughts have all been for our mother and sisters, their pain at losing you, and the other losses we have suffered over the years. Until this morning I had never troubled myself to acknowledge that you have felt it all, just as we have, and perhaps most of all.

I am bound for Pemberley this very hour, and I would say only that whether you ever choose to call Darcy House home again, I hope my absence in London might help to untwist some of the wires around your cage. God bless you.

Fitzwilliam Darcy

13

❧

Darcy House, London
17 January, 1812

Dear William,

I have been at Darcy House a week today and I can go no longer without answering your letter. It is not your absence from London that has made this time more bearable for me, so much as the efforts of Jane, Mary, Mamma, and my uncles. I confess I was not optimistic when Uncle Edward called all the family together, but it seems that he and Mamma are very serious about behaving like a proper family. All is well at Darcy House, though I know that Mamma, Jane, and Mary wish you would come back to London.

Despite our tranquility here at Darcy House, Richard and Uncle Henry have had a row, and Richard says he will be following you to Derbyshire ere long. I hope you and he shall lift one another's spirits at Pemberley. I find myself worrying about you; it feels strange to be at Darcy House, knowing I have driven you out of it. I know not whether it pleases me or pains me to know that you have been as hard on yourself as I have been on myself these ten days, but I hope you will be content at Pemberley.

I accept your apology, on the condition that you likewise accept mine. I cannot reflect with satisfaction on how I spoke to you that morning at my uncle's house, nor how I behaved myself. Your letter has given me some heart, for I believe you meant it sincerely, and thus I must show you equal sentiment.

I left Pemberley seven years ago because I did not fully understand my place in this world, or this family. I overheard a very serious conversation and misunderstood the particulars of what happened on the day of the carriage accident – in short, I came to believe that I was responsible for it, and that our family had been cursed as a result of it. I felt myself unworthy to take the Darcy name, which had just been offered to us – unworthy of anything from the Darcys. My uncle allowed me to be governed by my unchecked, juvenile emotions. I do not blame him; I have always known that he needed me, and it pains me to think that I could almost regret the choice I made, which brought him so much comfort.

Only Richard and Charlotte knew of my despair – and the adults – Jane has only just learned of it, and Mary has never asked me for any explanation. It has been a burden I have remained perversely determined to carry with me all these years, but I shall let it bind my heart no more. What I am attempting to say is that my behavior toward you, both at the ball and the morning after, was simply the inevitable boiling over of so many years of strife in our family. That you did not know me cemented my conviction that you did not want me, that my position in this family is as precarious as I feared.

I have examined my own actions, my own heart, and the anger I showed you is a mere veil covering a devastating need for acceptance. You said at the ball you have two sisters; imagine what I felt on discovering it was you who spoke those words. I have wielded my dislike and distrust of you as a shield, and it has not served me well, for I have still been wounded. I have been determined to refute the idea that I might actually desire your good opinion, and knowing that I only ever had it when you did not know me has been a difficult discovery, but I am willing to forgive everything if you are in earnest.

I hope you will write soon, and that we might be friends.

Elizabeth Bennet

***

Pemberley, Derbyshire
23 January, 1812

Dear Elizabeth,

Thank you for your letter. I received a packet from Jane, Mary, and our mother a few days ahead of your letter, and was disappointed not to find anything from you. Having now received your letter and read it several times through, I can see you must have put considerable time and thought into it, and I can only thank you for having the generosity to believe that I am worth the effort.

As you have so graciously accepted my apology, I can do no less for you. I have spent the better part of the last fortnight thinking over my own shame; to own the truth, it is not a thing I have ever done to such a degree in the whole course of my life, and therefore very long overdue.

Despite the rancor of our argument, I believe I was already aware of my own boorishness as soon as I left your uncle's house, and though my apology was sincere, I have since then wallowed in a rather selfish style of repentance, chiefly occupied by the dismay of having made such a fool of myself. I have begun a more fruitful manner of introspection, and I hope you would be proud to know that it is all your doing.

I often think of my conversation with the starling – that is, the Elizabeth I was able to speak so easily with. The minute our dance had ended, I desired to already be speaking with that woman again, and I am wishing every day for such conversation. Is that not strange that I saw you more clearly through your mask, than I ever have before?

I hope we might reach such an understanding again, and I fear I have expressed myself rather poorly by suggesting that it would only be for the benefit of our family; I wish for myself that we might be friends, as you say. As it was when we were masked, while I am at such a distance in my self-imposed exile, I am able to say to you what I truly think and feel.

It was brave of you to tell me why you left Pemberley, and I only wish I had known sooner. Richard arrived at Pemberley this morning, and has told me how he came to know of it so long ago. Dearest Elizabeth, how I wish I had been the one to speak with you that day, to allay your fear and guilt. It breaks my heart to think of you carrying such a burden, and I believe I must join the rest of our family in reminding you that it was not your fault – you were an innocent. You are not cursed, not unless you choose to persist in believing that you are. To know that you have carried such a burden for these seven years, when I might have prevented it merely by being a more attentive brother from the beginning – I cannot express the pain I feel at my own part in your distress.

I hope by now you have made amends with Mary, for though she was cross with you at the ball, she has long been your champion; last autumn at Pemberley she was so determined we should all be a family again, and after all her years of reading us your letters and singing your praises to us, I cannot bear for you two to be at odds now.

Richard is waiting in the doorway, now – he bids me send you his regards, and to tell Mrs. Reynolds that he has wheedled her gooseberry tart recipe from my cook to give to his own. I shall write you more when I have flogged him for his insolence, and gotten through the dinner – even now he is reminding me of the myriad matters we must discuss.

For now,
Fitzwilliam Darcy

Postscript,
I shall have to delay the sending of this missive a few days yet, but the recompense shall be in the delivery, for Richard means to return to London the day after next. I would ask you for a favor, that you keep an eye on Richard when he returns. He is in low spirits, and though he would confess to nothing, I suspect him of being rather lovelorn. I have my suspicions, but I leave it to your judgement, which I shall own is rather superior. I should wish to hear anything you choose to share of your time in London, as I shall be very dull at Pemberley,

with only matters of business to occupy my time, and perhaps the library.

***

Darcy House, London
1 February, 1812

Dear William,

I beg you would not seek to assuage my guilt by taking any of it on yourself. I think it unfair for you to blame yourself for not being the one to offer me comfort when I learned the details of the accident, though the sentiment is generous. I believe you are growing into quite a philosopher at Pemberley, and I shall decorate the margins of this letter with some small sketches of how I imagine your ponderous pose, like the Greeks of old.

You may also imagine my chagrin, after such shocking speeches as I have made about you, to discover you possess such hidden depths. We are to be friends, and I cannot tell you how it pleases me. There is much truth in what you wrote last, that just as I spoke so candidly to you from behind the mask, I might do likewise in a letter. Like you, I have thought nearly daily of that night, of our dance together, and even of our brief conversation at Christmas, when you thought I was Rose. You thought Rose was me, because you saw only what you expected to see, and when we danced together I suppose neither of us expected we might ever speak so openly.

I must mention Richard, for I have done as you asked in observing him. I took a different meaning from the request when first I read it; he has been a caller daily at Darcy House, and I have begun to wonder just what you were asking. In truth, I suspect some partiality between Jane and Richard. I suppose it must not be what you wish to hear, as I know you desired Jane should prefer Mr. Bingley. I beg you would not mention it to anyone just yet – it is a new development, and even Jane herself seems unaware of it. I have seen the looks they exchange, and I can only hope you would approve.

I have had some opportunity to observe Jane with Mr. Bingley as well, these three weeks. William, she is quite at a loss to keep up with his boundless energy, despite her being genuinely happier than she has been in so long. She is doing well, and I believe her time in London has lifted her spirits already, but she shall never be so gregarious or optimistic as Mr. Bingley – though I suspect he might know another lady who is.

Mr. Bingley has been a frequent guest at Darcy House since my coming here, and he is often bringing his mother and sister, as well as his friend, my cousin Collins. Though Mr. Collins's company is very agreeable, Mrs. and Miss Bingley are not my favorite acquaintances. I am winking at you from afar, for surely you must know me capable of saying far worse, but I am determined to exercise some restraint, and leave the full extent of their churlishness to your imagination.

On the subject of disagreeable mothers and daughters – forgive me – I must mention our Aunt Catherine and Cousin Anne. They were very cross with you for leaving London so suddenly, and I take the liberty of disparaging them just a little, because I know Lady Catherine vowed to write you, and I am so very curious – I imagine she was so severe! Poor Cousin John! He begins to fear Cousin Anne will begin to think of him, a fate he deems worse than the admiration of Miss Bingley!

Do write again soon, if you can bear my impudence. Until then, I shall be shamelessly enjoying some gooseberry tarts!

Elizabeth

***

Pemberley, Derbyshire
9 February, 1812

Dear Elizabeth,

Thank you for your last letter. You have confirmed a suspicion I have held since Richard's visit, and you need not fear I shall interfere – I am pleased to hear of it from you, for I have received far more discreet accounts from Mother and Jane. I shall keep my knowledge a secret for now, with a hope that you will keep me abreast of any further developments.

I confess I had once believed Richard's interest to lie elsewhere, and had genuinely thought Bingley a good match for Jane, but someone I admire very dearly has inspired me to leave it be. Jane was cross with me after I left London, but the tone of her letters has grown more cheerful, and I do wish for her happiness, even if she does not find it in the way I had wished. I would, of course, wish the same for Bingley, and for you, Elizabeth.

As to the letter from Aunt Catherine, I am torn between my wish to satisfy your curiosity, and proper decorum – the letter was harsh, unsurprising, and upon reading it I was embarrassed on her behalf. She seeks to press me into making an offer I could never desire, arousing false jealousy by mentioning Cousin John, though I cannot imagine that should John truly wish to make Anne his viscountess, Aunt Catherine would still think me a better prospect.

I am much occupied in estate matters – and, yes, the reading of some philosophy in the very postures your amusing drawings depicted. Being separated from my family is rendered more bearable not only by the satisfaction of my own productivity here, but in looking forward to your letters. I imagine all the ladies I hold dear, so happily ensconced in Darcy House, breathing life

into the place after so long. It is just what I would wish.
I look forward to your next.

William

***

Darcy House, London
14 February, 1812

Dear William,

It is kind of you to anticipate my letters as eagerly as I await yours. And how much I have to write!

Things are progressing well with Richard and Jane — I shall not betray any confidences, but if you are indeed in favor of the notion, I think you need not fear being disappointed. You were not incorrect in suspecting Richard's interests once lay elsewhere, but they have taken a turn, to everyone's satisfaction — and relief!

Our Uncle Henry has relented a great deal in his matrimonial designs for us all, and though I have come to understand his motives better, I am still relieved that he has taken a more laissez faire approach. Poor Uncle Henry — I think Mamma and our lady grandmother have rather given him the business about his desire to see us all wed, and he has promised not to force anything — much to Aunt Catherine's dismay! She only calls at Darcy House to press for news of you, and Cousin Anne is far from pleasant on such occasions. She has made the connection between my presence at Darcy House, and your absence. I think she means to punish me with her haughty incivility, but she fails to realize how well I like to laugh at human folly.

The Bingleys and Mr. Collins continue calling often on us, and we are quite as snug as you might imagine. Miss Bingley is making significant progress toward capturing John's... heart? I must admit it has made her vastly more pleasant company. I had supposed her cool civility toward me to result from her awareness of my falling out with Jane years ago, but I think I have grown enough these last several weeks to admit to a change in my opinion of her.

Her mother is a different case entirely. Mrs. Bingley, we have discovered, is an old acquaintance of my Uncle Edward's, and though he is on affable terms with her, Mamma dislikes her tremendously and will say nothing about it to us. Perhaps you might pay me back in kind, and attempt to discover the truth?

Uncle has another most unexpected admirer — Mr. Collins! Cousin Will has been so attentive to us all, but I have begun to tease him that he comes to

Darcy House only hoping for a chance to see my uncle, for they are often speaking together to the exclusion of everyone else! They speak of business – Miss Bingley thinks it very odious! – and even our lady grandmother declared it quite infamous when Cousin Will declared he should like the life of a merchant over that of a landowner. She still teases Uncle – her 'old beau' – and I think ere long she will have a new follower in Cousin Will.

I wonder if you have had any letters from Mr. Bingley since you went away? Cousin Will has told Mr. Bingley of an estate near his own, and though Mr. Bingley is most interested in the prospect of Netherfield Park, he says he shall not act until you can advise him on the matter. He seemed not to know when you shall return, but none of us really know your plans.

I hope whatever occupies your days is pleasant enough. I had intended, on speculating that you had become a philosopher, resolved to begin reading some weighty tomes myself, but alas, Mary has been plying me with novels that we might discuss them together. She has always been a bluestocking, but now she is a romantic besides! We shall begin Udolpho next week, though Charlotte has told me already what lies behind the black veil, and I gave her quite a pinch for it.

Your novel-frenzied friend,
Elizabeth

***

Pemberley, Derbyshire
20 February, 1812

Dear Elizabeth,

Your last letter was a balm to my spirits. I confess I have put aside my philosophical tomes for a reading of A Sentimental Journey, *and certain passages have drawn me into such a pensive reverie. I hope I am right inferring from your letters that my beautiful starling no longer feels trapped in her cage.*

To hear that you are happy at Darcy House, to imagine my dear ladies so flooded with happy visitors warms my heart, and assures me that I have done right in returning to Pemberley for some weeks of personal reflection. In truth, I ache at the thought that I might never have been out onto such a path of self-improvement, were it not for the pain I caused you, and though I regret our quarrel, I find myself grateful at how my eyes have been opened.

I must apologize for our cousin Anne's behavior toward you. However she came to the conclusion that you are to blame for my absence, I hope I have made it clear to all of our family that it was my own conduct that drove me to Pemberley. I cannot give you any firm answer as to when I might return, for it depends upon a matter of some delicacy. I am content enough to pass my days visiting the tenants and their families, surveying the estate and grounds on horseback, and attempting to be a dedicated master of Pemberley as my father was.

Until I return, I hope you will continue delighting me with your letters.

William

***

Darcy House, London
26 February, 1812

Dear William,

I have crumpled up half a dozen letters to you this morning. I fear I may disappoint, for though I have much to say about our friends and our family, and should wish to indulge your request of a delightful letter, I have not the spirit to put anything to paper.

We are happy enough, to be sure, but it is not the same at all, telling you of all our happy times together, when you are not here to enjoy it all with us. I know not what delicate matter keeps you away, nor have I any right to ask, but I do wish you would come home. I know I am not alone in such a wish, though I am a selfish creature and ask only for my own sake, and yours.

Mamma and Jane and Mary will likely be writing to you soon, for John has made Miss Bingley an offer, and we are all in uproar. Lady Catherine has been in high dudgeon, and used some language to Mrs. Bingley that was at once quite shocking, and marvelously impressive – yet another sight I wish you were here to see, for I am sure we should all be laughing together.

But I must leave it for now, for the thought of describing such merriment to you while you remain in your self-imposed exile begins to give me pain, and I fear I might be paining you as well. I shall leave off for now, and attempt a more diverting letter another time.

Until then I remain your unfettered starling,

Elizabeth

14

❦

Lady Anne Darcy sighed to herself as she took a seat in her brother's drawing room. The dinner to celebrate John's engagement was a grand affair, and she had done her best to compliment Lady Phyllis's elegant arrangements, and to be of good cheer for her daughters' sake, but inside she was miserable.

She was happy for John and Miss Bingley, to be sure. She knew his first marriage had not been for love, but she believed he might have found it this time. Caroline Bingley was a good sort of girl – a little haughty for a tradesman's daughter, but ambitious and clever enough to take on the role of countess someday with aplomb.

Miss Bingley had been a friend to Jane when she needed one the most, which endeared her to Anne. Indeed, Anne had once thought her a pretty, bright enough creature to turn William's head, and though Miss Bingley had seemed keen for a brief time, her head had been turned by John years ago. Anne could not think her mercenary; she respected the fact that Miss Bingley had not tried to catch William's eye after her hopes with John were disappointed. And it had all worked out nicely – except for the late Lucy Fitzwilliam.

Anne hung back, letting Lady Phyllis and Charlotte take the lead in becoming acquainted with Miss Bingley while the gentlemen tarried over their brandy and cigars. It was charming, seeing Caroline so readily accepted into their family; it was only the mother, Mrs. Bingley, who gave Anne discomfort.

She looked up with a smile as her mother approached, strutting in her usual confident way with her walking stick. "Ah, my dear, how wretched you look tonight," Lady Eleanor whispered as she sat down on the sofa beside Anne.

"I am well, Mamma. I believe Caroline will be good for John."

"I never suspected you of sulking all night because of *that*. If you had disapproved of the match, you might have simply not attended, just as Catherine and her daughter."

176

"I was no supporter of Catherine's designs in that direction," Anne said softly. She had never favored Catherine's desire for a match between her daughter and William, either, but neither could she support the idea of such a thing for John. They each deserved love, beyond what Anne de Bourgh could give them.

"What is it, then? I was too far down the table to speak with you, but you looked so glum at dinner, my dear. But of course, you must be missing William."

It was not uncommon for him to be away – when they were all at Pemberley, William would occasionally attend house parties in the area, or visit friends from Cambridge. "I do miss him of course, but he wished me to spend some time with the girls all together, and it is sweet of him to want that for us – I hope I am making the most of it."

Lady Eleanor glanced over at the girls, and Elizabeth caught their eye and smiled widely. "She has always adored you, Anne. It is good to see her looking happy. I gather it is the work of William's absence?"

Anne looked warily at her mother, wondering how much she knew. "I do not think she takes any satisfaction in it. They have been exchanging letters and I think they are beginning to find their footing with one another. I am resolved to give it a few weeks more, and then write to him to beg his return."

"Well, if it is not his absence that has you down, pray tell me what is the matter."

Anne looked down and wrung her hands in her lap. "It is Mrs. Bingley," she breathed. "Seeing her and Edward... it is so strange, after all these years. Surely you know... Madeline Bingley was once Madeline Fisher, the young lady who broke Edward's heart all those years ago. The woman who Lizzy believes inspired her mother's curse."

Lady Eleanor began to mutter some rather indelicate things, and someone gasped – Anne looked up to see Lizzy on her way to speak to them – she had frozen in her tracks, and then she abruptly quit the room.

***

Elizabeth nearly collided with seven smoky-smelling gentlemen as she hurried down the corridor, and Richard caught her by the shoulder as she moved past. "Lizzy, are you unwell?"

"No. I only needed some air," Elizabeth snapped, folding her arms and glaring at the floor.

"Shall I ring for the carriage, dear? I can take you back to Darcy House early, if your mother is not ready to depart," Uncle Edward said.

She knew she ought to appreciate the gesture, but she only glowered at him. "I should hate to tear you away from Madeline Fisher's company. How could you not tell me?"

Uncle Edward sputtered with indignation. Richard linked his arm through Elizabeth's and began to lead her down the corridor. "Come, let us get you some air."

Elizabeth resisted only a little, for the sake of her dignity, before she allowed Richard to steer her out to the garden, but in her high temper she continued to glare at him.

"I am not going to kiss you again, if that is what you fear," Richard chided her as they stepped outside.

"I know."

"I still owe you an apology for that, actually."

"*I know.*"

Richard laughed. "Well, I *am* sorry, Lizzy. I do not know what came over me – I did not know what my father was about, pushing you at all those dreadful specimens. I wanted to protect you and... and to own the truth, it felt safer than following my heart."

"Oh."

"You may speak your mind – I assure you, Darcy has already given me the business for it, so you may say what you will."

"Does William know about it?"

"He saw it and confronted me the next day, after you quarreled with him."

"Oh." Elizabeth could scarcely formulate an appropriate reply. "Does Jane know?"

"I thought it right to be honest, after all she has confided in me about Wickham."

"Well... good. I am glad you have been open with one another." Elizabeth sighed and sat down on a bench just under the sconce on the outer wall, and Richard sat down next to her.

"I am sorry, Lizzy. I have gone on about myself, when I meant to ask you what that was just now between you and Sir Edward."

"Oh – oh, Richard," she sighed, feeling entirely overwhelmed. "Mamma said that Mrs. Bingley is the lady who broke Uncle's heart, the woman my mother cursed on her deathbed."

"Oh. That is... unexpected."

"It is terrible! How can he bear to see her?"

"He must be civil to her; her daughter is marrying into this family, and her son may yet as well."

"She would certainly like that! Mr. Bingley turned his eye from Jane to Mary as soon as you returned to London, and yet Mrs. Bingley would push him at me! It is so odd. I have never quite trusted her, and now I know why."

"I should say I know why," Richard laughed. "You are a lovely creature with a handsome dowry."

"The same could be said of my sisters!"

Richard looked askance at her. "Do you really not know?"

"Know what?"

"Lizzy, what are your sisters' portions?"

"The same as mine. Ten thousand each from the Darcys, and the same from Uncle Edward."

He shook his head. "You, Lizzy, have *twenty* from Sir Edward."

Elizabeth was stunned. "I do not know what to say. I have more than my sisters? I cannot like it."

"Mr. Bingley has piles of money; it will not be why he makes his choice, and neither of your sisters deserve a man who would be daunted by them having less than you."

"I hope you will not be," Elizabeth said, and then clapped a hand over her mouth. "I am sorry. That was...."

"Well-deserved, I daresay. No, I shall not be daunted by it. That was never the reason – Jane shall make a splendid match, regardless of her portion, when she at last decides she is quite over George Wickham."

This last had been said with disdain, and Elizabeth could see the hurt in Richard's eyes. "I *do* believe she is close."

"That is kind of you to say. I am in no hurry Lizzy, and as my father has been harangued by the women to relent in his great mission, you need not fear, either. Although... I would warn you to be on your guard with Mrs. Bingley."

"I certainly shall! She would push her daughter at a viscount, her son at an heiress, and throw herself at a wealthy, beknighted merchant she once spurned – if fortune hunting were a competitive sport, Mrs. Bingley would be a formidable contender."

There were footfalls on the garden terrace, and then the clink of Lady Eleanor's cane. Their grandmother stepped into the light, her expression droll. "So, this is where we come to speak the perfectly obvious? What a novelty!"

Elizabeth grinned at her grandmother's affectionate sarcasm. "I am sorry, Grandmamma."

"Oh, you must never apologize for agreeing with me, dear, though I gather you have had words with my old beau this evening?"

"I – I have."

"Well then. Let us send Richard back in to the ladies and have a little chat about it."

Richard smirked at them, taking his cue to leave with a teasing bow as he turned away.

"So, after two months of living in such perfect harmony with your family, you have discovered something to grow maudlin over once again? Is that it?"

"I think I have some right to be upset," Elizabeth replied. "This is the woman who broke my uncle's heart, who...."

"My dear, *your uncle* has some right to be upset."

"Have I not? She saw my mother on her deathbed, she –"

Lady Eleanor waved her off. "Yes, yes, the curse. Need I inform you that this is nonsense?"

Elizabeth let out a heavy sigh. "William wrote me that I am only cursed if I choose to believe I am cursed. Oh, Grandmamma, I do not know. That is, I *do* know that William is right, but sometimes I cannot help but think how many terrible things have happened to our family over the years, and now this...."

"William said that, did he? Well, I am glad it appears I have not waited so long in vain for him to exhibit some good sense." Lady Eleanor harrumphed.

"His advice was sensible, and very kind," Elizabeth sighed.

"Indeed! Well, well. You must take it from a very old woman, Lizzy, bad things happen in every family. I have been around a while, and I could tell you such stories! Well, all I will say is that I love my children dearly, but it seems they have let a snake into their midst, and I have tried to warn them. I daresay it happens all the time in the *ton*, but not to us. You need not be cross with Edward – remember who your friends are."

Elizabeth nodded. "I think I see."

"Good girl."

When Elizabeth and her grandmother returned to the drawing room the younger portion of their party was dancing, with Mary plucking at the pianoforte. Mr. Bingley, seated in a chair positioned to admire Mary, now stood to ask Elizabeth to join the dance with him, and as she accepted his hand she caught sight of her uncle – he was actually standing up with Mrs. Bingley!

Elizabeth had not long to muddle through the lively reel with Mr. Bingley, who, unaware of her distress, chatted amiably how well Mary was playing. When the dance ended a few minutes later, Elizabeth began to move toward the instrument, hoping to lead Mr. Bingley back to Mary. They were intercepted by his mother, who took Elizabeth's hand in hers. "What a lovely couple you make together! It is such a delight to see all the young people enjoying themselves."

"Yes," Elizabeth replied coldly, withdrawing her hand. "It is pleasant to see the *young* people enjoying the dance. I daresay I spy the most ideal partner for Mr. Bingley coming this way." Mary approached with a quizzical look, but Elizabeth kept her steely gaze on Mrs. Bingley a moment longer before turning around and walking away.

***

Madeline Bingley wrinkled her nose with distaste as she sat down on the shabby sofa in her sister's poky drawing room, in what was likely the least respectable house she had ever entered. Across the room, Evelyn Younge silently glared at her. Madeline held her sister's eye with a confident stare of superiority. Her younger sister would not be given the satisfaction of seeing that Madeline had actually sunk so low as to come all the way to such an unfashionable neighborhood in order to beg a favor.

To Madeline's satisfaction, it was Evelyn who broke the silence at last. "It has been two years, Maddy. What do you want?"

Madeline smoothed out her dress and smiled. "I have been back in Town for two months now, and I had expected that you would come to see me. When you did not, I grew concerned. I know how much you have always enjoyed visiting Mayfair – it must be such a welcome change of pace for you!"

Evelyn folded her arms and glowered. Though she was not yet thirty, she looked like the older of the two sisters – life had not been kind to her. "Us war widows have not as much to live on as widows of wealthy merchants. I suppose I got sick of always being reminded."

Madeline maintained her unperturbed expression. "I recall when last we met, you had found yourself a new sailor, who is very much alive. I hope you have not been keeping away because the scoundrel up and left you!"

"George ain't left me," Evelyn growled.

"Well, that is good to hear. Is he home? I should love to wish both of you joy. When is the wedding?"

Evelyn stared blankly back at her. Madeline softened her smile just a little as she began to twist the knife. "Of course, you are wearing no ring. But I suppose you would not marry him, would you, and lose your annuity as Captain Younge's widow? It must be *all* you have to live off of. Though certainly George must have been able to find some work since returning from his years at sea." Madeline again paused to calmly regard her sister as the silence intensified. "Oh dear – gambling, is he? I am very sorry to hear it. As it happens, I *did* happen to consider the differences in life between a war widow and the widow of a wealthy merchant. Only tell me what it is I can do for you, sister."

"And I might just as well ask you what you want. You never do anything for anyone if there is not something in it for you. Say I did want your help – what would it really cost me?"

Madeline laughed. "Oh sister, no need to be like that. Trust me, I believe you might actually enjoy this nearly as much as I. I merely need to ask you a few questions about George, perhaps a favor or two. No part of it shall be so disagreeable for you, I am sure. You need only name your price."

"I will not betray him, if that is what you are asking. We cannot wed, but he loves me. You will not pay me off to leave him."

"Good Lord, is that what you think? No sister, I am sure the two of you are quite perfect for one another, and just as much so for the task I would ask of you. What say you to a new house? A bigger house, a better house – a more fashionable address. I am sure he would not dislike it, and it might be just the thing to help us on."

Evelyn squinted warily at Madeline. "Mayfair?"

Madeline scoffed. "Portman Square. Respectable, but a comfortable distance away. I know of a house available that shall not cost me more than half my allowance."

"You have given this some thought. A hundred pounds, up front, and Portman Square will suit. And you speak to George and I together."

Madeline clapped her hands with satisfaction. "That suits me perfectly. Be ready to move one week from today. I will hire the servants. Yes, they will be my spies, in case you are wondering – you will not betray me in this. As far as the servants and neighbors are concerned, you are many years older, perhaps forty. George is your nephew, and his name is Thomas… something. Thomas Smythe, or the like – he is a respectable widower, and you his doting spinster aunt."

"We may require some new clothes to play our parts appropriately."

Madeline rolled her eyes and opened up her reticule. She handed her sisters a handful of ten-pound notes before she rose and made ready to leave. "I shall send a note with further instructions. And, Sister – I look forward to learning why my new in-laws think George Wickham is dead."

***

Another week of nearly daily visits with all her family passed happily enough for Elizabeth. She was every day expecting a letter from William, which would complete her happiness, or nearly so.

What she really wished was for him to come home. She was entirely content at Darcy House now, and would be going about her day in perfect harmony with her mother and sisters, when suddenly it would strike her that it simply felt wrong without William there; he had gone away so that she might be at ease there, but somehow, in two long months, she had come to realize it was his return that would most put her at ease now. His penitence served a purpose no longer; she needed his presence.

She and her mother and sisters were to remain at home that day, awaiting callers, and ere long Richard appeared, with eyes only for Jane. Soon after brought Mr. Bingley and his mother, and as the eager gentleman sought Mary out at once, his mother seated herself on the sofa between Elizabeth and Lady Anne.

"Well, my dear friends, what do you think – I daresay I felt rather warm this morning. What do you say to an early spring? What a fine thing it would be for all the young lovers, eh?"

Elizabeth had been rebuked by her grandmother and her uncle, but she could not help herself. "I am feeling rather cold today," she quipped, and her mother gave her a subtle warning look.

"I hope this weather change is not the reason for Miss Bingley and Mr. Collins's absence on this visit," Lady Anne said.

"Caroline is never ill, she is far too resourceful for all that. No, she has gone shopping with the countess and her daughter. I am sure I shall only get in the way, pushing in like that!"

"Who could ever think such a thing," Lady Anne replied flatly.

"That is kind of you to say. I am all aflutter this morning; I have been worked up into such a state ever since Caroline became engaged. Two daughters soon to be married! If only you knew, Lady Anne! Oh, I am so proud, but I shall miss my dearest girl." Mrs. Bingley concluded her obviously rehearsed speech and reached into her reticule to withdraw a handkerchief. As she dabbed at nonexistent tears, Elizabeth and her mother immediately noticed the small monogram on the corner of the handkerchief: EG.

Elizabeth watched her mother's eyes go wide, but Lady Anne had made no reply when a footman entered the room to inform them that there was an unexpected visitor in the foyer. As Lady Anne left the room, Elizabeth glanced at Mrs. Bingley with blatant disdain. She did not know what sort of scheme the woman was about, but she had no desire to find out; she stood up without another word and crossed the room.

Mary was sitting at the pianoforte, idly plucking the keys as she whispered with Mr. Bingley, who sat at her side smiling idiotically; he was besotted, and she had no wish to interrupt their interlude, for the pair seemed oblivious to everyone else in the room. Neither did Elizabeth wish to encourage Mrs. Bingley's machinations, and so she joined Richard and Jane across the room.

They were not speaking, but simply staring contentedly at one another; Elizabeth rolled her eyes as she joined them. "Good Heavens, say something," she chided, her voice hushed. "I shall not speak with Mrs. Bingley for all the world!"

"Lizzy!" Jane laughed. "I am sure she is not so very bad. Uncle seems fond of her."

"Elizabeth," Richard said, "you have been churlish all week!"

"Have I?"

He winked at her and Jane. "Or perhaps you are pining for Mr. Collins, in his unusual absence?"

"Oh yes," said Jane. "Why is he not here, as he always is?"

"I daresay the poor man has grown tired of keeping me company while the rest of the party makes doe eyes at one another," Elizabeth said, waggling her eyebrows.

"Doe eyes," Jane exclaimed – perhaps a little too loudly – before dissolving in giggles.

"Jane has Fitzwilliam eyes," Richard said, "wise and generous."

Jane swatted at him. "You know that is quite impossible!"

Richard shrugged at them both. Elizabeth laughed and nudged him. "It is odd that Mr. Collins did not come with Mr. Bingley today."

Richard responded with an irreverent smile. "Our lady grandmother told me that Mr. Collins was to go and tour one of Sir Edward's warehouses. He is strangely fascinated by the industry, and Grandmother is strangely fascinated by him. She quite looked as if Mr. Collins had just taken the Tennis Court Oath."

Jane and Elizabeth exchanged a look of mirth, and were still snorting with laughter when their mother returned to the room with a genteel woman in her late thirties, whom she introduced as Mrs. Younge.

Mrs. Younge approached Elizabeth directly and took her by the hand. "Upon my word, you are the very image of Fanny Bennet. Oh, what a pleasure it is to make your acquaintance, child."

Elizabeth beheld the woman in astonishment. "You knew my mother?"

"Aye, she was a dear friend since the time that we were young. I had moved away before she died, but I heard of it from friends in the area, and how it broke my heart! Well now, are these your sisters? I daresay the fair ones favor their father."

"This is my eldest, Jane," Lady Anne said, "and Mary is there at the pianoforte." Lady Anne was pale, her voice tense as she went through the rest of the introductions.

Mrs. Younge took a seat near Elizabeth, as both Mary and Jane moved closer to hear what she would say. "I heard the Bennet girls were in London – some mention of you in the papers, attending such grand parties – I can only imagine what dear Fanny would have to say about that! I hope I am not too forward, but I felt I had to meet you, as I never had the chance to say goodbye to Fanny all those years ago."

Mrs. Younge spent the next quarter of an hour answering questions for the three sisters, sharing memories of their mother with a pleasant, reminiscent smile. Mrs. Bingley stared icily at Elizabeth for nearly the duration of the conversation before she and her son took their leave, but Mrs. Younge was more reluctant to go, and seemed especially affectionate to Elizabeth as she took her leave.

***

The next day, Elizabeth visited Mrs. Younge in Portman Square, though her sisters could not resist the hope of another call from their beaux, and so remained at home. Mrs. Younge was not offended by Jane and Mary's absence, recalling with fondness how much dear Fanny used to enjoy her gentlemen callers. She offered Elizabeth some excellent tea and cakes, and after speaking for some time about her dear friend, she expressed a desire to become better acquainted with Elizabeth.

"Your sisters are very lucky in their beaux," she observed, "but have you one of your own?"

"No indeed, but I am perfectly happy just as I am. I shall end an old maid, and dote upon my sisters' children."

"Pah! You are too lovely not to marry. You must be like Fanny in that respect too, never settling for less than the best, eh?"

"My mother wed quite young, I understand."

"Oh, yes – that is true. I had quite forgotten how young she was. Well, he was such a fine man, your father. So devoted to you girls!"

Elizabeth smiled. She had heard a different story from her uncle, who had once told her, when the twins were young and at a particularly rowdy age, that her father had been just as beleaguered by his own children, and had wished them boys besides.

"You are too kind," Elizabeth replied, wondering if perhaps time and affection had muddied Mrs. Younge's memory. Noticing the time, she thanked her new friend for the refreshments and returned to Darcy House, promising to visit the lonely old widow again soon.

Elizabeth freshened up in her room upon returning, and as her mother and sisters had left word that they should be walking in the park, Elizabeth decided to pass the hours before dinner in the library. Perhaps she would finally crack open a philosophy book, that she might discuss it with William when next he wrote.

She stopped short as she entered the library, for there in the window seat, reading a book, sat William.

"I was just thinking about you," Elizabeth blurted out as she grinned at him.

William shut his book and set it aside, smiling back at her. "Likewise. Imagine my astonishment when I returned home to surprise you all and found the house empty."

"No fanfare at all – how shocking for you," Elizabeth teased.

"Ah, I have had a healthy dose of shocking while I waited for you." He gestured with the book.

Elizabeth laughed. "You were reading *Udolpho*? Mary and I finished it last week."

"Yes, and now we shall have such an interesting dinner conversation."

"Oh, do save it for when our lady grandmother is present."

"Undoubtedly," he quipped with a smirk.

Elizabeth had taken a few hesitant steps from the door as they spoke, but now she came fully into the room, and William met her halfway. He hesitantly took her hand in his and smiled down at her. "I am glad that you are happy to see me," he said.

"And are you enjoying my surprise?"

"Very much. I had hoped it would be a pleasant one."

She swatted at him. "Of course it is a pleasant surprise. Did I not tell you I wished you would come home?"

"Yes. I departed Pemberley not an hour after receiving your last letter."

"Oh, William…."

"I thought I would stay away until you wanted me here. You *do* want me here?"

Elizabeth blushed and looked down at her feet, laughing nervously. "Very much. This is your home."

"But… with me present, do you feel that it could remain *your* home?"

She looked up at William, whose eyes searched her own. She was reminded of their dance at the ball, when she had seen only his eyes, piercing her soul. It seemed so long ago, and yet she lost all sense of the time that had passed since then. She had, through their letters in his absence, come to hold just as high a regard for him as she had on the Twelfth Night… and yet perhaps there was something more. Unable to give voice to what she was feeling, she simply nodded and peered up at him; they held one another's gaze a moment longer, until some commotion in the corridor alerted them to the rest of their family returning to the house.

***

That evening was one of the merriest Darcy House had ever seen. Though Lady Anne had written to Brook Street and Matlock House, the earl insisted that the family allow his sister one night of peace with her children, and only Lady Eleanor acted otherwise by attending her daughter and grandchildren for dinner.

The meal was an intimate one, and lively throughout. The three sisters took turns – though not always without overlap – in regaling their brother with stories of their activities over the last two months, as Lady Anne and the dowager countess occasionally peppered the conversation with their own opinions, adding just the right amount of sugar and salt to the two hours of spirited raillery.

Mary had the most to say, for Mr. Bingley had promised to write to William and ask permission to court her; now William was here, and he instantly gave his hearty consent.

"Well," Lady Eleanor quipped, "at least here is a tradesman who looks to purchase an estate – not like your Mr. Collins, Lizzy, who would sell Longbourn and build warehouses in the image of your uncle's!"

As Elizabeth felt William gazing at her with a curious look, she replied, "He is not *my* Mr. Collins, Grandmamma, and he has already plundered Longbourn of its treasures for my sisters and I; he may do what he likes with the house."

"Besides," Mary said, "you have always been Uncle Edward's biggest supporter!"

"Yes, well," the dowager countess said with a sniff and a sly grin, "you should have seen the sight of him twenty years ago!"

"Mamma!" Lady Anne flushed crimson and looked down at her plate.

William looked over at their grandmother with bemusement. "It is the future. Perhaps I might pay Mr. Collins a visit, and discuss investment opportunities with him."

"Ha!" Elizabeth gave a triumphant laugh as she briefly met William's eye across the table, before giving her grandmother a smirk. "You see?"

The dowager countess harrumphed. "Indeed I do."

Lady Anne had recovered from her momentary embarrassment, and turned the subject to Richard; it was a topic upon which even timid Jane could be quite voluble.

Elizabeth watched with pleasure as William listened to Jane, and then spoke to his sister with such gentle approval. Elizabeth knew she had been wrong to accuse him of disregarding Jane's feelings, but at present she was a great deal happier to have been proven wrong than right in the matter.

They remained at table for above two hours and withdrew to the drawing room afterward, where Jane delighted them with a performance at the pianoforte.

Seated near Elizabeth on the sofa, Williams eyes were all for Jane, and when she had finished playing, he leapt to his feet. "That was magnificent, Jane. It is good to hear you playing again, and as beautifully as ever."

"Thank you, William. Shall I play again?"

"I should like that – I should like it even better if you played something we might all dance to."

Jane looked surprised, but quickly complied, and William approached their grandmother, bowed and extended her his hand.

"You silly boy, what are you about? My dancing days are long over!"

"I have it on good authority that you danced with Lord Chawton at the Twelfth Night ball."

"Well, that is very different. They say he propositions every lady he dances with and I wanted to see if it was true." She reached over and stomped the walking stick that had been leaning against her chair. "It is not."

Mary dissolved into giggles, and waved William away as he turned to her. Their mother did likewise, laughing with the rest of them, and finally William approached Elizabeth. "I am in high spirits, Lizzy. Will you not indulge me?"

She peered up at him; she had been hoping he would ask her, and yet fearing it all the while. She hesitated, but she could not decline, and as she began the steps of a lively reel with William, Mary coaxed their mother into standing up too.

Elizabeth was relieved that her mother and sister had joined them in making merry, for she could scarcely look at William without causing her heart to pound and her mind to spin as she pushed away thoughts of the Twelfth Night. Amidst all this, her grandmother watched her throughout, her expression inscrutable.

Mary and Elizabeth performed a lively duet after the dance, and by the time their little party resolved to retire, it was very late. Lady Eleanor professed it vulgar to travel even a few blocks at such an hour, and declared that she would stay the night. As the family all began to make their way upstairs, Lady Eleanor discreetly detained Elizabeth.

"A moment, my dear," the dowager countess said, taking Elizabeth by the arm. Elizabeth obediently followed her grandmother back into the drawing room. "I think I see what you are about, child, but I wonder if you do."

Elizabeth only shook her head at Lady Eleanor. "I do not understand."

"I thought that might be the case, my dear," her grandmother said, sitting down beside her. "It often is, when one first falls in love."

"Grandmamma!"

"Hush, Lizzy, this is important, and I will speak my peace on the matter. I saw how you looked at William when he said he wished to dance, and it was the same way you looked at him on the Twelfth Night, right before you told your uncle you wished him added to your list."

"I did not know who he was."

"But you know now, is that not so? And very well, I would wager. I hear you have been exchanging letters since he went away, and I saw how you looked at one another at dinner, as if the entire conversation was a private joke you were sharing."

"I am fond of William – for the first time in my life, I have come to hold him in such high esteem – that is all."

Lady Eleanor harrumphed. "Is that so? Or have you simply not made up your mind yet? You had better give it some thought, my dear, because I can promise you, the way William looked at you tonight, he is thinking about it."

"Surely not!"

"And why not? You are not his true kin, you do not even share his name. You are beautiful, he is handsome, and you are both rich, so why not? It might seem strange to some, but how does it feel to you?"

"I do not know," Elizabeth said, wringing her hands as she began to feel some trepidation. "It is all so new, so sudden. I have been content to merely enjoy my growing regard for him, without even considering...."

"Mmm," the dowager nodded sagely. "That is just how it begins, my dear."

***

Elizabeth lay awake in her bed for hours, thinking of her grandmother's words. *Give it some thought* – she could do little else! She tossed and turned in her bed, thinking of the handsome knight, of William's face as they conversed at dinner, and of the way it had felt to dance with him once again, his tall, strong body so near to hers. Finally she could bear it no longer and lit a candle, that she might sit up in her bed, reading over the letters he had written her, searching for some clue.

What her grandmother had suggested was certainly not something she had ever considered – but no, that was not true. She *had* thought of it, when he was only the handsome knight – she had thought of little else the night of the ball. He was her brother, but he was not – *oh, it is all so very muddled, but somehow I have lost myself, and my heart.*

Determined to put the attraction from her mind, Elizabeth resolved to fetch the dullest possible book from the library, in the hope that sleep may yet find her. She put on her robe and crept down the hallway.

William was there, sitting just where he had been that afternoon. He looked up at the sound of her footfalls, before she could recover from her surprise and sneak away. "Lizzy," he breathed.

He was less formally attired than she was accustomed to seeing him, wearing only a loose white shirt and breeches, and the heat she felt on her face told her she ought not to be there dressed for bed as she was.

When she did not speak or move, he set aside his book and beckoned her to join him. "It is a fine thing you are here, else I am sure I should read entirely too much of *Udolpho* and have lurid nightmares."

She smiled at his jest and took a few timid steps into the room, though she knew not what to say or how to behave. Their time in the library earlier that day had felt so natural, so easy, and now it had all been turned upside down by her grandmother's comments. *Surely he cannot be thinking of....*

"I could not sleep," he said, once more gesturing for her to come and sit with him. "I had thought I was the only one still awake in the house."

"I had not expected to be discovered."

"Is it a habit of yours, sneaking about the house like Emily in the castle of Udolpho?"

Elizabeth sat down on the sofa, drawing her robe together about herself as she laughed. "I imagine the circumstances are rather different for me. I am here of my own free will, after all."

"And shall you remain, now that I am returned? When I asked you before, you seemed... uncertain."

"I was...." Elizabeth broke off, chewing her lip as she considered her answer. "I was surprised that you should ask it of me. It is your house, William."

He smiled warmly at her and opened the book in his lap once more. "'*If my happiness is dear to you,*'" he read, "'*you will always remember, nothing can contribute to it more, than to believe that you have recovered your own esteem.*' The passage is underlined."

Elizabeth blushed. Her relations had teased her at Christmas for her habit of writing in books, and though she had resolved to improve herself in many ways of late, this was not one of them. She shook her head at William as she approached the window seat and took the book from him, thinking to put it back on the shelf. "You had better leave off, or you *will* have proper gothic nightmares tonight." He caught her hand before she could return the book to the shelf, and drew her toward him until she was sitting by his side.

"I wonder, what could such a passage mean to you?"

Elizabeth distractedly ran her fingers over the embossed lettering on the cover of the book in her lap. "It made me think of us – of our situation. We have forgiven each other, but it occurred to me that I have also wanted you to forgive yourself. It is a new sentiment, much to my chagrin, that I should be thinking of your feelings at all, but it is the truth. Where I have long been angry with you, now that I am not, I would not have you angry with yourself, and I believe you rather were."

She supposed her idle fingers tracing the letters on the book had bothered him, for he laid his hand on hers to still her nervous fidgeting, before he looked earnestly at her. "It is just what I would say to you as well, Elizabeth. Nothing would contribute to my happiness more than to know that you hold yourself – both of us – in high esteem, despite everything that has happened in the past."

"I do, William." She closed her eyes and let out a shaky breath, thinking again of her grandmother's – *warning? advice? omen?*

As he entwined his fingers with hers, Elizabeth felt herself leaning closer to William. "I have experienced such a rapid reversal of feelings for you that I… I cannot but think of all the years wasted. Had I truly known you…."

He stroked her hair as she lay her head on his shoulder. "Had I been a better man when it mattered the most, I might have spared you such suffering."

He gently nudged her head off his shoulder and cupped her face in his hand. "Elizabeth," he breathed, "I had never imagined it, but I have come to admire you, most ardently."

He held her gaze, searching her eyes for so long that Elizabeth could not say which of them leaned in first, for she lost all sense when his lips met hers. She kissed him back, gripping the thin cloth of his loose-fitting shirt as he wrapped his arms around her.

What began as a chaste kiss soon became more, his hands running up her back and into her hair as his lips caressed hers. She could think of nothing but giving in to the strange new sensations she was experiencing, and leaned her body against his, her fingers curling around the back of his neck until at last she broke away from him to catch her breath.

His hands did not leave her shoulders, and he looked at her as if he would speak, when something caught his eye and he jerked his head toward the open door. Elizabeth tore her gaze from him, distracted by the sound of hushed voices down the corridor, and the flickering shadows on the wall outside in the corridor, as if someone were approaching with a candle. She instinctively moved away from William, and had only just regained her composure when Mary entered the room, one hand clutching her robe around herself and the other holding a candle aloft. "Lizzy, William!" Mary looked momentarily stunned to discover them thus, yet there was something frantic about her. "Come quickly," she said. "It is Grandmamma!"

Mary quickly hurried away, and William was instantly up; he extended his hand to help Elizabeth to her feet. They rushed into the corridor after Mary, who was even now leading their mother into Lady Eleanor's bedchamber. Elizabeth's hand instinctively sought William's. As they made their way down the corridor, there came a chilling moan of pain, and Elizabeth flinched, stumbling into William. The sound rang in her ears and she squeezed her eyes shut as she clung to William, losing all sense of where she was.

"Elizabeth?" William tipped her chin up until she would look at him. "Elizabeth, what is it?"

"I... I do not know – it is as if I suddenly remembered being somewhere else and... I do not know, screaming in the dark." William looked at her with anxious concern, and Elizabeth was filled with a strange sense of dread she could not explain. "Heaven help me, I am truly cursed."

15

Elizabeth awoke in her own bed just after dawn and sat up with a start. She was still in the nightgown and robe she had been wearing the night before, and someone had lain her across her bed with a blanket put over her. The fire was roaring, as if it had been recently seen to, and she smiled to herself, both touched and amazed that someone had remembered to attend to it during all the chaos.

She rubbed at her eyes and pulled herself out of bed, determined that she could not be sluggish at such a time. She rang for her maid, resolved that she must dress at once and attend her grandmother. Her maid soon had her dressed for the morning, and assured Elizabeth that black would not be necessary any time soon, for Lady Eleanor was awake, and William and Jane were with her.

Elizabeth hastened to her grandmother's room, where Jane and William were seated on either side of Lady Eleanor's bed, speaking softly with her. All three of them looked up with relief when Elizabeth entered the room and came to stand beside her sister.

Lady Eleanor's left ankle was bandaged and propped up on a stack of pillows; her shoulder was also bandaged, but she otherwise looked well. "Oh, Grandmamma, what has happened?"

"Good morning, my dear. I understand I am not the only one who took a little fall last night."

"I swooned – it was so silly of me. But you had a fall, too?"

"Much to my chagrin, I did," Lady Eleanor drawled.

William looked over at Elizabeth. "She tripped and fell last night, and Mary's room is on the other side – she woke when she heard our grandmother cry out. We thought she was having a fit of apoplexy, but she was merely panicked from the pain of twisting her ankle."

"And do not forget about my shoulder – I have dislocated it, and that great brute of a doctor has most obligingly put it back into place." She gave a feeble harrumph.

Elizabeth blinked. "Oh, Grandmamma, how awful! I am so sorry."

"What ever for? It was all my own foolishness. I was cold, and I woke and got up to stoke the fire – the fireplace is much nearer my bed, in my chamber at Matlock, you see. Much better arrangements! Well, as

I was walking back to bed, I tripped on the rug – again, the placement is different than I am accustomed to. And down I went like an avalanche of old bones!"

William grimaced at Lady Eleanor's banter. "She fell near the fireplace, so she was quite warm when we found her, and we feared it was fever."

"Oh yes, you feared it was quite the end of me," Lady Eleanor laughed. "But I am still here and that is how it is going to stay, young man. You all simply need me far too much, and if the good Lord tried to take me now, I should be quite put out!"

William and Elizabeth chuckled and Jane shook her head with suppressed laughter. "You gave us quite a fright!"

"Oh, but I am so sorry to have been sleeping through it all! William, Jane, you have not been here all night," Elizabeth said.

"Anne and Mary went off to bed a few hours ago, but these two would not leave me in peace," Lady Eleanor chortled. "William snores, and talks in his sleep besides!"

Elizabeth noticed William's look of apprehension at this, and she began to fear what he might have said at such a time. She glanced at Jane, whose face betrayed nothing. "You ought to rest," Elizabeth said. "Jane, William, I can stay with Grandmamma."

"Yes, go, go! We cannot have Richard see you looking so tired, Jane, my dear, and William, I believe you have a rather large frog to go and remove from your throat, anyhow. Lizzy shall stay with me, and I shall take more of Dr. Purcell's wonderful elixir, by and by."

William nodded and offered Jane his arm. "Shall I send up two breakfast trays?"

"As long as there are no eggs! I can only abide them as they are served at Matlock!"

Barely able to meet William's eye, Elizabeth thanked him, and took a seat near her grandmother.

When Jane and William were out of the room, Lady Eleanor fixed Elizabeth with an arch look. "Well, child, what have you to tell me?"

"Oh, Grandmamma, I am so very sorry. I ought to have been with you last night, as everyone else was."

"My goodness, that is not at all what I mean. It is well you slept through it, for I am sure there were so many people in and out of my room, we might have begun selling tickets! No dear, you know what I am asking."

Elizabeth shifted uncomfortably in her chair. "I have thought about it, as you asked me to."

"I had surmised that. Mary said you and William had been in the library together when she woke and came to attend me."

Elizabeth could not meet her grandmother's eye, but instead

focused on Lady Eleanor's wrinkled old hands, which she had laid on top of Elizabeth's with a gentle pat. "Oh, Grandmamma, I have been so wrong about him. All these years I despised him, but he has a kind and honorable heart. My feelings for him are so different now."

"And what do you mean to do about it?"

"I hardly know. Perhaps it is better forgotten, after last night. I – we – he kissed me, and then just afterward, you had your fall." Elizabeth hung her head in shame at the admission.

Lady Eleanor groaned and slapped Elizabeth on the wrist. "Look at me, child! If you say one word about the curse again, I am sure I shall get up out of this bed and throttle you myself."

"But...."

"Do not dispute me, child. I am quite right, and I mean to carry my point. Did not William tell you that you are only cursed if you choose to believe it? Perhaps, by and by, I shall decide I cursed myself, by declaring I should not dance with William last night, and then twisting my ankle. And then where does it all stop? No, we shall have none of that nonsense, Lizzy. If you are afraid of something, simply say so, without seeking something to blame it on."

Elizabeth regarded her grandmother with astonishment. "That is very good advice."

"Well, you need not sound so surprised," Lady Eleanor drawled.

Elizabeth smiled weakly. "I *am* afraid of something. When William kissed me, I was so happy, but then I knew, deep down, that I ought not to be. He is my brother, in the eyes of the world. I am sure Mamma would be horrified, and Mary and Jane."

"Is that all that scares you?"

"No. No, I am also frightened because it is so very sudden. For years I have thought the very worst of him – this esteem for him is all so new. How can I be sure it will last? What if our kiss was just some new mischief to send our family back into chaos?"

"Well, I do agree you ought not get up to mischief of *that* sort in the middle of the night – though it is how I caught my late husband – at any rate, best not to make a habit out of it, my dear. It seems to me you ought to take it slowly with William, rebuilding the trust between you, and letting the love grow that way."

"Love! I said nothing of the kind. Esteem, perhaps – I cannot own to more than that. I cannot even be sure I trust him, or myself...."

Lady Eleanor sighed and shook her head. "Upon my word, you young people take everything so seriously nowadays. Every courtship is a Greek tragedy! I blame all the mania of novel-reading; you and William have done yourselves no favors there!"

Elizabeth smirked and shook her head. "Grandmamma, I am quite serious! If you wish to speak of love and courtship, I shall leave and send in one of my sisters."

Lady Eleanor made a droll face and patted Elizabeth's hand. "I surrender, my dear – I shall be somber as you like. Tell me, what do you mean to do about William?"

"I have scarcely had time to consider it. I really wish to go back home and think it all over, in peace and solitude."

"Go back home? You mean, to your uncle's house? You might have been justified in running away when you were a scared little girl, but you are older and wiser now, Lizzy. Would you really wound your mother like that again?"

Elizabeth frowned and furrowed her brow, but felt that the harder she tried to think on it, the more muddled her mind felt. "I do not wish to hurt Mamma, but I fear that I may do so anyhow, if I remain. What if William and I quarrel again, or we… meet in the library, again? Would that not wound her, as well?"

Lady Eleanor gave a little shrug, which was as close as she ever got to admitting it when another person had out-reasoned her. "You must speak with your mother, Lizzy. I am grown tired, child, and I believe I may require more medicine for my present relief – and where is this breakfast William promised us?"

"Shall I go and inquire?" Elizabeth stood, suddenly eager to be away, but Lady Eleanor caught her by the hand. "You are an obstinate, headstrong girl, and I daresay you will do as you like, but Lizzy, I beg you would speak with your mother."

"It is too humiliating," Elizabeth sighed. "But you are right. I shall give her an explanation, before I leave here. I think it right for me to go, Grandmamma. It is so much to think on, and I would not wish to give anyone pain, but I cannot promise that I would not make it all a thousand times worse if I stayed here in such a state of mind. I shall tell Mamma that I am not ready to reside with William – that I am not sure I look upon him as a brother – that much is true."

Lady Eleanor nodded. "Very good, Lizzy. I cannot entirely like it, but you are quite resolved, and I must respect that. Only have a care, child, when you speak with your mother. I would not see her hurt."

"Not for all the world," Elizabeth promised.

***

Elizabeth was grateful that despite her recent petulance, her uncle sent an immediate reply and allowed her to return to Upper Brook Street – to return home – at once, without asking questions. And yet, she knew it could not possibly last. She steeled herself, as she unpacked her trunks in her bedroom, knowing that her uncle would eventually require some explanation.

It was not long after she had unpacked, having twice denied Rose entry to her room, that her uncle called her down to his library. She expected him to be cross with her, and was surprised by what she saw in his countenance. He looked concerned, but not defeated, and indeed there was a certain clarity about his eyes as he studied her, that she had not often found there before.

"Well, Lizzy," he began, "I have your note here, and a longer one from your mother. I am pleased that you confided in her before you left Hanover Square, and yet I get the distinct impression that there is more to it than you have revealed."

"You think me dishonest?"

He laughed gently at her. "No one is calling you a liar, child. I only wish you to know that you may confide in me fully; you have always done so before, and it is not like you to state your feelings so... succinctly."

Elizabeth squirmed in her seat. "There is nothing else to confide. I merely thought it best I return home, Uncle. William and I have resolved our quarrel from January, and have written some very conciliatory letters to one another, but now that he is back in London I think it too soon for me to be residing at Darcy House, under the same roof as he. I do not look on him as a brother, though I have grown fonder of him, and I had thought some distance might be the best answer. After all, I have distrusted and disliked him for years, and it has only been two months that I have begun to feel otherwise."

"And all this, you discerned within a single day of his returning to London?"

"Yes, sir."

Her uncle raised an eyebrow and gave her an arch look. "Did you quarrel again?"

"No, sir."

"Have you spoken much?"

"A little."

"Hmm." He frowned at her, drumming his fingers on the desk.

Elizabeth tried to keep her countenance, knowing that her uncle may suspect there was something more, but that he would be horrified if he knew the truth. And it might all be for naught. She had not even begun to examine her burgeoning attraction to William – she may yet be able to coax herself out of it, and she would not embarrass herself before all the family only for it to come to nothing.

"Am I... am I in trouble?"

"No, my dear, you are not in trouble. I cannot force a confidence from you, though I remain convinced there is something else you will not say. I am not angry with you, only disappointed."

"But you know that is so much worse!"

"Well, Lizzy, what is to be, then? You may stay here – you shall always be welcome, my dear – but I shall not pretend I am not hurt by your determination to be secretive. I have ever been your confidante, and Heaven knows you have been mine these last seven years."

Feeling cornered, Elizabeth stood to go. "Perhaps I should *not* have been your confidante so often, Uncle. Have you ever considered that? It has given me so much to be afraid of." At that, she turned and fled to her room, and saw no one for the rest of the day.

***

Edward was shown into Lady Eleanor's chamber, where she looked less feeble old woman of five and seventy, and more like a queen, reclining in the height of luxury. Her bandaged ankle was propped up on a stack of pillows, as was her back, and she had a little bell just within her reach on the side table, which he imagined was giving the servants no little trouble indeed.

Lady Anne was seated at her mother's side, reading, and both of the ladies smiled at him as he entered the room. "Ah, here is my old beau! What lovely flowers, Edward," the dowager countess cried. "You must put them here beside me, and move away these awful roses Catherine sent."

"Mamma!" Lady Anne gave Edward a droll look of exasperation as she carried the roses away and drew up another chair for Edward.

He sat down beside Lady Eleanor and Anne moved back to her own chair just opposite him. Edward and Anne exchanged a kindred look. "I had no doubt you would be well," he told the dowager countess. "But I shall confess, it is a relief to behold you thus. I was rather astonished that Lizzy would choose to leave Darcy House at such a time, though I am sure she would have remained, had your condition been truly dire."

Lady Eleanor fairly rumbled with laughter. "Aha, see how he gets right to the point, Anne? I do love it when a man is direct!"

Anne smiled sadly. "I was surprised she wished to leave, but we spoke of it. She has grown so much since she went away from Pemberley, and I am sure she knows what is best for herself now. At any rate, she is not *so* very far away – I am sure we shall meet every day, or nearly so."

Edward nodded. "Of course, of course. I only wondered what she told you – what explanation she gave for wishing to return to Brook Street."

"I am curious myself," Lady Eleanor said with a twinkle in her eye.

"Why, that she was not yet confident enough in her fragile new accord with William – that she did not yet feel like a true sister to him. I am disappointed, of course," Anne said gently. "They have had but two months of writing letters, after so many years. Of course she needs more time, and I have always desired her comfort and happiness."

Edward nodded. "I shall be direct, as you say, Lady Eleanor – I got the distinct impression there was something Lizzy was not telling me."

"Oh, as to that," Anne said, "there *was* something else. Lizzy asked Jane if she had any memory of a dark corridor, and a woman screaming. Edward, could she have possibly remembered?"

Edward sat back heavily. Whatever he had suspected, it was not this. "I shall never forget that night. I knew it was wrong of us to bring the girls into Fanny's room. What did Jane say?"

"Nothing at all, but she began to breathe very heavily and tremble all over, and then she left the room. Lizzy was very angry with herself for mentioning it at all. I told her it was not impossible that she may have some trace of a recollection, though we had tried to avoid exposing them to such a shocking scene."

Edward shook his head. "Another way I have failed them."

"No, Edward," Anne said, leaning over her mother and extending her hand toward him.

Lady Eleanor had been silently watching their exchange, and now she cleared her throat. "Well, as you have chosen to hold such a conversation in my sick room, I had inferred you might want my opinion on the matter. You would not be the first to seek such sage counsel, you know."

"Has she spoken with you?"

"She came to me yesterday, before she spoke to Anne," Lady Eleanor replied triumphantly.

"Well?"

"*Well*, our dear Lizzy chose to confide in the wisest member of this family, and you would have me betray her confidence?"

"Mamma!" Anne scowled and looked expectantly at her mother.

"It is William, is it not?" Edward smiled knowingly at Lady Eleanor.

"As my daughter says, Lizzy does *not* look upon William as a brother, and how could she? He was away at school when she was at Pemberley, and she has been in London these seven years. He is not brotherly with her, as he is with Jane and Mary."

"But they were getting along so well," Anne insisted. "Surely their letters brought them closer. Poor Lizzy, I am sure she was simply frightened by your injury in the middle of the night, and ran away just as she did when she was a girl."

"She was frightened by *something* in the middle of the night – and I do not think it was what she was reading in the library." Lady Eleanor raised an eyebrow at them, and made a great show of fidgeting with her blankets and pillows before she continued. "Of course, I understand she had some company in the library last night. I am sure it was a great comfort to her."

Edward leaned forward, looking at Lady Eleanor with interest. "Oh?"

The dowager countess sniffed. "Nothing to alarm you, I am sure," she said archly. "They are *so much* brother and sister, are they not?"

Anne let out a strangled sound, somewhere between a gasp and a whimper. "Are you saying…? But *he is her brother*," she sighed, burying her face in her hands.

"Anne," Edward breathed; he walked around Lady Eleanor's bed to go to Anne's side and stood next to her, stroking her hand. "This is my fault. I ought never to have allowed her to leave Pemberley. She has not been brought up with him, the way Jane and Mary have. Surely *they* would not…."

"No indeed," Anne said. "Though I cannot believe anything untoward could happen between William and Lizzy, either."

"If it did, I am sure she would be frightened out of her wits over it," Lady Eleanor observed.

Edward sighed. "That, too, is likely my fault. If Lizzy has… feelings for William, of that nature, she has every reason to be wary. I have given her no good reason to look upon the prospect of love without apprehension."

Anne peered up at him. "What do you mean?"

"I… I have done this. I have ruined that poor girl. When I asked her to confide in me yesterday, she told me that perhaps I ought not to have confided so much in her, since she has resided in London. It stung, but she was not wrong. No thirteen-year-old girl should be made so fully aware of what an unhappy marriage looks like. I was too caught up in my own suffering to see the damage I was doing, the difficulty I was setting her up for."

"How astute you are," Lady Eleanor quipped. "She would have done much better living in the dower house with me all those years; what good it has done Phyllis! But now look at the state of things. Henry is pressuring her into the very thing Edward has made her fear the most, and Anne, my dearest child, you have expected her to treat William like a brother when in fact they are strangers, thrown together in a time of great upheaval. I wonder no one expected such a thing!"

Anne chewed her lip for a moment before looking to Edward. "Henry," she muttered. "Oh yes, we must speak to Henry about it. I am sure he shall know just what is to be done. He spoke to Lizzy about

William the night of the ball, you know."

"I did not know that," Edward replied with no little curiosity. "Well, I had better go and speak with him, and get it all sorted out."

"Seriously?" Lady Eleanor threw her hands up in exasperation, and then winced at the pain in her shoulder.

"Oh, Mamma," Anne cried. "You must not tire yourself. Here, have another dose of Doctor Purcell's elixir, and rest yourself." She poured a small amount of the liquid into a cup of tea, and offered it to the dowager countess, who was scowling fearsomely. "Here, Mamma, drink this now."

"I thank you for your candor, my lady," Edward said, and kissed Lady Eleanor's hand. "I believe it shall all turn out well. We have been idle too long, but now we must act."

***

Madeline Bingley made herself at home in her sister's drawing room – after all, she was paying for the place. *Money well spent, if it shall bring down everyone Fanny Bennet ever held dear.* She smiled at her sister and sipped her tea. "We have had a stroke of luck, Evelyn. The little minx has left Darcy House – now is our time to strike."

Evelyn crossed her arms and scowled, but George Wickham leaned forward with a look of great interest. "Well, my dear benefactress, only tell me how I can best please you, and you may depend upon it being done in a trice."

Evelyn grimaced at George. "Must you always be so eager?"

"Come now, my love," he said, patting Evelyn's hand. "Your sister has been very kind to us. I see no reason not to return her generosity with acquiescence."

Madeline watched with amusement as Evelyn shifted uncomfortably in her seat. She would not like what Madeline was going to propose, but then, it had been many years since Evelyn had acted sensibly, in her own best interest. Evelyn cared for nothing but George, a trait Madeline supposed that the two lovers had in common.

What a relief that I have never lost my head over a man. Aloud, she said, "Your affection is truly touching, but the next phase will be a delicate one. I wonder – perhaps it is better to leave it. I fear Evelyn is not willing, and it is hardly worth doing with half a heart." She slowly rose as if to leave, waiting for them to protest.

George smiled widely at her and laid his hand over hers. "Mrs. Bingley, do stay. Evelyn and I are keen to hear your plan; is it not so, my dear?"

Evelyn offered them a derisive smile. "You are determined to underestimate me, Maddy. Let us hear it, then."

Madeline gave them a sweet smile. "Well, if you are quite sure."

"We are at your disposal," George said smoothly.

"Well, then. Now that Miss Bennet has so obligingly removed herself from the Darcys' protection, it is time for you to introduce your *nephew*, Evelyn. It will need to look like a chance encounter, nothing too obvious. George, you must be charming, but do not appear too eager or you shall frighten her off. Appeal to her sentiment. She lost her aunt a year ago," Madeline said, this last bit bringing a genuine smile to her lips. "Work with that – say you lost your wife, or the like."

George nodded and struck a dramatic pose. "The grieving widower – I can do that."

"Do not overdo it – moderation is the key. The more you say, the more you shall have to keep track of. Keep her talking, and see what you can discover."

"What would she best like to hear? What are her passions, her pursuits?"

"The usual things – music, dancing, reading, walking in the park. For having such a high opinion of herself, she is no different than any other girl at such an age. I daresay she is rather spoiled, coming from such wealth, and you had better appear to have a great deal of it yourself, or she will think you a fortune hunter."

George grinned and rubbed his hands together, as Evelyn sneered at his enthusiasm. "I shall play up the dead wife angle, get her chasing me."

"Good, yes."

Evelyn did not conceal her displeasure. "To what end?"

"Miss Bennet's, I should hope. I daresay, sister, you are hardly George's only conquest. How long shall it take you to gain her trust, lure her into an elopement, and ruin her?"

He laughed. "Is she comely?"

"Does it matter?"

"Pretty girls require a little more finesse than the plain ones. Is that not right, Evelyn?"

George reached for her, but Evelyn swatted him away, pushing her elbow into his as she said, "The girl trusts me. Two weeks, three at the most."

Madeline grinned with satisfaction. Three weeks at the most, and Elizabeth Bennet would be finished. With her out of the way, Edward would soon be toppled – he was already eating out of the palm of Madeline's hand. It was hardly an effort for her. All her pretty words of regret were true – she *did* wish she had chosen Edward over her late husband, though he need not know *why*. James Bingley's fortune has certainly been enough to tempt her, but Edward had been given a knighthood and made friends in very high places – what a different life she might have had, had Fanny Bennet not spoiled it all for her.

"So," Evelyn said, interrupting Madeline's reverie. "How are we going to split her dowry? Fifty-fifty, or three equal shares?"

It was all Madeline could do not to laugh. Miss Bennet's family might indulge her a great deal, but there was no way the little chit would see a penny of her dowry if she wed so far beneath them. More likely it would be split between her two sisters – a fine thing for Mary, Charles, and by extension, Madeline herself. *Of course, George had better remain ignorant of that, else he would lose his motivation.*

"I am feeling generous," she drawled, "but not quite out of my senses. We shall divide her thirty thousand pounds right down the middle, and if you go back on the bargain, I shall have you turned out of this house in an instant."

"We are family," George said smoothly. "We should never think of betraying your trust."

"What is to become of the girl, after?"

Madeline looked askance at her sister. "Whatever usually becomes of such women, I imagine. You need not... keep her. I leave it to you to decide."

George furrowed his brow. "And how do I know Darcy will not come after me?"

"You know him better than I, and have evaded him these two years or more. I am sure you shall manage. Of course, you must be wishing to avoid the sister, though I can assure you she is no longer pining over your untimely demise."

Wickham tried to appear aloof, but his eyes gave him away. "I would prefer to give them all a wide berth, for if I am recognized, it is all for naught."

"She has not seen you since she was a girl," Evelyn chided him. "You look nothing like your younger self. You have grown tan, and changed your hair – she will not know you, so long as we can get her alone."

"The Darcys are at home on Monday, Tuesday, and Thursday to receive callers – visiting Miss Bennet at her uncle's home would be safest on those days. Inviting her here would be safer still. Keep your eyes open and your wits about you, and try not to slip up. You have three weeks to bring her down, or I shall expose you to the mercy of the Darcys. The earl's younger son is courting Jane Darcy – I am sure he would love you to... remain deceased."

Wickham laughed, but Madeline knew she had struck a chord, and she rose to take her leave with a triumphant heart.

***

After spending her first day at home entirely in her room, Elizabeth was determined to raise her own spirits and put aside the tumultuous thoughts that had taken hold in her heart and mind, if only for a little while. Rose was hoping for a visit from Mr. Collins, who had apparently been a very frequent visitor at Brook Street since Elizabeth had gone to Darcy House, and a fast friend to her uncle.

For her part, Elizabeth wished for a visit from her sisters. They had been gentle and understanding with her, Mary most of all, when she had bid them farewell before departing the previous day, but still Elizabeth feared there may grow another rift between them, and all because of her foolishness. She felt as if she were thirteen all over again, embroiling herself in problems too complicated to understand, and running away.

Determined not to dwell on such things while it was so fine outside, Elizabeth declared she would walk out, and thought that a visit with Mrs. Younge might do her some good. As she approached Mrs. Younge's modestly genteel house in Portman square, Elizabeth thought she saw the old widow's face appear in the window, and waved to her, but a moment later she was gone. By the time Elizabeth had reached the front steps of the house, Mrs. Younge herself was just exiting it – on the arms of a very handsome man.

"Miss Bennet, good day to you, my dear." Mrs. Younge sang out as she made her way down the stairs where Elizabeth waited for her. "You must have had the same idea as we have, to be out and about in the sunshine. The almanac is predicting a freeze next week, you know, but Thomas and I think there is nothing at all in it. Better to be out of doors and active! Well now, at last I have the good fortune of presenting my favorite nephew, Mr. Thomas Smythe. Tom, this is Miss Elizabeth Bennet, the new young friend I was telling you about."

Mr. Smythe smiled at Elizabeth, a fine sight indeed. He was tanned, tall and lean, dressed impeccably; he wore his hair long and his sideburns large and well-manicured, in the new fashion. He was, in short, incredibly handsome, and evidently a gentleman of some standing. He gave a gallant bow. "How do you do, Miss Bennet? I have heard nothing but praise of you and your sisters this last week, and I have been hoping for some opportunity to thank you for your attention to my aunt. I am all she has, and I am often fearing it is not enough. But who could complain with a friend like you for company?"

Elizabeth made her curtsey and continued to drink in the sight of Mr. Smythe before recollecting herself enough to speak. "It is a pleasure to meet you, sir. I apologize if I – that is, I had thought you looked familiar, but I am sure I am mistaken."

Mr. Smythe laughed affably. "Have no fear, Miss Bennet; it happens rather a lot. I am told I have one of those faces that always resembles someone or other. But though we have only just met, I hope you will do us both the honor of walking with us? We are for Hyde Park this morning. Do you fancy a turn about the Serpentine?"

"I should love to," Elizabeth said with a smile, and took his proffered arm.

As they began their walk, Mrs. Younge addressed Elizabeth. "I wonder if everybody thinks they know dear Tom because he looks like something straight from a fashion plate, does he not?"

Mr. Smythe laughed. "Aunt! I am quite self-conscious, I am sure. You must not misrepresent me to such a lovely young lady! I am trying to present myself credibly, you know, now that I am back in London."

"Back in London?" Inexplicably embarrassed, Elizabeth latched on to something that they might speak of, beyond the very fine appearance of the gentlemen beside her.

"I have been away, at my estate in Cornwall. To own the truth, I have only just come out of mourning, Miss Bennet. Indeed, I wonder now if it was not a mistake to bring my aunt with me when I purchased some new clothes, for it has never been my experience to be looking so very dapper. My late wife was a gentlewoman, but she had much simpler taste."

"Oh – I am so sorry. I cannot imagine how awful it must be to lose a wife. My aunt passed away last year, and my uncle was mad with grief."

"Had they been wed long?"

"Sixteen years," Elizabeth replied.

"Your uncle has my condolences," Mr. Smythe replied with a tender look. "And yet, I could almost envy him. I had but sixteen weeks with my dear Susan."

"How tragic! She must have been so young!"

"She was, and very beautiful besides. I did not know her well – it was an arranged match, but I think we might have done well together, had we only the time to grow acquainted. Your uncle is a fortunate man to have had so many years with your aunt."

"As much as you have sung Sir Edward's praises," Mrs. Younge said, "she must have been a very lucky woman."

"She was one of a kind," Elizabeth mused. "I learned a great deal from her." She felt strangely unsettled, and was relieved when Mr. Smythe turned the subject.

"Enough of such sad talk, I say. It is a beautiful day, and I have gone far too long without such very fine company. Let us speak of other things. I should like to know you better, Miss Bennet. If you are fond of music and dancing, books and poetry, and long walks on sunny days, I daresay we shall get on famously!"

And so they did. They walked together for more than an hour in Hyde Park, and though Mrs. Younge was rather more reticent than had been her custom with Elizabeth, Mr. Smythe's pleasant conversation more than made up for it. By the end of their time together, she felt that they had been acquainted for ages, for they had discovered they possessed a great deal in common. They admired the same writers and composers, were both fond of walking in the park, and studying human character; indeed, they were both quite interested in the other, and Mrs. Younge appeared to be so fond of each of them as to approve heartily. They walked her back to Brook Street after their time in the park, and to Elizabeth's delight, Mr. Smythe asked if he might call again.

***

Darcy tried to smile at his cousin as Richard sauntered into the library, but it was no use. He knew Richard would see right through him.

"Well, Darcy, what have you to say for yourself?"

Darcy sighed as Richard went through his usual routine of pouring them both a drink before he came to sit across from Darcy. "Nothing. Nothing has changed since we spoke at Pemberley – not for me, at least."

Richard laughed. "And you resent my change of heart? I would have expected you to be relieved by the, ah... transfer of my affections from one sister to the other."

Darcy took a drink. "If it is genuine, you have my blessing."

"It is. I want you to know that. I care for Lizzy – I would have been happy to protect her, as father desired, but I could not have loved her as I do Jane. She and I are kindred spirits."

"And your father has accepted your decision?"

"He accepted it when Lizzy was at Darcy House, and you were at Pemberley. Now... well, we shall have to see. She shall reach her majority in a couple of months; it is a miracle she has not been worked on by some villain already, inattentive to her as Sir Edward has been."

Darcy flinched. "Sir Edward is a good man, made better by the influence of the family since I went away, from what I hear."

"Yes, I suppose it is so – he has been roused at last from years of indolence – of course he will protect her," Richard replied, without appearing to wholly believe it.

Darcy stared down at his glass, swirling the amber liquid around. "Once again, it is me she needs protection from."

"What happened? Jane said so little – only that Lizzy was upset about our grandmother's injury, but I know Lizzy is made of sterner stuff than that."

Darcy consider simply refusing to answer, but if Richard were to hear of it from Elizabeth, he knew there would be hell to pay. "We were in the library together when our grandmother was injured."

"What, in the middle of the night? Darcy, are you mad?"

"I... I might be. Richard, I kissed her."

Richard pounded his fist on the table. "What?"

"You do not understand –"

"She is your sister!"

"*She is not my sister*," Darcy exploded. "I should never behave in such a way to Jane or Mary, of course. But Elizabeth is different. Richard, I love her."

"Two months ago, you despised her. We sat together in this very room and you disparaged her to me."

"Two months ago, I was consumed by prejudice that she has stripped away. She has made me a better man."

"What, with a few paltry letters? Darcy, this is madness."

Darcy shook his head and waved Richard off. "I do not expect you to understand."

Richard sneered. "Do not try that with me, Darcy, I invented that gambit."

"Well? Can you not try to think on it from my perspective? At least when *I* kissed her, she kissed me back."

Richard downed his drink and poured himself another. "If I were not so devoted to Jane, that would hurt, Darcy."

"Well... good."

Richard sighed, shook his head, and then smiled. "We had better make up and be friends again – if you have cocked this up, you are going to need someone in your corner. But Darcy, you had better tell me everything."

Darcy did just that, starting with the exchange of letters and his own introspection at Pemberley, his first encounter with Elizabeth in the library, and then the second. Afterward, Richard let out a low whistle. "Well, well. It is... not something I would ever have thought – it shall take some getting used to. However, I will admit, I have often hoped to see you in love, and in some doubt of a return. It has clearly done you some good."

"Done me some good?" Darcy thundered at his cousin. "I am miserable, Richard."

Richard laughed. "That is how you know it is love, or at least that is what our lady grandmother would say. What does she know of your troubles, by the by?"

"As little as possible, I hope. I would not trouble her at such a time."

"And no one else in the family is aware of what has happened? There is going to be an explosion, you know, when all this comes out."

Darcy sighed. "As I told you, I left our grandmother's room that morning to rest, after staying with her all night. I woke a few hours later and Elizabeth was gone. She told Mother that she did not wish to reside under the same roof as me, and that is all. I cannot imagine Sir Edward knows anything of it, for he was here yesterday and said nothing of it – we spoke in passing, but he was affable as ever."

"Well, I should say that is good news. If it stays between you and she, you may yet work it all out. The question is, what do you want to do about it?"

"What can I do? I have frightened her away, when the trust between us was so new I fear it shall never be repaired."

Richard laughed again. "Lord, to have your problems for a day!"

"I am quite serious."

"Oh, I should never doubt that. Only think, Darcy – Lizzy does not suffer fools, and Lady Olivia taught her a thing or two about the art of the set down."

"I have firsthand experience."

"Exactly so! But what has she done this time? She has not told you off – by all accounts, she has not told anyone at all. If she were only angry with you, the whole family would have heard of it."

"So... what does it mean?"

Richard shrugged. "That she is not angry. I would advise giving her time, Darcy. That has been my approach with Jane, you know. I did not attempt to compromise her as soon as I realized I fancied her." Darcy glared at his cousin, who raised his hands in mock surrender. "Right, but we will laugh about it someday. All I am saying is, if Lizzy is not going to talk to anyone about it, she must intend to think it through herself, and I believe that is a good sign. Give her some time."

"It has been three days!"

"She has hated you for years – and you are her brother."

"Damn and blast!"

"You know I am right. Give it a week, Darcy. Let her think on it, and see what she says of it to her sisters."

Darcy shook his head. "I do not know...."

"I learned the hard way, did I not? It was all for the best, but there is no need for you to repeat my mistakes with her. Just give it a week Darcy – what more could go amiss in a week?"

16

❧❧

Elizabeth did her best to return to her usual good cheer in the week after she returned to her uncle's house, and the easiest way of accomplishing it was to put all thoughts of William from her mind entirely. She was every day hoping to see Charlotte, the one person in her family she felt she could trust entirely to confide in; however, every day brought some new visitor to Brook Street, to keep her at home.

Her mother and sisters visited her twice, and while Elizabeth was relieved that they desired to remain on intimate terms with her, it was difficult to push William from her mind during their visits. Her mother and sisters made some subtle mentions of him, but Elizabeth would not allow herself to ask for any further information than they offered, for she was determined to betray nothing of her tempestuous feelings.

On the days that did not bring visitors from Darcy House, she had callers from Portman Square. Mrs. Younge accompanied her nephew on the first visit, and seemed delighted, if a little overwhelmed, to meet Sir Edward, her late friend's brother. Poor Uncle Edward! He was very gracious, though by all appearances he did not truly recall Mrs. Younge from amongst his late sister's wide circle of acquaintance in Meryton.

After that, Mr. Smythe called again by himself, with the evident purpose of recommending himself to Elizabeth. She was disappointed that Mrs. Younge had not accompanied him, fearing she might have been embarrassed that Sir Edward did not remember her from their youth.

For his part, Uncle Edward had been rather occupied that week, calling on the Darcys, the Bingleys, and the Fitzwilliams when he was not in his office or at his warehouses. He had met Mr. Smythe but briefly, and had the same reaction as Elizabeth; he found Mr. Smythe's face almost familiar, causing Elizabeth and her guest to share a private laugh.

Her uncle was at home for Mr. Smythe's next visit, and Will Collins joined them soon afterward for an appointment with Sir Edward. Though her uncle had promised her cousin the opportunity to tour one of his merchant vessels, and take tea on board with the captain, Cousin Will would tarry in the drawing room, despite his anticipation.

"It is a pleasure to meet you," he said, addressing Mr. Smythe. "I hope you aunt is in good health – I have heard much of her from all my fair cousins."

"She is well, though she was a little over-tired this morning, and urged me to go along without her."

"I understand she was acquainted with the Bennets. As you may know, I am the late Mr. Bennet's heir, and have resided at Longbourn these seventeen years. I should like to meet your aunt, for I daresay we may have some acquaintance in common."

"Perhaps you may, though it is not likely," Mr. Smythe replied. "I understand she left Hertfordshire some twenty years ago."

Here Uncle Edward interjected, "Was Smythe her maiden name? I am trying to recall – but Fanny had so many friends in the village when she was young...."

"So I hear," Mr. Smythe replied with a little chuckle, before turning the subject. "I hear you are for the docks today, then? I had hoped Miss Bennet might be permitted to walk with me."

"I should like that very much," Elizabeth said.

Cousin Will looked at his pocket watch. "What do you say, Sir Edward? We might spare an hour – let us all go to the park for a walk – you and I can see the ship after, and I am sure Miss Rose must be wishing for some fresh air as much as the rest of us."

"Well, I know you are eager to be getting on, but I do not see why we should not all go together – capital idea!"

Elizabeth could sense that Mr. Smythe was a little disappointed that he would have to share her company with so many chaperones, though she herself was not vexed about it. She liked Cousin Will, and found his influence on her uncle rather interesting, for he rendered Sir Edward so lively and voluble.

Rose was delighted to discover her inclusion in the plan, and though she was rather smitten at the sight of Mr. Smythe, Elizabeth had no doubt where *his* interest lay, for he helped her into her pelisse and offered her his arm as they departed the house with a professed determination to make himself agreeable to her, and it was such a welcome distraction from her troubles that she was equally resolved to be very well pleased indeed.

***

"I hope your aunt is in good health," Elizabeth said, smiling up at Mr. Smythe.

"She is, thank you. She found it too cold to walk out this morning. I thought she was being overly cautious, but it *is* a bit chilly." He drew his coat tighter about him and gave an exaggerated shiver.

Elizabeth laughed and shook her head at his teasing. "You puzzle me exceedingly, Mr. Smythe. I believe you said your estate is in Cornwall, and you are so affected by the cold here in London, but I had taken your accent to have the tones of a northerner."

Mr. Smythe looked surprised, and then broke into a smile. "I should have guessed you would be so perspicacious. Indeed, I resided in the north of England as a child. My parents died while I was away at Eton, and by the time I had left Cambridge, I had inherited a small estate in the south, from a distant relation."

"But tell me of your estate. What is it called?"

"Thornwall," he said slowly.

She blinked at him. "Thornwall, in Cornwall?"

He grinned and nodded. "Oh yes, it is a very handsome house, and very well fortified, with a great wall surrounding the place and a fearsome hedge of briar roses around the perimeter to hold off brigands and pirates!"

Elizabeth laughed and shook her head. "You are putting me on!"

He shrugged, giving her a rueful smile. "I *will* tell you of my estate someday, I promise. For now, I had better not. I do not like to speak of it – you must understand, my late wife was perhaps a little *too* interested – that is, I did not mean to suggest that you are the same...."

Elizabeth was taken aback, and knew not whether to laugh or apologize. That he should think *her* a fortune hunter! She was rather heartened by what might have been a rather insulting presumption, were it not for her relief at his apparent ignorance of her own circumstances.

"I hope I did not offend you, Miss Bennet. You must forgive me; I have been out of the habit of speaking to handsome young ladies for quite some time."

"Let us resolve that neither of us has given the other offense, and speak of happier tidings."

"Your cousin Mr. Collins is an interesting fellow," said he.

"Oh, yes – Uncle Edward is vastly fond of him, and I think it rather charming, the two of them." She gestured backward, and they each glanced back over their shoulder – some twenty paces behind them, Sir Edward, Will Collins, and Rose were engaged in an exceedingly animated conversation.

"I wonder that he should take such an interest in your uncle, when there are two such beautiful ladies to be met with in the house."

"Oh – he is a dear friend, but I am sure that is all. He has been very kind to me and both of my sisters."

"Yes, that is right. I had forgotten that you have two sisters – you scarcely mention them. You were also raised in the north for a time, I understand, and your sisters as well. There was a family – the Darnleys?"

"The Darcys. Yes, they raised us, though I came to London seven years ago."

"Not the Darcys of Pemberley?"

"Yes. Do you know them?"

"I know *of* them. I had a dear friend when I was at Cambridge, who was intimately acquainted with their family. Oh, but I am sure you would know him. You would have been very young, I am sure, but do you recall a man called George Wickham?"

"I do, a little. In truth, I can barely remember his face; he was already away at school when I came to Pemberley, though we met sometimes at Christmas or over the summer when I was a girl. William and my cousins were fond of him growing up, and he was betrothed to my sister Jane."

"Yes – I heard she is a great beauty. As to his friendship with your brother and cousins, I cannot say – that is, I had better not. He is gone now, poor Wickham; I suppose I ought to leave it."

Elizabeth peered up at Mr. Smythe with unconcealed curiosity. "What is it?"

"Only that Wickham once confided in me that he and Mr. Darcy were not always on the best of terms, nor Mr. Darcy's cousins. He was so violently in love with his dear Jane, and the young men in the family, I understand, were very proud, and thought Wickham not worthy of her. Of course, I have no wish to impugn your relations – that was several years ago, and perhaps they have grown in generosity since then – perhaps Wickham's loss has taught them to value their former friend in memory."

Elizabeth was quiet for a minute, processing what Mr. Smythe had told her. Though she had begun to think better of William these past two months – perhaps a little *too* well – she nonetheless felt vindicated in her previous opinion of him. She had resented William's interference in George Wickham's career, which cost him his life. To hear that it had been done in such an unfeeling manner was a shock, and yet at the time she had believed him fully capable of such hatefulness. Yet now, her opinion of William was so drastically changed that she could not believe it without a tremendous pain in her heart.

"I apologize," said Mr. Smythe, "if I have offended you once more, Miss Bennet. I have been thinking about you a great deal since first we met, and now that I am with you, I cannot seem to speak without doing myself discredit. Truly, I meant not to disparage any of your family."

Elizabeth blushed and looked away. "You have not offended me – I was merely thinking how very sorry I have been for Jane since she lost her betrothed."

"A sentiment I can understand. Was she very attached to him? I know he worshipped her."

"I believe it was entirely mutual. She was not her former self for years after he was lost at sea, though being in London has done a great deal to cheer her. I own it has done my heart good to see her slowly returning to joy. Goodness, I must sound so silly!"

"No indeed. I am moved by your affection for your sister. I can well understand her being devastated at such a loss – even I was low for many months when I heard of it, for George Wickham was one of the finest men I have ever known. Jane is very lucky to have a sister like you."

Elizabeth smiled warmly as he gave her a charming look, and drew her a little closer. "The wind begins to sting a little, does it not?"

"I am quite well; do you wish to turn back?"

"Not for all the world. I am sure I could endure a blizzard if it brought me your company!" He laughed and glanced back over his shoulder at Uncle Edward, Cousin Will, and Rose. "They seem not to feel the cold at all – I must accept that I am being quite a ninny. How absorbed they are in whatever it is that they are discussing. Indeed, I believe we might say just about anything to one another, and they should be none the wiser."

Elizabeth arched an eyebrow at him. "I hope you are not scandalized by my abysmal chaperones, sir."

"Let us just see." Speaking a little louder, he grinned over his shoulder and said, "My darling Elizabeth, I hope your bags are all packed for Gretna, for I am quite ready to carry you off!"

Elizabeth pressed her hands against his chest and gave him a little shove as she burst out laughing. Recollecting herself, she looked around, but fortunately the chilly weather had rendered the park rather empty, save their little party. "Hush," she chided, "you will get us into trouble!"

Mr. Smythe laughed and, glancing back to confirm her uncle's distraction, he gave her hand a cheeky squeeze. "We cannot have that! Your cousin Collins would call me out, I am sure of it!"

"No indeed!" Elizabeth dissolved in laughter again. "Cousin Will would never fight anybody, I am sure. He is too gentle, too eager to approve of everyone."

Mr. Smythe raised his eyebrows and gave her a dubious look. "Is he? I daresay he did not seem too fond of me. You must warn me, Miss Bennet, if he may think me a rival."

"You are quite mistaken, I am sure." She looked away for a moment, smiling to herself. He had all but declared his interest in her!

"Tell me about your brother, then. I hope he is not so very proud and disagreeable, as I have heard."

"I have thought him both at times, though I am fond of him." She hesitated, hardly knowing what she had said or how to proceed, how to account for her true feelings when all she had done was try to suppress them. How came she to be talking about William to Mr. Smythe? Blushing, she said, "I have not always gotten along with him so well as I do now."

"He has improved in essentials?"

"No, in essentials I believe he is much the same as he ever was – rather, my coming to know him better has improved my opinion of him. He is proud, but where there is a real superiority of mind, pride will always be under good regulation. He is headstrong, to be sure, but it is a family trait, I think."

"I had imagined him to be an imposing and protective brother, given his disapproval of your sister's betrothal."

Elizabeth knew not what to say. She had been angry for this very reason for so long, and yet she realized that she no longer wished to be angry with William about the past. She shrugged at Mr. Smythe. "I suppose it matters not. I believe Jane is soon to be wed, and I am sure she and Cousin Richard have nothing to repine anymore."

Mr. Smythe's expression grew severe for a moment, before he shook his head and looked away. "I suppose it was Mr. Darcy's plan all along, for the cousin to have her," he muttered.

Elizabeth was beginning to grow uncomfortable with Mr. Smythe, and even the cold was beginning to bother her. "William is an attentive brother, but I am sure he would not go so far as to concoct any scheme against Mr. Wickham – I am sure he only meant to help, to care for Jane." She chewed her lip, thinking of William's design on Jane and Mr. Bingley. Certainly he could not have meant to push Mr. Wickham aside for Richard all along. Indeed, it was rather forward of Mr. Smythe to remark upon it at all! "William is a kind and attentive brother," she repeated firmly.

"I see," Mr. Smythe said with a gentle smile. "I hope I have not offended you again – I believe I must rethink my plans to carry you off to Gretna, for Mr. Darcy may be Mr. Collins's second."

Elizabeth laughed weakly, relieved he had at least attempted to put her at ease, but she had begun to wary of his company. She observed that it might be time for her to return home and warm herself by the fire.

***

It was chilly out, despite the coming spring, and Sir Edward was obliged to use his walking stick as they meandered through Green Park. Rose took Mr. Collins's arm, and stared ahead at Elizabeth and Mr. Smythe. "Soon it will be my turn," she sighed.

Mr. Collins laughed indulgently at her. "You envy our cousin, I take it?"

"How could I not?"

"Very easily, I think," Mr. Collins said, and looked skeptically at Sir Edward. "I cannot like this Smythe fellow."

"Ha! Now who is jealous?"

"Rose!" Sir Edward scowled at his daughter, but she only grinned playfully at them. "I jest, Papa!"

"Well, I am not in jest at all," Mr. Collins replied, giving Rose a look of patient concern before addressing Sir Edward. "I think it all very odd."

"How so? He seems a pleasant, harmless fellow, and Lizzy likes him."

"With all due respect, Sir Edward, I think it all stinks. What do we really know of this man? His aunt, this Mrs. Younge, appears out of nowhere, recommends herself to my cousins with all this talk of their mother, and then singles out the most well-dowered of the three sisters to introduce to her nephew? Forgive me, sir, for I am only a distant and recently discovered relation, and my claim on Miss Bennet's interest must be small in comparison to your own and that of her excellent extended family, yet I fear it would be remiss of me not to make my concerns known to you."

Edward nodded appreciatively, knowing the young man was quite right. Again he felt a pang in his heart, for this young fellow who had been acquainted with Elizabeth not three full months was already taking more of an interest in her affairs than he himself had ever done.

"Your judgment is a fair one," he admitted. "If Mr. Smythe begins to form any serious designs upon her, I shall be obliged to make some inquiries. At present, I admit I am finding my niece rather difficult to read. She seems to enjoy this young man's company, though he is but a relatively new acquaintance. However, I had thought her interests might lie elsewhere."

"Has Lizzy some other suitor?" Rose's interest in the conversation had apparently redoubled, and she stared expectantly at her father.

Sir Edward raised his eyebrows and gave his daughter a stern look. "You ought not to be privy to such a conversation, my dear, and while I will not satisfy any of your impertinent questions, I would remind you that if you thought to repeat anything you have heard, you should not receive one shilling of your allowance until Christmas, I am sure."

"Papa!"

Mr. Collins chuckled, and clucked his tongue at Rose. "Your father is right, my dear. We speak out of concern and affection for Cousin Elizabeth, but it is your father's place to put her on her guard."

Rose gave them a penitent look. "Very well."

"Lizzy is a good girl," Edward replied. "Stubborn, indeed, but she would never get into any serious mischief. She has long declared herself completely uninterested in any kind of romance, so perhaps we ought to leave it be for now." Though he did not say so aloud, Edward had spoken with Henry at length about the possibility of a match between William and Elizabeth, and though he had never imagined such a thing before, he now rather hoped it would come to pass. If Elizabeth had developed feelings for William, this Smythe fellow could be no great threat.

Ere long, the conversation turned from Elizabeth to matters of business, for Mr. Collins was quite fascinated by the operations of Gardiner Imports, and Sir Edward was delighted at having an audience. It was not the sort of thing that was much talked of amongst his more lofty connections, though he saw no shame at all in engaging in trade, for he had done so very well in it himself, and would not be made to feel ashamed of it. It was, in short, the one part of himself he could be proud of – he was not gifted in matters of romance, and neither had he been an ideal parent or guardian, but he was an excellent businessman.

That Mr. Collins, a landed gentleman, should take such an eager interest was eminently flattering, as well as small confirmation of what Edward himself had long believed, that future generations may not be so fettered by such rigid social structures, that society would move forward progressively, celebrating self-made men. It would be ten years or more before Sir Edward could expect to have such a discussion with his own young son, and yet Will Collins was such an enthusiastic novice.

"I have never felt myself designed for a pastoral life," Mr. Collins admitted. "My father was an indolent master, and aside from the establishment of a horse breeding enterprise, there was much potential in Longbourn that he never strived to reach. I understand the previous master, your late brother-in-law, was much the same."

"Thomas was... lackadaisical at times, yes."

"I meant no disrespect, of course. I only wished to say that it has been some years since Longbourn was all that it could be, and while I have had a poor example of land management in my late honored father, I find that what I most lack is not the experience, but the interest in what ought to be done. It is not that I do not desire some useful employment, but that perhaps agriculture might not be the best outlet for my aptitude. I had once wished to join the church, which was not clever enough for my mother – she thought I might become a barrister, had I not inherited so young, but that would have been rather too smart *for me."*

Rose listened to Mr. Collins with unusual interest. "And should you have liked to go into trade, like Papa?"

"Why, yes, Miss Rose, I think I should. The world is changing; trade will not hold its stigma forever, you know. Not when it is the backbone of the nation. There is a great deal more in it to interest me, in terms of employing one's mental abilities. I think I should do very well at it. The entail was broken with my inheritance, you know, and the more time I spend in London, the more I begin to consider selling the place entirely, and taking up some more fulfilling employment here in the city."

"I do love London," Rose declared, "though I have scarcely been anywhere else."

"Scarcely been elsewhere?" Sir Edward laughed. "I am sure you have been to Derbyshire a dozen times, and to some seaside place or other nearly every summer!"

Rose laughed, and Mr. Collins did likewise. "I begin to envy you, Miss Rose. I have never seen the seaside."

"Why ever not? You are a man, and might do as you like, whenever you like."

Sir Edward gave his daughter another warning look. "Rose!"

Mr. Collins only laughed again. "Would that it were so! Even while I am at my leisure here in London, I do have some responsibilities, and am often writing to my steward. I would like to travel more, but I think I should like to reside here in London best of all."

From here the conversation turned to more general remarks on the attractions and diversions of Town. Edward and Rose were both effusive in recommending the bustling city they called home to Mr. Collins, who was determined to discover as much of the city as he could, and to be delighted by all of it.

Edward did his best to keep a watchful eye on Elizabeth all the while, and after three quarters of an hour in the park, he decided it best to suggest their return, for Elizabeth had seen enough of her new beau for the day, and even appeared to be rather bored of his conversation – this was some relief to Sir Edward. She did not seem to repine the loss of her admirer's company at all, and Sir Edward breathed a sigh of relief as he offered his niece his arm, to walk her and Rose home before continuing on his errand with Mr. Collins.

***

Elizabeth finally went to see her cousin Charlotte that afternoon. Aunt Phyllis had other callers, and so Elizabeth lured her cousin out into the courtyard for a tête-à-tête. Charlotte had doubled up her shawls, and drew them tighter around her. "Lizzy, it is chilly out here – whatever is the matter?"

"Oh, *everything*, Charlotte," Elizabeth replied, her posture utterly defeated.

Charlotte looked alarmed, and gestured for Elizabeth to sit down with her in a pair of garden chairs at the back of the courtyard. "Tell me everything, cousin"

"I hardly know where to begin."

"Well, if you cannot simply start at the beginning, suppose you tell me what has put you into this panic," Charlotte said gently. "Surely something must have upset you today."

"I went walking in the park with Uncle Edward and Rose, and Cousin Will… and a gentleman."

"What gentleman?"

"His name is Mr. Smythe – he is Mrs. Younge's nephew. She introduced us last week, and he has called on me twice."

"Well! So that is what you have been up to all week – I was missing you, you know. Tell me of this Mr. Smythe – I hope *he* has not caused your distress."

"Perhaps a little – nothing untoward, only we were speaking of my family and… William."

"And this upset you? Has it something to do with why you left Darcy House? It is not like you to be so mysterious, Lizzy."

Elizabeth leaned back heavily in the wrought iron garden chair, and let out a deep exhale. "Mysterious? Charlotte, I have been such a fool."

"It would not be the first time, dear Cousin, but I shall love you anyhow. Tell me what happened."

"You know I had been writing to William, when he was away at Pemberley."

"Yes, it all seemed to be going well since your quarrel."

"Charlotte, there is something I never told you about my quarrel with William – indeed, I have not told anybody."

"I heard he did not recognize you – he thought you were Rose, and Rose was you."

"Yes, that is true, but at the Twelfth Night, he did not know me at all, nor I him. Charlotte, when we danced that night I… I was attracted to him," Elizabeth said, her heart aching as she forced the words out. "We spoke so candidly, so warmly – there was a spark between us, an instant connection."

"And neither of you discerned the other's identity?"

"Not until the next day, after I had said such dreadful things – and then I was so angry with him for being the handsome knight I had admired, that is why I struck him. After feeling what I felt toward him at the ball, and learning that all those feelings had been for *him*, I was mortified."

"And very angry, I hear."

"Yes, I was, but, Charlotte, I think I was rather heartbroken over it. And since we have been writing letters, my opinion of him has undergone such a material change. I have come to see so much good in him, to care for him. He came back to London because I asked it of him – because I missed him, Charlotte, as I never knew I could miss a person. When he came home, it was as if somebody had struck a match inside me. The house seemed lit up by his presence, and I have never known a more pleasant time there than our family dinner that night. Being in his company felt right for the first time in my life, and I did not want the evening to end. I could not sleep at all, and I went into the library late that night – he was there, Charlotte, and… we kissed."

Charlotte took Elizabeth's hand and grinned. "Oh, Lizzy! My dear friend, I am so happy for you! You are in love!"

Elizabeth burst into tears, and could not speak sensibly for several minutes. Finally, Charlotte reached forward and gently lifted Elizabeth's chin, forcing her to look up. Elizabeth met her cousin's eye, and Charlotte tilted her head as she asked, "Oh my – you have not yet admitted it to yourself, have you?"

"How could I? He is my brother."

"You have been assiduously denying that statement for months – years, even! No, Lizzy, you shall have to do better than that."

Elizabeth wiped away her tears and glowered at her cousin. "Please, Charlotte, do not tease me. I am so tired of feeling angry and confused all the time, and now I am just frightened. Whatever am I to do?"

Charlotte simply laughed. "Marry him, Lizzy. He's damned handsome, and I would do it myself if it did not put me at risk of being absolutely murdered by Cousin Anne."

Elizabeth was astonished in a number of ways, and knew not what to remark upon first. She could only shake her head and stare, wide-eyed, at her cousin.

"Do I shock you, then?" Charlotte gave another gentle laugh, and squeezed Elizabeth's hand. "Truly, Lizzy, I do not understand what is causing all this confusion for you, when it seems so very simple."

"One evening, Charlotte, *one evening* spent in his presence, after seven years of dislike and distrust – how can I put it all aside so quickly? How could I have even considered throwing myself at him in such a manner?" Elizabeth unconsciously brought her fingers to her lips, remembering what it had felt like to kiss William, to be in his arms.

"How indeed! It is not uncommon, Lizzy, for handsome men and pretty ladies to be attracted to one another, and discovering some common ground, as you have, it is a natural step toward acting on those... other feelings."

"Charlotte!"

"What? It is the truth. I may be a spinster in the making, but I am still older and wiser than you, Lizzy. At any rate, you and William have been making eyes at one another since Christmas dinner."

"He thought I was Rose!"

"He thought that you were worth staring at, and that is precisely what he did for most of the night."

"Can you not understand my apprehension at all? We have only just begun to find our footing with one another, and *he is my brother* in the eyes of all the family. I like him very well, but two months of exchanging letters and one evening of merriment is not enough to commit to something more, not when I have seen how very wrong it can go. I should hate for us to end up like my aunt and uncle."

"Which aunt and uncle? You may have one rather discouraging example of an unhappy marriage, but you have also had two very superior pictures of domestic felicity before you, with my father and your Aunt Phyllis, and the Darcys who raised you."

"Your father and my Aunt Phyllis knew one another for ten years before they wed. My Uncle Edward married Aunt Olivia after two weeks!"

"You have known William nearly all your life!"

Elizabeth shook her head again. "And yet, I have only liked him for the last two months! It is not enough, Charlotte."

Charlotte really began to look quite cross. She took a deep breath, closing her eyes, and then finally opened them again, her countenance softening. "I am sorry, Lizzy. I am trying to understand you – you must recall that not every young lady would scorn such an opportunity, but I am determined to see your side of the matter, if it will bring you any comfort. Go on then, tell me what else is on your mind, for there must be something more to have you so worked up, and set against poor William."

"I do not know exactly," Elizabeth said, chewing her lip. "I met Mr. Smythe, who I thought was very agreeable, and today he made some confusing insinuations about William."

"Are they acquainted?"

"No, not at all. They have a mutual acquaintance, one that has given Mr. Smythe some insight, apparently, into William's behavior when he was a young man."

"I cannot think it right of him to say such things about William, to ingratiate himself with you by disparaging a family member."

"His assertions made me uncomfortable. To own the truth, it made me wish to sever the acquaintance entirely, though he is so handsome.

When I think about it… he said nothing of William that I had not once thought myself, and yet I realized that I have no wish to hold a grudge any longer against him. I have come to think better of him, to esteem him…."

"Do not use that insipid word again," Charlotte cried. "*You love him.*"

"What if I do? Whatever will our family say? He ought to have been my brother, but I do not feel he ever could be, not when I feel as I do about him."

"Then say so, Lizzy! Never in your life have you been so hesitant to make your sentiments known on any subject, and it ought to be the occasion on which you are the most vocal. Get rid of this rotten Mr. Smythe, and do not let go of William."

Elizabeth laughed in spite of herself. "I wonder if you are secretly a romantic."

"If I was, I should never admit it. At my age, prudence may prove to be the order of the day. If I grow any more desperate, I may take a crack at your Cousin Collins!"

"He should be so lucky," Elizabeth giggled.

Charlotte grinned, her posture relaxing from their moment of tension before, and then she grew serious once more. "Truly, Lizzy, you need not fret over it. *Talk to William.* You have only run away from him, and it shall solve nothing. Have we not all resolved to rise above the mistakes of our past?"

Elizabeth sighed. "I hardly know what to say, but I shall think on it, I promise I shall."

***

Henry Fitzwilliam slowly shut the window pane, flinching against the breeze; it was worth the chill, after what he had just overheard. He picked up the almanac off of his desk and leafed through it for a moment, and then smiled to himself as he came out of his study.

The walk to Darcy House was a brisk one, and had Richard not accompanied him, the earl's confident self-satisfaction would have carried him thither all the same. Richard went directly to see Jane, having something very particular to ask her; the earl was shown into his sister's private parlor, where she was seated by the fire.

"Henry, it is good to see you. Have you come to look in on Mamma?"

"I have come for a number of reasons, though Richard had one in particular."

Anne's eyes lit with joy. "Truly?"

"He is with Jane now."

"Oh, my dear girl – I know she shall be so happy, at last."

"Perhaps while Richard is making his declaration, I might have a word with you. Do you mind if I shut the door?"

"I suspected you would ask," Anne replied. "I take it you have spoken with Edward?"

"Yes, he called a few days ago, and I have been mulling the matter over in my mind. I have gained some new insight, as it were, just this afternoon, and I believe I have a plan."

Anne frowned skeptically at him, then looked away. "A plan? Can you tell me, Brother, what is it you hope to accomplish?"

Henry hesitated, noticing his sister wringing her hands and staring down at the rug. "Surely you would not wish them separated?"

"I hardly know. I have always considered Elizabeth to be William's sister, but it appears I am outnumbered in that opinion."

"My dear sister," Henry said, taking a seat beside her. "I understand your feelings, though they are born out of sentiment, rather than being rooted in reality, I fear. I have had it from Elizabeth's own lips that she does not think of William as a brother – that she never has, and never could. She is fond of him, yes, in a different way."

Anne gasped. "She told you this?"

"Not exactly, but I heard her say as much to Charlotte. Thank Heaven the two of them are thick as thieves!"

"Oh, but why can she not be open with us?"

"Do not fret, Sister. We all had our secrets from Mamma, did we not? And we had not nearly so much strife in the family." He shook his head and scowled. "Elizabeth ought never have come to London to live with Edward. He loves her, but he has failed her for years, and I have been trying, through some scheme or other, to get her out of his house – she ought to marry, as I have been saying all along, but when I put Richard forward, nobody would hear of it! We all want what is best for her, and we had better come to some agreement on the matter, and soon."

"I wish you would not say such things about Edward. There is no reason to push her to marry, when I am sure Lizzy is content with him."

"Edward is my friend, but he is an indolent guardian, and it is a miracle Elizabeth has not fallen prey to a fortune hunter already – had we not been in mourning for George, and then Olivia, had she been out more, I shudder to think of what might have happened."

"Henry!"

"Do you not want grandchildren, Anne?"

"Henry, you are horrible!"

"I am an old man who wants his children and nieces and nephew to find love and happiness – and security! If I have to pair them all up amongst themselves and march them down the aisle, then by God, that is what I shall do!"

Anne sighed. "I could approve of it, if I were to hear it from her, or him – or both, that would be ideal. Oh, why must they be so secretive?"

Henry laughed and made a droll face at her. "Yes, I recall when you met George, the first thing you did was run to Mamma, telling her of your passion for him."

"That was different."

"No, it was not. Listen to me, Anne. I cannot speak for William, but I can tell you that Elizabeth is not going to confide in you until she has come to some understanding with William, and she will not accomplish that until she has some opportunity to sort through her feelings and find the courage to speak to him. *We* may very well be the last to hear of anything, when it comes to matters of the heart."

"I suppose you are right. Jane was terrified to tell us of her feelings for George Wickham, and yet we were so supportive."

"Fear is never rational my dear, and neither is Elizabeth just now."

Anne chewed her lip. "It would not seem strange, Lizzy and William?"

"Seem strange to whom?"

"To all the world, I suppose. They are nearly brother and sister in the eyes of society, I am sure."

"Hang society!"

"I suppose that is just what Lizzy and William would say, too," she mused.

"You see? Aha, I see it in your eyes; you know I am right."

Anne gave him a playful huff. "You are worse than Mamma."

"Fighting words indeed! Come now, Anne, I would have you say that you support them."

"If it is what they want, I shall, but it seems to me that if that were so, Lizzy would not have left us."

"It is *precisely* why she left you, but that is beside the point. I shall need your cooperation, Sister, for I mean to tell you my plan...."

17

☙✦❧

Darcy paced the drawing room of Matlock House, peering out of the window and watching the snowfall grow heavier, waiting for Elizabeth and Sir Edward to arrive. What madness on his uncle's part, expecting anybody to leave their home on such a night!

He could not repine that Aunt Catherine and her daughter had left Matlock House, unable to resist the temptation of dining with a marquess, despite the family's celebration. However, the Bingleys had been sensible in declining the invitation, and he could scarcely account for his mother's uncharacteristic insistence that they attend. Even Mary, who had remained at home with their grandmother, had been adamant that the others attend the earl, who was eager to celebrate Richard and Jane's betrothal.

Across the room, Richard tore himself away from Jane and the other ladies and approached Darcy. "I believe it is your turn to congratulate me, Cousin."

Darcy peered out the window, glowering at the snow. "What madness to travel in this weather! I am happy for you, truly Richard, but if any harm befalls Elizabeth, I shall box your father's ears!"

Richard laughed and clapped Darcy on the shoulder. "They are just coming from across the square. I thought you would be eager to see her."

"Not if it puts her at risk. I have done my week of waiting, as you said, and I cannot help but feel a sense of foreboding, as if the rug is about to be pulled from under my feet."

"Look, there is Sir Edward's carriage now. She is safe and sound, and in very fine looks!"

"She is freezing – see how she runs for the house!"

"You ought to go and warm her."

Darcy scowled. "Do not be vulgar, Richard – and do not think to take any liberties with Jane, either. She is still my sister!"

"There's the affable Darcy we all know and love," Richard guffawed. "You know just how to woo a lady!"

Darcy rolled his eyes at Richard and moved away; Sir Edward and Elizabeth were in the house now, and making their entrance. Lady

Anne and Jane were the first to greet them, and Darcy waited patiently from the back of the room as Elizabeth offered Jane her effusive congratulations. He watched her, mesmerized by the way she moved through the room; he silently willed her to look his way.

She glanced around, and finally caught his eye; her cheeks flushed red and she gave him just the trace of a smile with her perfect lips before she looked away. He watched her still, and she gazed back at him again; this time her bright eyes locked on his, beckoning like a siren's call. At that moment, Darcy knew he was utterly lost.

He went to her, but had scarcely the time to speak before dinner was called. Heartened by the disappointment in her face when they were interrupted, he offered his arm to lead her into the dining room. "We are an intimate family party tonight," said he. "I hope you would sit with me, Elizabeth. I have missed you."

She gazed up at him and smiled, blushing once more. "And I you, William."

***

Elizabeth reminded herself to breathe as William led her into the dining room. He guided her to a chair between himself and Jane, with Uncle Edward on his other side. Charlotte quickly inserted herself between her brothers to take the chair opposite Elizabeth, and Lady Anne was left to sit on the countess's right-hand side, across from Uncle Edward. Though she was seated farthest from Jane and Elizabeth, their mother warmly regarded them with a wide smile as she took her place.

The Earl was grinning at them too, and patted Jane's hand as he took his place at the head of the table. "Oh, my dear girls, what a happy day!"

Elizabeth grinned at her uncle – she had never in her life seen him so very giddy, and yet his peculiarly high spirits served to put her own strangely at ease. He signaled the footmen to begin pouring wine, and before their food could make it to the table, Richard had leapt to his feet at his father's side, holding his glass aloft as he smiled down at Jane.

"You see before you the happiest of men," Richard declared with a broad smile. "I would have you all know that this morning I officially tendered the resignation of my commission – I am no longer a Colonel, merely *Mr.* Fitzwilliam, and the most beautiful woman I have ever beheld shall soon become *Mrs.* Fitzwilliam."

The earl and countess began to cheer with undignified enthusiasm, and before long the others at the table had joined in. Jane bowed her head to conceal her blushing laughter, and finally Richard, laughing along with them, waved his hand in the air.

"Yes, yes, it is long overdue, but it is done. The Scottish pile shall be sold next week, and then you are all very welcome to join us for some very merry house-hunting."

"Not in this weather," Aunt Phyllis harrumphed, giving a fair impression of the absent Lady Eleanor.

Richard shook his head in good humor and sat down, his eyes never leaving Jane. Elizabeth watched her sister meet Richard's gaze, and break into the most breathtakingly beautiful smile. Elizabeth felt her eyes begin to mist over, and she dabbed them discreetly.

William had been relatively silent until now; he cleared his throat and raised his glass at Richard. "I am delighted for you both," said he. "Perhaps, by and by, I shall give some little offense to my neighbors, and we may yet have a house become vacant right next door!"

Jane and Richard both gaped at William for a moment before sputtering with laughter. "Invite Aunt Catherine around more often," John drawled, "I am sure you shall meet with success ere long."

Beside him, Lady Anne swatted at her nephew. "That is hardly fair – Catherine is not present to defend herself."

John made a droll face and turned the subject. "Speaking of nefarious schemes, and those who are not present to defend themselves...." He flicked his gaze over to Richard. "Shall I have any success, do you think, in persuading you and the ladies to consider a double wedding?"

"Oh, but I should like nothing better," Jane exclaimed. "How happy Caroline will be!"

"I hoped you might say that," John replied. "And if Mary would keep up, Caroline's brother might wish to join us at the altar as well!" John laughed and looked around, and then seemed to abruptly realize that Mary was not actually present at the table to respond to his teasing. He looked momentarily embarrassed, and the rest of the family chided him with laughter.

Elizabeth had relaxed enough to join in the merriment, and even braved a glance at William. He felt her gaze and looked over, still laughing at John. Waggling his eyebrows at Elizabeth, William cast a mischievous sideward glance at his cousins and screwed up his face, as Elizabeth laughed at him, and smiled in spite of herself, relieved she could feel so at ease with him after their last encounter.

At length, the earl cleared his throat and loudly addressed the entire table. "It occurs to me you were all quite cross with me not so very long ago, yet now we jest about the very outcome I desired in the first place. Well, I have never been one to say I told you so, but now is as good a time as any," he said with a laugh. "Two sons married, and two nieces as well ere long!"

"Mr. Bingley and Mary are only courting, Brother," Lady Anne reminded him.

"Well, at least it is something," the earl said. "Now I can only wonder who should be next. William? Lizzy?"

"Father!" All three of his children regarded him with varying degrees of amusement and chagrin.

"Well," he huffed. "William has no mind to heed Catherine's wishes regarding her daughter, so surely he must have some other young lady in mind, now that he is back in London. And Miss Lizzy here has been receiving a gentleman caller, or so I hear."

Four sets of eyes peered across the table at her, and Elizabeth unconsciously sank down a little in her chair, afraid to look over and meet William's eye – she stared down at her plate of untouched food, groaning internally. Further down the table, Uncle Edward came to Elizabeth's defense, to her complete and fervently grateful astonishment. "Lizzy has no designs at all upon *that* fellow, I am sure – he really had her looking quite cross when last they met, just like every gentleman you have suggested for her, Henry."

The earl gave an indignant snort, fell silent a moment, and then laughed it off. "You have got me there, old friend," he said, and took a long drink of wine.

Charlotte inclined her head, attempting to make Elizabeth meet her eye, and slowly she smiled. "What if it is me, Papa?" Charlotte teased. Elizabeth looked over and mouthed a small, silent *thank you* to her cousin for the deflection, and Charlotte continued. "I may yet set my cap at Mr. Collins, for all I have been hearing of Longbourn lately."

Uncle Edward laughed. "I do believe he means to quit the place ere long, or so he tells me. He wishes to reside here in London."

"Most convenient," Charlotte quipped with a smirk, eliciting more laughter from around the table.

"I only wish you as happy as your brothers, my dear," the earl said gently. "Set your cap at whoever you like – even William here is fair game!"

Charlotte blanched, and the rest of their party fell silent for a moment; Elizabeth flinched as the air in the room began to feel heavier. Elizabeth's instincts screamed at her to run away, to simply get up from the table and run as far away from the dining room as she could, and she looked down at her lap in some confusion for a moment, until William very subtly reached over and took her hand in his.

He gave her hand a squeeze and entwined his fingers with hers as he turned to address her uncle. "You say Collins means to quit Longbourn? It *would* be a most convenient thing, for I understand our mutual friend Bingley wishes to purchase an estate. Perhaps it may all work out to everyone's satisfaction."

"As to that, Collins tells me he is urging Mr. Bingley to go up to Hertfordshire with him when the weather clears up, and take a look at a neighboring estate – Netherfield, I believe it is called. It is vacant now, and as I recall, very grand indeed."

William finally released Elizabeth's hand as he continued conversing with her uncle, and the rest of the meal passed without any more discussion of marriage, nor any further cause of alarm to Elizabeth, and though she could scarcely touch her food, she took comfort in the wine.

***

As they were a small party, there was no separation of the sexes after supper, and everyone stood to adjourn to the drawing room together. William offered Elizabeth his arm once more, but moved rather slowly, until all the others had gone through before them.

"Are you quite well, Elizabeth?"

"I am, thank you," she said softly.

"You are not angry with me? All week, I have been rather afraid you were."

"I am not. I have felt many things, but not anger – not at you, I promise."

He lowered his arm to take her hand in his. "I am so relieved," he breathed. "I was afraid I had driven you away."

"No, I merely needed some distance – some time to think on everything that has happened."

"And have you?" William held Elizabeth's gaze. "Elizabeth, I would know what you are thinking."

She could only offer him a wistful smile as they finally stepped into the drawing room together. "So would I." In the drawing room, they took a seat together on the sofa, in view of the pianoforte.

Jane and Charlotte had positioned themselves at the instrument, and Richard leaned against it, whispering happily to Jane until he was needed to turn the pages. John sat down in an armchair across the room in a posture of ennui, and picked up a book, while the earl quickly summoned his wife, sister and Sir Edward to make up a game of whist with him. Elizabeth gave them all an arch look, suspecting there was some scheme afoot to leave her with none but William for conversation.

On the other hand, perhaps the strange sense of something in the air existed only in her mind. Determined to simply enjoy her family truly acting like one, for once, Elizabeth smiled at William, hoping they might continue to speak naturally. Jane and Charlotte began to play and sing, and William watched their performance appreciatively for a few minutes, as nobody else appeared to do, aside from Richard. At length,

William turned to Elizabeth and whispered, "I hope you will come home soon, to have your share in the wedding planning."

Elizabeth let out a shaky breath. *Home.*

"How happy Jane looks – I thought I should never see it again," he said.

Her heart pounded, and she gazed at William with admiration that she could not conceal – to her relief, his eyes were still fixed on Jane at the instrument, and she was at some liberty to simply marvel at him a moment longer. *Of course Mr. Smythe was wrong – so very wrong indeed!* She had been wrong, too, for it was clear to her now that William had always wanted Jane's happiness. He was the very best of men.

He looked her way, and caught her out. Laughing softly, he asked, "Why do you stare at me so?"

"I... I was merely thinking about somebody who annoyed me."

William raised his eyebrows with a look of alarm. "You were staring at me, thinking of someone who annoyed you?"

Elizabeth gasped with startled laughter, and brought her hands up to her cheeks to hide her face. "No, that is not what I meant to say." She chuckled to herself at William's momentary panic, and after a minute he joined in her mirth.

Jane missed a few notes of the song she was playing with Charlotte as she turned to glance back at William and Elizabeth, and Elizabeth could have sworn she saw Uncle Henry, across the room playing at whist, give her mother a roguish wink. She glanced over at John, and her cousin made a great show of raising his book higher in front of his face.

Jane and Charlotte's duet ended, and Charlotte began a song by herself as Richard led Jane to the furthest sofa from William and Elizabeth, who gazed at her family with affectionate defiance before she turned her eyes on William. Making a slight gesture with her head, she rolled her eyes and clucked her tongue at all their family and then looked back at him. William smirked. "Yes," he murmured.

Elizabeth shook her head, and as a gust of wind rattled the nearby windowpane, she suddenly stood up and said – rather loudly, for the benefit of her impertinent relations, "My, how it is snowing! It is quite a blizzard."

The earl drew his attention away from the game of whist for a moment and turned to look out another window near his seat. "Indeed it is," he cried. "I daresay you shall all have to stay the night!"

"Surely not," Uncle Edward cried.

"No, no, we insist – is it not so, Phyllis?"

"It would be safest."

"You and William take the two guest rooms. Lizzy can share with

Charlotte, and Anne, you and Jane can take my niece's room – Catherine and Anne will surely be just as trapped, at the Marquess's house," Uncle Henry declared.

Uncle Edward looked at Lady Anne, who gave a little nod of her head, and the earl took that for agreement enough to consider the matter quite settled. Elizabeth glanced over at William; he gave a little roll of his eyes and gestured with his head toward the window farthest from the others. Elizabeth moved that way, peering out the window at the heavy snow blowing about in the wind outside.

A moment later, William joined her, his hands behind his back as he stood at her side, watching the snow. "They are all acting strangely, are they not?"

"I do love our family, but I daresay they are always rather strange."

William laughed. "That sounds like something Richard would say."

"Or our lady grandmother!"

"She misses you, you know. You should come and see her. She has tolerated visits from Aunt Catherine and Cousin Anne every day, and grows crankier at the conclusion of each visit."

Elizabeth laughed softly, still staring out at the snow. "Do not speak of Anne de Bourgh," she chided, before biting her lip, wondering if she ought to have said something so rude.

"I shall never disagree with that."

"Is there anything you *would* speak of?"

William waited to speak until Elizabeth had turned to look at him. "We could speak of your gentleman caller," he whispered.

Elizabeth wrung her hands. "Oh dear, only if you do not call him *that*. To own the truth, when I said before that I was thinking of someone who had annoyed me, it was Mr. Smythe that I meant. I was civil to him because I am fond of his aunt, but he really made me so cross today, and I should not like to see him again."

William looked concerned, and reached out to place a hand on her shoulder. "Has he hurt you, Elizabeth? I swear to God, I will call him out."

Elizabeth raised her hand to place it atop his, on her shoulder. "No – nothing like that, I assure you. He only made some impertinent remarks about my family, that is all." She chewed her lip for a moment. It was odd, for Mr. Smythe had clearly been in jest when he suggested that Mr. Collins might call him out, and it occurred to her now that it had been a rather cruel jest for him to make at her cousin's expense, for Will Collins was a kind young man and did not deserve such derision from a stranger.

"What sort of remarks?" William asked.

"Honestly, the more I think upon it, the more I find fault in his conversation. He insulted Cousin Will – truly, Cousin Will likes *absolutely everybody*, but not Mr. Smythe, and that alone is remarkable. Mr. Smythe made a jest at Cousin Will's expense that was not very kind, nor entirely appropriate. And then, there was a comment in passing about Rose – I cannot quite recall, but that it was unseemly, considering she is not yet out in society." Elizabeth stopped, not wishing to tell William what Mr. Smythe had said of *him*, and said only, "I should like not to meet with him again."

"I cannot like this, Elizabeth. I should go and have a talk with this Mr. Smythe." William removed his hand from her shoulder and brought it down to his side, where he found her fingers and laced them with his, positioning his body so that the gesture might not be observed.

Elizabeth ran her thumb across the top of his hand. "There is no need, William. He... he does not matter."

William moved closer, his voice trembling. "You were only civil to him because his aunt is your friend... not because of what happened between us?"

Elizabeth drew nearer the window and stared out at the snow. "No, it was only a chance meeting, and not a pleasant one."

"And, after what happened, could you ever come home?"

There was that word again – *home*. "You want me there?"

"I do want you," he breathed. "I only wonder what this Mr. Smythe might want."

"What does it matter," she sighed, "I love you, William!"

Elizabeth froze and clapped a hand over her mouth, not able to meet William's eye; she turned her face away, and found eight sets of eyes fixed on them. For a moment, one might have heard a pin drop in the Matlock Drawing room, and then everything suddenly resumed as if nothing had happened – Charlotte continued playing, the earl and his companions went back to the game of whist, Jane and Richard lost themselves in one another's gaze again, and John once more picked up his book, in which he'd likely not turned a single page.

Elizabeth let out a shaky breath and looked up at William. "Excuse yourself – say you are going to bed. I shall send Charlotte after you, and as soon as I can get away I shall meet you in the library," he whispered, giving her hand another squeeze.

"Yes, Charlotte shall cover for me."

***

Elizabeth paced the length of Charlotte's bedchamber until at last her cousin slipped into the room. "William sent me to come and speak with you."

Elizabeth rushed to her cousin's side, falling into her ready embrace. She buried her face in Charlotte's shoulder and exhaled. "Good God, what have I done?"

"Delighted everyone who is still downstairs," Charlotte quipped.

Elizabeth could only groan. "I am mortified!"

"Why? Is Jane mortified at being in love with Richard? Is Mary ashamed of her affection for Mr. Bingley?"

Elizabeth shook her head and laughed as she pulled away from Charlotte. "I suppose you are right, only it was such a shocking thing of me to do. Good Heavens, what did Mamma say about it?"

"I daresay they are already planning your wedding at the whist table even now. Poor cousin William!"

Elizabeth sat down heavily on Charlotte's bed, holding her head in her hands. "I was so anxious at the prospect of seeing him – truly, I did wish to speak with him, but I had no notion that *that* would come out."

Charlotte sat down at her side. "I think it a rather good job that it did."

Elizabeth took a deep breath. "I suppose... I suppose it *is* a relief to have said it."

"There now! See, now that you have admitted it, you have nothing to fear. Nothing can hurt you now, for Cousin William's reaction was *most* assuring."

Elizabeth chewed her lip. "He asked me to meet him in the library."

"Then go, get out of here," Charlotte said, shooing Elizabeth away with a giggle.

***

The earl and countess were close behind their daughter in retiring for the evening, and John as well. Lady Anne was engrossed in conversation with Sir Edward, as Jane was with Richard, and so Darcy simply slipped unnoticed from the drawing room. He knew it could not be possible that they were all truly so unaware of him, though his demeanor was far more stoic than what he felt inside. Nonetheless, he was happy to be away from them, and let out a deep, discomposed breath as he made his way down the corridor, his mind a whirl.

Elizabeth was waiting for him in the library, and as soon as he shut the door behind him, it occurred to him that he knew not what to say – he ought to have some fine speech to make, yet he was unprepared. She stood in the center of the room, peered nervously up at him, and he went straight toward her, taking her in his arms at once. "I love you," he said, kissing her face as he held her. "I love you, Elizabeth Bennet." He kissed her face again. "Elizabeth Darcy." Again. "I love you, I love you, I love you." Again, again, again he kissed her face, and finally, her lips.

Elizabeth leaned in, clinging to him, returning his kisses with a force of passion beyond anything he had dared to wish for. His hands were in her hair, on her neck, and finally they slid down her back, gripping her hips as he pulled her closer. Her body responded to his, and in a moment he had lifted her up; her legs wrapped around his waist as his lips trailed down her cheekbones and then down her neck, which she craned back, allowing his mouth to travel lower still.

Only when a moan of pleasure escaped her lips did he stop, feeling a certain stirring himself. He set her down, both of them breathing heavily as they leaned into one another. Finally she looked up at him and smiled. "Did you say, Elizabeth Darcy?"

He gazed down at her, running his hands up her arms until they rested on her shoulders. "Would you like that?"

"Not... not just yet, but... soon, yes. Could you... could you wait?"

Though his body protested otherwise, he said, "For you, Elizabeth, I could wait as long as you wish, so long as I know you will be mine someday."

Her smile widened, and she kissed him again.

***

Lady Anne and Sir Edward exchanged a knowing look as William slipped silently out of the room. "Jane, my dear, we had better retire."

"Yes, Mamma," Jane said, and she stood, smiling up at Richard as he whispered some parting compliment.

Richard bid Anne and Edward goodnight as well, and was granted permission to walk Jane upstairs. As Anne rose to follow them, Edward caught her by the hand. "Stay a while and watch the snow with me, my old friend. I daresay we have much to discuss."

Anne smiled fondly at him, and extended her hand. "Indeed we have, but not here. Upstairs in the gallery, there is a window overlooking the square – it was my favorite place when I was a girl."

"Lead the way," Edward said, taking her hand with an affectionate look.

The house was quiet, the only light upstairs coming from the library as Anne led Edward around the corner, to the gallery. Wide windows stretched from the floor to the ceiling, and Anne drew near them, looking out on the snowy square.

Edward came and stood at her side. "What a night, Anne. Can you believe it? William and Lizzy! And all three of our girls in love, likely to be wed by summer."

Anne reached out and slipped her hand into his once more, enjoying the warmth of him as her breath frosted over the icy window panes. "I never thought I would see our family so happy again."

"Nor I, my dear. And yet I must brace myself for what is coming next – endless talk of wedding clothes!"

She laughed. "Oh, yes. I imagine we shall have to ransack your warehouses, Edward."

"You may take what you like, I am sure."

Anne gave a sigh of contentment, and wrapped her fingers around Edward's. "It is strange to think they shall all leave me."

"Not Lizzy, surely."

"No, not exactly, but it will be different. I suppose if anyone is to come first in her heart, I am glad it is William."

Edward squeezed her hand, leaning in until their shoulders touched. "I am glad to hear you say that. I thought... I thought it might bother you. For them to grow up together, and then... well, I was not sure, after seventeen years, that it would be so easy for them to... to add romance to their relationship."

Anne rested her head on Edward's shoulder and sighed happily as she watched the snow swirling through the air outside. Her shawl had slipped off of her shoulder and she shivered, but Edward reached around her to fix her shawl and then rested his hand on her shoulder, his arm across her back.

She looked up at him, but he was staring out at the snow. "We have a very strange family, do we not?" Edward chuckled, and she was near enough to feel the deep rumble in his chest. She had not been held by a man in more than three years, and her heart felt as if it would burst open after being closed away for so long. "I love them all so dearly," she sighed, wondering if she could be as brave as her daughter. "I love you, Edward."

He wrapped his arm tighter around her and kissed the top of her head before resting his own head there, and staring out the window with her. "I know, Anne," he breathed. "And I love you, too."

Anne closed her eyes. She slipped her hand into the pocket of her gown, reaching for the handkerchief she had been carrying with her since Christmas, and, letting out a heavy exhale before drawing in a deep breath of absolute tranquility, she gently ran her thumb over the handkerchief, feeling the embroidery on the initials EG.

***

Elizabeth giggled and leaned back against Charlotte's door after she closed it behind her. Charlotte was seated on her bed, nearly swallowed up by her blankets, with a candle lit on her end stand, waiting expectantly for her cousin's return. "Well?"

Elizabeth stretched, and feigned a yawn. "I am so tired."

Charlotte hurled a pillow at her. "Not so fast – tell me everything."

Elizabeth smiled as she threw herself heavily down on the bed, causing Charlotte to bounce. "Well, we kissed passionately for half an hour."

"Sounds like an excellent sort of conversation. Pray, did you do any actual speaking?"

"A little – but only as much as was necessary."

"And?"

"He loves me!"

"Obviously." Charlotte stuck out her tongue at Elizabeth.

"Indeed not! I was rather terrified, Charlotte."

"And now you need only fear the wedding preparations – and Aunt Catherine!"

Elizabeth wiggled on her back as she laughed, and Charlotte nudged her playfully. "I am still not ready for all that – not yet at least. I did manage to tell William that I still need time. I know there is still so much we do not know about each other, but I should like to find it all out," she said with a wicked laugh.

Charlotte hummed thoughtfully to herself. "What was it like?"

"The kiss?"

"Yes."

"Mmm... wonderful. My whole body felt warm and I wanted to touch him and be touched, and...." Elizabeth suddenly stopped, feeling her face grow hot as she realized she could not possibly give voice to the rest of it.

Charlotte giggled. "Oh my."

"Oh Charlotte, if only there were such a man for you!"

"Indeed! I daresay if there was, I should not be speaking of *waiting* for anything – or be speaking much at all," she laughed.

"I cannot believe it! You *are* a romantic, Charlotte, and I never knew it!"

Charlotte's face grew serious. "I should like romance as much as anyone, Lizzy, even though I know well enough to be practical. I may be older, but I am still a girl, and matters of the heart are more to me than just a jest over supper. I do not know why it should astonish anybody that I have not yet resigned myself to either cheerful spinsterhood, or a marriage of convenience."

"Oh, Charlotte," Elizabeth sighed, taking her cousin's hands. "I did not mean it like that – I am sorry."

"I know, dearest. I only wish... well, never mind that. I am happy for you, now let us get some sleep."

***

Richard could not sleep for thinking of Jane, envious that he had not gotten to sneak away with his lady love as Darcy had. He was on the verge of creeping from his room to see if anyone was still awake and about, when there came voices in the corridor. He opened the door and stepped out into the hall; in the light of the single sconce still lit, he could make out the figures of Aunt Catherine and her daughter, lurking outside one of the guest rooms.

Richard hung back in the shadows for a moment, listening.

"Now is your chance, Anne," Lady Catherine hissed at her daughter.

"But the maid said Sir Edward is staying the night as well. What if it is not the right room?"

"Nonsense, child. Fitzwilliam always favors the blue room when he stays." Lady Catherine reached up and pulled back the sleeves on Anne's night dress, and began to push her at the door, when Richard stepped forward. He cleared his throat as he strode up to them, and Anne froze as her hand rested on the door knob.

"Aunt Catherine," Richard hissed. "We had not expected you back before morning. Why did the marquess send you home in all this weather?"

"Never you mind," his aunt snapped back. "I hardly anticipated coming home to find my sister and her *daughter* in my own dear girl's bed."

"And so you thought to send her in to Darcy's bed? I think Anne had better share with you, Aunt, and now I must retire, and consider whether I need to tell my father about this in the morning. I am sure you were only over tired, and confused," he said firmly.

Anne glared at him, drawing away from Darcy's door and stomping on Richard's foot as she swept past him toward her mother's room. "We shall see who speaks to Henry in the morning," Lady Catherine said imperiously, before following her daughter.

Richard stood watch, making sure they did indeed return to their room, and then knocked on Darcy's door. There was no answer – he turned the knob and was relieved to find that at least the door was locked, and he needn't stand vigil for his cousin all night. He returned to his room, walking past Jane's door with a heavy longing in his heart.

***

Darcy sat down to breakfast a happy man the next morning. Only Richard and Charlotte were awake, fixing plates for themselves at the sideboard when Darcy entered. "Good morning," he said cheerfully.

"It may be for you," Richard said as he turned around and sat down at the table. "And if it is, I believe you have me to thank, Cousin."

"Is that so? I had rather intended to direct my gratitude elsewhere."

"That you may," Richard said with a wry look. "And yet, I must claim a share myself, for I saved you most heroically from a fate worse than death last night, I am sure."

"Good Heavens, Richard," Charlotte laughed. "Was the house ablaze, I wonder?"

"Not unless Aunt Catherine and her daughter set a fire themselves, once I caught them out trying to sneak into Darcy's room."

Charlotte momentarily lost her composure as she drank her coffee, but Darcy calmly sipped at his own. "It is fortunate that I locked my door."

"Why did you? Has she tried something before?"

"I had wondered if she might. Anne has been to Darcy House every day for a week on the pretense of visiting our grandmother, but she always seeks me out, and with Jane and Mary both receiving their eager beaux, I am forced to be sociable so that she cannot get me alone."

"How tragic for you," Charlotte chortled.

Richard laughed and shrugged. "Well, I hope you settle things quickly with Lizzy, before Anne tries again. After everything that has happened... I hardly know, but we are all so very happy, and I feel the strangest sense of dread."

"Brother, it is far too early to be so maudlin," Charlotte drawled.

Darcy stirred his coffee contemplatively; he had felt the same just last evening. "Elizabeth wishes to take some time yet," he said after a moment. "I shall simply have to speak to Uncle. He clearly favors my intentions toward Elizabeth, from what I could discern last evening."

Richard and Charlotte exchanged a look of private mirth. "Lizzy told me the same, that she needs time," Charlotte said to Darcy.

He regarded his cousins with some amusement. "Were you all in on it, then?"

"Of course, yes, all of us," Charlotte replied. "Well, perhaps not John, at first, but I think he seemed to catch on rather quickly."

"No, he knew," Richard guffawed.

Charlotte laughed. "And Jane was in on it too? I was not sure."

"Nor I, but I think so. She did me very proud, indeed!"

Darcy shook his head and pretended to peruse the newspaper. "What scandalous relations I have," he drawled.

"You certainly have one," Richard said, snatching away Darcy's newspaper. "I have some idea about what to do with Cousin Anne – you know there will only be a row if Father tries to intercede on your behalf – what if we were to provide Anne some... distraction, while you settle things with Lizzy?"

Darcy considered. "You may be right – so much has gone wrong, it does seem strange that it should be smooth sailing from here, and I cannot risk anything else going amiss with Elizabeth. If Anne were to catch wind of it, she might very well make all of us miserable, perhaps Elizabeth most of all."

Richard grinned. "Two words: *Elliot de Bourgh.*"

Charlotte leaned forward with interest. "Who is Elliot de Bourgh?"

Darcy laughed. "There would definitely be a row between Uncle Henry and Lady Catherine."

"Perhaps not – but it would amuse me to find out."

Charlotte swatted at her brother. "Who is Elliot de Bourgh?"

Richard gave her a mysterious smirk before wagging his eyebrows at Darcy. "I am for York next week anyhow, to meet with the fellow who is buying the Scottish estate – come with me, let us visit our old friend. If what Lady Catherine has always feared does indeed come to pass, it shall bode well for you, your sanity, and dear Lizzy as well."

Darcy chuckled. "An entertaining notion, and your estimation is likely accurate; I am sure it could be managed, though I should rather pity poor Elliot."

"No indeed! I daresay he would put up with a great deal to get Rosings Park back into his family's hands."

"But I cannot be away from Elizabeth a whole fortnight."

"A whole fortnight? No – nine days, ten at the most. We could make it in four days there, and the same back again, and we could easily accomplish all our business in the space of one or two days more. Did not Lizzy say she needs time? Give her some – they say absence makes the heart grow fonder."

Darcy nodded. "I shall send word to Elliot and his father – he will need to be ready to travel the morning after we arrive – I shall give you eight days, and that is all."

Richard extended his hand for Darcy to shake. "Eight days it is, Darcy. I shall meet with my buyer and then help you work on Elliot, though I doubt it will take much." He grinned, then drew a little flask out of his coat pocket and poured a generous amount of the amber liquid into his coffee. "The Fitzwilliam cousins, going north on a quest – to track down the man who can woo Anne de Bourgh best!"

Charlotte gaped at her brother, laughing despite her evident confusion. "Will someone please tell me what is going on?"

18

❧❦

The rest of the family had finally made their way down to breakfast, with two notable exceptions, who were not missed at all. The Darcys and Gardiners had just begun to speak of returning home at last, when Mary was shown into the drawing room.

"Here you all are," Mary said. "Grandmamma is quite beside herself, and sent me over directly. Oh – Jane, Richard!" Mary came forward to embrace them and offer her congratulations. "I wished to be here last night, but I knew there should hardly be room for me to stay over – oh!" She leaned in, whispering in Jane's ear. Jane nodded, casting a glance at Elizabeth and William, who were seated nearby; Mary giggled and waved at them.

Elizabeth looked at William and laughed, sliding her hand toward his – he captured it, and gave it a quick kiss. After exchanging more whispers with their mother, Mary soon came over to William and Elizabeth, smirking merrily. "Oh, not you, too," Elizabeth said, rolling her eyes and giving her sister a playful smile.

Her eyes sparkled with mischief. "Yes indeed, me too."

"And so you have come all this way to tease me? I wonder that it was safe to come out at all, as heavily as it snowed last night."

William leaned closer to Elizabeth and discreetly wrapped his arm around her. "It may yet be too dangerous for any of us to leave the house," he whispered in her ear.

"How odd – it is the first day of spring, yet there must be a foot of snow on the ground, I am sure," Mary said. "It was really quite a beautiful sight when I stepped outside this morning. It reminded me of when we were young, at Pemberley."

"Ah, yes," Elizabeth mused dreamily as she leaned nearer to William. "We used to have the most remarkable snowball fights."

"I remember having snowball fights with Richard and John," William said, "and later, with Jane and Mary, but never with you."

"We must remedy that," Elizabeth teased him.

Charlotte was moving that way, and she stopped when she heard Elizabeth speak. "What's this, Cousin? Planning some mischief?"

"Mmm, perhaps." Elizabeth stood up and peered out the window – the road had been mostly cleared, but there was still a beautiful and enticing blanket of snow on the ground in the square.

"I say *yes*," Mary whispered, and as Elizabeth offered her a smirk in return, Mary caught her by one hand, and Charlotte by the other. Laughing, the three girls hurried from the room – Charlotte latched on to Jane on their way out, and the four of them donned their warmest coats before running out of the house, and out onto the square.

Elizabeth followed her sisters and Charlotte out to the middle of the square, the four of them kicking up snow as they ran, and when they reached it, Charlotte spun about with her arms in the air. The snow was still gently falling, and Mary had not exaggerated the amount of it already on the ground.

The rest of their family trickled out of Matlock house. The girls made their way back toward the edge of the square as the earl and countess lingered on the steps with Lady Anne and Sir Edward. John and Richard came bolting around them, down the steps, and across the road with William following behind at a more sedate pace.

"Have some decorum, children," the earl cried out to them.

Charlotte was the first to throw a snowball, packing it quickly and tossing it across the road at her father. It fell short of the stairs, but Lady Phyllis give a cheeky smile and scooped some snow off of the railing of the stairs, smashing it into the earl's chest. Aunt Phyllis caught Lady Anne by the hand and led her down the steps, and she in turn latched on to Sir Edward; soon even the Earl was forced to make his way out to enjoy the snow.

The Fitzwilliam brothers had just reached the ladies, and Richard stopped just short of Jane, heaving himself backward. He moved his arms and legs through the loosely packed snow, making a snow angel, while John kicked more loose snow back at him.

Jane laughed at her fiancé, and he kicked his leg up behind hers, causing her to tumble down onto the snow beside him with a loud squawk. The earl chided them again as he approached the square. "I daresay half the neighborhood will see you – look, you already have an audience." Uncle Henry pointed across the square, at the Gardiner House on Upper Brook Street. There in the window was Rose, her hands pressed up against the glass, watching them.

Elizabeth gave a little jump of glee and waved her hands in the air, beckoning Rose to join them. She let out a little cry of delight, and a moment later felt an arm catch her around the waist – she looked up at William and smiled at the sight of him with snowflakes in his hair.

"If we were home at Pemberley, I would take you skating on a day like this," he whispered in her ear. "Quite alone."

Elizabeth blushed and drew away from him just a little. He had been openly affectionate with her since she had come down to breakfast, but despite their activities the prior evening – or perhaps because of them – she was still adjusting to keeping her composure while in such close physical proximity. Out in the open as they were, she could not let herself be tempted. As she moved away from his embrace, she noticed he still held one arm behind his back, and asked, "What have you there?"

He raised his hand to reveal a very well-packed snowball. Again he leaned in to whisper, "Who shall my target be?"

Elizabeth looked around, tapping her chin as she considered. Rose was just that moment coming out of the Gardiner house, still putting her gloves on, and Elizabeth gestured in her cousin's direction – Rose would take it in good humor.

"She is too far," he whispered. "Try again."

Elizabeth cast her eyes across the square. The earl and countess had hung back as her sisters and cousins frolicked in the snow, and at the center of the square her mother and Uncle Edward had drifted toward a little copse of trees – Elizabeth noticed with no little curiosity that they were holding hands.

"I should think it an easy decision," William chided her, and pointed at the earl as he took him and hurled the snowball into the air. The earl was struck square in his belly, and cried out in exaggerated indignation. For a moment his children and nieces all stared at him in alarm before breaking out into laughter. William had already crouched down to begin packing another, which he launched at Richard.

Rose ran to join them, and for several minutes a cheerful chaos ensued. Elizabeth happily ignored the cold in her fingers and on her face as she pelted her companions with snowballs, everyone ignoring the earl's banter about decorum as he dodged their projectiles. Their amusement came to a halt when a carriage came down the road and stopped outside Matlock House; they all turned to watch as two gentlemen and two ladies descended the carriage and approached the snowy square.

Jane ran up to them, squealing with delight, while Rose, John, and Mary were close behind. Mr. Collins and Mr. Bingley doffed their hats. "We were just coming to see you," Caroline cried out, embracing Jane and then Mary, before attaching herself to John with a look of great affection.

Mr. Collins began to approach Sir Edward, waving at him, and at Elizabeth as well, when he was struck by a snowball; Rose laughed until she fell backward in the snow, and the countess kicked more snow at her with a grin. Elizabeth looked up at William and they beamed happily at one another before going to greet their friends. She gave a sigh of contentment as she took in the scene before her, with everyone she held dear so merry together – she had never felt so much a part of a true family until this moment, and she squeezed William's hand. "I love you," she whispered.

He smiled bashfully at her. "It is good to hear you say that – although I still think my way of saying it was rather a little better."

She blushed at the recollection. "I cannot disagree, though at present, neither can I indulge you." She gave him a cheeky wink before moving away to speak with Mr. Collins and Mr. Bingley.

Their merry party was soon broken up when the sun broke through the clouds, promising to melt the snow, and the countess invited everybody in to warm themselves by the fire with some tea.

Mrs. Bingley had attached herself to Sir Edward, who declined the earl's invitation, stating that he had business to attend to, and William offered to escort Elizabeth back to her uncle's house. Mr. Collins followed as well, speaking with Uncle Edward and Rose, as Elizabeth and William lagged behind.

"There is something I must tell you," William said as he took Elizabeth's hand.

"What is it?"

"Richard has asked me to travel with him to Yorkshire, on some business."

"Oh. And have you agreed?"

"I have, but I should be too happy to tell him that you have refused to allow it."

"Is that so? I do not know what to make of having so much authority," she laughed.

He looked earnestly at her. "Truly, my love – would it bother you if I went away for a week or so? Eight days, nine at the most... You said you wished for some time, and I thought perhaps it would be good for us, as separation has been before."

"Will you write me?"

"Every day, if you wish."

"Will you miss me?"

He raised her hand to his lips and gave it a quick kiss. "I will do little else."

Elizabeth smiled. "I cannot object to you going, any more than Jane could object to Richard going – rather less, I think."

"That part is entirely up to you," William teased her.

"I shall miss you, but a week, or even nine days, is not so very long. I confess I might benefit from some time to adjust my mind to everything that has happened."

"I hope you do not regret any of it."

"No, not at all – only it is all so new, so unexpected."

"But... you are happy? I could make you happy?"

"Oh yes, William. You make me very happy."

"And shall you be back at Darcy House when I return?"

Elizabeth chewed her lip. "Perhaps not – not yet. But I shall visit every day to look in on Grandmamma, and to see Mamma and Jane and Mary."

"Shall you write to me?"

Elizabeth laughed. "I suppose, if you give me the direction. Shall you have time to receive one of my letters?"

"Richard and I mean to depart within the hour. If you write tomorrow, you can forward it along to Bourghleigh Hall, near York."

"And what is at Bourghleigh Hall, near York?"

"Something – someone who is going to make Aunt Catherine very angry."

Elizabeth laughed again. "I approve already."

***

William wrote every day of his journey to York, both of his travels with Richard and of his affection for Elizabeth. She was not surprised that his feelings, like hers, had begun on the night of the ball, and he used some incredibly risqué language in describing the anticipation he felt at returning just in time to dance with her again at Richard and Jane's engagement ball, or even to explore a library with her. His fourth letter confirmed his arrival at Bourghleigh, though by the time it arrived in London, Elizabeth knew William must be on his return journey already.

She visited Darcy House daily. Wedding preparations for Jane and Richard were already underway, and when it became too overpowering, Elizabeth made her escape to speak with her grandmother, who was every day asking to look at Elizabeth's letters from Darcy, and laughing wickedly when she was refused.

William had been gone a week when Lady Eleanor's injuries had healed enough for her to return to Matlock House, and on that morning Elizabeth remained at home. Cousin Will paid them a visit, eager to confide to Elizabeth, Rose, and Uncle Edward that his friend Mr. Bingley had gone to Darcy House that morning on a *particular errand*. Elizabeth was delighted, Uncle Edward beamed with pride, and Rose declared herself thoroughly envious; Cousin Will met all of their reactions with equal affability.

They had been chatting together for half an hour when another caller was admitted to the room – it was Mr. Smythe, carrying a bouquet of flowers. He had called twice that week, while Elizabeth was at Darcy House, but she had not responded to the calling cards he left – indeed, she had forgotten about the man entirely.

Clearly he had not forgotten her; he appeared as keen as ever to recommend himself to Elizabeth. He greeted them all warmly before taking a step toward Elizabeth and offering her the flowers. "I fear I offended you, when last we met," he said breathily. "The opposite of my intentions, I assure you."

Uncle Edward stepped forward to intervene. "Yes, well, young man, whatever your intentions, I think I had better ask you to desist, and hint that my niece is very soon to be engaged."

Elizabeth looked with wide eyes at her uncle, both surprised to hear him speaking so sternly, and still unaccustomed to her amorous accord with William. She was not sure that she would *soon* be engaged, but this was hardly the time to refute it, when it suited her purposes so well.

"Engaged?" Mr. Smythe looked at her with astonishment, and then his eyes sought Mr. Collins. "I see," he said coldly. "I have clearly misunderstood you, dear Miss Bennet."

"Sir, I must ask you to leave," Uncle Edward said, folding his arms in an imposing stance between Elizabeth and Mr. Smythe. "It would be best if you did not return."

Mr. Smythe's countenance looked rather hateful for a moment, before he schooled his expression into one of guarded disappointment. "Very well, sir," he said, giving Elizabeth one last glance before tossing the bouquet of flowers into the fire and storming out of the room.

The room was silent for a moment, and then Rose began to shift her gaze between Elizabeth and Sir Edward, laughing nervously. Sir Edward gave Rose a quelling look, and she was obliged to lean on Mr. Collins for support.

***

William and Richard were away for nine days, returning late in the afternoon on the day of Richard and Jane's engagement ball. Elizabeth was disappointed that she would have no opportunity to see William until that evening, as her preparations for the night were well underway, and this time Rose was getting ready alongside her.

Rose was a fortnight away from her seventeenth birthday, and after a week of alternately begging and cajoling her father, and seemingly being on the verge of tears every moment, she had been granted permission to attend the ball. Her toilette proved to be a massive undertaking, though Elizabeth attempted to remind her blissfully frantic cousin that this night was not her official debut, and was indeed meant to honor Jane and Richard.

"Yes, I know that, Lizzy," Rose huffed, trying on her fourth gown. "I am sure I could not upstage Jane for all the world. She is so very beautiful! Now what do you think of this one?"

Elizabeth gave an affectionate roll of her eyes. "It is just as lovely as the first three, I am sure."

"Ugh," Rose cried, and tossed the gown aside in favor of the first one she had tried on. Elizabeth shook her head, nearly causing the maid to burn her with the curling tongs. "Have a care, Lizzy," Rose laughed. "I daresay it shall be a big night for you, too."

Elizabeth smiled to herself, thinking of William. The distance between them had indeed given her time to consider everything that had passed between them, and she sincerely hoped they would be afforded some opportunity to speak privately that night, for she had come to feel that she could wait no longer.

***

The party from Darcy House arrived fashionably late; Charlotte had already left the receiving line to mingle in the ballroom with Elizabeth when the Darcys arrived. Elizabeth felt her gaze drawn to William the moment he entered the room, and she felt the need to instantly be at his side, perhaps asking for some further elaboration on some of his rather saucy insinuations in the letters he had written her while he had been away in York.

She felt a little thrill in her chest at the recollection of his letters, and would have gone to his side directly, had Charlotte not latched on to her arm. "Heaven and Earth! Lizzy, *who is that?*"

It was only then that Elizabeth noticed the man with William – a tall, broad-shouldered, tanned gentleman who walked with Lady Anne on his arm, though he was a whole head taller than she. He was muscular, yet graceful in his step, dressed exceedingly well, and seemed to already be attracting a great deal of attention from at least one half of the crush in the ballroom. Elizabeth laughed at the sight of such masculine perfection. "That must be William and Richard's secret weapon, Elliot de Bourgh."

Charlotte sighed. "Oh my. He is... very welcome at Matlock House."

"I am sure he is! Cousin, do you need some air?"

"I think I rather do," Charlotte drawled, "though I should hate to turn my eyes away from him. What a pity he is meant for Cousin Anne."

"I am not entirely sure I understand this scheme of theirs," Elizabeth admitted. "I can see why they might assume Mr. de Bourgh could draw cousin Anne's attention away from William, but would she really have him? He *is* still a second son, is he not?"

"Who cares?" Charlotte nearly panted.

"Very good point," Elizabeth agreed. "I would still argue that William is the handsomest man in the room, but Mr. de Bourgh might be the second most."

"Had I been in any doubt of your affection, that should be the confirmation of it," Charlotte whispered, "for you are utterly wrong. Never before have I seen – Good Heavens, he is looking over here! Smile, Lizzy."

"You smile, Charlotte. It seems such a waste that he should be for Anne, even if his family does want to get their hands on Rosings Park."

"Your wisdom does you great credit," Charlotte said with a wink and a sly smile. "And so much the better, because he is coming this way."

Rose materialized at their side, clinging to Elizabeth's arm. "You have had your share of balls and parties this season, Lizzy," she whispered. "I hope you will remember that some of us have not had our fair share yet." She straightened her shoulders, pushing her chest out as the Darcys and Mr. de Bourgh approached.

Elizabeth laughed and gave her cousins each a little nudge. "Poor Mr. Collins, will none of you think of him now?"

***

"Well Darcy, which one is she?" Elliot de Bourgh scanned the ballroom, smiling and nodding at any lady that caught his eye, and there were a great many.

"Over there by the fireplace, speaking with her mother – she is wearing the purple gown with gold striping."

Darcy saw a brief look of distaste flicker across Elliot's countenance before he schooled his expression into a more neutral look. "She is much changed since last we met, ten years ago."

"As are you, I daresay," William drawled.

"I have grown, I think, for the better," Elliot laughed.

"Do you remain willing…?"

"If everything you and Richard have told me is true, I can expect to invest half of her dowry in recouping the losses my late uncle's estate has suffered in the years of our aunt's mismanagement, and still keep a house in Town besides. It is what my father wishes, and I have yet to meet anyone I really like – yes, I would say I am still willing. I have been since she was of age, but her mother would not hear of it."

"Shall we go and speak with her?"

Elliot shook his head. "Not yet." He glanced around the ballroom. "Which one is your lady, and which one is Richard's?"

"You have already met Jane. She is engaged to Richard. Her sister Elizabeth, who has long resided in London, is just over there, in the magnificent green dress, speaking with Richard's sister."

"That is Richard's sister?"

"Yes, Lady Charlotte Fitzwilliam."

"I like the sight of *her*," Elliot said with a grin. "See how the two ladies with her are laughing. She is witty and amusing like Richard, I can tell."

"Yes, but Anne –"

"Anne has not thought of me in ten years, I am sure. I cannot make it too easy on her. The sport shall be better if I get her chasing me."

By now William's mother and sisters had gone ahead to greet Elizabeth and Charlotte, and by the time William and Elliot reached them, Richard and Mr. Bingley had approached their ladies to claim the first dance, which was just beginning.

Elizabeth was watching him with a wide smile, an expression his cousin Charlotte was mirroring as Darcy performed the introductions. "It is a pleasure to meet you," Charlotte said, blushing crimson as she curtseyed to Elliot de Bourgh.

"The pleasure is mine," said he, "and it would be greater still if you would dance with me, Lady Charlotte." He flexed his arm as he extended Charlotte his hand.

"Yes, it would," Charlotte breathed, taking his hand and making eyes at him as if he had just made her an indecent proposal.

Elizabeth was biting her lip to contain her mirth, and Darcy quickly whisked her away to dance before she began laughing outright. "I take it that was not part of your plan," Elizabeth quipped as they began the steps of the dance.

"No, it was not... but that is Elliot de Bourgh."

She laughed once more. "He is Cousin Anne's relation, but you seem to know him well. I think you wrote that you were acquainted at Cambridge?"

"He and Richard were both a year ahead of me, and by then we all knew of Aunt Catherine's dislike for all her in-laws – Richard decided to befriend him his first year at Cambridge on a lark, and over the years we both came to find his company some of our favorite amongst all our acquaintance. He is a good man."

"He seems popular with the ladies," Elizabeth said. "I wonder that he is not married already."

"I have remained single all of these years, Elizabeth, because I have always known exactly what I wanted in a woman, and have only just recently, at last, discovered all that and more. Elliot is much the same. He is remarkably intelligent, but... odd."

"What do you mean by odd – should I be worried for Charlotte?"

"What I mean is that he is clever, but not in the usual way. Your cleverness comes with a wit that absolutely sparkles in conversation. Elliot has never had to be adept at conversation in order to attract those that would speak with him, if you take my meaning. He knows what little compliments might please the ladies, but when his conversation is inevitably too intellectual, and his sense of humor rather dark – well, he has learned to often say less, and let people come to conclusions based on his appearance, rather than his mind."

"Poor man! But he seems to be doing well enough with Charlotte," Elizabeth whispered, looking around to see if the other dancers were listening to their conversation.

"He is rather wasted on Anne," Darcy admitted in a low voice. "His father is pressuring him to marry, and has long had his eye on his late brother Sir Lewis's estate. Aunt Catherine has avoided Elliot assiduously these ten years or more for fear of Anne growing attached to him. She despises the de Bourghs, though, I rather wonder she has not grown weary all these years of trying to push Anne at me, when she might at least have her daughter married to a willing and respectable gentleman."

"Perhaps, like me, she considers you a more desirable man," Elizabeth said, biting her lip very prettily.

William felt his cheeks grow warm as he gazed down at Elizabeth with adoration. "Do you really think so?"

"Can you doubt it? I think you are very fine to look upon, and I am in no way dismayed by your intelligent conversation. Elliot de Bourgh is tolerable, I suppose, but he is not handsome enough to tempt me."

Darcy laughed, spinning Elizabeth with the other dancers. "My goodness," Elizabeth whispered. "Aunt Catherine certainly appears to be giving Uncle Henry the business over there." She gestured with her head, and Darcy looked down the ballroom, to where Lady Catherine was indeed having what appeared to be an extremely unpleasant conversation with the Earl of Matlock.

Nearby, Anne was seated beside Mrs. Bingley, her eyes fixed on Elliot de Bourgh. He and Charlotte were dancing nearby; they were, by all appearances, getting along famously – Charlotte was looking at Elliot in much the same way as women always did, but Elliot looked more at ease than he ever had in such a situation.

"I worry for Charlotte," Darcy observed to Elizabeth. "I know she is aware of the plan, but I think I had better speak to her after this, and give her some gentle reminder – or perhaps it would be better coming from you, woman to woman. I would hate to see her wounded."

"It is so endearing, William, to see you looking out for her. I should not like to see her hurt, either. It is strange, for I know you brought him here to distract Anne, so that she might not hinder our progress as we grow better acquainted, and yet I wonder...."

She gave him such a tantalizing look that he let out a shaky breath, wishing they were alone. "What is it, my love?"

"I was only thinking that if our attachment was made known, if Aunt Catherine and Cousin Anne were made to admit their defeat, there should be no reason for us to fear their interference, and yet it would make your bringing Elliot de Bourgh here all for naught. Unless...." she glanced back at Charlotte, and then smiled up at Darcy and gave him a saucy wink.

They went down the dance together, and when they had gotten to the end of it, Darcy pulled her away from the other dancers and led her to a corner of the room. "If our attachment was made known...?"

Elizabeth smiled at him, chewing her lip again. "I told you I needed time, but with every letter I received from you, I...." She fell silent as two garishly dressed matrons walked past, gossiping. "Not here," she whispered, and discreetly took his hand and led him out onto the balcony. *The same balcony where....*

"There, now," Elizabeth said when they were alone together.

Before she could say more, Darcy reached up and placed a finger on her lips to still her. "A moment, my love. There is a matter of great import, to which I must attend."

"Oh?"

He led her by the hand to the little stone bench, and sat down beside her. Without saying a word, he took her in his arms and kissed her. She was as responsive as she had been that night in the library, and so incredibly warm. She broke away from him and gave a happy little sigh, then looked about, suddenly seeming to realize where they were. "Oh dear – oh, William, the Twelfth Night... tell me you did not see...."

"I did," he sighed.

"Oh, my love. I did not – that is –"

"I know," he said, cupping her hands in his. "I came out here that night, having just overheard what you really thought of me. Richard said I should try to get along with you for his sake, and I was beastly about it. Then I came out here and saw – well, I thought that in my attempt to dissuade him from pursuing you, Elizabeth, I had pushed him into the arms of the beautiful, mysterious starling who had captivated me and utterly captured my heart."

"Would that it had been you, that night."

He laughed. "That would have been a disaster."

"I suppose it would have *then*. But now...."

"Now, I think you had better explain what you meant when you said that we should make our attachment known."

"I think you know what I mean," she breathed, wrapping her arms around him. "After nine days away from you, and everything you wrote in your letters, I find I cannot wait much longer." She kissed him briefly on the lips, then on the jaw, and then pressed her body against him as she nibbled at his ear, her breath hot on his neck.

Darcy groaned as he held her close, his breathing ragged. "Elizabeth, we must marry at once!"

She laughed and rubbed her nose against his cheek. "After all our uncle's scheming, it would serve him right if we took off for Gretna Green directly!"

He hugged her close, humming happily. "Say the word, Elizabeth, and I shall call for the carriage at once."

She laughed. "Who do you think would be the angriest?"

"It would be a ten-way tie at the least. Our lady grandmother would absolutely throttle me."

"Do you know, she asked to see the letters you sent me!"

Darcy blushed, remembering a few especially amorous lines he had penned in his first letter, with their evening in the library so fresh in his mind. "Oh dear."

"Oh, yes," she laughed, eyeing him flirtatiously. "I could hardly keep my countenance. There was one passage in particular, about the very promising possibilities of the Pemberley library...."

Darcy pulled her closer for one more kiss, before standing up. "We had better go and speak to Sir Edward at once."

Elizabeth leapt to her feet as if entirely unaffected by the tone the conversation had taken. "Would Jane and Richard be very angry if we make the announcement tonight?"

"At the moment, Elizabeth, I cannot say I much care," he growled, giving her a little squeeze before they returned to the ballroom.

***

The announcement was made at dinner, and the reactions of all their family were duly predictable – in short, everyone was elated except for Aunt Catherine. Even Cousin Anne was well enough distracted by Elliot de Bourgh to show no distress at all.

After the meal the dancing resumed, and Darcy was on the point of asking Elizabeth to join him alongside their mother and Sir Edward, when Mr. Collins approached him.

"Mr. Darcy, Cousin Elizabeth, my congratulations. But I am interfering with your elegant dancing – my apologies, of course, only I had rather hoped to have a word with you, Mr. Darcy."

Elizabeth smiled warmly at her cousin before looking up at Darcy. "Go on, then. I see poor Mr. de Bourgh over there looking rather in need of rescue."

Darcy looked around, and saw that Elliot was indeed looking beleaguered by the conversation of all three of the Bingleys at once. He looked back at Elizabeth appreciatively. "He shall be eternally grateful, I am sure."

As Elizabeth moved away, Mr. Collins said, "I wonder if there is somewhere private we might speak? Would your uncle the earl allow us the use of his study for just a few minutes?"

Darcy began to grow concerned, but acquiesced, and led Mr. Collins out of the ballroom and down the corridor, toward his uncle's study. Inside, he offered Mr. Collins a seat and a drink, but he declined both. "I will be brief, Mr. Darcy. As you are now engaged to my cousin, I think it right to bring this to you. Sir Edward is a dear friend, and while I hold him in high esteem, I have received the impression that he may not share my concerns in this matter. In short, I wonder if you have heard anything of Mr. Smythe?"

"I have," Darcy admitted with some trepidation; he helped himself to a glass of his uncle's brandy.

"Very good – I am sure my cousin Elizabeth would not conceal it from you – not to imply that there is anything untoward, at least not on her part...."

"I have heard that he has paid her some unwanted attention."

"He has, and yet I think there is more in it than she might realize. After meeting Mr. Smythe about a fortnight ago, and forming a most unfavorable impression, I was relieved when Cousin Elizabeth seemed impervious to his charms, and I am sure that is why her excellent uncle pressed the matter no further. However, Mr. Smythe paid her another visit a couple days ago, and it was not a pleasant one. Sir Edward asked him not to call again, but I fear they have not seen the last of him, for there was such a look about him. An evil look."

Darcy felt his blood began to boil, but attempted to remain calm. "I see."

"There is more. His aunt, this *Mrs. Younge*.... I thought it strange that she should put herself forward with my three cousins, and then single Cousin Elizabeth out, and after Elizabeth had left the protection of Darcy House, there was this chance meeting with Mrs. Younge pushing her nephew at Elizabeth. Far too convenient!"

"Indeed," Darcy said, sensing there was more still.

"As you know, I have lived at Longbourn since shortly after Elizabeth and her family ceased to reside there. It occurred to me to send some inquiries to my friends and neighbors, asking after a Mrs. Younge, or perhaps a Miss Smythe, who might have been friends with

Fanny Bennet. Nobody in the neighborhood had ever heard of such a person."

"So she is an impostor, and he a fortune hunter."

"I thought so, and yet it is undeniable that the pair of them *do* seem to possess certain information about Elizabeth's family history, at least enough to pass themselves off credibly."

"What does this man look like?"

"About your height, very tanned – he claims he is from Cornwall, and yet even Elizabeth has observed his northern accent. He wears his hair long, with very pronounced sideburns, and dresses rather like a dandy."

"Green eyes?"

"Yes, I think so."

Darcy closed his eyes and ran his hands through his hair. "Cleft chin?"

"A little, yes."

Darcy paced the room for a few minutes, downed his brandy, poured himself another, and then downed that one.

"Mr. Darcy, I must –"

"No. Speak of this to no one, Mr. Collins. And… thank you." Darcy strode out of the room; he needed to speak with Richard at once.

19

~&~

Darcy had obtained Mrs. Younge's address from Elizabeth at the ball, and he set out for Portman Square first thing the next morning. As he approached the house Elizabeth had specified, he encountered George Wickham descending the stairs; the bastard actually had the cheek to smile at him.

"Good morning, Darcy. You look like hell."

Darcy grimaced. He had been up half the night, preparing for this moment, and yet it was all he could do not to simply pull out his pistol and end the wastrel once and for all. "Perhaps I only need a drink. Shall you invite me in?"

Wickham grinned viciously at him. "I suppose my errands can wait," he drawled. "Do come in, Darcy. I am rather proud of my new home. Let us step into my study."

Darcy followed Wickham into the house, wondering how the profligate could afford such a residence. The study was just off of the foyer, and Wickham strode around a large oak desk, making a great show of stopping to admire himself in the mirror before sitting down at the desk, leaning back in his chair, and propping his feet up. "To what do I owe the pleasure, Darcy?"

"What do you want?"

"I say, Darcy, you came to visit me."

"And I did not come to play games. You ought not even be in England! But here you are, hardly surprised to see me, so I will ask again – what do you want?"

Wickham stroked his chin, pretending to consider. "What *do* I want? I suppose I am in a position to be choosy. Do I want to Jane back? What an uproar that would cause the good Colonel and his family, if I were to come forward and stake my prior claim. Ah, but then you would be in quite a bit of hot water yourself, when you are made to explain to your dear sister that I am not really dead. Yet I wonder… is she the sister I want? It is a difficult decision, Darcy. I might have Eliza, who is just as fetching, in her own way. She is keen on me, Darcy, and I have spoken to her of you often enough to know I could easily make two of your three sisters into your enemies very easily. It would certainly be amusing."

"Enough! I have already paid you to stay away, and now you would ask for more?"

"Yes, that was your mistake, Darcy – you underestimated me. Did you really think I could be bought so cheaply?"

"*Cheaply?* Considering your origins, I gave you a *fortune*! I put you on a boat bound for America with ten thousand pounds in your pocket, more money than the son of a steward could ever expect! That was the arrangement, Wickham."

"Yes, and now it is not. You put me on the boat in Portsmouth, but by the time we docked in Plymouth, I had rather changed my mind."

"And what has kept you silent all this time? It has been nearly three years."

"Well, spending your ten thousand pounds *has* taken time. I suppose you would not know – *you* have an endless supply of money."

"And you thought you should like a little more yourself?"

"No indeed – I should like a *lot* more, and your sister Eliza has thirty thousand pounds and an absolutely delectable figure."

Darcy tried to keep his composure, but the thought of Wickham going anywhere near Elizabeth made him sick. "How dare you!"

Wickham only laughed. "You hadn't noticed? More's the pity. Well, I have lost interest in one of your sisters – though I do not know if she has lost interest in me. I could be made to give them both up, though I had other plans in store for one of them."

"How much do you want?"

"I believe I am in a position to say that thirty thousand pounds is rather my minimum, as I might have as much anyhow, if things go a different way."

"Ten thousand of her dowry would come from me, and I can guarantee that you would never see a shilling of it. As to the other twenty, I am sure her uncle could be made to feel the same."

"Proud Mr. Darcy would let his sister live in penury? No, I think your dignity could not allow it, nor all the tender-hearted ladies in your family. How broken-hearted poor Jane would be over the matter!"

"Ten thousand, and this time you sail directly for Australia."

"Fifteen, and I shall write you when I arrive in Boston."

"You had your chance at America!"

"And you have had your chance at an amicable solution. I should really hate to see any discord in your family."

Darcy gave a heavy sigh. "One thousand up front, and another thousand every month forwarded to you in Boston for a year, and if you ever set foot on British soil again —"

"Make it two thousand up front and I shall board a ship today."

Darcy stood and nodded. "I will not offer to shake hands on the bargain, as I know such a gesture means nothing to a man with no honor."

Wickham feigned indignation. "You wound me, Darcy."

"I would like to."

Wickham laughed. "Always a pleasure doing business with you."

"This will be the last transaction between us. I shall return in two hours. Be ready to leave for the shipyard."

Wickham nodded, his lips curling into a sinister smile. "I am ready to travel even now."

***

Darcy walked slowly down the street, away from Portman Square, knowing it very likely that he was being watched from the window of Wickham's study. He hoped he had given a convincing performance, and that Wickham believed he was hastening home to collect his funds. He was, in fact, returning to Darcy House to assemble what he needed to ensure that Wickham was finally removed from his family's lives forever.

He checked his pocket watch; it was half past nine. By now, Richard should have arrived at the Gardiner residence, ostensibly bringing Charlotte to visit Elizabeth, and with three of his most trusted men posted outside. Darcy would be there within half an hour, and they could proceed.

Jane was in the corridor as he entered the house, and though she smiled up at him, he instantly sensed that aught was amiss with his sister. "Good morning, Jane. Are you well?"

"I am, Brother, though a little tired. You look as if you have hardly slept yourself. There were noises last night, as if people were coming and going from the house after we came back from the ball."

"I had some business with my agent, and a few others. I am sorry if it woke you."

"Were you up so late? I hope there is nothing wrong, Brother."

Jane was looking up so earnestly at him, such tender, trusting compassion in her eyes; it broke his heart. The letters he had dispatched last evening, following his one-sided conversation with Richard at the ball, had ensured that his secret would remain just that. This would all soon be resolved; Wickham would once again disappear without Jane being any the wiser. And yet, as he peered down at his sister, her eyes almost resembling Elizabeth's, he was filled with a sudden and terrible remorse.

Elizabeth and Jane trusted him implicitly. They thought him a finer man than he was, and he could not stay silent. He could not deserve their love if he would withhold the truth. "Jane, my dear," he sighed, "I have an appointment I must get to, but first we had better speak privately. Would you come into my study?"

***

Matlock House was already in uproar when a trembling footman braved the earl's displeasure, interrupting the heated argument to announce that three officers were waiting for Richard in the drawing room.

The earl pounded his fist on his desk, his face pink with rage; the footman gave Richard a quick, imploring look and then scurried away. "You do not think you can just leave at a time like this?"

"I have an appointment, Father, as I have told you. It is a matter of some urgency."

"More urgent than your sister's disappearance?"

In truth, Richard did not know. Darcy had been strangely cryptic the night before. He had asked Richard to bring Charlotte to visit Elizabeth – which was now quite impossible – and to have three of his most trusted men posted guard outside. Darcy was to meet him at ten o'clock to explain the rest. Whatever it was, he had known at the time it did not bode well, and the nagging sense of suspicion in him now told him there was one possibility, an absolutely catastrophic one, that might indeed outweigh his sister's elopement.

"Well?" The earl snarled at Richard. "Have you nothing to say for yourself, when you have brought this fellow into our midst, knowing very well it would not only go against my wishes, but sow discord with your aunt and cousin? And for what?"

Richard met his father's ire with fury of his own. "You might have put your foot down years ago, regarding Aunt Catherine's ambitions to have Darcy for her daughter! You might have pressed for the de Bourgh alliance in the first place – her reasons for opposing it have ever been foolhardy and selfish! Darcy was never going to have Anne, but Elliot might have."

"And so you would take matters into your own hands without consulting me? I am your father!"

"Yes, and I am very much your son, am I not? I, too, can scheme and sneak and try to arrange people's lives for them, just as you have taught me."

The earl cuffed his son. "My schemes *work*, damn you!"

"Father," John said, stepping in between them. "This serves nothing. De Bourgh is not a villain, and Richard's intentions were good, if misguided. Charlotte is gone of her own free will, and if you wish, I will go after them – I am sure I can catch them up before they reach Gretna. But what would it serve?"

The earl sputtered with rage. "*What would it serve?* Your sister's honor, this family's reputation, our fortunes...." He grabbed Richard by the collar and sneered at him. "I have done so much for you, and this is how I am repaid?"

"Henry, enough," the dowager countess bellowed from the corner. "We have been silent out of respect, and so you would forget that there are women in the room?" Lady Phyllis laid a hand on her mother-in-law's arm, but Lady Eleanor shook it off and stood, stomping her cane in indignation.

The earl released his son gruffly, sparing a hard look for John as well, and Richard gave his lady grandmother an appreciative nod. Lady Eleanor grimaced at all of them. "This is unseemly, Henry – this may be your house now, but I shall not sit by and abide such violence! John was quite right to ask, to what end? Charlotte is of age, and have you not always feared she would end an old maid?"

"Better a spinster than a whore!"

"Henry, that is enough," Lady Phyllis said again, rising to stand beside Lady Eleanor. "John, ride out at once. Tell Mr. de Bourgh that if he returns with Charlotte, we would be happy to begin planning proper wedding proceedings for them immediately. There is no need for all this."

"I should say not," Lady Catherine clipped, striding into the room, dragging her weeping daughter by the arm. "See here, Anne? Do you see *now* what sort of man Elliot de Bourgh is? You would lament over him running off with your artful, grasping cousin Charlotte – see what ignominy you have been spared!"

"Go back to your room, Catherine," the earl growled.

"I have just as much right to a say in this conversation as anyone else," she snapped. "Your son has brought this matter upon me, much as he has done the rest of you. I am only sorry for you, that my daughter was spared, while yours was less fortunate."

Anne de Bourgh stamped her foot and screeched, *"Less fortunate?* She stole him from me, Mamma! First Eliza stole Darcy, and now Charlotte has taken Cousin Elliot away from me!"

"Hush, child! You ought to be grateful it was not you that barbarian carried off! I only hope your prospects are not so materially damaged by having a fallen cousin!"

"Catherine, shut up," the dowager countess sighed. "You give me such headaches. As of this morning, your life and Anne's are no different than when you woke yesterday morning, with not a thought in your head for Elliot de Bourgh."

"But I wanted him," Anne shrieked. "He is twice the man Darcy is, and Mamma will not listen!"

"This is madness," John said, pounding his fist against the wall. "I am going to ride for Gretna and bring them back. The countess is quite right. With all your marriage mania, Father, you might have given her some little encouragement when you saw, as we all did, how well they were getting on last night. You are glib enough with a joke at her expense, and when she finally captures a man's notice she is made to feel she must run off in secret. I cannot wonder why."

As John opened the door to go, Richard could see Sergeant Drew, Major Pruett, and Lieutenant Buchanan waiting in the hallway. His family were all still shouting at one another, and so he made his escape. *This had better be worth it, Darcy.*

***

Jane had fled the room in tears, and Darcy knew he could not have pressed her to hear his apology, even if he had the time to offer one. He checked his pocket watch – it was nearly ten; he needed to leave immediately to meet Richard at Upper Brook Street. He had prepared everything he would need the night before – every document he had on Wickham, every debt accrued before he went to sea, and in the six months between his returning from service, and his slithering back to Pemberley to ask for more money before he would honor his engagement to Jane. Despite having written Jane that his fortune had been made in his years at sea, Wickham had returned to England just after the death of Darcy's father, gambling away what little he had earned, and Darcy held a great deal of proof of Wickham's other misdeeds from that time period. He had hoped never to use them, but he had kept everything, knowing there would always be a chance....

He slipped the packet into his briefcase and prepared to leave for Upper Brook Street at once. As he left his study, he caught sight of his mother and Mary in the drawing room. "William," his mother cried. "Where are you going? Jane was so very upset."

"I am sorry, Mother – it could not be helped. I have some business, and then I shall return and explain it all, and makes amends with Jane. I swear it. You had all better stay at home until I come back."

"Jane went to see Richard, at Matlock House," Mary said. "She was angry with you, but she would not tell us why – only that she could not bear to be anywhere near you."

"William," his mother said firmly. "You had better tell us what all this is about. First Lizzy, now Jane?"

They were interrupted. A footman cleared his throat, and offered

Darcy a note, which he tore open at once. "Good God!"

"What is it, William?"

Darcy looked up at his mother and sister as his face twisted in despair. "I ought to have been there already," he breathed.

"Brother," Mary whimpered, "whatever is the matter?"

"George Wickham is alive," he said bluntly, "and he has attempted to abduct Elizabeth."

***

Richard checked his pocket watch as he and his trusted former subordinates departed Matlock House and set off across the square. It was a quarter till ten; he was already late.

"What is all this about," Major Pruett asked.

"I do not know yet," Richard admitted, "but I daresay it is nothing good. In fact, I suspect it may be rather serious. We better make haste."

It was quiet on the square. It occurred to Richard that nearly all of their neighbors in Grosvenor Square had actually been at the ball last night, and likely they were all still abed, for the festivities had gone late. There was hardly anybody about; pedestrians and carriages were rather thin on the street that morning, save for one equipage, which Richard did not recognize, parked in front of Sir Edward's house. He quickened his step.

"Drew, Buchanan, go left. Watch the coachman. Pruett, you and I will go right." Richard would have preferred more cover on the street – it was impossible to make his way there with any degree of stealth, and he was forced to make up for it with speed. As he rounded the square toward Upper Brook Street, he saw a man descend the front steps of the Gardiner residence and shove Elizabeth into the carriage. Richard broke into a sprint, and the man looked over at the sound of his footfalls. It was George Wickham.

Wickham laughed when he saw Richard come around the back of the carriage; he pushed Elizabeth into the equipage and swiftly drew a gun out of his breast pocket. He trained it on Richard, who likewise had drawn his own weapon. At his side, Major Pruett had done the same. The two men stopped not five yards distant from Wickham, their pistols trained on him, and Richard slowly began to inch to the side, that he might get a visual on Elizabeth.

Wickham likewise moved toward the carriage, sneering at him. "Well, well, Richard – it has been a while, has it not? I hear you think to claim my fiancée as your bride. What a pity another of her paramours might turn up dead."

Slowly, a little white hand emerged from the open door of the carriage and Elizabeth peered out – she grabbed Wickham by the scruff of the neck and jerked his head back, while her other hand brought a comically small purse gun to his exposed throat. "I think not," she snarled. She pressed the gun against his skin. "My cousin Collins gave me this," she said with a vicious laugh. "It turns out, you were as right about him as he was about you."

The coachman had stood and leaned around, his own gun pointed down at Elizabeth. She drew back into the carriage, kicking at the back of Wickham's leg, causing him to stumble.

At that moment, Lieutenant Buchanan moved from behind the front of the carriage. He seized the coachman by the ankle and pulled him from the top. A shot rang out as the coachman toppled down from the carriage; his bullet ricocheted off the metal fence in front of the house, and struck him in the neck. Lieutenant Buchanan quickly took the man's weapon and restrained him.

Wickham regained his footing and hesitated, pointing his gun between Richard and Elizabeth. Richard fired a warning shot at the ground. "Drop your weapon, Wickham."

Wickham ignored him and seized Elizabeth from the carriage, putting her body in front of his, and raising his gun to her head before she could turn hers on him. "Tell your men to stand down, Richard!"

Richard kept his eyes locked on Wickham, betraying nothing as he turned his pistol to the side and gestured for Major Pruett beside him to lower his weapon as well. Behind Wickham, Sergeant Drew slowly crept forward, getting close enough to strike Wickham on the top of the head with the butt of his gun.

Elizabeth shrieked and moved away from Wickham as he collapsed beside her, still trying to keep her little purse gun pointed on the villain. Richard rose from his semi-recumbent posture and rushed to Elizabeth's side. "Take him," he commanded his men. "Bring him inside and tie him up in the cellar."

Richard wrapped his arms around Elizabeth, who was not crying, but shaking violently in his arms. "You are safe, Lizzy," he said, kissing her on the top of her head. Elizabeth drew away from him, a queer look on her face. "There is a length of rope in the carriage," she whispered, her voice numb. He nodded, and took the little gun from her hands with an appreciative smile. "Collins, eh?"

She smiled weakly at him. "I daresay he would rather not hear how close I came to using it. I am so glad I had it in my reticule. He had my arms pinned behind my back as he brought me out; had you not come, I was waiting for him to put me in the carriage, thinking it would be my chance to pull the gun from my reticle."

"Lizzy, I am so proud of you," Richard said, hugging her close. "My old friend, I cannot think what would have happened if…."

She shook her head and turned away, leaning in to the carriage; she took the length of rope that had been on the seat. Her eyes were wide and her face pale as she handed it to him, and he had no need to ask what she was thinking at such a moment.

"Come," he said, wrapping his arm protectively around her, "let us get you inside."

Pruett and Drew had hoisted Wickham's inert body off the ground, as Buchanan did likewise with the coachman. "Take them in through the back," Richard said. "Tie them up in the cellar, nice and tight. Pruett, Buchanan, stay with them, and Drew, report back to me."

Elizabeth looked up at the window, and Richard followed her gaze – Rose's horror struck face appeared in the window like a ghost. A moment later, a maid belatedly burst out the door with another pistol just like Elizabeth's; the poor girl looked rather stunned to see that it was all over. Richard laughed and looked down at his cousin. "I see Rose got one too, eh?"

***

Richard led Elizabeth into the house, and guided her to a sofa near the fire in the drawing room. No sooner had he wrapped a blanket around her than Rose flew into the room, and was at Elizabeth's side in an instant. "Oh Lizzy, I was so scared," she wailed.

"I should wager Lizzy was rather scared, too, Rose."

"Oh, Lizzy!"

Elizabeth gave a wry smile. "As a matter of fact, I was not. I was angry, but I was not frightened." She could sense that Richard was disconcerted by her unlikely calm, but in truth she was so stunned she could scarcely feel anything at all, other than relieved that it was over. "Where is William?"

Richard checked his watch. "That is a very good question – he ought to be here any minute. Perhaps I should send word to Darcy House, if he has been detained – my father is already on the warpath this morning, and I was late myself because of it."

"What happened?"

"Nothing to worry yourself over. You should sit and calm your nerves. You there, maid, give Miss Rose her gun back, and go see about some tea. But wait – a coffee for me, and two hot chocolates, I think, for your ladies." Richard turned back to Elizabeth, and she could tell his mind was racing. "Where is your uncle?"

"He received word that there was a burglary at one of his warehouses, and left not twenty minutes ago," Elizabeth said slowly. "I suppose that was a ruse, so that I might be taken." She looked down at her shaking hands, and Rose covered them with her own, leaning against Elizabeth on the sofa.

Richard let out a string of oaths, and strode over to Elizabeth's little writing desk in the corner. He wrote out several notes, and bellowed for one of the footmen. "You there, boy. Get another of the servants to help you in the delivery of these. This to Darcy House, this to Sir Edward, this to the magistrate, and this to Matlock House – in that order."

Elizabeth was still sitting numbly with Rose when their refreshments were brought in. The maid gave her a reassuring smile as she pushed a plate of Elizabeth's favorite strawberry tarts at her, and Richard pulled a flask out of his pocket, pouring a generous dose into Elizabeth's hot chocolate. "Drink this, my dear," he said.

Elizabeth did as she was bid. A moment later, one of Richard's companions returned to the room. "The prisoners are secure, sir."

"Very good, Drew. You are to report to Number 4, Bow Street, and return at once with one of the runners. Ask for John Renard. And, Drew – he need not know that Wickham is still in the house. *He got away.*"

"Yes, sir."

When Sergeant Drew had left, Elizabeth looked at Richard. "Please, sit down; you are making me nervous."

"I am sorry, Elizabeth." Richard sat down in a chair nearby. "I am only anxious for Darcy to arrive, and before I question Wickham, I should very much like to ask my cousin just why that villain is even alive."

"So Mr. Smythe… he is George Wickham?" Elizabeth was still reeling. "Was he not lost at sea three years ago?"

"Would that he was! Darcy better have a damned good explanation."

A carriage pulled up in front of the house, and Rose ran to the window. "It is Mr. Collins!"

Elizabeth sat in awkward silence for a moment with Richard; she could feel the anger radiating out of him, and she began to grow rather distressed herself. Was this what William had meant to tell her when he promised to call this morning? Did Jane know? How would this affect Jane's engagement to Richard? The questions swirled around in her head, without connecting to any sensible answers.

Mr. Collins hesitated as he stepped into the drawing room, instantly sensing the tension. His eyes flew to the little purse gun that was still in Rose's hand, folded in her lap.

"Sally," Rose gasped, "Please, take this back to my dressing table."

"Yes, Miss."

Mr. Collins's gaze flicked between the three of them for a moment before his eyes settled on Elizabeth. "Cousin, what has happened? I had an ill feeling this morning, and I could not get that villain Smythe off my mind."

"Yes, he was here," Elizabeth said.

"His name is George Wickham," Richard spat. "He is the son of the former Mr. Darcy's steward, and was engaged to Jane Darcy until, we were told, nearly three years ago, that he had died at sea."

"And he has come here, masquerading to Elizabeth as someone else all this time?"

"That is correct," came a deep voice. William strode into the room, Uncle Edward trailing behind him.

Her uncle looked out of breath, and placed a hand on William's shoulder. "I was making my way home when I received your message, Richard. He lured me out to my warehouses, and I fell into his trap like a useless old fool," her uncle groaned. "I am so sorry, Elizabeth."

Elizabeth nodded, feeling tears finally begin to prick her eyes, and she threw herself into her uncle's arms. William moved closer, stroking Elizabeth's hair even as her uncle embraced her. She broke away from Uncle Edward at last and looked up at William with so many questions on her tongue, she could not speak at all.

He looked dejectedly at her for a moment. "I am sorry, Elizabeth. I ought to have been here in time to stop him. Can you forgive me?"

Before Elizabeth could speak, Richard began to rail at William. "What the devil is all this about, William? If I find out that you knew the bastard was alive, I am going to kill you with my bare hands."

"Richard, stop," Elizabeth cried.

"No, Lizzy, I shall have my answer. Now, William."

"Everybody calm down," Mr. Collins shouted. The room fell silent, though the tension hung about them still.

"Thank you, Mr. Collins," William said. "I believe I owe you a debt of gratitude for your warning to me last night. You have, quite possibly, saved Elizabeth's life, and I cannot express to you what it means to me."

Mr. Collins gave a very cordial bow. "I am honored to be of assistance."

William extended Mr. Collins his hand. "If there is ever anything I can do, anything at all –"

Mr. Collins shook William's hand and nodded. "I see I have come at a difficult time. Sir Edward, I wonder if Miss Rose might like to play for me in the music room?"

Sir Edward nodded. "Yes – thank you, Will. *Door open*, Rose."

Elizabeth stared at her uncle, her emotions a jumble at the sight of him looking so stricken. "Rose saw... you will want to talk to her later," she whispered.

Uncle Edward looked back at her with tired eyes. "And what exactly did she see?"

William had drawn closer to Elizabeth, and wrapped his hand around hers, clearly both eager and afraid to hear her answer.

"Mr. Smythe – Mr. Wickham came into the house, and I told him that he should not be here. He told me Mrs. Younge had wished to visit me, had fallen on the stairs outside, and that she required my assistance. I cannot think why, but I picked up my reticule as I went outside, and Mrs. Younge was not there. There was a carriage waiting, the door open. He seized my arms and pinned them behind my back, and dragged me down the steps. As he was putting me into the carriage, I saw Richard running across the square. I... I scarcely remember the rest, it all happened so fast." She looked over to Richard, who filled William and her uncle in on the rest.

No sooner was this done than the magistrate, Mr. Moore, arrived and Elizabeth was obliged to repeat her story over again, as the magistrate took notes. When Mr. Moore had finished, he asked, "And where is Mr. Wickham now, and the wounded driver?"

Elizabeth glanced up at Richard, remembering what he had told Sergeant Drew. "They got away," she said evenly.

Richard gave her an almost imperceptible nod, then told the magistrate, "My men and I gave chase, but we lost them after a few blocks."

"And you say your cousin saw this from the window, Miss Bennet?"

"Yes," Elizabeth said. Richard quietly slipped out of the drawing room and walked into the music room. He leaned down and whispered something to Rose, and led her back into the room; she gave her statement, which corroborated Elizabeth's entirely.

"You did very well, girls," Uncle Edward said after the magistrate left. "Mr. Collins, I wonder if my daughter might need some fresh air." Rose smiled widely, and Mr. Collins seemed eager to please both of them. As Rose and Mr. Collins left the room, Uncle Edward looked between Elizabeth and Richard. "Just to be clear, you have told the magistrate these villains got away, but before that, you told me they are within the house even still."

"I am not ready to turn him over until I have had a few words with him," Richard growled.

"I believe I shall as well," Uncle Edward said gruffly. "And you, William? What is your part in all this?"

Elizabeth peered up at William, wishing to know as much herself. "Did you know?"

"I knew he was not dead, yes."

Richard exploded, and lunged at his cousin. "Damn you, Darcy! You did not think to tell anyone?"

William dodged Richard's attack and pushed him backward, his temper rising. "I put him on a ship for America after he came back from his service, gambled away his earnings in London for six months, and then asked me to triple Jane's dowry, effectively depriving Mary and Elizabeth of their portions."

Richard glowered at William. "And you let your sister think for three long years that he was dead? What is the matter with you, Darcy?"

"You know damn well he was never good enough for Jane, Richard!"

Elizabeth gasped. "William, how could you? Jane was devastated!"

"Should I have let her marry that villain? I knew what he was, even then. He has always been a wastrel and a liar, and I could not let Jane throw herself away on such a man. I tried to warn father, but he would hear nothing against Wickham. I hoped he would die at sea, and when he came back, demanding more money, I knew it would never stop. Better for Jane to think him dead, than to learn the hard way what he is really like."

"That is insane," Richard bellowed. "Did you not see how miserable she was? How could you have allowed such a thing?"

William looked to Elizabeth, his eyes wide with panic. She wished to say something to put him at ease – in truth, she wished to throw herself into his arms, but she could not reconcile what she was hearing with everything she had come to feel for William. "I thought I knew you," she breathed, and William looked as though she had struck him.

"I wanted to tell you," he sighed.

"Like hell you did," Richard snarled.

"Gentlemen!" Sir Edward thundered. He gestured to the window. To Elizabeth's relief, she saw her mother walking up to the house. Elizabeth met her in the foyer, and burst into tears in her mother's arms.

***

While Elizabeth was speaking with her mother, Sir Edward, Richard and Darcy met with Inspector Renard, who arrived shortly after Lady Anne.

Sir Edward could do little more than listen as Darcy detailed his plan – he listed Wickham's many debts, which he had collected over the years. Darcy intended to search out any new debts Wickham had accrued more recently, in the hope that it would be enough to put him away in Marshalsea for quite some time.

"If we find him, of course," was Richard's contribution. Inspector Renard outlined a plan to investigate any debts incurred under the names Wickham or Smythe, and promised to report back the next day. The meeting was a brief one, both due to Darcy's premeditated arrangement, and likely also the hostile air in the room.

Sir Edward was angrier than he had ever been on his nieces' behalf, both Jane and Elizabeth. And yet, the two young men he rather wanted to horsewhip were just as likely to do far worse to each other – though he was furious at being the last to know about Wickham, he decided it best to steer everyone's anger toward the man tied up in his cellar.

The three men went down there, where Wickham was tied to a chair and guarded by two soldiers who seemed to take their orders from Richard. The coachman that Wickham had employed as his getaway driver was tied up on the floor beside him. "Please," the coachman cried, showing them where his neck had been wounded. "Please, I need a surgeon."

"Buchanan," Richard drawled. "You stitched me up on the field once, a couple years ago. Can you do it?"

"Yes, sir."

"Sorry, old boy," Richard taunted the coachman. "If we take you to a doctor, who knows what song you would sing? We need to keep your co-conspirator here with us a little longer. Take him into the next room, Buchanan. And *you*," he said, pointing to Wickham. Sir Edward hung back, watching with a rising ire in his chest as Richard went forward and taunted the villain. "I have been long overdue in welcoming you back to England," Richard growled before he punched Wickham in the face.

Wickham spat blood at Richard's foot, and Richard hit him again. Darcy came forward and pulled Richard back by the shoulder, away from Wickham. "I need to question him, Richard."

For a moment Richard turned and looked as if he would lash out at Darcy, but he did not. He cracked his knuckles loudly, and then clenched his fists. "This is not over, Wickham," he said, backing away. "Darcy has some questions to put to you, and I shall decide if I like the answers or not."

Darcy began by asking Wickham questions about the nature of his debts accrued while in London, but the villain was not very forthcoming. Richard was clearly growing impatient, and took another swing at Wickham, but elicited no information. Sir Edward waved Darcy off, and began a different approach.

"I want to know what Mrs. Younge has to do with all this."

"She is innocent."

"Oh, is she? She is no friend of my sister's, and I think we both know that. How came she to have so much information about my family?"

"One of the servants gave this to us," Major Pruett said, handing Sir Edward a letter. "Wickham gave it to them, to give to you."

Sir Edward opened the letter and read it over. It appeared to be written in Elizabeth's hand – but no, it was quite similar, though not exact. It was addressed to himself, explaining Elizabeth's violent passion for Mr. Smythe, and her intention of eloping with him – it went so far as to suggest that she forfeited all claim to her dowry, and urged

Sir Edward to divide her portion between her two sisters.

"This was meant to be left behind, had you succeeded in your abduction?"

Wickham said nothing, and only shrugged at them, smiling wickedly. Richard struck him in the face again, the force of his blow sending the chair backward. There was a loud thud as Wickham's head hit the ground, but the villain only laughed again. Richard kicked him several times in the stomach, until he began to choke on his own blood.

"That is enough," Darcy said, and Richard set Wickham's chair upright. The scoundrel's body sagged now, blood pouring down his face and mouth.

Sir Edward regarded him thoughtfully. "Did you read this letter?"

"No – it was meant to explain Eliza's absence."

"I wonder who wrote such a thing. It could not possibly have been your co-conspirator, Mrs. Younge, for I am sure you were only in it for the financial gain, and yet right here it says that Lizzy wishes me to give her dowry entirely to her sisters. Why should you relinquish the claim on such a substantial sum?"

Wickham looked genuinely surprised, and sputtered as he coughed up more blood. "That bitch!"

"What bitch?" Richard growled.

Wickham smiled over at Darcy. "Your best friend's mother, Madeline Bingley. She is Evelyn's sister, and she copied one of Eliza's notes to Evelyn, practicing getting her hand just right. *Filthy, lying whore!* It was all her plan; Evelyn wanted nothing to do with the idea, she would tell you anything you wish to know. I went along with it for the money, but it was all Madeline's plan. She sought us out, to bring you all down, and I could not pass up the opportunity."

Sir Edward staggered backward as if he was the one who had been struck. That was how Mrs. Younge seemed to have just enough information to pass herself off as a friend of Fanny's – Madeline knew a little of his sister's history, and Wickham must have filled in the blanks. They had all had the wool pulled over their eyes, and it had almost cost him Elizabeth.

When Sir Edward said nothing, Richard hit Wickham again. "I have a few more questions for this bastard. Leave me."

Darcy leaned in to Richard, whispered something, and Richard nodded. "I shall try to find out," he said. Darcy muttered something else, and Richard only shook his head. "*You owe me this,*" he hissed, and gave Darcy a dark look and a rough shove.

At that, Darcy approached Sir Edward, who was still reeling from this new information. "Uncle, let us rejoin the ladies upstairs. You will not want to see any more, I think."

***

Darcy led Sir Edward back upstairs in search of Elizabeth; he tried to push from his mind what his cousin was likely doing to George Wickham at present. *Nothing the blackguard does not deserve.*

Elizabeth was in the drawing room, laying on the sofa with her head in Lady Anne's lap. It was plain to see that Elizabeth had been weeping a great deal. She sat up from her recumbent position as Darcy and Sir Edward entered.

Sir Edward looked over at Darcy. "I shall give you two a moment," he said. "I am going to my study."

Darcy nodded gratefully, and went to sit down beside Elizabeth. He took her hands in his and gently nudged her forehead with his, hoping she would look up at him. Finally she met his eye, and fresh tears began to stream down her face as she leaned into him. "Oh, William, how could you not tell me?"

"I was coming to tell you, even this morning. I ought to have gotten here before that villain laid a hand on you."

"I know – I understand. Mamma told me you were detained, that you told Jane the truth."

"She has every right to be angry with me; so do you all. To own the truth, I considered simply not telling her, and even though it would have gotten me here faster, I cannot regret it, now that I know that you are safe. I cannot regret being honest with Jane – I thought it was what you would want of me. I truly believed I might resolve the matter in some degree of secrecy – I did not think he would come here. I had instructed him to wait in Portman Square, with the promise of another bribe."

"Another bribe? The first one obviously worked so well! You would teach him to be forever coming back, wreaking havoc and asking for more?"

"Lizzy," Lady Anne hissed. Darcy leaned over and looked imploringly at his mother. He needed to be alone with Elizabeth. She seemed to understand, and nodded. "I shall go and look in on your uncle, Lizzy."

After Lady Anne left the room, Darcy turned his attention back to Elizabeth. As much as he wanted to explain himself to her, he could only take her in his arms and kiss her deeply. Her back and shoulders relaxed and she gave into his embrace, and a moment later he grew emboldened, and pulled her onto his lap, their lips never parting. There was a trace of desperation in the force of her kiss, and he likewise felt as a man drowning; he needed her, he needed not to stop.

Finally Elizabeth drew away, her breathing ragged; she pulled herself off of his lap and crossed her arms. "I am still angry at you, William."

"That was anger?"

"How could you do this? Have you any idea, you who have lived with her the most, what Jane has suffered these last three years? Longer still – for two years she pined for him, while he was at sea, when you might have spared her that simply by being honest with her about your reservations as to his true character. Five years of her life have been wasted, and for what? It is everything I feared, everything I believed about you when first you came to London, that you are determined to manage the lives of others as you see fit, without a second thought for anyone else's feelings."

"You would have me speak to a seventeen-year-old girl about his depravity, when even my own parents would not hear of it? I was protecting her!"

"You conspired to fake her fiancé's death! Yes, you should have simply been open with her, when she was at enough of an age to be deemed an adult in the eyes of society. If Uncle Edward does not relay the particulars of today's events to Rose in full, I shall do so myself. She, of all people, ought to understand exactly how the world works, as Jane ought to have been told. You could have prevented everyone so much pain."

Darcy stood and began to pace the room. "Since you feel the need to bring up past grievances, I might as well inquire why you have been so angry at me for failing to recognize you after three years of separation, when you yourself saw Wickham on several occasions, and continued thinking him a stranger."

"Are you quite serious? I had not seen him in seven years, since I was a child! I saw him perhaps twice a year, at the most, before I went away. How could I be expected to know his face?"

Darcy sighed heavily. Wickham *was* much changed – he had grown tanned at sea, and wore his hair differently. It was an awful thing of him to say, and he knew it. "I apologize, Elizabeth."

"Oh."

"I am not angry with you – I have no right to be. In truth, I admire your courage today. I have never been prouder of anybody in my entire life. In contrast, I have never been more ashamed of my own actions."

Elizabeth's lip quivered. "I bared my soul to you, William. I told you my darkest secrets, everything. In all the times we wrote and spoke of Jane, you had every opportunity to tell me the truth. You had three years to tell her!"

"You are right, Elizabeth, and you must believe I will do whatever is in my power to make amends to you, and to Jane. I had no idea it would come to this."

"You... you must have had some sort of plan, when you promised to visit today, and asked Richard to bring his men."

"I had. I met with Wickham this morning, and I promised him a substantial bribe if he would truly disappear this time. I told him I would return in two hours. I knew it was possible he would come here, and so I asked Richard to arrive early, but I had rather hoped I was convincing enough – that he would simply await my return to Portman Square. If Wickham had not come here, it was my intention to take Richard's men and collect him by force, and then assemble certain information to ensure he rots in debtors' prison."

Elizabeth wrapped her arms around her chest and chewed her lip. "I see. You might have accomplished it – for all you knew, it would be carried out without a hitch, and yet you told Jane the truth anyhow. You might have concealed it from her still."

"Yes. And we will still carry out the rest of the plan. He will be imprisoned, and soon. Inspector Renard has his men on the case, and already I hold enough markers to get him several years at Marshalsea. I want him in there forever."

Elizabeth nodded sadly. "Poor Jane," she sighed. "I wish to go to her."

"You should," Darcy said, stepping closer to Elizabeth. She looked longingly at him, and he quickly closed the gap between them and took her in his arms. He kissed the top of her head as she buried her face in his chest, and Darcy felt he could be content to remain in such a pose forever. "Stay at Darcy House tonight, with Jane. Take Rose, too. I shall stay here with your uncle and guard the prisoner. Inspector Renard should have an update for us in the morning, or with any luck, this evening."

"Very well, William." She looked searchingly up at him.

"Elizabeth… do you still wish to marry me?"

She laughed. "For Heaven's sake, William, of course. We have only had a little row; I daresay it shall not be our last."

"I should rather wish it was."

"No indeed," she said with a smirk. "Whenever we quarrel, we shall have the pleasure of making up afterwards."

"And how shall that go?"

She grinned, and stood up on her toes, pulling his face down toward hers. "Something like this…."

***

Determined to give William some privacy, Anne went down the hall and knocked on the door to Edward's study. There was no answer, but she let herself in. He was sitting at his desk, staring down at a revolver in his hands. "Edward!" He looked up as Anne rushed to his side. "What are you doing?"

"Thinking," he said, his voice heavy with emotion.

"Edward...."

"I have failed Lizzy again. I fell right into that villain's trap, getting lured out of the house by his false note, and if it had not been for Richard, Darcy, and Collins – in short, every man in her life *except* me... God knows what might have become of our dear girl. I am a useless, miserable old man." He ran his fingers across the barrel of the gun. "Perhaps it is time I took some sort of action, did something good for this family."

"Edward, no!" Anne took the gun away from him and set it on a shelf across the room. "How could you even think such a thing?"

"How could I not? I looked into that villain's eyes, Anne, and I wanted to murder him. I saw in him all the years of pain and suffering this family has endured, and his part in it, and I wanted to kill him. What is to stop me? He is in my house, he is my prisoner, and when Richard is done, if there is anything left of the wretch, what is to stop me from sending the officers away and simply putting a bullet in the blackguard?"

Anne's heart twisted and she let out a sigh of relief; she could not bear to admit that she had been thinking of something else entirely. "Edward, that is not who you are. They can put him in prison – let that be enough for you. I beg you, do not take his life, Edward."

He stood from his chair and took Anne in his arms, weeping softly on her shoulder. "You are a good woman, Anne, to love such a stupid old man."

She cupped his face in her hands. "Do not say that, Edward. How many years have I listened to you speak of yourself so meanly? Olivia broke you down, just as the years have broken me."

"You are not broken," he breathed. "You are the strongest woman I know and I... I need you, Anne."

She closed her eyes as he caressed her cheek, and a moment later she felt his lips brush hers, tentatively at first, and then, as she leaned her body against his, with a greater intensity. A moment later he had swept aside the books and papers from his desk, and hoisted her onto it. "I need you, Anne," he breathed in her ear.

***

Madeline Bingley awoke in good cheer, having slept late after the previous evening's festivities. After she dressed and ate breakfast with Charles and Caroline, she expressed a wish to call on the Darcys. She rather expected them not to be at home, and sure enough, they were not.

"I wonder if they have gone to Grosvenor Square," she mused. "Shall we call at Sir Edward's house?"

"If that is where Mary is to be found," Charles said, "that is where I wish to be."

It was certainly where Madeline wished to be. By now, she supposed, Wickham was on his way to Gretna Green with Elizabeth. She had left him with a note, written in her best imitation of Elizabeth's hand, and Sir Edward had likely discovered it and summoned the Darcys at once. Now, she would be there to privately bask in her success, and lend Sir Edward what comfort her feminine wiles could muster.

They were shown into the house, where they met with Elizabeth and Mr. Darcy in the drawing room, alone. Madeline tried not to lose her composure when she saw Elizabeth standing there, and despite her mounting panic, she calmly replied, "Good day to you, Miss Bennet, Mr. Darcy. I was rather hoping to meet with your sisters."

"They are at Matlock House," Elizabeth said with her usual coldness, though her countenance betrayed no distress, or even awareness of what ought to have been afoot.

"I see," Madeline said, calculating her next move.

"Perhaps we should go there," Caroline said, smiling over at Charles. "Then we might both be satisfied."

Charles turned to address Mr. Darcy. They had not been invited to sit down yet, and he asked, "Is something the matter, Darcy?"

"Not at all," Darcy replied. Sir Edward and Lady Anne entered the room through a side door, and though Sir Edward looked greatly pleased to see them, Lady Anne's countenance instantly took on the same standoffishness as her wretched daughter's. "Edward, I think I should take Lizzy home."

"No indeed, my love," Sir Edward told Lady Anne, as Madeline flinched. "I would much rather you and Lizzy stay, and visit with the Bingleys. We have much to talk of, Madeline. Do sit down. Mr. Bingley, Miss Bingley, you are both marrying into this family, are you not?"

"How wonderful that it has brought us closer," Madeline said carefully, taking a seat between her two stepchildren on the sofa. She was beginning to feel very uneasy, for Edward took a seat beside Lady Anne on the opposite sofa, and placed his arm around her, smiling all the while at his guests.

Even Elizabeth and Mr. Darcy were regarding them with no little curiosity, and Madeline was on the brink of suggesting they depart again, when Sir Edward spoke. "It is interesting you should call today, on such an eventful day here. I was just discussing you with George Wickham about an hour ago."

Madeline stood to flee, and Mr. Darcy instantly put himself between her and the door. She cast a wild look back at her step-son. "Charles, it is time for us to go."

"Darcy, Sir Edward, with all due respect, I do not understand," Charles stammered.

"You shall be made to understand, and I shall have a few questions to put to you later, I think. I begin to wonder now about your interest in this family, and your sister's, having discovered what your stepmother's has been."

"Charles," Mr. Darcy said. "Three years ago I told my family that George Wickham died at sea. He did not. He attempted to extort money from me, and I put him on a ship bound for America. He returned to England, and since that time has begun to conspire with your stepmother against my family's interest. Richard caught him this morning attempting to abduct Elizabeth, and when we captured him, he confessed that he and a woman named Mrs. Younge have conspired with your mother, to abscond with my fiancée. You are my friend, Charles, but Sir Edward has a right to wonder where your loyalty lies."

Madeline closed her eyes at the sound of Charles and Caroline's protests. "Mother! How could you?" Caroline screeched. "This is to be my family!"

"Is it true, Mother?" Charles grabbed her roughly by the shoulders. "Is it true?"

Madeline wrested herself away from him and turned to Sir Edward, letting her face show him the full force of her hatred. "You have deserved it," she spat at him. "Your wretched sister cursed me from her deathbed. You came to me six month later, trying to make trouble with James, and a week later my father died, though he had been a picture of health. My husband died ten years to the day after Fanny. And you – you have just continued to rise!"

Sir Edward did not react, but turned to Mr. Darcy and said, "Wickham has already indicated that Mrs. Younge will cooperate with us to save herself. As for this one, I think you had better summon the magistrate."

Thirty minutes later, Madeline was clapped in irons and escorted from Sir Edward's house. The last thing she saw as she looked back over her shoulder was Sir Edward standing at the top of the stairs, his arm still wrapped around Lady Anne Darcy had better summon the magistrate."

Thirty minutes later, Madeline was clapped in irons and escorted from Sir Edward's house. The last thing she saw as she looked back over her shoulder was Sir Edward standing at the top of the stairs, his arm still wrapped around Lady Anne Darcy.

20

⊱✧⊰

Elizabeth woke with a start, instantly relieved to be spared from the nefarious specters that had haunted her dreams. Instead, sunlight was streaming through the window, warming her face. She was at Matlock House, having slept once more in Charlotte's bed, only it was Jane who lay sleeping beside her. Elizabeth gently laid her hand across Jane's forehead – the fever had subsided, and Jane seemed to be resting peacefully.

Soon Jane began to stir, and Elizabeth waited, wishing her sister would be well, and yet impatiently hoping that Jane would confide in her.

Jane gave a little groan. "Lizzy?"

Elizabeth stroked Jane's hair as her sister's eyes flickered open and she slowly sat up, getting her bearings. "How do you feel, dearest?"

"A little better, I think, but I should like some water. We slept at Matlock House?"

"Do you not remember?"

"Oh – I swooned, on the stairs."

Elizabeth and her mother had arrived yesterday to chaos at Matlock House; the uproar following Charlotte's elopement had been too great for anyone in the house to offer Jane any succor after her quarrel with William, but in her anger, Jane had refused to return to Darcy House, until Elizabeth and their mother had arrived, and practically dragged her from the place. They had gotten as far as the front stairs of Matlock House when they encountered Richard returning home. Jane was already was so overcome by everything that had transpired that she was beginning to seem very ill indeed, and the sight of so much blood on Richard's sleeves had been the final straw.

"Do you want to talk about yesterday?" Lizzy asked as she got up from the bed to pour a glass of water from the pitcher on Charlotte's dressing table.

Jane sighed and took a long drink of water from the glass Elizabeth handed her. She leaned into her sister's embrace. "I hardly know," Jane finally said. "I wished to speak of it yesterday, to no avail, and now I feel as though everything I felt yesterday and could not give voice to has simply burned through me."

"Perhaps it has. You were running a fever last night, after we brought you upstairs. It gave us all quite a fright, Jane. Dr. Purcell was here, and left you some of his elixir. Mamma was quite beside herself."

"Oh dear. Poor Mamma."

"Poor Jane," Elizabeth replied.

Jane took her hand. "Poor Lizzy, too, I think."

"Will you talk to William and Richard today?"

"I do not know," Jane said blankly.

"Speaking to William made me feel better yesterday. I had quite a shock, and I know you must have done as well."

"A shock? Oh, yes. I feel as though the last five years of my life have been turned upside down in one fell swoop. Oh, to be seventeen again! At least, I am sure that is how I *ought* to feel, is it not? George Wickham was ever a villain, and William thought me quite a fool for loving George as I did. And yet, he let me pass five years of my life in such foolishness. I might have married another, had many children, had a... much happier life. Instead, I have devoted myself to the memory of a blackguard, a monster who has come back and tried to steal my own sister from me. And yet I would weep to see his blood on Richard's hands. Am I such a fool as to miss him still? How am I ever to face anyone who knows what my foolishness has been? What could William, or Richard, or anyone else, say to me that changes anything?"

Elizabeth knew not what to say to such a speech, but tightened her arms around Jane, who began to weep softly onto her shoulder.

"Oh, Lizzy, everything I have thought and felt and done has all been for naught, and now it is all utterly shattered."

"That is not true, Jane. You have fallen in love with Richard. Even when you believed Wickham to be a good man, and forever lost to you, you found a way to move on and return to happiness. How can that be shaken?"

"Because now I must always wonder what might have been, if I had known the truth, if I had not been so blind, not been lied to. Would Richard and I have married sooner? Would I have... I hardly know – would I have had an entirely different life? Why was it not so? Was I not worthy of the truth? I have loved so deeply, so devotedly, and I have been utterly betrayed by those I have trusted. The worst of it is, Lizzy, I know it is expected of me to simply alter every happy memory, every tender sentiment I ever held for *that man*, and turn it to hate in the work of a moment, but I cannot do it."

Elizabeth could do nothing but hold Jane close and stroke her hair, as the force of Jane's sobs shook both of their bodies. Having no words of wisdom for her older sister, though she desperately wished it otherwise, Elizabeth was left to wish she could do more than whisper comforting platitudes in her sister's ear.

At length, Jane collected herself and drew away. "Oh Lizzy, wretched as I am, I ought to ask how you are feeling. Mary and Mamma came to Matlock yesterday after I did, and they said that George tried to kidnap you. You must have been so frightened!"

"Everyone tells me it must be so, and I think perhaps I was, a little. I was very angry, above anything. I felt a rage I have never felt in all my life, and when I held that gun to his throat...."

Jane made a strangled sound and fell back against her pillows and covered her face in her hands.

"I am sorry Jane. I thought you knew."

Jane slowly pulled back her fingers. "I did not know that part – I heard that Richard saved you."

"Well, he saved me from having to pull the trigger."

Jane groaned again, her face twisting in despair. "Could you really have done it, Lizzy?"

Elizabeth furrowed her brow as she thought about it. *Oh yes, I would have done it.* "It would have been hard to face you, once I learned who he really was. I suppose it would be hard to face anyone, after... doing such a thing."

"And yet, he would have deserved it," Jane sighed, pulling the blankets closer around herself. "He was a villain all along."

"He did not act alone, you know."

Jane tilted her head and looked askance at Elizabeth. "What do you mean?"

"Do you remember Mrs. Younge, who visited Darcy House? The so-called friend of our late mother's? It was she who introduced me to Wickham – well, to Mr. Smythe, as he called himself. They knew I was not likely to recognize him after all these years, and they had their information from Madeline Bingley. She is the same woman that our mother cursed all those years ago as she lay dying, and in a way I suppose this has brought the curse full circle."

"Lizzy," Jane softly chided her, "I thought you had ceased to cling to this notion of a curse."

"And so I have, Jane, even when there is more reason than ever to allow myself the comfort of wallowing in it, at last I reject the notion. As you said earlier, I have also wondered how I am to live with everything that has happened, and in truth, I have spent seven years avoiding it. I can well understand the sense of lost time, of wondering what if I had been just a little stronger, a little wiser, more of an adult... but, Jane, everything in the past, for better or worse, has led us here."

"And what happens next?"

"You shall have to make that choice yourself – so must we all. For my part, I am going to marry William as soon as it can be arranged. I am going to come home, Jane, and I think I am going to fill Pemberley with children as soon as I can manage it. What happened yesterday will not change me; George Wickham will hold no place of triumph in the course of my life."

Elizabeth had not noticed the door open, nor had she heard Lady Eleanor's footfall on the carpet, but she looked up at the sound of her grandmother's applause. "Well, my dear," she chortled, "I had only come to be sure there was no talk of curses in here this morning, but do carry on."

***

That morning brought the return of Inspector Renard to Upper Brook Street. He met with Darcy, Richard, and Sir Edward, having taken Evelyn Younge's sworn testimony and obtained her cooperation in providing a list of Wickham's creditors.

"What became of Madeline Bingley?" Sir Edward asked.

"Even with her sister's sworn testimony, there was insubstantial evidence of any wrongdoing on her part – the carriage was hired under Wickham's name, and the only documentation of their dealings was Mrs. Bingley's renting a house for Mrs. Younge; a suspiciously generous thing, but not actually a crime. The magistrate might have let her go free, had it not been for her rancor over being brought in the first place. She had worked herself into such a state that Mr. Moore was obliged to have her installed in Bedlam, and her reaction to being transported there will likely ensure her stay is of some duration."

"Would a sworn statement from Mr. Wickham sway the case against her?"

"It might, if we could locate the devil. My men have been looking, but after his attempt at removing Miss Bennet from this house, the trail on him goes quite cold." The inspector raised his eyebrow provokingly at them.

"As it happens, he came back just this morning," Richard said smoothly. "I cannot think why, but we apprehended him, and he is in the cellar."

"Excellent," Inspector Renard said. "What a stroke of luck for you, I am sure."

Despite Richard's levity, Darcy remained stoic. "He will be transported to Marshalsea directly upon his removal from this house?"

"Exactly so. We have your evidence against him, both in the attempted abduction, and his many debts. If he does not swing, he will rot in Marshalsea."

Darcy nodded. Between the debts Wickham had accrued in London over the last two years, the great many outstanding bills he had acquired at the tailor since entering Madeline's employ, as well as the markers Darcy already held, Wickham's debt was well in excess of ten thousand pounds. And, of course, he had attempted to abduct the niece of an earl – the courts would never forgive him that. Richard had found it more satisfying to simply beat the scoundrel – so much so that he was very nearly ready to forgive Darcy the secrecy entirely – but Darcy was interested in true justice being served, at long last.

Shortly after the inspector carried Wickham away to meet his fate, Charles Bingley and his sister called, and were shown into the drawing room. They took their seats nervously, and Darcy offered Bingley a reassuring smile, thinking it an odd reversal that *he* should be seeking to put *Bingley* more at ease.

"I came to offer my apologies, again, for everything that transpired yesterday at my stepmother's behest. I beg no forgiveness on her part, but mean to assure you that Caroline and I have broken with her entirely – she shall receive no support from our family – that is, *you* are our family now, as far as we are concerned. Jane and Elizabeth Darcy are to be my sisters, and anyone who would do them harm is my enemy."

"And mine," Miss Bingley said. "Mr. Fitzwilliam – Richard – you are to be my brother, and Jane and Eliza my cousins. I pray you would not hold our stepmother's offenses against *us*. If Mary were to change her mind, or John...." A tear rolled down Miss Bingley's cheek, and Sir Edward stepped forward to hand her a pocket square, but found he had none. Darcy offered his own, and shook hands warmly with Bingley.

"You have been my friend for many years, and I know you incapable of deceit. You are as welcome in this family as ever," Darcy said with feeling.

Richard likewise extended his hand to Miss Bingley, after she had dabbed away her tears. "I cannot speak for my brother, but I look forward to welcoming you into the family. Jane shall be your sister as well as your cousin, and I know it shall not cease to delight her."

Edward smiled indulgently at them all. "I had word from Lady Anne this morning – they all stayed the night at Matlock House, she and the girls. I cannot be the only person here who would rather be walking there...."

Sir Edward received no arguments against walking there directly.

***

The arrival of Sir Edward, William, Richard and the Bingley

siblings at Matlock House was overshadowed by the return of the Viscount, who had caught up with Charlotte and Elliot the previous evening and ridden all through the night to bring them back. The earl was still in high dudgeon, but Richard would not see him while Jane was still within the house.

After Richard's anger was spent on Wickham, he and Darcy had reached a tentative accord the night before over Sir Edward's finest brandy, but it rested on Jane's forgiveness, which Darcy was eager to seek when he arrived at his Uncle's house. He found Elizabeth standing with Lady Eleanor in the corridor outside the earl's study, and when they noticed him and Richard approaching, they began to act as though they had not been listening to the shouting coming from the other side of the door.

Darcy smiled as he took in the sight of his beloved. She was wearing an ill-fitting gown of Charlotte's, and yet she looked resplendent as she tried to play off her mischief. "William, it is good to see you," she said, her face lit with joy as she slipped into his embrace. Their grandmother paused to roll her eyes at them, before pressing her ear back to the door, her hand creeping ever closer to the doorknob.

Richard bid Elizabeth good morning and inquired after Jane. "I should like to see her before Father realizes I have returned."

Elizabeth nodded. "I do not know if she will speak to you, but I will advise her to come down. First, I think I must clear the drawing room. I am sure Mr. and Miss Bingley must be wanting to walk out with John and Mary on such a fine day, and no doubt Mamma and Uncle Edward will be willing chaperones, though from the looks they have been exchanging, I daresay they are in as much need of chaperoning as anybody."

Darcy watched, too enchanted by Elizabeth's poise to feel much of the anger still radiating from Richard, as Elizabeth went into the drawing room and convinced their relations and visitors alike to go forth and enjoy the sunshine. Sir Edward led Lady Anne out of the room, the young people trailing behind, and his mother stopped to give Darcy's hand a gentle squeeze.

"Will you speak to Jane?"

"If she will see me. I heard she was unwell last night?"

"She was overwhelmed from the day, as we all were, but poor Jane most of all. The doctor has been in to see her – she would heal best, I think, if she was reminded that her brother loves her, as I know you do."

"She is certainly owed some explanation," Richard growled at Darcy's side. Lady Anne looked thoughtfully at him, and rested her hand on his cheek for a moment, but said nothing. Richard seemed to understand her, and gave a little nod.

After the others had gone, Darcy and Richard sat down in the drawing room, and soon after, Elizabeth led Jane into the room. Darcy's heart tore at the sight of her. She was pale, her face puffy from weeping, and she could neither meet his eye nor their cousin's. Richard was at her side in an instant, leading her to a sofa near the fire, and he sat protectively beside her, his face schooled into an expression that betrayed nothing beyond his concern for Jane.

Elizabeth came and sat beside Darcy, her hands slipping into his, and she rested her chin on his shoulder as she leaned into him, whispering, "You need only speak your heart, my love. Be open with her, as you have been with me, and I am sure you will be forgiven. There is much love in this family, but too much secrecy. What is the point of so much devotion if we cannot all share our burdens with one another?"

Darcy closed his eyes and let out a breath he had not realized he had been holding. She was too perfect for him, the way she could speak to his heart so eloquently, and he wanted nothing more than to be alone with her, to show her in every sense what she meant to him, but first, he meant to throw himself upon his sister's mercy.

He leaned forward, resting his elbows on his knees, and waited for Jane to finally meet his eye. "I do not deserve your forgiveness, Jane, but I must beg it of you anyhow."

Jane shook her head at him. "How can I forgive such deception? What explanation can you possibly offer me for what you have done?"

"Only that I was trying to protect you," he said.

"To protect me? You have humiliated me, and that you thought I needed to be thus shielded only deepens my shame. I cannot understand why you could not tell me the truth. Our conversation yesterday ought to have taken place five years ago. It sickens me to think of all the years of pointless misery I have endured, and that you, whom I have loved as a true brother, and trusted as I have our father, you have brought this on me – to what end?"

"It is true, you ought to have been made to understand the truth, and all I can say in my defense is that I love you, Sister, and I have feared losing your esteem since the moment that monster George Wickham staked his own claim on your gentle heart. I knew what he was, an artful and selfish creature, a depraved man, a spendthrift and a wastrel, and many times I nearly fell out with our father over him."

"This is true," Richard admitted to Jane. "We have always known what he was like."

"You must not think yourself any more deceived by *him* than our father," Darcy sighed. "Father knew Wickham all his life, and supported him until the last. If I could not convince him that Wickham was a scoundrel, how could I hope to persuade a young girl in love?"

Fresh tears slid down Jane's face, and as Richard attempted to soothe her, Darcy turned to Elizabeth. She offered him the trace of a sad smile, and laced her fingers with his.

"When I saw how he had deceived you, just as he had our father, I realized I had not been the sort of brother I ought to have been. I thought that the best I could do to atone for my failure was to shield you from Wickham's true nature. I knew he would disgrace you if he went into the church, a man with his proclivities. And, in truth, I fought hard for our father to push Wickham toward a naval career because I hoped... I hoped he would die at sea. In that way, you might have held on to whatever happy memories you had of him, without having to experience the calamity of ever becoming his wife."

Jane covered her face with her hands and continued to weep, and Darcy leaned forward, whispering, "Whatever pain you are feeling now would have been manifested a hundred times over if you had married him, Jane, I swear it."

Jane lowered her hands from her face, which was contorted with misery. "Why was it for you to decide, to gamble with my life, my heart? My life had been a lie these five years," she cried, and Darcy recoiled from her outburst. "You tell me I have been pining for a man whose true nature you kept hidden from me, that every day I spent in mourning, you made the choice to continue your deception, and I am supposed to be grateful for your protection?"

"It has been my duty to protect you," Darcy said, trying to subdue his frustration. He stood and began to pace the room. "I was so young when we lost Father, Jane. At three and twenty I became not only the master of Pemberley, bearing the myriad responsibilities which that entails, but the head of our family besides. All this, and my heart was broken at his passing. I was trying to survive, Jane, to do my best for all those dependent on me. I know I have not been perfect, I have made mistakes, but the grief in my heart was still fresh when Wickham came crawling back, asking for more money... that must be some defense, if I may be permitted to make any. I knew you shared my grief over Father, and I thought that to include Wickham in that grief a better thing for you than to mourn father while discovering the truth of George Wickham's character. I have tried to be a true brother to you, Jane, and if the decision I made to protect you was the wrong choice, I have made it out of love. I would halve any burden of yours, bear it all myself, even...."

Darcy broke off, feeling tears begin to prick at his own eyes, and though Jane would not look at him, Elizabeth sat regarding him with a look of dismay, her hand extended toward him. He moved toward her, capturing her hand in his, and Elizabeth stood to embrace him. "Oh William," she breathed. "I never knew – I never thought of what you must have suffered. I believed you devoid of every proper feeling, berated you every time I visited, and yet, I see now how you bore it with such fortitude…." She stood on her toes to plant a quick kiss on his cheek, her little fingers grazing his neck, before she turned and knelt in front of her sister.

"Oh, Jane," Elizabeth sighed. "William is right, you know. If I, of all people, can see it now… you must believe it, Jane. We were all suffering our own private pain, and look where it has gotten us. You have devoted yourself to the love of a man that did not exist, just as I have spent so many years despising a man I did not even know. We have invested our emotion in mere illusions, and I…." Elizabeth's voice began to crack, though she did not shed any tears as she laid her head on Jane's lap. "I am so sorry."

Richard looked up at Darcy, his brow knot with worry and remorse, and he nodded. Darcy moved toward them, offering Elizabeth his hand to help her to her feet. "We are past that now, my love," he whispered to her.

"I suppose we are," she replied. "But it is a choice we have had to make. To put the past away, to really see one another, after looking at everything through the fog of so many years of sorrow…." She stroked his cheek again before looking down at Jane. "Do you see, dearest?"

Jane wiped the tears from her face and let out a shaky breath as she looked up at Darcy. "Yes, but… it still hurts."

"Jane, Wickham was destined to hurt you from the minute he saw what I did not, that you had blossomed into a woman. The pain you are feeling now, after years of healing, would have left a deeper wound then, than it shall now, I would stake my life on it, because in all those years you have grown stronger. I cannot defend my actions any further, except to say that I am proud of the woman I have watched you become these five years. I believe that you are a woman who will fight for her own happiness. Whether that includes my forgiveness, I cannot say, but I have done what I have done out of love, and I pray that someday you will see it as such."

Richard looked thoughtfully at Darcy, and addressed himself to Jane. "My love," he said, taking her hands in his. "Think on this – If you had known what Wickham was, could you have ever opened your heart to me?"

"I… I do not know. If you had intervened five years ago… oh, William, I was already so in love with George by then. I might not have listened to you – it might have been me he tried to carry off to Gretna. I would not have been so easily persuaded to throw him off in favor of Richard, because I could not love him until my heart had been broken and made new." She looked hesitantly from Darcy to Richard. "I do not know what my life would have been like if William had separated George and I sooner, but I know it would not be much like the life I have now, and until yesterday morning I rather liked that life."

Richard's face contorted with despair. "Until yesterday? Jane, do you no longer wish to marry me?"

"Of course I do," she gasped. "Oh dear – what I meant to say is that, well... Lizzy is right. We have all been fooled by illusions in our years of grief. We have all failed to understand one another. You told me this morning, Lizzy, that you will not let what Wickham has done change you. I rather like that, but you are stronger and braver than I, and I do not know if I can do it."

"I did not know if I could do it, either," Elizabeth admitted. "I was already in the middle before I knew I had begun. But you might have the advantage, in learning from my foolishness."

Darcy heaved a heavy sigh. He was not one for making such speeches, and the force of his emotion left him feeling depleted. There was one woman in the world whose love and forgiveness he could depend upon, and without her at his side, both in body and spirit, he knew not how he would get on. "If I could do it all again, Jane, I would have sent Wickham away as soon as he began to woo you, forced Uncle Henry to sell the Scottish pile sooner to keep Richard out of the army, and even now I should be bouncing one of your children on my knee. In that respect, I know I have robbed you of much, and know I can never fully make amends. I am sorry, Jane."

Elizabeth and Richard both nodded encouragingly at Jane, and finally she stood and wrapped her arms around Darcy. "Oh, Brother," she cried. "Oh, my dear brother. All shall be well, if only because Lizzy commands it."

Elizabeth laughed, and added her own arms to their embrace, whispering gentle assurances to Jane that all would indeed be well.

When Jane pulled away from him, Richard stepped forward and extended his hand for Darcy to shake. "I cannot say I would have done much better in your position, Darcy, such as it was at the time. If Jane can forgive you, so must I. And now, I think perhaps you had better leave us."

Darcy signaled his agreement, and Elizabeth gave Jane a parting kiss on the cheek before taking William's hand and leading him out of the room.

***

Elizabeth and William enjoyed a private moment in the corridor, and were interrupted a moment later by Charlotte stepping out of her father's study. She smirked at their passionate embrace and shook her head. "Amateurs."

Elizabeth laughed and swatted at her cousin. "Ah, but we have permission."

Charlotte merely rolled her eyes at Elizabeth, and glanced up at William. "Father knows you are here, for Grandmamma has given you up. He is asking for you, but fear not – our lady grandmother has teased him into some semblance of his usual humor. You ought to go in; the negotiations have turned rather serious, and I have been kicked out of the proceedings. I should not deprive my brothers of their time with Jane and Caroline, but I would steal Lizzy…."

William looked down at Elizabeth with a twinkle of mirth in his eyes. "I had better go in; I feel rather responsible for poor Elliot."

"As well you should! Is this not the very outcome we desired?"

"Lizzy, you sly thing!" Charlotte giggled, and looped her arm through Elizabeth's and led her out to the garden. "I should warn you," Charlotte teased, "that if Father's window is open, he shall hear every word we say."

Elizabeth laughed. "Do you intend to tell me anything more shocking than that you have attempted to elope?"

"I *could*," Charlotte said, and waggled her eyebrows.

Elizabeth gasped. "No!"

Charlotte grinned at her. "I shall only say this, Lizzy: John may have intercepted us by last evening, but I am marrying a man of strong passions, and it is particularly imperative that we do wed."

"Charlotte!" Elizabeth laughed, and blushed to think of the thoughts she had recently come to harbor of William.

"Suffice it to say, if you need any advice before your wedding…." She leaned in and whispered to Elizabeth a great many things far more shocking than even William's most detailed letters had contained, and Elizabeth was red all over and rather warm inside by the end of it.

When at last they went back inside, William was just emerging from the study with Elliot, the earl, and the countess. Elizabeth went to him at once, her head and heart still aflutter from Charlotte's information. "I hope the earl was not too severe upon you," she whispered in his ear. "Although, if he was, I should have to offer you some consolation…."

William wrapped his arms around her. "I ought to say he was ghastly, if only to enjoy your comfort," he whispered back. "However, he was not difficult to reason with, and I believe he will be generous to them. After all, he has accomplished his great mission, and now has five weddings in the family to look forward to."

Elizabeth laughed, running her fingers through William's hair. "He ought to be the happiest man alive!"

They were alone in the corridor, and William kissed Elizabeth, giving her bottom a generous squeeze. "No, my love – *I* am the happiest man alive."

Elizabeth brushed her lips against his neck, her hands working their way into his coat. "If you are not," she breathed, "I shall make sure that you very soon will be."

Epilogue

❧❦

August 1812, Netherfield Park, Hertfordshire

Mary and Charles Bingley returned from their honeymoon in want of some society. Two blissful weeks passed, full of all the lively activities a summer in the country could promise for five newlywed couples, as well as the earl, countess, and dowager countess of Matlock, Lady Anne Darcy, Sir Edward, and Rose Gardiner.

Yet none of them could be happier, in his estimation, than the Bingleys' neighbor and cousin, William Collins, who felt himself quite the mastermind of the whole scheme; when Sir Edward and Lady Anne announced their engagement at supper one night, he knew it was time that he, the only man amongst them not experiencing or anticipating marital bliss, took some action to change that.

As the gentlemen lingered after supper with cigars and brandy, it was no secret that his seven merry companions were wishing every moment to return to their ladies, but Williams Collins could not be satisfied until he knew he should leave the room with just as much a right to such happy hopes as the rest of them. He began by addressing himself to Darcy. "You told me in April, sir, that if ever there was a favor I could ask of you...."

Darcy nodded encouragingly at him. "Yes, of course."

"In fact, there is something I should like to ask of you, Cousin."

"You preserved my wife from danger – you may ask me anything," Darcy said earnestly.

Mr. Collins grinned at him as their companions looked on with interest. "I should like to ask if you have any interest in buying Longbourn. A belated wedding present for Lizzy, perhaps – and a worthy investment should you have a second son."

"Let him get through the first one, Will," Richard laughed.

Darcy puffed thoughtfully at his cigar. "It is a worthy notion, though I could wish it closer to Derbyshire."

"It is close to family," Charles playfully protested. "I am fond of Netherfield, even if it is three days' journey north to see the rest of you lot." He laughed to himself. "Perhaps if Mary and I have a daughter, and she is half as pretty as her mother, your second son might not think it a punishment to have Longbourn."

"No more wedding planning, I beg of you, sir," the earl cried, laughing into his third glass of brandy.

"I can hardly give you an answer at present, though I can guess what my wife will tell me," Darcy mused with a smirk. "Let us meet tomorrow, and have a good look at the place. I should like to know your price."

"And I should like to know," Sir Edward chortled, "Where you mean to live, sir? Are you still so keen on London?"

"I am, sir, and I have just the place in mind."

"Is that so?"

"Number twenty-six, Upper Brook Street."

"I was not aware my house was for sale," Sir Edward laughed.

"Yet I had understood that Cousin Darcy was to make the dower house at Pemberley ready to receive you and your bride," Mr. Collins countered. He sipped nervously at his brandy, his throat burning, wishing Sir Edward might seriously consider what he was summoning the courage to ask.

"It is true, I will be spending less time in London when Anne and I are wed."

"And Rose shall be very sorry for it. Yet think of what our life might be, if we were to reside there. We might be as custodians to the house until young Tom is of age, more than ten years hence. By that time, the money I could invest in *Gardiner and Collins Imports*, from selling Longbourn, would surely redouble, and then I could buy her the palace she deserves."

"A palace, eh?" The earl winked at Collins, and he wondered what he had said amiss.

Sir Edward set aside his cigar and steepled his fingers as he leveled a curious glance at Mr. Collins. "Well, now, as to all that... I thought you would never ask."

***

Lady Eleanor had a great deal of advice for Charlotte on how to ensure her child would be healthy – and male – and she had been dispensing it at length to the entire room, insisting that after so many weddings, it was quite impossible that Charlotte could be the only young lady present in need of such comprehensive instruction. Elizabeth Darcy felt her hands drifting toward her belly, but she caught herself – she could not betray anything, not until she was sure, and then she hoped for some chance to tell William in private, before Lady Eleanor wheedled it out of her.

Jane and Mary seemed to be bearing the turn of conversation with some composure, though poor Caroline Fitzwilliam was not yet accustomed to the dowager countess's forthrightness.

"Mamma," Lady Anne sighed, squeezing at her temples as she always did when her mother's exuberance became too much for her. "Surely Rose should not be hearing these things."

"I am sure she should," Lady Eleanor said unapologetically. "I was already a mother at her age, and mistress of Matlock besides. Keep up, my dear," she said, giving Rose a quick wink.

"She is seventeen," the countess chided. "I know very well, Mamma, that you did not even wed until twenty."

Lady Eleanor waved her away. "Oh, who can remember! And you, Miss Rose – I have my eye on you,"

The drawing room doors opened, and the gentlemen all poured into the room, each of them with someone to seek out directly. Uncle Edward lingered near the door, gesturing to his daughter. "Rose, my dear, come here. Mr. Collins wishes a private word with you – he is in the library." He gave her an affectionate pat on the cheek as she hastened from the room, while Lady Eleanor threw back her shoulders and gave them all a look of triumph.

William made his way to Elizabeth's side, and leaned in to whisper to her, "I had hoped we might escape there ourselves tonight – what say you, my love?"

A thrill of anticipation coursed through Elizabeth as she considered his saucy suggestion. "We have a whole bedchamber to ourselves," she whispered back, feeling her cheeks grow warm. The weeks of their short engagement had seen them press their luck at every family gathering, until at last they had been wed, and no longer needed to sneak about. And yet….

She met his eye with a mischievous smirk, and he grinned at seeing her so flustered. He cast a quick look around, and, seeing that nobody was looking their way, he leaned in and kissed her just below the earlobe. "Tomorrow, we might even have a chance to explore Longbourn…."

Elizabeth shivered with delight, knowing she could only surrender.

About the Author

❧

Jayne Bamber is a life-long Austen fan, and a total sucker for costume dramas. Jayne read her first Austen variation as a teenager and has spent more than a decade devouring as many of them as she can. This of course has led her to the ultimate conclusion of her addiction, writing one herself.

Jayne's favorite Austen work is Sense and Sensibility, though Sanditon is a strong second. Despite her love for Pride and Prejudice, Jayne realizes that she is no Lizzy Bennet, and is in fact growing up to be Mrs. Bennet more and more each day.

After years of dating Wickhams, Collinses, and the occasional Tilney-that-got-away, Jayne married her very own Darcy (tinged with just the right amount of Mr. Palmer) and the two live together in Texas with a pair of badly behaved rat terriers, and a desire to expand their menagerie of fur babies.

Printed in Great Britain
by Amazon